Charles Dickens's A CHRISTMAS CAROL is the most famous celebration of Christmas—and family love—ever written. Tight-fisted Scrooge, humble Bob Cratchit, and little Tiny Tim are among Dickens's most beloved characters, showing us the real nature of charity, the power of tenderness, the wisdom of innocence in a hardhearted world. Now, in a volume selected and introduced by children's literature expert U. C. Knoepflmacher of Princeton University, Dickens's classic story is presented alongside four other great Victorian tales:

John Ruskin's THE KING OF THE GOLDEN RIVER, which, like A CHRISTMAS CAROL, celebrates the victory of charity over cruelty, as the kindly Gluck strives against miserly Schwartz and Hans;

W. M. Thackeray's THE ROSE AND THE RING, set in the kingdom of Paflagonia, a story about the romance of a prince and princess who have been identically cursed at birth;

George MacDonald's THE LIGHT PRINCESS, the wry tale of a girl who takes everything in life too lightly because she, quite literally, lacks gravity;

And MOPSA THE FAIRY, Jean Ingelow's neglected master-piece about a boy's dream journey through a series of fairy kingdoms—a story which deliberately evokes and subverts the greatest of all Victorian fairy tales, ALICE'S ADVENTURES IN WONDERLAND.

These are the tales Dickens's audience loved to read to one another, stories in which ghosts, fairies, adults, and children freely mingle—and create, with magical wishfulness, en-chanting places where all things are possible.

Bantam Classics
Ask your bookseller for these other British Classics

BEOWULF AND OTHER OLD ENGLISH POEMS
  Translated by Constance B. Hieatt

THE CANTERBURY TALES by Geoffrey Chaucer

ROBINSON CRUSOE by Daniel Defoe

GULLIVER'S TRAVELS AND OTHER WRITINGS by Jonathan Swift

PRIDE AND PREJUDICE by Jane Austen
EMMA by Jane Austen
SENSE AND SENSIBILITY by Jane Austen
MANSFIELD PARK by Jane Austen

FRANKENSTEIN by Mary Shelley

JANE EYRE by Charlotte Brontë
WUTHERING HEIGHTS by Emily Brontë

DAVID COPPERFIELD by Charles Dickens
GREAT EXPECTATIONS by Charles Dickens
HARD TIMES by Charles Dickens
OLIVER TWIST by Charles Dickens
A TALE OF TWO CITIES by Charles Dickens
NICHOLAS NICKLEBY by Charles Dickens
BLEAK HOUSE by Charles Dickens
THE PICKWICK PAPERS by Charles Dickens
A CHRISTMAS CAROL by Charles Dickens

SILAS MARNER by George Eliot

FAR FROM THE MADDING CROWD by Thomas Hardy
TESS OF THE D'URBERVILLES by Thomas Hardy
JUDE THE OBSCURE by Thomas Hardy
THE MAYOR OF CASTERBRIDGE by Thomas Hardy
THE RETURN OF THE NATIVE by Thomas Hardy

HEART OF DARKNESS and THE SECRET SHARER by Joseph Conrad
LORD JIM by Joseph Conrad

DR. JEKYLL AND MR. HYDE by Robert Louis Stevenson
TREASURE ISLAND by Robert Louis Stevenson
KIDNAPPED by Robert Louis Stevenson

DRACULA by Bram Stoker

CAPTAINS COURAGEOUS by Rudyard Kipling
KIM by Rudyard Kipling

ALICE'S ADVENTURES IN WONDERLAND and THROUGH THE
  LOOKING-GLASS by Lewis Carroll

THE MOONSTONE by Wilkie Collins

THE PICTURE OF DORIAN GRAY AND OTHER WRITINGS
  by Oscar Wilde

THE TIME MACHINE by H. G. Wells
THE INVISIBLE MAN by H. G. Wells

THE WIND IN THE WILLOWS by Kenneth Grahame

LADY CHATTERLEY'S LOVER by D. H. Lawrence

A Christmas Carol by Charles Dickens

and Other Victorian Fairy Tales by John Ruskin, W. M. Thackeray, George MacDonald, and Jean Ingelow

Selected with an Introduction
by U. C. Knoepflmacher

BANTAM BOOKS
TORONTO · NEW YORK · LONDON · SYDNEY

A CHRISTMAS CAROL
AND OTHER VICTORIAN FAIRY TALES
A Bantam Book

PRINTING HISTORY

A Christmas Carol was first published in 1843.
The King of the Golden River was first published in 1851.
The Rose and the Ring was first published in 1854.
"The Light Princess" was first published in 1864.
Mopsa the Fairy was first published in 1869.

Bantam Classic edition / November 1983

Cover painting, *Many Happy Returns of the Day* by W. P. Frith,
Harrogate Art Gallery, North Yorkshire, England. Reproduced
by kind permission of the Council of the Borough of Harrogate.

ISBN 0-553-21126-9

Published simultaneously in the United States and Canada

Bantam Books are published by Bantam Books, Inc. Its trademark,
consisting of the words "Bantam Books" and the portrayal of
a rooster, is Registered in U.S. Patent and Trademark Office
and in other countries. Marca Registrada. Bantam Books, Inc.,
666 Fifth Avenue, New York, New York 10103.

PRINTED IN THE UNITED STATES OF AMERICA

O   0 9 8 7 6 5 4 3 2 1

Contents

Introduction

When Charles Dickens published *A Christmas Carol* in December of 1843, as the first of his five annual Christmas books, he evoked a response that almost rivaled the reception accorded to his celebrated *The Pickwick Papers*, seven years earlier. Once again, Dickens had managed to devise a brand-new literary form. His fairy tale was simultaneously realistic and dreamlike. In it he managed to acknowledge the stark social realities of the 1840s and yet express, at the same time, the wishful desire to dissolve that present through the fluidity of a myth of rebirth and renovation. The mixture was exquisitely suited to the aspirations of his reading public. Victorian reviewers were ecstatic. "Who can listen to objections regarding such a book as this?" asked W. M. Thackeray in a review for *Fraser's Magazine*. "It seems to be a national benefit, and to every man or woman who reads it a personal kindness." And, lest his assertion be open to challenge, Thackeray turned to the testimony of other witnesses: "The last two people I heard speak of it were women; neither knew the other, or the author, and both said, by way of criticism, 'God bless him!' A Scotch philosopher, who nationally does not keep Christmas Day, on reading the book, sent out for a turkey, and asked two friends to dine—this is a fact! Many men were known to sit down after perusing it, and write off letters to their friends, not about business, but out of their fulness of heart, and to wish old acquaintances a happy Christmas. Had the book appeared a fortnight earlier, all the prize cattle would have been gobbled up in pure love and friendship, Epping denuded of sausages, and not a turkey left in Norfolk."

Although Thackeray ends this tribute with characteristic playfulness, his testimonial is indeed based on "fact." The Scotch philosopher converted to Christmas spirit and Christmas feastings was none other than Thomas Carlyle. Jane Welsh Carlyle wrote in amazement that her dyspeptic husband, upon reading *A Christmas Carol*, was so violently "seized with a perfect *convulsion* of hospitality" that he "actually insisted on *improvising two* dinner-parties with only a day between." She was delighted but also dismayed (for she did not know how to stuff a turkey). Thackeray's reliance on the example of Carlyle as a reader transformed by the power of Dickens's art is deliberate. In *Past and Present*, a work published earlier in 1843, the "Scotch philosopher" had inveighed against the ills of his age. Although he, too, had delved into the spirit of times past to give shape to his hopes for a better society of the future, his skepticism remained dominant. Thackeray thus subtly equates Carlyle with Scrooge, another figure of disbelief and doubt who fails to observe Christmas Day. Scrooge's intense skepticism propels him at first to dismiss Marley's ghost as an empirically verifiable phenomenon. Just as an adult reader may want to resist Dickens's powers of fantasy, so does Scrooge try to resist the hallucinatory fascination that his partner's ghost has for his awakened imagination: "You may be an undigested bit of beef," he protests to Marley, "a blot of mustard, a crumb of cheese, a fragment of an underdone potato." But Scrooge's resistance crumbles. The rigid conventions by which he has governed his life are relentlessly eroded by the successive visits of his supernatural guests, the spirits of Past, Present, and Future released by his unconscious.

Dickens's fable of transformation continues to exert its hold on our own collective imagination. In our minds Christmas and Dickens have long ago somehow become synonymous. "Scrooge" has become a household word for that repressed and oppressive social self we yearn to shed in an annual ritual of renovation. Curiously enough, *A Christmas Carol* has become a secular parable that appeals to would-be believers of all denominations. (My grandfather, an orthodox Jew who certainly did not "keep Christmas Day," nonetheless religiously read the story on that day to his children in *fin-de-siècle* Vienna.) That the Christian elements are there is undeniable, of course. The tale involves a conversion, the resurrection of an old man who can again become "as humble as little children." In *The Life of Our Lord*, a little book that he privately wrote for his children a few years after the publication of *A Christmas Carol*, Dickens gave special prominence to the words of Jesus, "Whosoever shall receive one such little child in my name receiveth me." Dickens added,

"Our Saviour loved the child and all children." It is through his rekindled love for Tiny Tim, to whom he becomes "a second father," that Scrooge illustrates this doctrine. Early in the book Marley's crippled ghost appears, weighted down by his chain of adult transgressions, "cash-boxes, keys, padlocks, ledgers, deeds, and heavy purses wrought in steel." The very first sentence in the *Carol* insists, laconically and implacably, "Marley was dead: to begin with." Yet this grim beginning is overcome. The story ends by lingering on a Tiny Tim "who did NOT die"; its last sentence invoking the blessings uttered by this innocent, who can now look forward to a future without crutches. By severing himself from the ways of his dead partner and by adopting Tiny Tim's innocent faith, Scrooge attains a salvation that is this-worldly rather than other-worldly. Made immortal through Dickens's art, Scrooge survives as an emblem for our own yearning for renewal and liberation.

If *A Christmas Carol* has at its core the liberal theology that Dickens shared with other Victorians, the book's mythic energies stem from more universal psychological sources. It is noteworthy that the three spirits who visit Scrooge in this "Ghost Story of Christmas" (the *Carol*'s original subtitle) are ghosts rather than angelic messengers. Indeed, in an earlier and inferior version of this myth, the "Story of the Goblins Who Stole a Sexton," interpolated in *The Pickwick Papers*, the role of the ghostly visitors was filled by underground gnomes who abduct the Scrooge-like Gabriel Grub on Christmas Eve and torture him into becoming a good-natured and contented man. Like the three spirits, the goblins who terrorize Grub the Grave-Digger confront him with consequences of a denial of those primal and elementary memories too easily buried by a hardened adult psyche. The greater scope of *A Christmas Carol* allowed Dickens to give much wider play to that process of repression and to locate Scrooge's loss in his inability, as an adult, to cling to the child's capacity for absolute and unqualified belief.

The Spirit of Christmas Past thus forces Scrooge to behold himself in his former, more vulnerable yet also more inviolable, incarnation as a "solitary child, neglected by his friends." Dickens invites the reader to recognize in that earlier abandonment the sources of Scrooge's defensive recoiling from human contact. Yet Scrooge's younger self, we are also asked to notice, was never wholly deserted. His little sister Fan—whose commitment to him, we now realize, is still being honored in the present by her son, Scrooge's nephew Fred—acted as a buffer between him and the stern father who had banished him to school. It is she who persuaded their father to allow her to bring her brother back home. Before his inevitable maturity (" 'And you're to be a man!' said the child, opening her eyes"), brother and sister could rekindle their childhood oneness and delay the onslaught of time, their eventual severance as adults. But the child Ebenezer could rely on the support of other companions as well. Figures from fairy tales and juvenile romances—Ali Baba and the Sultan's groom from *The Arabian Nights*, Valentine and his wild brother Orson, and that fellow solitary, Robinson Crusoe—appeared to the boy as vivid and actual presences. Indeed, it is the reality that these fictional personages once held for him that will eventually allow Scrooge to reactivate the dormant powers of belief stirred by his ghostly visitors.

As Scrooge nostalgically reimmerses himself in a recreation of the tales that sustained his childhood imagination, he suddenly, "with a rapidity of transition very foreign to his character," bursts into tears. It is his first real catharsis. Yet Scrooge not only pities "his former self," the youthful self he now at last allows to resurface, but also remembers a present child, the young boy whom he had so harshly repulsed in the first chapter. Contritely, he acknowledges his relation to that living child: "There was a boy singing a Christmas Carol at my door last night. I should like to have given him something: that's all." It is not all, of course. But Scrooge has taken an important first step in the process of reclaiming his emotional core.

A Christmas Carol is a fable for adults in need of such a reclamation. It is written by a man who persistently remembered having once been an imaginative and contented little boy. Like the four authors of the tales for children also included in this collection, Dickens set out to recover the child's innocence and strong capacity for make-believe. That recovery was, for Dickens and his fellow Victorians, absolutely essential to the adult's mental well-being. Like his creator, Ebenezer Scrooge must rescue and reanimate the suppressed "transition" that converts a healthy child into a healthy adult. In *Dickens and the Invisible World: Fairy*

Tales, Fantasy, and Novel-Making, Harry Stone has shown the crucial role played by the fairy stories and romances that nourished Dickens's early imagination. Again and again, Dickens relied on his childhood imaginings to give shape to his mature art. For he understood what Scrooge must come to recognize: the need and the value of our repeated return as grownups to the magical thinking of the child.

The metamorphic power of *A Christmas Carol* depends on that intuitive understanding. Scrooge is suitably horrified when the Spirit of Christmas Present forces him to behold "two children; wretched, abject, frightful, hideous, miserable." The boy, Ignorance, and the girl, Want, are premature adults, the products of a civilization that stifles its young and stunts them into grotesque aberrations. At the end of the story, however, as a playful Scrooge gleefully indulges his newfound willingness to regress, such phantasms can be exorcised. Linear time has been annulled for the reborn child-man: " 'I don't know what day of the month it is!' said Scrooge. 'I don't know how long I have been among the Spirits. I don't know anything. I'm quite a baby. Never mind. I don't care. I'd rather be a baby. Hallo! Whoop! Hallow here!' " The new Scrooge no longer repels child visitors from his door. As he beckons the boy decked out in Sunday clothes, he heaps encomia upon encomia with exaggerated but infectious playfulness: the "fine fellow" he welcomes with such relish soon becomes "an intelligent boy," "a remarkable boy," "a delightful boy." Scrooge's delight emanates from the irrepressible sense of wonder and well-being he has recovered. Though he earnestly assumes the new role of adult benefactor and philanthropist, he has been internally renovated by his ability to retrieve the child within. The dismal realities of Victorian England can be dissolved.

At the end of *A Christmas Carol* the reinstated imagination of the child once again reigns triumphant. Seizing on the figure of Tiny Tim as an embodiment of that triumph, Thackeray concluded his review of the story by asserting, "There is not a reader in England but that little creature will be a bond of union between the author and him." Thackeray's insight still holds true. For if the healed Scrooge acts as the agent for our deep yearning for psychic integration, the healed child symbolically satisfies that yearning for reader and author alike, a yearning shared by grownup and child, by "all of us," "Every One!"

The transformational process that plays so central a role in *A Christmas Carol* is just as integral to the other four major Victorian fantasies reproduced in this volume—John Ruskin's *The King of the Golden River* (1851), William Makepeace Thackeray's *The Rose and the Ring* (1854), George MacDonald's "The Light Princess" (1864), and Jean Ingelow's *Mopsa the Fairy* (1869). Each of these works involves the same traffic between illusion and realism, the child's wonder and the adult's skepticism. And, once again, it is the agency of fairytale magic that helps bridge these contrary states.

In depicting Scrooge's conversion, Dickens began from the adult's vantage point. Ruskin, Thackeray, MacDonald, and Ingelow, however, reverse that perspective from the start. Their protagonists are boys and girls still situated in the realm of innocence Scrooge was forced to regain. Their movement, therefore, is not backward but forward to maturation and mastery. If Dickens addressed the same adult audience who read his major novels, the other four fantasists regarded the child or adolescent as their prime reader. Just as Lewis Carroll's Alice books began as stories privately told to Alice Liddell, so did the works of Ruskin, Thackeray, MacDonald, and Ingelow posit a special and privileged child auditor. Ruskin addressed the ten-year-old Effie Gray when he, as a young man of twenty-two still unsure of his own vocation and goals, wrote *The King of the Golden River* (by the time the work was lavishly published ten years later, he had achieved notoriety as an art critic). Thackeray fashioned *The Rose and the Ring* as a Christmas pantomime for his daughters Minny and Anny, as well as for a younger child, the American Edith Story, before he decided to share the work with a wider public. MacDonald seems to have tried out "The Light Princess" on his own children (who were also exposed, in the same year, to a trial reading of *Alice in Wonderland* by his friend Lewis Carroll). Jean Ingelow dedicated *Mopsa the Fairy* to a "little cousin," Janet Holloway; when she speaks of Jack as a boy "whom I knew very well," she is presumably drawing on memories of her favorite brother William Frederick, who had been nine years her younger.

By embracing the child's point of view, however, these

four authors enlist the same regressive capacities that animated Dickens's art. Indeed, as in the case of Dickens, it is precisely their ability to hold on simultaneously to childhood wishfulness and to the grown-up's more sober notions about reality that gives their writing its elasticity and richness. Conflict and harmony are allowed to interpenetrate and coexist. Like Scrooge, Ruskin's Gluck, Thackeray's Giglio and Rosalba, MacDonald's Light Princess and her sober Prince, Ingelow's Mopsa and Jack, all must effect a blending that involves the mundane and the extraordinary; freedom and responsibility; the modalities of male and female; the child's magical thinking and the adult's awareness of mutability, compromise, and death. The quality and extent of that blending may vary greatly, as does each story's narrative mode. Yet Ruskin's earnest didacticism, the comic mixtures fashioned by Thackeray and MacDonald, and Ingelow's lyrical fusion and eventual sundering of separate realities have a common goal. Like Dickens's *Carol,* these stories express a profound yearning for the dissolution of the false values of a civilization alienated from its primitive strengths.

Just as *A Christmas Carol* is rooted in the romances Dickens read as a child, so is *The King of the Golden River* an imitation of the Grimm fairy tales (illustrated by the famous Cruikshank) that gripped Ruskin's childhood imagination. The androgynous Gluck—who looks very much like a little girl in the drawings Ruskin commissioned from Richard Doyle, Cruikshank's successor—is immediately set in apposition to his sadistic older brothers. A Cinderella figure, frail and vulnerable, Gluck will be rewarded by "the little man," the "golden dwarf, about a foot and a half high," whom he has unwittingly freed from the malicious enchantment of a much "stronger" fairy king. Whereas the story's first supernatural visitor, South-West Wind, Esquire, acted as an analogue to the phallic violence of Gluck's adult brothers, Schwartz and Hans, the King of the Golden River is to be seen as Gluck's own counterpart, himself a victim in need of liberation. Although his powers by far exceed those of the passive boy, he merely turns the destructive nature of the two Black Brothers against itself. When Gluck feebly remonstrates with the dwarf-king for having been "so cruel," he is reminded that the transgressions of Hans and Schwartz—like those of Dickens's Marley—were simply self-defeating.

Gluck is Ruskin's version of Tiny Tim. At the end of *The King of the Golden River* he is left in charge of the fertile valley his older brothers had desecrated and polluted. Like Dickens, Ruskin relies on a biblical rhetoric in depicting the recovery of a lost Eden: "And, when he came in sight of the Treasure Valley, behold, a river, like the Golden River, was springing from a new cleft of the rocks above it, and was flowing in innumerable streams among the dry heaps of red sand." Yet this miraculous transformation is the product of what Carlyle called a "natural supernaturalism." Gluck has found neither the material treasure his brothers sought nor St. Matthew's heavenly riches. He is merely reinstated in a pastoral world he now administers as benignly as Scrooge administered his city wealth: "And Gluck went, and dwelt in the valley, and the poor were never driven from his door: so that his barns became full of corn, and his house of treasure." No wife joins Gluck as fellow guardian of the womblike valley's natural riches. Instead, the asexual youth reigns as a matriarchal as well as a patriarchal provider. As the young Ruskin's tribute to the still younger Effie Gray (whom he later married, with disastrous consequences), *The King of the Golden River* not only tries to remove the discord between the adult's acquired rapacity and the child's innate benevolence but also attempts to eradicate all distinctions of gender. Although this parable significantly anticipates the matured Ruskin's organicist thinking about economics, ecology, and religion, it can also be read as his attempt to exorcise a male sexuality he regarded as unduly aggressive.

No such softening shapes Thackeray's persistently ironic *The Rose and the Ring*, a work that capitalizes on the very frictions that Ruskin is so eager to remove. Like Schwartz and Hans, the kings Valoroso and Padella are power-hungry usurpers. But instead of dwelling on a single dispossessed child like Gluck, Thackeray charts the separate fates of male and female heirs and carefully distinguishes young Giglio and Rosalba from another pair of adolescents, Bulbo and Angelica. And whereas the prepubescent Gluck remains arrested, it is the growth of his young protagonists that concerns Thackeray. That growth is supervised by a Fairy Blackstick who uses her magic sparingly. Though powerful enough to turn men into metal, the fairy wisely allows "things to take their natural course" in promoting the maturation of her nurslings. Scarcely

using her wand "except as a cane to walk about with," she
bequeaths a "little *misfortune*" to her godchildren in order to
instruct them in self-reliance. Like Thackeray, she clearly
regards the magical rose and ring as crutches for those infirmer
minds who, like Bulbo and Angelica, cannot do without the
props of make-believe.

It would be a mistake, however, to read *The Rose and the
Ring* as an anti–fairy tale. Thackeray does not intend to
subvert the magic he praised in Dickens's *Christmas Carol*
and the drawings of fairy tale illustrators such as Richard
Doyle. In "De Juventute," an essay written before *The Rose
and the Ring*, he expressed his desire to fashion a story that
would appeal equally to child and adult, thereby establishing
a lifelong tie "between writer and reader." Thackeray's own
drawings reinforce this duality. The Fairy Blackstick, Rosalba,
and Giglio are represented realistically, while all others are
rendered as caricatures (Bulbo's enormous head, so dispropor-
tionate to his body, makes him resemble a giant baby). By
playfully calling attention to his story's exaggerations and
contradictions, Thackeray attempts to find a middle way between child and adult. Laughter dissolves all boundaries. The
mockery of male prowess renders hero-worship impossible
for both the reader nursed on boyish adventure stories and
the reader of military gazettes (the story debunks the contem-
porary war in Crimea). The boastful and sadistic Count
Hogginarmo gets eaten up by lions who purr like contented
kittens when stroked by Rosalba; but the true dramatic con-
test is between two strong female figures, represented without any of Ruskin's restraint, the greedy, sex-starved, but
resourceful Gruffanuff (a fairy-tale version of Thackeray's more
famous Becky Sharp) and the potent Fairy Blackstick. If the
latter's spells paradoxically allow her wards to grow up in a
world devoid of magic, Thackeray, too, cautiously steers between the realms of innocence and experience, subscribing to
neither, and yet to both.

MacDonald's "The Light Princess" opens on a comic note
that appears to be Thackerayan. Here, also, the tone seems
unmistakeably tongue-in-cheek. The king and queen who
quarrel in the beginning chapters are as bourgeois a couple as
King Valoroso and his wife (though here the queen is obviously
more acute than her dull-witted mate). In their metaphysical
differences, the disputing court-philosophers Hum-Drum and

Kopy-Keck recall Thwackum and Square in Fielding's *Tom Jones*, a work also embedded in *The Rose and the Ring*, where Giglio's imprudence and innate goodness distinctly resemble Tom's. If Thackeray parodied Shakespearean plays such as *Hamlet* or *Henry IV*, MacDonald seems eager to subvert the trappings of the Grimm fairy tale that Ruskin so earnestly adapted for his own purposes. MacDonald self-consciously exploits a running pun in his multiple permutations of the words "light" and "grave." Still, though initially lighthearted, he unexpectedly switches into a Ruskin-like gravity when the princess finds her vitality drained by the drying lake. Here, as in *The King of the Golden River*, the fate of the protagonist becomes identified with the natural and symbolic agent of water. Only by confronting death and rebirth can the princess be converted to a proper balance between thoughtless levity and emotional depth.

Like MacDonald's tale, Jean Ingelow's *Mopsa the Fairy* is a work full of surprises. Our expectations are consistently subverted. What begins as a boy's tale of adventure gradually turns into a mythic fable that probes into the burdens placed on an emerging female imagination. The little fairy girl whom Jack, the quintessential British boy, has patronized begins to outstrip her stolid protector. As the two children venture deeper and deeper into the heartland of a series of fairy provinces, Mopsa discovers that she is fated to rule as a powerful, yet also powerless, fairy queen. A poet of considerable renown in her own day, Jean Ingelow relied on ellipsis and indirection to enflesh the insight of Wordsworth's famous "Ode: Intimations of Immortality": "Our birth is but a sleep and a forgetting: / The soul that rises with us, our life's star, / Hath had elsewhere its setting, / And cometh from afar."

Transported afar, Jack, "the growing Boy" of Wordsworth's poem, is allowed to rise to an intimation of the primordial reality where Mopsa must forever remain. But his glimpse of that immortal domain is short-lived. Reluctantly, he must return from this female realm of the imagination to the practical, everyday world ruled by his father, a Victorian paterfamilias. As he returns to the house of his parents Jack is stripped of his former powers. He ceases to be an imaginative voyager and begins "to forget . . . even his little Mopsa, more and more." Read in one fashion, Ingelow's inventive and original fairy tale is by far the most fantastical of the fables included in this collection. Yet in its resigned acceptance of the chasm that eventually separates Mopsa from Jack, the imagination from actuality, *Mopsa the Fairy* is also more reality oriented than the works of Dickens, Ruskin, MacDonald, and even Thackeray. As an imaginative work that ultimately prizes Jack's acquiescence to the ordinary and matter-of-fact world in which he will slowly grow up, Ingelow's book relies on paradox to span the opposition between the contrary states that so fascinated her contemporaries and that still engross us today.

U. C. KNOEPFLMACHER

Princeton University

A CHRISTMAS CAROL
BY CHARLES DICKENS

PREFACE

I have endeavoured in this Ghostly little book, to rise the Ghost of an Idea, which shall not put my readers out of humour with themselves, with each other, with the season, or with me. May it haunt their house pleasantly, and no one wish to lay it.

Their faithful Friend and Servant,
C.D.

December 1843

STAVE ONE

MARLEY'S GHOST

Marley was dead: to begin with. There is no doubt whatever about that. The register of his burial was signed by the clergyman, the clerk, the undertaker, and the chief mourner. Scrooge signed it: and Scrooge's name was good upon 'Change, for anything he chose to put his hand to. Old Marley was as dead as a door-nail.

Mind! I don't mean to say that I know, of my own knowledge, what there is particularly dead about a door-nail. I might have been inclined, myself, to regard a coffin-nail as the deadest piece of ironmongery in the trade. But the wisdom of our ancestors is in the simile; and my unhallowed hands shall not disturb it, or the Country's done for. You will therefore permit me to repeat, emphatically, that Marley was as dead as a door-nail.

Scrooge knew he was dead? Of course he did. How could it be otherwise? Scrooge and he were partners for I don't know how many years. Scrooge was his sole executor, his sole administrator, his sole assign, his sole residuary legatee, his sole friend and sole mourner. And even Scrooge was not so dreadfully cut up by the sad event, but that he was an excellent man of business on the very day of the funeral, and solemnised it with an undoubted bargain.

The mention of Marley's funeral brings me back to the point I started from. There is no doubt that Marley was dead. This must be distinctly understood, or nothing wonderful can come of the story I am going to relate. If we were not perfectly convinced that Hamlet's Father died before the play began, there would be nothing more remarkable in his taking a stroll at night, in an easterly wind, upon his own ramparts, than there would be in any other middle-aged gentleman rashly turning out after dark in a breezy spot—say Saint

Paul's Churchyard for instance—literally to astonish his son's weak mind.

Scrooge never painted out Old Marley's name. There it stood, years afterwards, above the warehouse door: Scrooge and Marley. The firm was known as Scrooge and Marley. Sometimes people new to the business called Scrooge Scrooge, and sometimes Marley, but he answered to both names: it was all the same to him.

Oh! but he was a tight-fisted hand at the grindstone, Scrooge! a squeezing, wrenching, grasping, scraping, clutching, covetous old sinner! Hard and sharp as flint, from which no steel had ever struck out generous fire; secret, and self-contained, and solitary as an oyster. The cold within him froze his old features, nipped his pointed nose, shrivelled his cheek, stiffened his gait; made his eyes red, his thin lips blue; and spoke out shrewdly in his grating voice. A frosty rime was on his head, and on his eyebrows, and his wiry chin. He carried his own low temperature always about with him; he iced his office in the dog-days; and didn't thaw it one degree at Christmas.

· External heat and cold had little influence on Scrooge. No warmth could warm, nor wintry weather chill him. No wind that blew was bitterer than he, no falling snow was more intent upon its purpose, no pelting rain less open to entreaty. Foul weather didn't know where to have him. The heaviest rain, and snow, and hail, and sleet, could boast of the advantage over him in only one respect. They often "came down" handsomely, and Scrooge never did.

Nobody ever stopped him in the street to say, with gladsome looks, "My dear Scrooge, how are you? when will you come to see me?" No beggars implored him to bestow a trifle, no children asked him what it was o'clock, no man or woman ever once in all his life inquired the way to such and such a place, of Scrooge. Even the blindmen's dogs appeared to know him; and when they saw him coming on, would tug their owners into doorways and up courts; and then would wag their tails as though they said, "no eye at all is better than an evil eye, dark master!"

But what did Scrooge care? It was the very thing he liked. To edge his way along the crowded paths of life, warning all human sympathy to keep its distance, was what the knowing ones call "nuts" to Scrooge.

Once upon a time—of all the good days in the year, on Christmas Eve—old Scrooge sat busy in his counting-house. It was cold, bleak, biting weather: foggy withal: and he could hear the people in the court outside, go wheezing up and down, beating their hands upon their breasts, and stamping their feet upon the pavement-stones to warm them. The city clocks had only just gone three, but it was quite dark already: it had not been light all day: and candles were flaring in the windows of the neighbouring offices, like ruddy smears upon the palpable brown air. The fog came pouring in at every chink and keyhole, and was so dense without, that although the court was of the narrowest, the houses opposite were mere phantoms. To see the dingy cloud come drooping down, obscuring everything, one might have thought that Nature lived hard by, and was brewing on a large scale.

The door of Scrooge's counting-house was open that he might keep his eye upon his clerk, who in a dismal little cell beyond, a sort of tank, was copying letters. Scrooge had a very small fire, but the clerk's fire was so very much smaller that it looked like one coal. But he couldn't replenish it, for Scrooge kept the coal-box in his own room; and so surely as the clerk came in with the shovel, the master predicted that it would be necessary for them to part. Wherefore the clerk put on his white comforter, and tried to warm himself at the candle; in which effort, not being a man of a strong imagination, he failed.

"A merry Christmas, uncle! God save you!" cried a cheerful voice. It was the voice of Scrooge's nephew, who came upon him so quickly that this was the first intimation he had of his approach.

"Bah!" said Scrooge, "Humbug!"

He had so heated himself with rapid walking in the fog and frost, this nephew of Scrooge's, that he was all in a glow; his face was ruddy and handsome; his eyes sparkled, and his breath smoked again.

"Christmas a humbug, uncle!" said Scrooge's nephew. "You don't mean that, I am sure?"

"I do," said Scrooge. "Merry Christmas! What right have you to be merry? what reason have you to be merry? You're poor enough."

"Come, then," returned the nephew gaily. "What right

have you to be dismal? what reason have you to be morose? You're rich enough."

Scrooge having no better answer ready on the spur of the moment, said, "Bah!" again; and followed it up with "Humbug."

"Don't be cross, uncle," said the nephew.

"What else can I be" returned the uncle, "when I live in such a world of fools as this? Merry Christmas! Out upon merry Christmas! What's Christmas time to you but a time for paying bills without money; a time for finding yourself a year older, and not an hour richer; a time for balancing your books and having every item in 'em through a round dozen of months presented dead against you? If I could work my will," said Scrooge, indignantly, "every idiot who goes about with 'Merry Christmas,' on his lips, should be boiled with his own pudding, and buried with a stake of holly through his heart. He should!"

"Uncle!" pleaded the nephew.

"Nephew!" returned the uncle, sternly, "keep Christmas in your own way, and let me keep it in mine."

"Keep it!" repeated Scrooge's nephew. "But you don't keep it."

"Let me leave it alone, then," said Scrooge. "Much good may it do you! Much good it has ever done you!"

"There are many things from which I might have derived good, by which I have not profited, I dare say," returned the nephew: "Christmas among the rest. But I am sure I have always thought of Christmas time, when it has come round—apart from the veneration due to its sacred name and origin, if anything belonging to it can be apart from that—as a good time: a kind, forgiving, charitable, pleasant time: the only time I know of, in the long calendar of the year, when men and women seem by one consent to open their shut-up hearts freely, and to think of people below them as if they really were fellow-passengers to the grave, and not another race of creatures bound on other journeys. And therefore, uncle, though it has never put a scrap of gold or silver in my pocket, I believe that it *has* done me good, and *will* do me good; and I say, God bless it!"

The clerk in the tank involuntarily applauded: becoming immediately sensible of the impropriety, he poked the fire, and extinguished the last frail spark for ever.

"Let me hear another sound from *you*" said Scrooge, "and

you'll keep your Christmas by losing your situation. You're quite a powerful speaker, sir," he added, turning to his nephew. "I wonder you don't go into Parliament."

"Don't be angry, uncle. Come! Dine with us to-morrow."

Scrooge said that he would see him—yes, indeed he did. He went the whole length of the expression, and said that he would see him in that extremity first.

"But why?" cried Scrooge's nephew. "Why?"

"Why did you get married?" said Scrooge.

"Because I fell in love."

"Because you fell in love!" growled Scrooge, as if that were the only one thing in the world more ridiculous than a merry Christmas. "Good afternoon!"

"Nay, uncle, but you never came to see me before that happened. Why give it as a reason for not coming now?"

"Good afternoon," said Scrooge.

"I want nothing from you; I ask nothing of you; why cannot we be friends?"

"Good afternoon," said Scrooge.

"I am sorry, with all my heart, to find you so resolute. We have never had any quarrel, to which I have been a party. But I have made the trial in homage to Christmas, and I'll keep my Christmas humour to the last. So A Merry Christmas, uncle!"

"Good afternoon!" said Scrooge.

"And A Happy New Year!"

"Good afternoon!" said Scrooge.

His nephew left the room without an angry word, notwithstanding. He stopped at the outer door to bestow the greetings of the season on the clerk, who, cold as he was, was warmer than Scrooge; for he returned them cordially.

"There's another fellow," muttered Scrooge; who overheard him: "my clerk, with fifteen shillings a-week, and a wife and family, talking about a merry Christmas. I'll retire to Bedlam."

This lunatic, in letting Scrooge's nephew out, had let two other people in. They were portly gentlemen, pleasant to behold, and now stood, with their hats off, in Scrooge's office. They had books and papers in their hands, and bowed to him.

"Scrooge and Marley's, I believe," said one of the gentlemen, referring to his list. "Have I the pleasure of addressing Mr. Scrooge, or Mr. Marley?"

"Mr. Marley has been dead these seven years," Scrooge replied. "He died seven years ago, this very night."

"We have no doubt his liberality is well represented by his surviving partner," said the gentleman, presenting his credentials.

It certainly was; for they had been two kindred spirits. At the ominous word "liberality," Scrooge frowned, and shook his head, and handed the credentials back.

"At this festive season of the year, Mr. Scrooge," said the gentleman, taking up a pen, "it is more than usually desirable that we should make some slight provision for the poor and destitute, who suffer greatly at the present time. Many thousands are in want of common necessaries; hundreds of thousands are in want of common comforts, sir."

"Are there no prisons?" asked Scrooge.

"Plenty of prisons," said the gentleman, laying down the pen again.

"And the Union workhouses?" demanded Scrooge. "Are they still in operation?"

"They are. Still," returned the gentleman, "I wish I could say they were not."

"The Treadmill and the Poor Law are in full vigour, then?" said Scrooge.

"Both very busy, sir."

"Oh! I was afraid, from what you said at first, that something had occurred to stop them in their useful course," said Scrooge. "I'm very glad to hear it."

"Under the impression that they scarcely furnish Christian cheer of mind or body to the multitude," returned the gentleman, "a few of us are endeavouring to raise a fund to buy the Poor some meat and drink, and means of warmth. We choose this time because it is a time, of all others, when Want is keenly felt, and Abundance rejoices. What shall I put you down for?"

"Nothing!" Scrooge replied.

"You wish to be anonymous?"

"I wish to be left alone," said Scrooge. "Since you ask me what I wish, gentlemen, that is my answer. I don't make merry myself at Christmas, and I can't afford to make idle people merry. I help to support the establishments I have mentioned: they cost enough: and those who are badly off must go there."

"Many can't go there; and many would rather die."

"If they would rather die," said Scrooge, "they had better do it, and decrease the surplus population. Besides—excuse me—I don't know that."

"But you might know it," observed the gentleman.

"It's not my business," Scrooge returned. "It's enough for a man to understand his own business, and not to interfere with other people's. Mine occupies me constantly. Good afternoon, gentlemen!"

Seeing clearly that it would be useless to pursue their point, the gentlemen withdrew. Scrooge resumed his labours with an improved opinion of himself, and in a more facetious temper than was usual with him.

Meanwhile the fog and darkness thickened so, that people ran about with flaring links, proffering their services to go before horses in carriages, and conduct them on their way. The ancient tower of a church, whose gruff old bell was always peeping slily down at Scrooge out of a gothic window in the wall, became invisible, and struck the hours and quarters in the clouds, with tremulous vibrations afterwards, as if its teeth were chattering in its frozen head up there. The cold became intense. In the main street, at the corner of the court, some labourers were repairing the gas-pipes, and had lighted a great fire in a brazier, round which a party of ragged men and boys were gathered: warming their hands and winking their eyes before the blaze in rapture. The water-plug being left in solitude, its overflowings sullenly congealed, and turned to misanthropic ice. The brightness of the shops where holly sprigs and berries crackled in the lamp-heat of the windows, made pale faces ruddy as they passed. Poulterers' and grocers' trades became a splendid joke: a glorious pageant, with which it was next to impossible to believe that such dull principles as bargain and sale had anything to do. The Lord Mayor, in the stronghold of the mighty Mansion House, gave orders to his fifty cooks and butlers to keep Christmas as a Lord Mayor's household should; and even the little tailor, whom he had fined five shillings on the previous Monday for being drunk and blood-thirsty in the streets, stirred up to-morrow's pudding in his garret, while his lean wife and the baby sallied out to buy the beef.

Foggier yet, and colder! Piercing, searching, biting cold. If the good Saint Dunstan had but nipped the Evil Spirit's nose with a touch of such weather as that, instead of using his familiar weapons, then indeed he would have roared to lusty purpose. The owner of one scant young nose, gnawed and mumbled by the hungry cold as bones are gnawed by dogs, stooped down at Scrooge's keyhole to regale him with a Christmas carol: but at the first sound of—

> "God bless you merry gentlemen!
> May nothing you dismay!"

Scrooge seized the ruler with such energy of action, that the singer fled in terror, leaving the keyhole to the fog and even more congenial frost.

At length the hour of shutting up the counting-house arrived. With an ill-will Scrooge dismounted from his stool, and tacitly admitted the fact to the expectant clerk in the Tank, who instantly snuffed his candle out, and put on his hat.

"You'll want all day to-morrow, I suppose?" said Scrooge.

"If quite convenient, sir."

"It's not convenient," said Scrooge, "and it's not fair. If I was to stop half-a-crown for it, you'd think yourself ill used, I'll be bound?"

The clerk smiled faintly.

"And yet," said Scrooge, "you don't think *me* ill used, when I pay a day's wages for no work."

The clerk observed that it was only once a year.

"A poor excuse for picking a man's pocket every twenty-fifth of December!" said Scrooge, buttoning his great-coat to the chin. "But I suppose you must have the whole day. Be here all the earlier next morning!"

The clerk promised that he would; and Scrooge walked out with a growl. The office was closed in a twinkling, and the clerk, with the long ends of his white comforter dangling below his waist (for he boasted no great-coat), went down a slide on Cornhill, at the end of a lane of boys, twenty times, in honour of its being Christmas-eve, and then ran home to Camden Town as hard as he could pelt, to play at blindman's-buff.

Scrooge took his melancholy dinner in his usual melancholy tavern; and having read all the newspapers, and beguiled the rest of the evening with his banker's-book, went home to bed. He lived in chambers which had once belonged to his deceased partner. They were a gloomy suite of rooms, in a lowering pile of building up a yard, where it had so little business to be, that one could scarcely help fancying it must have run there when it was a young house, playing at hide-and-seek with other houses, and have forgotten the way out again. It was old enough now, and dreary enough, for nobody lived in it but Scrooge, the other rooms being all let out as offices. The yard was so dark that even Scrooge, who knew its every stone, was fain to grope with his hands. The fog and frost so hung about the black old gateway of the house, that it seemed as if the Genius of the Weather sat in mournful meditation on the threshold.

Now, it is a fact, that there was nothing at all particular about the knocker on the door, except that it was very large. It is also a fact, that Scrooge had seen it night and morning during his whole residence in that place; also that Scrooge had as little of what is called fancy about him as any man in the City of London, even including—which is a bold word—the corporation, aldermen, and livery. Let it also be borne in mind that Scrooge had not bestowed one thought on Marley, since his last mention of his seven-years' dead partner that afternoon. And then let any man explain to me, if he can, how it happened that Scrooge, having his key in the lock of the door, saw in the knocker, without its undergoing any intermediate process of change: not a knocker, but Marley's face.

Marley's face. It was not in impenetrable shadow as the other objects in the yard were, but had a dismal light about it, like a bad lobster in a dark cellar. It was not angry or ferocious, but looked at Scrooge as Marley used to look: with ghostly spectacles turned up upon its ghostly forehead. The hair was curiously stirred, as if by breath or hot-air; and though the eyes were wide open, they were perfectly motionless. That, and its livid colour, made it horrible; but its horror seemed to be, in spite of the face and beyond its control, rather than a part of its own expression.

As Scrooge looked fixedly at this phenomenon, it was a knocker again.

To say that he was not startled, or that his blood was not conscious of a terrible sensation to which it had been a stranger from infancy, would be untrue. But he put his hand upon the key he had relinquished, turned it sturdily, walked in, and lighted his candle.

He *did* pause, with a moment's irresolution, before he shut the door; and he *did* look cautiously behind it first, as if he half-expected to be terrified with the sight of Marley's pig-tail sticking out into the hall. But there was nothing on the back of the door, except the screws and nuts that held the knocker on; so he said "Pooh, pooh!" and closed it with a bang.

The sound resounded through the house like thunder. Every room above, and every cask in the wine-merchant's cellars below, appeared to have a separate peal of echoes of its own. Scrooge was not a man to be frightened by echoes. He fastened the door, and walked across the hall, and up the stairs: slowly too: trimming his candle as he went.

You may talk vaguely about driving a coach-and-six up a good old flight of stairs, or through a bad young Act of Parliament; but I mean to say you might have got a hearse up that staircase, and taken it broadwise, with the splinter-bar towards the wall, and the door towards the balustrades: and done it easy. There was plenty of width for that, and room to spare; which is perhaps the reason why Scrooge thought he saw a locomotive hearse going on before him in the gloom. Half a dozen gas-lamps out of the street wouldn't have lighted the entry too well, so you may suppose that it was pretty dark with Scrooge's dip.

Up Scrooge went, not caring a button for that: darkness is cheap, and Scrooge liked it. But before he shut his heavy door, he walked through his rooms to see that all was right. He had just enough recollection of the face to desire to do that.

Sitting room, bed-room, lumber-room. All as they should be. Nobody under the table, nobody under the sofa; a small fire in the grate; spoon and basin ready; and the little sauce-pan of gruel (Scrooge had a cold in his head) upon the hob. Nobody under the bed; nobody in the closet; nobody in his dressing-gown, which was hanging up in a suspicious attitude against the wall. Lumber-room as usual. Old fire-guard, old shoes, two fish-baskets, washing-stand on three legs, and a poker.

Quite satisfied, he closed his door, and locked himself in; double-locked himself in, which was not his custom. Thus secured against surprise, he took off his cravat; put on his dressing-gown and slippers, and his night-cap; and sat down before the fire to take his gruel.

It was a very low fire indeed; nothing on such a bitter night. He was obliged to sit close to it, and brood over it, before he could extract the least sensation of warmth from such a handful of fuel. The fireplace was an old one, built by some Dutch merchant long ago, and paved all round with quaint Dutch tiles, designed to illustrate the Scriptures. There were Cains and Abels; Pharaoh's daughters, Queens of Sheba, Angelic messengers descending through the air on clouds like feather-beds, Abrahams, Belshazzars, Apostles putting off to sea in butter-boats, hundreds of figures to attract his thoughts; and yet that face of Marley, seven years dead, came like the ancient Prophet's rod, and swallowed up the whole. If each smooth tile had been a blank at first, with power to shape some picture on its surface from the disjointed fragments of his thoughts, there would have been a copy of old Marley's head on every one.

"Humbug!" said Scrooge; and walked across the room.

After several turns, he sat down again. As he threw his head back in the chair, his glance happened to rest upon a bell, a disused bell, that hung in the room, and communicated for some purpose now forgotten with a chamber in the highest story of the building. It was with great astonishment, and with a strange, inexplicable dread, that as he looked, he saw this bell begin to swing. It swung so softly in the outset that it scarcely made a sound; but soon it rang out loudly, and so did every bell in the house.

This might have lasted half a minute, or a minute, but it seemed an hour. The bells ceased as they had begun, together. They were succeeded by a clanking noise, deep down below; as if some person were dragging a heavy chain over the casks in the wine-merchant's cellar. Scrooge then remembered to have heard that ghosts in haunted houses were described as dragging chains.

The cellar-door flew open with a booming sound, and then he heard the noise much louder, on the floors below; then coming up the stairs; then coming straight towards his door.

"It's humbug still!" said Scrooge. "I won't believe it."

His colour changed though, when, without a pause, it came on through the heavy door, and passed into the room before his eyes. Upon its coming in, the dying flame leaped up, as though it cried "I know him! Marley's Ghost!" and fell again.

The same face: the very same. Marley in his pig-tail, usual waistcoat, tights, and boots; the tassels on the latter bristling, like his pig-tail, and his coat-skirts, and the hair upon his head. The chain he drew was clasped about his middle. It was long, and wound about him like a tail; and it was made (for Scrooge observed it closely) of cash-boxes, keys, padlocks, ledgers, deeds, and heavy purses wrought in steel. His body was transparent: so that Scrooge, observing him, and looking through his waistcoat, could see the two buttons on his coat behind.

Scrooge had often heard it said that Marley had no bowels, but he had never believed it until now.

No, nor did he believe it even now. Though he looked the phantom through and through, and saw it standing before him; though he felt the chilling influence of its death-cold eyes; and marked the very texture of the folded kerchief bound about its head and chin, which wrapper he had not observed before: he was still incredulous, and fought against his senses.

"How now!" said Scrooge, caustic and cold as ever. "What do you want with me?"

"Much!"—Marley's voice, no doubt about it.

"Who are you?"

"Ask me who I *was*."

"Who *were* you then?" said Scrooge, raising his voice. "You're particular—for a shade." He was going to say "*to* a shade," but substituted this, as more appropriate.

"In life I was your partner, Jacob Marley."

"Can you—can you sit down?" asked Scrooge, looking doubtfully at him.

"I can."

"Do it then."

Scrooge asked the question, because he didn't know whether a ghost so transparent might find himself in a condition to take a chair; and felt that in the event of its being impossible, it might involve the necessity of an embarrassing explanation. But the ghost sat down on the opposite side of the fireplace, as if he were quite used to it.

"You don't believe in me," observed the Ghost.

"I don't," said Scrooge.

"What evidence would you have of my reality, beyond that of your senses?"

"I don't know," said Scrooge.

"Why do you doubt your senses?"

"Because," said Scrooge, "a little thing affects them. A slight disorder of the stomach makes them cheats. You may be an undigested bit of beef, a blot of mustard, a crumb of cheese, a fragment of an underdone potato. There's more of gravy than of grave about you, whatever you are!"

Scrooge was not much in the habit of cracking jokes, nor did he feel, in his heart, by any means waggish then. The truth is, that he tried to be smart, as a means of distracting his own attention, and keeping down his terror; for the spectre's voice disturbed the very marrow in his bones.

To sit, staring at those fixed, glazed eyes, in silence for a moment, would play, Scrooge felt, the very deuce with him. There was something very awful, too, in the spectre's being provided with an infernal atmosphere of its own. Scrooge could not feel it himself, but this was clearly the case; for though the Ghost sat perfectly motionless, its hair, and skirts, and tassels, were still agitated as by the hot vapour from an oven.

"You see this toothpick?" said Scrooge, returning quickly to the charge, for the reason just assigned; and wishing, though it were only for a second, to divert the vision's stony gaze from himself.

"I do," replied the Ghost.

"You are not looking at it," said Scrooge.

"But I see it," said the Ghost, "notwithstanding."

"Well!" returned Scrooge. "I have but to swallow this, and be for the rest of my days persecuted by a legion of goblins, all of my own creation. Humbug, I tell you—humbug!"

At this, the spirit raised a frightful cry, and shook its chain with such a dismal and appalling noise, that Scrooge held on tight to his chair, to save himself from falling in a swoon. But how much greater was his horror, when the phantom taking off the bandage round its head, as if it were too warm to wear in-doors, its lower jaw dropped down upon its breast!

Scrooge fell upon his knees, and clasped his hands before his face.

"Mercy!" he said. "Dreadful apparition, why do you trouble me?"

"Man of the worldly mind!" replied the Ghost, "do you believe in me or not?"

"I do," said Scrooge. "I must. But why do spirits walk the earth, and why do they come to me?"

"It is required of every man," the Ghost returned, "that the spirit within him should walk abroad among his fellowmen, and travel far and wide; and if that spirit goes not forth in life, it is condemned to do so after death. It is doomed to wander through the world—oh, woe is me!—and witness what it cannot share, but might have shared on earth, and turned to happiness!"

Again the spectre raised a cry, and shook its chain and wrung its shadowy hands.

"You are fettered," said Scrooge, trembling. "Tell me why?"

"I wear the chain I forged in life," replied the Ghost. "I made it link by link, and yard by yard; I girded it on of my own free will, and of my own free will I wore it. Is its pattern strange to *you*?"

Scrooge trembled more and more.

"Or would you know," pursued the Ghost, "the weight and length of the strong coil you bear yourself? It was full as heavy and as long as this, seven Christmas Eves ago. You have laboured on it, since. It is a ponderous chain!"

Scrooge glanced about him on the floor, in the expectation of finding himself surrounded by some fifty or sixty fathoms of iron cable: but he could see nothing.

"Jacob," he said, imploringly. "Old Jacob Marley, tell me more. Speak comfort to me, Jacob."

"I have none to give," the Ghost replied. "It comes from other regions, Ebenezer Scrooge, and is conveyed by other ministers, to other kinds of men. Nor can I tell you what I would. A very little more is all permitted to me. I cannot rest, I cannot stay, I cannot linger anywhere. My spirit never walked beyond our counting-house—mark me!—in life my spirit never roved beyond the narrow limits of our money-changing hole; and weary journeys lie before me!"

It was a habit with Scrooge, whenever he became thoughtful, to put his hands in his breeches pockets. Pondering on what the Ghost had said, he did so now, but without lifting up his eyes, or getting off his knees.

"You must have been very slow about it, Jacob," Scrooge observed, in a business-like manner, though with humility and deference.

"Slow!" the Ghost repeated.

"Seven years dead," mused Scrooge. "And travelling all the time?"

"The whole time," said the Ghost. "No rest, no peace. Incessant torture of remorse."

"You travel fast?" said Scrooge.

"On the wings of the wind," replied the Ghost.

"You might have got over a great quantity of ground in seven years," said Scrooge.

The Ghost, on hearing this, set up another cry, and clanked its chain so hideously in the dead silence of the night, that the Ward would have been justified in indicting it for a nuisance.

"Oh! captive, bound, and double-ironed," cried the phantom, "not to know, that ages of incessant labour by immortal creatures, for this earth must pass into eternity before the good of which it is susceptible is all developed. Not to know that any Christian spirit working kindly in its little sphere, whatever it may be, will find its mortal life too short for its vast means of usefulness. Not to know that no space of regret can make amends for one life's opportunity misused! Yet such was I! Oh! such was I!"

"But you were always a good man of business, Jacob," faultered Scrooge, who now began to apply this to himself.

"Business!" cried the Ghost, wringing its hands again. "Mankind was my business. The common welfare was my business; charity, mercy, forbearance, and benevolence, were, all, my business. The dealings of my trade were but a drop of water in the comprehensive ocean of my business!"

It held up its chain at arm's length, as if that were the cause of all its unavailing grief, and flung it heavily upon the ground again.

"At this time of the rolling year," the spectre said, "I suffer most. Why did I walk through crowds of fellow-beings with my eyes turned down, and never raise them to that blessed Star which led the Wise Men to a poor abode? Were there no poor homes to which its light would have conducted *me*!"

Scrooge was very much dismayed to hear the spectre going on at this rate, and began to quake exceedingly.

"Hear me!" cried the Ghost. "My time is nearly gone."

"I will," said Scrooge. "But don't be hard upon me! Don't be flowery, Jacob! Pray!"

"How it is that I appear before you in a shape that you can see, I may not tell. I have sat invisible beside you many and many a day."

It was not an agreeable idea. Scrooge shivered, and wiped the perspiration from his brow.

"That is no light part of my penance," pursued the Ghost. "I am here to-night to warn you, that you have yet a chance and hope of escaping my fate. A chance and hope of my procuring, Ebenezer."

"You were always a good friend to me," said Scrooge. "Thank'ee!"

"You will be haunted," resumed the Ghost, "by Three Spirits."

Scrooge's countenance fell almost as low as the Ghost's had done.

"Is that the chance and hope you mentioned, Jacob?" he demanded, in a faultering voice.

"It is."

"I—I think I'd rather not," said Scrooge.

"Without their visits," said the Ghost, "you cannot hope to shun the path I tread. Expect the first to-morrow, when the bell tolls one."

"Couldn't I take 'em all at once, and have it over, Jacob?" hinted Scrooge.

"Expect the second on the next night at the same hour. The third upon the next night when the last stroke of twelve has ceased to vibrate. Look to see me no more; and look that, for your own sake, you remember what has passed between us!"

When it had said these words, the spectre took its wrapper from the table, and bound it round its head, as before. Scrooge knew this, by the smart sound its teeth made, when the jaws were brought together by the bandage. He ventured to raise his eyes again, and found his supernatural visitor confronting him in an erect attitude, with its chain wound over and about its arm.

The apparition walked backward from him; and at every step it took, the window raised itself a little, so that when the spectre reached it, it was wide open. It beckoned Scrooge to approach, which he did. When they were within two paces of each other, Marley's Ghost held up its hand, warning him to come no nearer. Scrooge stopped.

Not so much in obedience, as in surprise and fear: for on the raising of the hand, he became sensible of confused noises in the air; incoherent sounds of lamentation and regret; wailings inexpressibly sorrowful and self-accusatory. The spectre, after listening for a moment, joined in the mournful dirge; and floated out upon the bleak, dark night.

Scrooge followed to the window: desperate in his curiosity. He looked out.

The air filled with phantoms, wandering hither and thither in restless haste, and moaning as they went. Every one of them wore chains like Marley's Ghost; some few (they might be guilty governments) were linked together; none were free. Many had been personally known to Scrooge in their lives. He had been quite familiar with one old ghost, in a white waistcoat, with a monstrous iron safe attached to its ankle, who cried piteously at being unable to assist a wretched woman with an infant, whom it saw below, upon a door-step. The misery with them all was, clearly, that they sought to interfere, for good, in human matters, and had lost the power for ever.

Whether these creatures faded into mist, or mist enshrouded them, he could not tell. But they and their spirit voices faded together; and the night became as it had been when he walked home.

Scrooge closed the window, and examined the door by which the Ghost had entered. It was double-locked, as he had locked it with his own hands, and the bolts were undisturbed. He tried to say "Humbug!" but stopped at the first syllable. And being, from the emotion he had undergone, or the fatigues of the day, or his glimpse of the Invisible World, or the dull conversation of the Ghost, or the lateness of the hour, much in need of repose; went straight to bed, without undressing, and fell asleep upon the instant.

STAVE TWO

THE FIRST OF THE THREE SPIRITS

When Scrooge awoke, it was so dark, that looking out of bed, he could scarcely distinguish the transparent window from the opaque walls of his chamber. He was endeavouring to pierce the darkness with his ferret eyes, when the chimes of a neighbouring church struck the four quarters. So he listened for the hour.

To his great astonishment the heavy bell went on from six to seven, and from seven to eight, and regularly up to twelve; then stopped. Twelve! It was past two when he went to bed. The clock was wrong. An icicle must have got into the works. Twelve!

He touched the spring of his repeater, to correct this most preposterous clock. Its rapid little pulse beat twelve; and stopped.

"Why, it isn't possible," said Scrooge, "that I can have slept through a whole day and far into another night. It isn't possible that anything has happened to the sun, and this is twelve at noon!"

The idea being an alarming one, he scrambled out of bed, and groped his way to the window. He was obliged to rub the frost off with the sleeve of his dressing-gown before he could see anything; and could see very little then. All he could make out was, that it was still very foggy and extremely cold, and that there was no noise of people running to and fro, and making a great stir, as there unquestionably would have been if night had beaten off bright day, and taken possession of the world. This was a great relief, because "three days after sight of this First of Exchange pay to Mr. Ebenezer Scrooge or his order," and so forth, would have become a mere United States' security if there were no days to count by.

Scrooge went to bed again, and thought, and thought, and thought it over and over and over, and could make nothing of it. The more he thought, the more perplexed he was; and the more he endeavoured not to think, the more he thought. Marley's Ghost bothered him exceedingly. Every time he resolved within himself, after mature inquiry, that it was all a dream, his mind flew back again, like a strong spring released, to its first position, and presented the same problem to be worked all through, "Was it a dream or not?"

Scrooge lay in this state until the chimes had gone three quarters more, when he remembered, on a sudden, that the Ghost had warned him of a visitation when the bell tolled one. He resolved to lie awake until the hour was passed; and, considering that he could no more go to sleep than go to Heaven, this was perhaps the wisest resolution in his power.

The quarter was so long, that he was more than once convinced he must have sunk into a doze unconsciously, and missed the clock. At length it broke upon his listening ear.

"Ding, dong!"

"A quarter past," said Scrooge, counting.

"Ding, dong!"

"Half past!" said Scrooge.

"Ding, dong!"

"A quarter to it," said Scrooge.

"Ding, dong!"

"The hour itself," said Scrooge, triumphantly, "and nothing else!"

He spoke before the hour bell sounded, which it now did with a deep, dull, hollow, melancholy ONE. Light flashed up in the room upon the instant, and the curtains of his bed were drawn.

The curtains of his bed were drawn aside, I tell you, by a hand. Not the curtains at his feet, nor the curtains at his back, but those to which his face was addressed. The curtains of his bed were drawn aside; and Scrooge, starting up into a half-recumbent attitude, found himself face to face with the unearthly visitor who drew them: as close to it as I am now to you, and I am standing in the spirit at your elbow.

It was a strange figure—like a child: yet not so like a child as like an old man, viewed through some supernatural medium, which gave him the appearance of having receded from the view, and being diminished to a child's proportions. Its hair, which hung about its neck and down its back, was white as if with age; and yet the face had not a wrinkle in it, and the

tenderest bloom was on the skin. The arms were very long
and muscular; the hands the same, as if its hold were of
uncommon strength. Its legs and feet, most delicately formed,
were, like those upper members, bare. It wore a tunic of the
purest white; and round its waist was bound a lustrous belt,
the sheen of which was beautiful. It held a branch of fresh
green holly in its hand; and, in singular contradiction of that
wintry emblem, had its dress trimmed with summer flowers.
But the strangest thing about it was, that from the crown of
its head there sprung a bright clear jet of light, by which all
this was visible; and which was doubtless the occasion of its
using, in its duller moments, a great extinguisher for a cap,
which it now held under its arm.

Even this, though, when Scrooge looked at it with increasing steadiness, was *not* its strangest quality. For as its belt
sparkled and glittered now in one part and now in another,
and what was light one instant, at another time was dark, so
the figure itself fluctuated in its distinctness: being now a
thing with one arm, now with one leg, now with twenty legs,
now a pair of legs without a head, now a head without a body:
of which dissolving parts, no outline would be visible in the
dense gloom wherein they melted away. And in the very
wonder of this, it would be itself again; distinct and clear as
ever.

"Are you the Spirit, sir, whose coming was foretold to me?"
asked Scrooge.

"I am!"

The voice was soft and gentle. Singularly low, as if instead
of being so close beside him, it were at a distance.

"Who, and what are you?" Scrooge demanded.

"I am the Ghost of Christmas Past."

"Long Past?" inquired Scrooge: observant of its dwarfish
stature.

"No. Your past."

Perhaps, Scrooge could not have told anybody why, if
anybody could have asked him; but he had a special desire to
see the Spirit in his cap; and begged him to be covered.

"What!" exclaimed the Ghost, "would you so soon put out,
with worldly hands, the light I give? Is it not enough that you
are one of those whose passions made this cap, and force me
through whole trains of years to wear it low upon my brow!"

Scrooge reverently disclaimed all intention to offend, or

any knowledge of having wilfully "bonneted" the Spirit at any period of his life. He then made bold to inquire what business brought him there.

"Your welfare!" said the Ghost.

Scrooge expressed himself much obliged, but could not help thinking that a night of unbroken rest would have been more conducive to that end. The Spirit must have heard him thinking for it said immediately:

"Your reclamation, then. Take heed!"

It put out its strong hand as it spoke, and clasped him gently by the arm.

"Rise! and walk with me!"

It would have been in vain for Scrooge to plead that the weather and the hour were not adapted to pedestrian purposes; that bed was warm, and the thermometer a long way below freezing; that he was clad but lightly in his slippers, dressing-gown, and nightcap; and that he had a cold upon him at that time. The grasp, though gentle as a woman's hand, was not to be resisted. He rose: but finding that the Spirit made towards the window, clasped its robe in supplication.

"I am a mortal," Scrooge remonstrated, "and liable to fall."

"Bear but a touch of my hand *there*," said the Spirit, laying it upon his heart, "and you shall be upheld in more than this!"

As the words were spoken, they passed through the wall, and stood upon an open country road, with fields on either hand. The city had entirely vanished. Not a vestige of it was to be seen. The darkness and the mist had vanished with it, for it was a clear, cold, winter day, with snow upon the ground.

"Good Heaven!" said Scrooge, clasping his hands together, as he looked about him. "I was bred in this place. I was a boy here!"

The Spirit gazed upon him mildly. Its gentle touch, though it had been light and instantaneous, appeared still present to the old man's sense of feeling. He was conscious of a thousand odours floating in the air, each one connected with a thousand thoughts, and hopes, and joys, and cares long, long, forgotten!

"Your lip is trembling," said the Ghost. "And what is that upon your cheek?"

Scrooge muttered, with an unusual catching in his voice,

that it was a pimple; and begged the Ghost to lead him where he would.

"You recollect the way?" inquired the Spirit.

"Remember it!" cried Scrooge with fervour—"I could walk it blindfold."

"Strange to have forgotten it for so many years!" observed the Ghost. "Let us go on."

They walked along the road; Scrooge recognising every gate, and post, and tree; until a little market-town appeared in the distance, with its bridge, its church, and winding river. Some shaggy ponies now were seen trotting towards them with boys upon their backs, who called to other boys in country gigs and carts, driven by farmers. All these boys were in great spirits, and shouted to each other, until the broad fields were so full of merry music, that the crisp air laughed to hear it.

"These are but shadows of the things that have been," said the Ghost. "They have no consciousness of us."

The jocund travellers came on; and as they came, Scrooge knew and named them every one. Why was he rejoiced beyond all bounds to see them! Why did his cold eye glisten, and his heart leap up as they went past! Why was he filled with gladness when he heard them give each other Merry Christmas, as they parted at cross-roads and bye-ways, for their several homes! What was merry Christmas to Scrooge? Out upon merry Christmas! What good had it ever done to him?

"The school is not quite deserted," said the Ghost. "A solitary child, neglected by his friends, is left there still."

Scrooge said he knew it. And he sobbed.

They left the high-road, by a well remembered lane, and soon approached a mansion of dull red brick, with a little weathercock-surmounted cupola on the roof, and a bell hanging in it. It was a large house, but one of broken fortunes; for the spacious offices were little used, their walls were damp and mossy, their windows broken, and their gates decayed. Fowls clucked and strutted in the stables; and the coach-houses and sheds were over-run with grass. Nor was it more retentive of its ancient state, within; for entering the dreary hall, and glancing through the open doors of many rooms, they found them poorly furnished, cold, and vast. There was an earthy savour in the air, a chilly bareness in the place, which associated itself somehow with too much getting up by candle-light, and not too much to eat.

They went, the Ghost and Scrooge, across the hall, to a door at the back of the house. It opened before them, and disclosed a long, bare, melancholy room, made barer still by lines of plain deal forms and desks. At one of these a lonely boy was reading near a feeble fire; and Scrooge sat down upon a form, and wept to see his poor forgotten self as he had used to be.

Not a latent echo in the house, not a squeak and scuffle from the mice behind the panelling, not a drip from the half-thawed water-spout in the dull yard behind, not a sigh among the leafless boughs of one despondent poplar, not the idle swinging of an empty store-house door, no, not a clicking in the fire, but fell upon the heart of Scrooge with a softening influence, and gave a freer passage to his tears.

The Spirit touched him on the arm, and pointed to his younger self, intent upon his reading. Suddenly a man, in foreign garments: wonderfully real and distinct to look at: stood outside the window, with an axe stuck in his belt, and leading an ass laden with wood by the bridle.

"Why, it's Ali Baba!" Scrooge exclaimed in ecstasy. "It's dear old honest Ali Baba! Yes, yes, I know! Onc Christmas time, when yonder solitary child was left here all alone, he *did* come, for the first time, just like that. Poor boy! And Valentine," said Scrooge, "and his wild brother, Orson; there they go! And what's his name, who was put down in his drawers, asleep, at the Gate of Damascus; don't you see him! And the Sultan's Groom turned upside-down by the Genii; there he is upon his head! Serve him right. I'm glad of it. What business had *he* to be married to the Princess!"

To hear Scrooge expending all the earnestness of his nature on such subjects, in a most extraordinary voice between laughing and crying; and to see his heightened and excited face; would have been a surprise to his business friends in the city, indeed.

"There's the Parrot!" cried Scrooge. "Green body and yellow tail, with a thing like a lettuce growing out of the top of his head; there he is! Poor Robin Crusoe, he called him, when he came home again after sailing round the island. 'Poor Robin Crusoe, where have you been, Robin Crusoe?' The man thought he was dreaming, but he wasn't. It was the Parrot, you know. There goes Friday, running for his life to the little creek! Halloa! Hoop! Halloo!"

Then, with a rapidity of transition very foreign to his usual character, he said, in pity for his former self, "Poor boy!" and cried again.

"I wish," Scrooge muttered, putting his hand in his pocket, and looking about him, after drying his eyes with his cuff: "but it's too late now."

"What is the matter?" asked the Spirit.

"Nothing," said Scrooge. "Nothing. There was a boy singing a Christmas Carol at my door last night. I should like to have given him something: that's all."

The Ghost smiled thoughtfully, and waved its hand: saying as it did so, "Let us see another Christmas!"

Scrooge's former self grew larger at the words, and the room became a little darker and more dirty. The panels shrunk, the windows cracked; fragments of plaster fell out of the ceiling, and the naked laths were shown instead; but how all this was brought about, Scrooge knew no more than you do. He only knew that it was quite correct; that everything had happened so; that there he was, alone again, when all the other boys had gone home for the jolly holidays.

He was not reading now, but walking up and down despairingly. Scrooge looked at the Ghost, and with a mournful shaking of his head, glanced anxiously towards the door.

It opened; and a little girl, much younger than the boy, came darting in, and putting her arms about his neck, and often kissing him, addressed him as her "Dear, dear brother."

"I have come to bring you home, dear brother!" said the child, clapping her tiny hands, and bending down to laugh. "To bring you home, home, home!"

"Home, little Fan?" returned the boy.

"Yes!" said the child, brimful of glee. "Home, for good and all. Home, for ever and ever. Father is so much kinder than he used to be, that home's like Heaven! He spoke so gently to me one dear night when I was going to bed, that I was not afraid to ask him once more if you might come home; and he said Yes, you should; and sent me in a coach to bring you. And you're to be a man!" said the child, opening her eyes, "and are never to come back here; but first, we're to be together all the Christmas long, and have the merriest time in all the world."

"You are quite a woman, little Fan!" exclaimed the boy.

She clapped her hands and laughed, and tried to touch his head; but being too little, laughed again, and stood on tiptoe to embrace him. Then she began to drag him, in her childish eagerness, towards the door; and he, nothing loth to go, accompanied her.

A terrible voice in the hall cried, "Bring down Master Scrooge's box, there!" and in the hall appeared the schoolmaster himself, who glared on Master Scrooge with a ferocious condescension, and threw him into a dreadful state of mind by shaking hands with him. He then conveyed him and his sister into the veriest old well of a shivering best-parlour that ever was seen, where the maps upon the wall, and the celestial and terrestrial globes in the windows were waxy with cold. Here he produced a decanter of curiously light wine, and a block of curiously heavy cake, and administered instalments of those dainties to the young people: at the same time, sending out a meagre servant to offer a glass of "something" to the postboy, who answered that he thanked the gentleman, but if it was the same tap as he had tasted before, he had rather not. Master Scrooge's trunk being by this time tied on to the top of the chaise, the children bade the schoolmaster good-bye right willingly; and getting into it, drove gaily down the garden-sweep: the quick wheels dashing the hoar-frost and snow from off the dark leaves of the evergreens like spray.

"Always a delicate creature, whom a breath might have withered," said the Ghost. "But she had a large heart!"

"So she had," cried Scrooge. "You're right. I'll not gainsay it, Spirit. God forbid!"

"She died a woman," said the Ghost, "and had, as I think, children."

"One child," Scrooge returned.

"True," said the Ghost. "Your nephew!"

Scrooge seemed uneasy in his mind; and answered briefly, "Yes."

Although they had but that moment left the school behind them, they were now in the busy thoroughfares of a city, where shadowy passengers passed and repassed; where shadowy carts and coaches battled for the way, and all the strife and tumult of a real city were. It was made plain enough, by the dressing of the shops, that here too it was Christmas time again; but it was evening, and the streets were lighted up.

The Ghost stopped at a certain warehouse door, and asked Scrooge if he knew it.

"Know it!" said Scrooge. "Was I apprenticed here?"

They went in. At sight of an old gentleman in a Welch wig, sitting behind such a high desk, that if he had been two inches taller he must have knocked his head against the ceiling, Scrooge cried in great excitement:

"Why, it's old Fezziwig! Bless his heart; it's Fezziwig alive again!"

Old Fezziwig laid down his pen, and looked up at the clock, which pointed to the hour of seven. He rubbed his hands; adjusted his capacious waistcoat; laughed all over himself, from his shoes to his organ of benevolence; and called out in a comfortable, oily, rich, fat, jovial voice:

"Yo ho, there! Ebenezer! Dick!"

Scrooge's former self, now grown a young man, came briskly in, accompanied by his fellow-'prentice.

"Dick Wilkins, to be sure!" said Scrooge to the Ghost. "Bless me, yes. There he is. He was very much attached to me, was Dick. Poor Dick! Dear, dear!"

"Yo ho, my boys!" said Fezziwig. "No more work tonight. Christmas Eve, Dick. Christmas, Ebenezer! Let's have the shutters up," cried old Fezziwig, with a sharp clap of his hands, "before a man can say, Jack Robinson!"

You wouldn't believe how those two fellows went at it! They charged into the street with the shutters—one, two, three—had 'em up in their places—four, five, six—barred 'em and pinned 'em—seven, eight, nine—and came back before you could have got to twelve, panting like race-horses.

"Hilli-ho!" cried old Fezziwig, skipping down from the high desk, with wonderful agility. "Clear away, my lads, and let's have lots of room here! Hilli-ho, Dick! Chirrup, Ebenezer!"

Clear away! There was nothing they wouldn't have cleared away, or couldn't have cleared away, with old Fezziwig looking on. It was done in a minute. Every movable was packed off, as if it were dismissed from public life for evermore; the floor was swept and watered, the lamps were trimmed, fuel was heaped upon the fire; and the warehouse was as snug, and warm, and dry, and bright a ball-room, as you would desire to see upon a winter's night.

In came a fiddler with a music-book, and went up to the lofty desk, and made an orchestra of it, and tuned like fifty stomach-aches. In came Mrs. Fezziwig, one vast substantial smile. In came the three Miss Fezziwigs, beaming and lovable. In came the six young followers whose hearts they broke. In came all the young men and women employed in the business. In came the housemaid, with her cousin, the baker. In came the cook, with her brother's particular friend, the milkman. In came the boy from over the way, who was suspected of not having board enough from his master; trying to hide himself behind the girl from next door but one, who was proved to have had her ears pulled by her Mistress. In they all came, one after another; some shyly, some boldly, some gracefully, some awkwardly, some pushing, some pulling; in they all came, anyhow and everyhow. Away they all went, twenty couple at once, hands half round and back again the other way; down the middle and up again; round and round in various stages of affectionate grouping; old top couple always turning up in the wrong place; new top couple starting off again, as soon as they got there; all top couples at last, and not a bottom one to help them. When this result was brought about, old Fezziwig, clapping his hands to stop the dance, cried out, "Well done!" and the fiddler plunged his hot face into a pot of porter, especially provided for that purpose. But scorning rest upon his reappearance, he instantly began again, though there were no dancers yet, as if the other fiddler had been carried home, exhausted, on a shutter; and he were a bran-new man resolved to beat him out of sight, or perish.

There were more dances, and there were forfeits, and more dances, and there was cake, and there was negus, and there was a great piece of Cold Roast, and there was a great piece of Cold Boiled, and there were mince-pies, and plenty of beer. But the great effect of the evening came after the Roast and Boiled, when the fiddler (an artful dog, mind! The sort of man who knew his business better than you or I could have told it him!) struck up "Sir Roger de Coverley." Then old Fezziwig stood out to dance with Mrs. Fezziwig. Top couple, too; with a good stiff piece of work cut out for them; three or four and twenty pair of partners; people who were not to be trifled with; people who *would* dance, and had no notion of walking.

But if they had been twice as many: ah, four times: old Fezziwig would have been a match for them, and so would Mrs. Fezziwig. As to *her*, she was worthy to be his partner in every sense of the term. If that's not high praise, tell me higher, and I'll use it. A positive light appeared to issue from Fezziwig's calves. They shone in every part of the dance like moons. You couldn't have predicted, at any given time, what would become of 'em next. And when old Fezziwig and Mrs. Fezziwig had gone all through the dance; advance and retire, hold hands with your partner; bow and curtsey; corkscrew; thread-the-needle, and back again to your place; Fezziwig "cut"—cut so deftly, that he appeared to wink with his legs, and came upon his feet again without a stagger.

When the clock struck eleven, this domestic ball broke up. Mr. and Mrs. Fezziwig took their stations, one on either side the door, and shaking hands with every person individually as he or she went out, wished him or her a Merry Christmas. When everybody had retired but the two 'prentices, they did the same to them; and thus the cheerful voices died away, and the lads were left to their beds; which were under a counter in the back-shop.

During the whole of this time, Scrooge had acted like a man out of his wits. His heart and soul were in the scene, and with his former self. He corroborated everything, remembered everything, enjoyed everything, and underwent the strangest agitation. It was not until now, when the bright faces of his former self and Dick were turned from them, that he remembered the Ghost, and became conscious that it was looking full upon him, while the light upon its head burnt very clear.

"A small matter," said the Ghost, "to make these silly folks so full of gratitude."

"Small!" echoed Scrooge.

The Spirit signed to him to listen to the two apprentices, who were pouring out their hearts in praise of Fezziwig: and when he had done so, said,

"Why! Is it not? He has spent but a few pounds of your mortal money: three or four, perhaps. Is that so much that he deserves this praise?"

"It isn't that," said Scrooge, heated by the remark, and speaking unconsciously like his former, not his latter, self. "It isn't that, Spirit. He has the power to render us happy or unhappy; to make our service light or burdensome; a pleasure or a toil. Say that his power lies in words and looks; in things so slight and insignificant that it is impossible to add and count 'em up: what then? The happiness he gives, is quite as great as if it cost a fortune."

He felt the Spirit's glance, and stopped.

"What is the matter?" asked the Ghost.

"Nothing particular," said Scrooge.

"Something, I think?" the Ghost insisted.

"No," said Scrooge, "No. I should like to be able to say a word or two to my clerk just now! That's all."

His former self turned down the lamps as he gave utterance to the wish; and Scrooge and the Ghost again stood side by side in the open air.

"My time grows short," observed the Spirit. "Quick!"

This was not addressed to Scrooge, or to any one whom he could see, but it produced an immediate effect. For again Scrooge saw himself. He was older now; a man in the prime of life. His face had not the harsh and rigid lines of later years; but it had begun to wear the signs of care and avarice. There was an eager, greedy, restless motion in the eye, which showed the passion that had taken root, and where the shadow of the growing tree would fall.

He was not alone, but sat by the side of a fair young girl in a mourning-dress: in whose eyes there were tears, which sparkled in the light that shone out of the Ghost of Christmas Past.

"It matters little," she said, softly. "To you, very little. Another idol has displaced me; and if it can cheer and comfort you in time to come, as I would have tried to do, I have no just cause to grieve."

"What Idol has displaced you?" he rejoined.

"A golden one."

"This is the even-handed dealing of the world!" he said. "There is nothing on which it is so hard as poverty; and there is nothing it professes to condemn with such severity as the pursuit of wealth!"

"You fear the world too much," she answered, gently. "All your other hopes have merged into the hope of being beyond the chance of its sordid reproach. I have seen your nobler aspirations fall off one by one, until the master-passion, Gain, engrosses you. Have I not?"

"What then?" he retorted. "Even if I have grown so much wiser, what then? I am not changed towards you."

She shook her head.

"Am I?"

"Our contract is an old one. It was made when we were both poor and content to be so, until, in good season, we could improve our worldly fortune by our patient industry. You *are* changed. When it was made, you were another man."

"I was a boy," he said impatiently.

"Your own feeling tells you that you were not what you are," she returned. "I am. That which promised happiness when we were one in heart, is fraught with misery now that we are two. How often and how keenly I have thought of this, I will not say. It is enough that I *have* thought of it, and can release you."

"Have I ever sought release?"

"In words. No. Never."

"In what, then?"

"In a changed nature; in an altered spirit; in another atmosphere of life; 'another Hope as its great end. In everything that made my love of any worth or value in your sight. If this had never been between us," said the girl, looking mildly, but with steadiness, upon him; "tell me, would you seek me out and try to win me now? Ah, no!"

He seemed to yield to the justice of this supposition, in spite of himself. But he said, with a struggle, "You think not."

"I would gladly think otherwise if I could," she answered. "Heaven knows! When *I* have learned a Truth like this, I know how strong and irresistible it must be. But if you were free to-day, to-morrow, yesterday, can even I believe that you would choose a dowerless girl—you who, in your very confidence with her, weigh everything by Gain: or, choosing her, if for a moment you were false enough to your one guiding principle to do so, do I not know that your repentance and regret would surely follow? I do; and I release you. With a full heart, for the love of him you once were."

He was about to speak; but with her head turned from him, she resumed.

"You may—the memory of what is past half makes me hope you will—have pain in this. A very, very brief time, and you will dismiss the recollection of it, gladly, as an unprofitable dream, from which it happened well that you awoke. May you be happy in the life you have chosen!"

She left him; and they parted.

"Spirit!" said Scrooge, "show me no more! Conduct me home. Why do you delight to torture me?"

"One shadow more!" exclaimed the Ghost.

"No more!" cried Scrooge. "No more. I don't wish to see it. Show me no more!"

But the relentless Ghost pinioned him in both his arms, and forced him to observe what happened next.

They were in another scene and place: a room, not very large or handsome, but full of comfort. Near to the winter fire sat a beautiful young girl, so like the last that Scrooge believed it was the same, until he saw *her*, now a comely matron, sitting opposite her daughter. The noise in this room was perfectly tumultuous, for there were more children there, than Scrooge in his agitated state of mind could count; and, unlike the celebrated herd in the poem, they were not forty children conducting themselves like one, but every child was conducting itself like forty. The consequences were uproarious beyond belief; but no one seemed to care; on the contrary, the mother and daughter laughed heartily, and enjoyed it very much; and the latter, soon beginning to mingle in the sports, got pillaged by the young brigands most ruthlessly. What would I not have given to be one of them! Though I never could have been so rude, no, no! I wouldn't for the wealth of all the world have crushed that braided hair, and torn it down; and for the precious little shoe, I wouldn't have plucked it off, God bless my soul! to save my life. As to measuring her waist in sport, as they did, bold young brood, I couldn't have done it; I should have expected my arm to have grown round it for a punishment, and never come straight again. And yet I should have dearly liked, I own, to have touched her lips; to have questioned her, that she might have opened them; to have looked upon the lashes of her downcast eyes, and never raised a blush; to have let loose waves of hair, an inch of which would be a keepsake beyond price: in short, I should have liked, I do confess, to have had the lightest licence of a child, and yet been man enough to know its value.

But now a knocking at the door was heard, and such a rush

immediately ensued that she with laughing face and plundered dress was borne towards it the centre of a flushed and boisterous group, just in time to greet the father, who came home attended by a man laden with Christmas toys and presents. Then the shouting and the struggling, and the onslaught that was made on the defenceless porter! The scaling him with chairs for ladders, to dive into his pockets, despoil him of brown-paper parcels, hold on tight by his cravat, hug him round the neck, pommel his back, and kick his legs in irrepressible affection! The shouts of wonder and delight with which the development of every package was received! The terrible announcement that the baby had been taken in the act of putting a doll's frying-pan into his mouth, and was more than suspected of having swallowed a fictitious turkey, glued on a wooden platter! The immense relief of finding this a false alarm! The joy, and gratitude, and ecstasy! They are all indescribable alike. It is enough that by degrees the children and their emotions got out of the parlour and by one stair at a time, up to the top of the house; where they went to bed, and so subsided.

And now Scrooge looked on more attentively than ever, when the master of the house, having his daughter leaning fondly on him, sat down with her and her mother at his own fireside; and when he thought that such another creature, quite as graceful and as full of promise, might have called him father, and been a spring-time in the haggard winter of his life, his sight grew very dim indeed.

"Belle," said the husband, turning to his wife with a smile, "I saw an old friend of yours this afternoon."

"Who was it?"

"Guess!"

"How can I? Tut, don't I know," she added in the same breath, laughing as he laughed. "Mr. Scrooge."

"Mr. Scrooge it was. I passed his office window; and as it was not shut up, and he had a candle inside, I could scarcely help seeing him. His partner lies upon the point of death, I hear; and there he sat alone. Quite alone in the world, I do believe."

"Spirit!" said Scrooge in a broken voice, "remove me from this place."

"I told you these were shadows of the things that have

been," said the Ghost. "That they are what they are, do not blame me!"

"Remove me!" Scrooge exclaimed. "I cannot bear it!"

He turned upon the Ghost, and seeing that it looked upon him with a face, in which in some strange way there were fragments of all the faces it had shown him, wrestled with it.

"Leave me! Take me back. Haunt me no longer!"

In the struggle, if that can be called a struggle in which the Ghost with no visible resistance on its own part was undisturbed by any effort of its adversary, Scrooge observed that its light was burning high and bright; and dimly connecting that with its influence over him, he seized the extinguisher-cap, and by a sudden action pressed it down upon its head.

The Spirit dropped beneath it, so that the extinguisher covered its whole form; but though Scrooge pressed it down with all his force, he could not hide the light: which streamed from under it, in a unbroken flood upon the ground.

He was conscious of being exhausted, and overcome by an irresistible drowsiness; and, further, of being in his own bedroom. He gave the cap a parting squeeze, in which his hand relaxed; and had barely time to reel to bed, before he sank into a heavy sleep.

STAVE THREE

THE SECOND OF THE THREE SPIRITS

Awaking in the middle of a prodigiously tough snore, and sitting up in bed to get his thoughts together, Scrooge had no occasion to be told that the bell was again upon the stroke of One. He felt that he was restored to consciousness in the right nick of time, for the especial purpose of holding a conference with the second messenger despatched to him through Jacob Marley's intervention. But, finding that he turned uncomfortably cold when he began to wonder which of his curtains this new spectre would draw back, he put them every one aside with his own hands; and lying down again, established a sharp look-out all round the bed. For he wished to challenge the Spirit on the moment of its appearance, and did not wish to be taken by surprise and made nervous.

Gentlemen of the free-and-easy sort, who plume themselves on being acquainted with a move or two, and being usually equal to the time-of-day, express the wide range of their capacity for adventure by observing that they are good for anything from pitch-and-toss to manslaughter; between which opposite extremes, no doubt, there lies a tolerably wide and comprehensive range of subjects. Without venturing for Scrooge quite as hardily as this, I don't mind calling on you to believe that he was ready for a good broad field of strange appearances, and that nothing between a baby and a rhinoceros would have astonished him very much.

Now, being prepared for almost anything, he was not by any means prepared for nothing; and, consequently, when the Bell struck One, and no shape appeared, he was taken with a violent fit of trembling. Five minutes, ten minutes, a quarter of an hour went by, yet nothing came. All this time, he lay upon his bed, the very core and centre of a blaze of ruddy light, which streamed upon it when the clock proclaimed the hour; and which being only light, was more alarming than a dozen ghosts, as he was powerless to make out what it meant, or would be at; and was sometimes apprehensive that he might be at that very moment an interesting case of spontaneous combustion, without having the consolation of knowing it. At last, however, he began to think—as you or I would have thought at first; for it is always the person not in the predicament who knows what ought to have been done in it, and would unquestionably have done it too—at last, I say, he began to think that the source and secret of this ghostly light might be in the adjoining room: from whence, on further tracing it, it seemed to shine. This idea taking full possession of his mind, he got up softly and shuffled in his slippers to the door.

The moment Scrooge's hand was on the lock, a strange voice called him by his name, and bade him enter. He obeyed.

It was his own room. There was no doubt about that. But it had undergone a surprising transformation. The walls and ceiling were so hung with living green, that it looked a perfect grove, from every part of which, bright gleaming berries glistened. The crisp leaves of holly, mistletoe, and ivy reflected back the light, as if so many little mirrors had been scattered there; and such a mighty blaze went roaring up the chimney, as that dull petrification of a hearth had never known in Scrooge's time, or Marley's, or for many and many a winter season gone. Heaped up on the floor, to form a kind of throne, were turkeys, geese, game, poultry, brawn, great joints of meat, sucking-pigs, long wreaths of sausages, mince-pies, plum-puddings, barrels of oysters, red-hot chestnuts, cherry-cheeked apples, juicy oranges, luscious pears, immense twelfth-cakes, and seething bowls of punch, that made the chamber dim with their delicious steam. In easy state upon this couch, there sat a jolly Giant, glorious to see; who bore a glowing torch, in shape not unlike Plenty's horn, and held it up, high up, to shed its light on Scrooge, as he came peeping round the door.

"Come in!" exclaimed the Ghost. "Come in! and know me better, man!"

Scrooge entered timidly, and hung his head before this Spirit. He was not the dogged Scrooge he had been; and though the Spirit's eyes were clear and kind, he did not like to meet them.

"I am the Ghost of Christmas Present," said the Spirit. "Look upon me!"

Scrooge reverently did so. It was clothed in one simple deep green robe, or mantle, bordered with white fur. This garment hung so loosely on the figure, that its capacious breast was bare, as if disdaining to be warded or concealed by any artifice. Its feet, observable beneath the ample folds of the garment, were also bare; and on its head it wore no other covering than a holly wreath, set here and there with shining icicles. Its dark brown curls were long and free: free as its genial face, its sparkling eye, its open hand, its cheery voice, its unconstrained demeanour, and its joyful air. Girded round its middle was an antique scabbard; but no sword was in it, and the ancient sheath was eaten up with rust.

"You have never seen the like of me before!" exclaimed the Spirit.

"Never," Scrooge made answer to it.

"Have never walked forth with the younger members of

my family; meaning (for I am very young) my elder brothers born in these later years?" pursued the Phantom.

"I don't think I have," said Scrooge. "I am afraid I have not. Have you had many brothers, Spirit?"

"More than eighteen hundred," said the Ghost.

"A tremendous family to provide for!" muttered Scrooge.

The Ghost of Christmas Present rose.

"Spirit," said Scrooge submissively, "conduct me where you will. I went forth last night on compulsion, and I learnt a lesson which is working now. To-night, if you have aught to teach me, let me profit by it."

"Touch my robe!"

Scrooge did as he was told, and held it fast.

Holly, mistletoe, red berries, ivy, turkeys, geese, game, poultry, brawn, meat, pigs, sausages, oysters, pies, puddings, fruit, and punch, all vanished instantly. So did the room, the fire, the ruddy glow, the hour of night, and they stood in the city streets on Christmas morning, where (for the weather was severe) the people made a rough, but brisk and not unpleasant kind of music, in scraping the snow from the pavement in front of their dwellings, and from the tops of their houses: whence it was mad delight to the boys to see it come plumping down into the road below, and splitting into artificial little snow-storms.

The house fronts looked black enough, and the windows blacker, contrasting with the smooth white sheet of snow upon the roofs, and with the dirtier snow upon the ground; which last deposit had been ploughed up in deep furrows by the heavy wheels of carts and waggons; furrows that crossed and re-crossed each other hundreds of times where the great streets branched off, and made intricate channels, hard to trace, in the thick yellow mud and icy water. The sky was gloomy, and the shortest streets were choked up with a dingy mist, half thawed, half frozen, whose heavier particles descended in a shower of sooty atoms, as if all the chimneys in Great Britain had, by one consent, caught fire, and were blazing away to their dear hearts' content. There was nothing very cheerful in the climate or the town, and yet was there an air of cheerfulness abroad that the clearest summer air and brightest summer sun might have endeavoured to diffuse in vain.

For the people who were shovelling away on the housetops

were jovial and full of glee; calling out to one another from the parapets, and now and then exchanging a facetious snowball—better-natured missile far than many a wordy jest—laughing heartily if it went right, and not less heartily if it went wrong. The poulterers' shops were still half open, and the fruiterers' were radiant in their glory. There were great round, pot-bellied baskets of chestnuts, shaped like the waist-coats of jolly old gentlemen, lolling at the doors, and tumbling out into the street in their apoplectic opulence. There were ruddy, brown-faced, broad-girthed Spanish Onions, shining in the fatness of their growth like Spanish Friars; and winking from their shelves in wanton slyness at the girls as they went by, and glanced demurely at the hung-up mistletoe. There were pears and apples, clustered high in blooming pyramids; there were bunches of grapes, made in the shopkeepers' benevolence to dangle from conspicuous hooks, that people's mouths might water gratis as they passed; there were piles of filberts, mossy and brown, recalling, in their fragrance, ancient walks among the woods, and pleasant shufflings ankle deep through withered leaves; there were Norfolk Biffins, squab and swarthy, setting off the yellow of the oranges and lemons, and, in the great compactness of their juicy persons, urgently entreating and beseeching to be carried home in paper bags and eaten after dinner. The very gold and silver fish, set forth among these choice fruits in a bowl, though members of a dull and stagnant-blooded race, appeared to know that there was something going on; and, to a fish, went gasping round and round their little world in slow and passionless excitement.

The Grocers'! oh the Grocers'! nearly closed, with perhaps two shutters down, or one; but through those gaps such glimpses! It was not alone that the scales descending on the counter made a merry sound, or that the twine and roller parted company so briskly, or that the canisters were rattled up and down like juggling tricks, or even that the blended scents of tea and coffee were so grateful to the nose, or even that the raisins were so plentiful and rare, the almonds so extremely white, the sticks of cinnamon so long and straight, the other spices so delicious, the candied fruits so caked and spotted with molten sugar as to make the coldest lookers-on feel faint and subsequently bilious. Nor was it that the figs were moist and pulpy, or that the French plums blushed in modest tartness from their highly-decorated boxes, or that everything was good to eat and in its Christmas dress: but the customers were all so hurried and so eager in the hopeful promise of the day, that they tumbled up against each other at the door, clashing their wicker baskets wildly, and left their purchases upon the counter, and came running back to fetch them, and committed hundreds of the like mistakes in the best humour possible; while the Grocer and his people were so frank and fresh that the polished hearts with which they fastened their aprons behind might have been their own, worn outside for general inspection, and for Christmas daws to peck at if they chose.

But soon the steeples called good people all, to church and chapel, and away they came, flocking through the streets in their best clothes, and with their gayest faces. And at the same time there emerged from scores of bye streets, lanes, and nameless turnings, innumerable people, carrying their dinners to the bakers' shops. The sight of these poor revellers appeared to interest the Spirit very much, for he stood with Scrooge beside him in a baker's doorway, and taking off the covers as their bearers passed, sprinkled incense on their dinners from his torch. And it was a very uncommon kind of torch, for once or twice when there were angry words between some dinner-carriers who had jostled each other, he shed a few drops of water on them from it, and their good humour was restored directly. For they said, it was a shame to quarrel upon Christmas Day. And so it was! God love it, so it was!

In time the bells ceased, and the bakers' were shut up; and yet there was a genial shadowing forth of all these dinners and the progress of their cooking, in the thawed blotch of wet above each baker's oven; where the pavement smoked as if its stones were cooking too.

"Is there a peculiar flavour in what you sprinkle from your torch?" asked Scrooge.

"There is. My own."

"Would it apply to any kind of dinner on this day?" asked Scrooge.

"To any kindly given. To a poor one most."

"Why to a poor one most?" asked Scrooge.

"Because it needs it most."

"Spirit," said Scrooge, after a moment's thought, "I wonder

you, of all the beings in the many worlds about us, should desire to cramp these people's opportunities of innocent enjoyment."

"I!" cried the Spirit.

"You would deprive them of their means of dining every seventh day, often the only day on which they can be said to dine at all," said Scrooge. "Wouldn't you?"

"I!" cried the Spirit.

"You seek to close these places on the Seventh Day?" said Scrooge. "And it comes to the same thing."

"*I* seek!" exclaimed the Spirit.

"Forgive me if I am wrong. It has been done in your name, or at least in that of your family," said Scrooge.

"There are some upon this earth of yours," returned the Spirit, "who lay claim to know us, and who do their deeds of passion, pride, ill-will, hatred, envy, bigotry, and selfishness in our name, who are as strange to us and all our kith and kin, as if they had never lived. Remember that, and charge their doings on themselves, not us."

Scrooge promised that he would; and they went on, invisible, as they had been before, into the suburbs of the town. It was a remarkable quality of the Ghost (which Scrooge had observed at the baker's) that notwithstanding his gigantic size, he could accommodate himself to any place with ease; and that he stood beneath a low roof quite as gracefully and like a supernatural creature, as it was possible he could have done in any lofty hall.

And perhaps it was the pleasure the good Spirit had in showing off this power of his, or else it was his own kind, generous, hearty nature, and his sympathy with all poor men, that led him straight to Scrooge's clerk's; for there he went, and took Scrooge with him, holding to his robe; and on the threshold of the door the Spirit smiled, and stopped to bless Bob Cratchit's dwelling with the sprinkling of his torch. Think of that! Bob had but fifteen "Bob" a-week himself; he pocketed on Saturdays but fifteen copies of his Christian name; and yet the Ghost of Christmas Present blessed his four-roomed house!

Then up rose Mrs. Cratchit, Cratchit's wife, dressed out but poorly in a twice-turned gown, but brave in ribbons, which are cheap and make a goodly show for sixpence; and she laid the cloth, assisted by Belinda Cratchit, second of her daughters, also brave in ribbons; while Master Peter Cratchit plunged a fork into the saucepan of potatoes, and getting the corners of his monstrous shirt-collar (Bob's private property, conferred upon his son and heir in honour of the day) into his mouth, rejoiced to find himself so gallantly attired, and yearned to show his linen in the fashionable Parks. And now two smaller Cratchits, boy and girl, came tearing in, screaming that outside the baker's they had smelt the goose, and known it for their own; and basking in luxurious thoughts of sage and onion, these young Cratchits danced about the table, and exalted Master Peter Cratchit to the skies, while he (not proud, although his collars nearly choked him) blew the fire, until the slow potatoes bubbling up, knocked loudly at the saucepan-lid to be let out and peeled.

"What has ever got your precious father then," said Mrs. Cratchit. "And your brother, Tiny Tim; and Martha warn't as late last Christmas Day by half-an-hour!"

"Here's Martha, mother!" said a girl, appearing as she spoke.

"Here's Martha, mother!" cried the two young Cratchits. "Hurrah! There's *such* a goose, Martha!"

"Why, bless your heart alive, my dear, how late you are!" said Mrs. Cratchit, kissing her a dozen times, and taking off her shawl and bonnet for her, with officious zeal.

"We'd a deal of work to finish up last night," replied the girl, "and had to clear away this morning, mother!"

"Well! Never mind so long as you are come," said Mrs. Cratchit. "Sit ye down before the fire, my dear, and have a warm, Lord bless ye!"

"No no! There's father coming," cried the two young Cratchits, who were everywhere at once. "Hide Martha, hide!"

So Martha hid herself, and in came little Bob, the father, with at least three feet of comforter exclusive of the fringe, hanging down before him; and his thread-bare clothes darned up and brushed, to look seasonable; and Tiny Tim upon his shoulder. Alas for Tiny Tim, he bore a little crutch, and had his limbs supported by an iron frame!

"Why, where's our Martha?" cried Bob Cratchit looking round.

"Not coming," said Mrs. Cratchit.

"Not coming!" said Bob, with a sudden declension in his

high spirits; for he had been Tim's blood horse all the way from church, and had come home rampant. "Not coming upon Christmas Day!"

Martha didn't like to see him disappointed, if it were only in joke; so she came out prematurely from behind the closet door, and ran into his arms, while the two young Cratchits hustled Tiny Tim, and bore him off into the wash-house, that he might hear the pudding singing in the copper.

"And how did little Tim behave?" asked Mrs. Cratchit, when she had rallied Bob on his credulity and Bob had hugged his daughter to his heart's content.

"As good as gold," said Bob, "and better. Somehow he gets thoughtful sitting by himself so much, and thinks the strangest things you ever heard. He told me, coming home, that he hoped the people saw him in the church, because he was a cripple, and it might be pleasant to them to remember upon Christmas Day, who made lame beggars walk and blind men see."

Bob's voice was tremulous when he told them this, and trembled more when he said that Tiny Tim was growing strong and hearty.

His active little crutch was heard upon the floor, and back came Tiny Tim before another word was spoken, escorted by his brother and sister to his stool before the fire; and while Bob, turning up his cuffs—as if, poor fellow, they were capable of being made more shabby—compounded some hot mixture in a jug with gin and lemons, and stirred it round and round and put it on the hob to simmer; Master Peter and the two ubiquitous young Cratchits went to fetch the goose, with which they soon returned in high procession.

Such a bustle ensued that you might have thought a goose the rarest of all birds; a feathered phenomenon, to which a black swan was a matter of course; and in truth it was something very like it in that house. Mrs. Cratchit made the gravy (ready beforehand in a little saucepan) hissing hot; Master Peter mashed the potatoes with incredible vigour; Miss Belinda sweetened up the apple-sauce; Martha dusted the hot plates; Bob took Tiny Tim beside him in a tiny corner at the table; the two young Cratchits set chairs for everybody, not forgetting themselves, and mounting guard upon their posts, crammed spoons into their mouths, lest they should shriek for goose before their turn came to be helped. At last the dishes were set on, and grace was said. It was succeeded by a breathless pause, as Mrs. Cratchit, looking slowly all along the carving-knife, prepared to plunge it in the breast; but when she did, and when the long expected gush of stuffing issued forth, one murmur of delight arose all round the board, and even Tiny Tim, excited by the two young Cratchits, beat on the table with the handle of his knife, and feebly cried Hurrah!

There never was such a goose. Bob said he didn't believe there ever was such a goose cooked. Its tenderness and flavour, size and cheapness, were the themes of universal admiration. Eked out by the apple-sauce and mashed potatoes, it was a sufficient dinner for the whole family; indeed, as Mrs. Cratchit said with great delight (surveying one small atom of a bone upon the dish), they hadn't ate it all at last! Yet every one had had enough, and the youngest Cratchits in particular, were steeped in sage and onion to the eyebrows! But now, the plates being changed by Miss Belinda, Mrs. Cratchit left the room alone—too nervous to bear witnesses—to take the pudding up, and bring it in.

Suppose it should not be done enough! Suppose it should break in turning out! Suppose somebody should have got over the wall of the back-yard, and stolen it, while they were merry with the goose: a supposition at which the two young Cratchits became livid! All sorts of horrors were supposed.

Hallo! A great deal of steam! The pudding was out of the copper. A smell like a washing-day! That was the cloth. A smell like an eating-house, and a pastry cook's next door to each other, with a laundress's next door to that! That was the pudding. In half a minute Mrs. Cratchit entered: flushed, but smiling proudly: with the pudding, like a speckled cannon-ball, so hard and firm, blazing in half of half-a-quartern of ignited brandy, and bedight with Christmas holly stuck into the top.

Oh, a wonderful pudding! Bob Cratchit said, and calmly too, that he regarded it as the greatest success achieved by Mrs. Cratchit since their marriage. Mrs. Cratchit said that now the weight was off her mind, she would confess she had had her doubts about the quantity of flour. Everybody had something to say about it, but nobody said or thought it was at all a small pudding for a large family. It would have been flat heresy to do so. Any Cratchit would have blushed to hint at such a thing.

At last the dinner was all done, the cloth was cleared, the hearth swept, and the fire made up. The compound in the jug being tasted, and considered perfect, apples and oranges were put upon the table, and a shovel-full of chestnuts on the fire. Then all the Cratchit family drew round the hearth, in what Bob Cratchit called a circle, meaning half a one; and at Bob Cratchit's elbow stood the family display of glass; two tumblers, and a custard-cup without a handle.

These held the hot stuff from the jug, however, as well as golden goblets would have done; and Bob served it out with beaming looks, while the chestnuts on the fire sputtered and crackled noisily. Then Bob proposed:

"A Merry Christmas to us all, my dears. God bless us!"

Which all the family re-echoed.

"God bless us every one!" said Tiny Tim, the last of all.

He sat very close to his father's side, upon his little stool. Bob held his withered little hand in his, as if he loved the child, and wished to keep him by his side, and dreaded that he might be taken from him.

"Spirit," said Scrooge, with an interest he had never felt before, "tell me if Tiny Tim will live."

"I see a vacant seat," replied the Ghost, "in the poor chimney corner, and a crutch without an owner, carefully preserved. If these shadows remain unaltered by the Future, the child will die."

"No, no," said Scrooge. "Oh no, kind Spirit! say he will be spared."

"If these shadows remain unaltered by the Future, none other of my race," returned the Ghost, "will find him here. What then? If he be like to die, he had better do it, and decrease the surplus population."

Scrooge hung his head to hear his own words quoted by the Spirit, and was overcome with penitence and grief.

"Man," said the Ghost, "if man you be in heart, not adamant, forbear that wicked cant until you have discovered What the surplus is, and Where it is. Will you decide what men shall live, what men shall die? It may be, that in the sight of Heaven, you are more worthless and less fit to live than millions like this poor man's child. Oh God! to hear the

Insect on the leaf pronouncing on the too much life among his hungry brothers in the dust!"

Scrooge bent before the Ghost's rebuke, and trembling cast his eyes upon the ground. But he raised them speedily, on hearing his own name.

"Mr. Scrooge!" said Bob; "I'll give you Mr. Scrooge, the Founder of the Feast!"

"The Founder of the Feast indeed!" cried Mrs. Cratchit, reddening. "I wish I had him here. I'd give him a piece of my mind to feast upon, and I hope he'd have a good appetite for it."

"My dear," said Bob, "the children; Christmas Day."

"It should be Christmas Day, I am sure," said she, "on which one drinks the health of such an odious, stingy, hard, unfeeling man as Mr. Scrooge. You know he is, Robert! Nobody knows it better than you do, poor fellow!"

"My dear," was Bob's mild answer, "Christmas Day."

"I'll drink his health for your sake and the Day's," said Mrs. Cratchit, "not for his. Long life to him! A merry Christmas and a happy new year!—he'll be very merry and very happy, I have no doubt!"

The children drank the toast after her. It was the first of their proceedings which had no heartiness in it. Tiny Tim drank it last of all, but he didn't care twopence for it. Scrooge was the Ogre of the family. The mention of his name cast a dark shadow on the party, which was not dispelled for full five minutes.

After it had passed away, they were ten times merrier than before, from the mere relief of Scrooge the Baleful being done with. Bob Cratchit told them how he had a situation in his eye for Master Peter, which would bring in, if obtained, full five-and-sixpence weekly. The two young Cratchits laughed tremendously at the idea of Peter's being a man of business; and Peter himself looked thoughtfully at the fire from between his collars, as if he were deliberating what particular investments he should favour when he came into the receipt of that bewildering income. Martha, who was a poor apprentice at a milliner's, then told them what kind of work she had to do, and how many hours she worked at a stretch, and how she meant to lie a-bed to-morrow morning for a good long rest; to-morrow being a holiday she passed at home. Also how she had seen a countess and a lord some days before, and

how the lord "was much about as tall as Peter"; at which
Peter pulled up his collars so high that you couldn't have
seen his head if you had been there. All this time the chestnuts and the jug went round and round; and bye and bye
they had a song, about a lost child travelling in the snow,
from Tiny Tim; who had a plaintive little voice, and sang it
very well indeed.

There was nothing of high mark in this. They were not a
handsome family; they were not well dressed; their shoes
were far from being water-proof; their clothes were scanty;
and Peter might have known, and very likely did, the inside
of a pawnbroker's. But they were happy, grateful, pleased
with one another, and contented with the time; and when
they faded, and looked happier yet in the bright sprinklings
of the Spirit's torch at parting, Scrooge had his eye upon
them, and especially on Tiny Tim, until the last.

By this time it was getting dark, and snowing pretty heavily;
and as Scrooge and the Spirit went along the streets, the
brightness of the roaring fires in kitchens, parlours, and all
sorts of rooms, was wonderful. Here, the flickering of the
blaze showed preparations for a cosy dinner, with hot plates
baking through and through before the fire, and deep red
curtains, ready to be drawn, to shut out cold and darkness.
There, all the children of the house were running out into the
snow to meet their married sisters, brothers, cousins, uncles,
aunts, and be the first to greet them. Here, again, were
shadows on the window-blind of guests assembling; and there
a group of handsome girls, all hooded and fur-booted, and all
chattering at once, tripped lightly off to some near neighbour's
house; where, woe upon the single man who saw them enter—
artful witches: well they knew it—in a glow!

But if you had judged from the numbers of people on their
way to friendly gatherings, you might have thought that no
one was at home to give them welcome when they got there,
instead of every house expecting company, and piling up its
fires half-chimney high. Blessings on it, how the Ghost exulted!
How it bared its breadth of breast, and opened its capacious
palm, and floated on, outpouring, with a generous hand, its
bright and harmless mirth on everything within its reach! The
very lamplighter, who ran on before dotting the dusky street
with specks of light, and who was dressed to spend the
evening somewhere, laughed out loudly as the Spirit passed:

though little kenned the lamplighter that he had any company but Christmas!

And now, without a word of warning from the Ghost, they stood upon a bleak and desert moor, where monstrous masses of rude stone were cast about, as though it were the burial-place of giants; and water spread itself wheresoever it listed—or would have done·so, but for the frost that held it prisoner; and nothing grew but moss and furze, and coarse, rank grass. Down in the west the setting sun had left a streak of fiery red, which glared upon the desolation for an instant, like a sullen eye, and frowning lower, lower, lower yet, was lost in the thick gloom of darkest night.

"What place is this?" asked Scrooge.

"A place where Miners live, who labour in the bowels of the earth," returned the Spirit. "But they know me. See!"

A light shone from the window of a hut, and swiftly they advanced towards it. Passing through the wall of mud and stone, they found a cheerful company assembled round a glowing fire. An old, old man and woman, with their children and their children's children, and another generation beyond that, all decked out gaily in their holiday attire. The old man, in a voice that seldom rose above the howling of the wind upon the barren waste, was singing them a Christmas song; it had been a very old song when he was a boy; and from time to time they all joined in the chorus. So surely as they raised their voices, the old man got quite blithe and loud; and so surely as they stopped, his vigour sang again.

The Spirit did not tarry here, but bade Scrooge hold his robe, and passing on above the moor, sped whither? Not to sea? To sea. To Scrooge's horror, looking back, he saw the last of the land, a frightful range of rocks, behind them; and his ears were deafened by the thundering of water, as it rolled, and roared, and raged among the dreadful caverns it had worn, and fiercely tried to undermine the earth.

Built upon a dismal reef of sunken rocks, some league or so from shore, on which the waters chafed and dashed, the wild year through, there stood a solitary lighthouse. Great heaps of sea-weed clung to its base, and storm-birds—born of the wind one might suppose, as sea-weed of the water—rose and fell about it, like the waves they skimmed.

But even here, two men who watched the light had made a fire, that through the loophole in the thick stone wall shed out a ray of brightness on the awful sea. Joining their horny hands over the rough table at which they sat, they wished each other Merry Christmas in their can of grog; and one of them: the elder, too, with his face all damaged and scarred with hard weather, as the figure-head of an old ship might be: struck up a sturdy song that was like a Gale in itself.

Again the Ghost sped on, above the black and heaving sea—on, on—until, being far away, as he told Scrooge, from any shore, they lighted on a ship. They stood beside the helmsman at the wheel, the look-out in the bow, the officers who had the watch; dark, ghostly figures in their several stations; but every man among them hummed a Christmas tune, or had a Christmas thought, or spoke below his breath to his companion of some bygone Christmas Day, with homeward hopes belonging to it. And every man on board, waking or sleeping, good or bad, had had a kinder word for another on that day than on any day in the year; and had shared to some extent in its festivities; and had remembered those he cared for at a distance, and had known that they delighted to remember him.

It was a great surprise to Scrooge, while listening to the moaning of the wind, and thinking what a solemn thing it was to move on through the lonely darkness over an unknown abyss, whose depths were secrets as profound as Death: it was a great surprise to Scrooge, while thus engaged, to hear a hearty laugh. It was a much greater surprise to Scrooge to recognise it as his own nephew's, and to find himself in a bright, dry, gleaming room, with the Spirit standing smiling by his side, and looking at that same nephew with approving affability!

"Ha, ha!" laughed Scrooge's nephew. "Ha, ha, ha!"

If you should happen, by any unlikely chance, to know a man more blest in a laugh than Scrooge's nephew, all I can say is, I should like to know him too. Introduce him to me, and I'll cultivate his acquaintance.

It is a fair, even-handed, noble adjustment of things, that while there is infection in disease and sorrow, there is nothing in the world so irresistibly contagious as laughter and good-humour. When Scrooge's nephew laughed in this way: holding his sides, rolling his head, and twisting his face into the most extravagant contortions: Scrooge's niece, by marriage, laughed as heartily as he. And their assembled friends being not a bit behindhand, roared out, lustily.

"Ha, ha! Ha, ha, ha, ha!"

"He said that Christmas was a humbug, as I live!" cried Scrooge's nephew. "He believed it too!"

"More shame for him, Fred!" said Scrooge's niece, indignantly. Bless those women; they never do anything by halves. They are always in earnest.

She was very pretty: exceedingly pretty. With a dimpled, surprised-looking, capital face; a ripe little mouth, that seemed made to be kissed—as no doubt it was; all kinds of good little dots about her chin, that melted into one another when she laughed; and the sunniest pair of eyes you ever saw in any little creature's head. Altogether she was what you would have called provoking, you know; but satisfactory too. Oh, perfectly satisfactory!

"He's a comical old fellow," said Scrooge's nephew, "that's the truth: and not so pleasant as he might be. However, his offences carry their own punishment, and I have nothing to say against him."

"I'm sure he is very rich, Fred," hinted Scrooge's niece. "At least you always tell *me* so."

"What of that, my dear!" said Scrooge's nephew. "His wealth is of no use to him. He don't do any good with it. He don't make himself comfortable with it. He hasn't the satisfaction of thinking—ha, ha, ha!—that he is ever going to benefit Us with it."

"I have no patience with him," observed Scrooge's niece. Scrooge's niece's sisters, and all the other ladies, expressed the same opinion.

"Oh, I have!" said Scrooge's nephew. "I am sorry for him; I couldn't be angry with him if I tried. Who suffers by his ill whims! Himself, always. Here, he takes it into his head to dislike us, and he won't come and dine with us. What's the consequence? He don't lose much of a dinner."

"Indeed, I think he loses a very good dinner," interrupted Scrooge's niece. Everybody else said the same, and they must be allowed to have been competent judges, because they had just had dinner; and, with the dessert upon the table, were clustered round the fire, by lamplight.

"Well! I'm very glad to hear it," said Scrooge's nephew,

"because I haven't great faith in these young housekeepers. What do *you* say, Topper?"

Topper had clearly got his eye upon one of Scrooge's niece's sisters, for he answered that a bachelor was a wretched outcast, who had no right to express an opinion on the subject. Whereat Scrooge's niece's sister—the plump one with the lace tucker: not the one with the roses—blushed.

"Do go on, Fred," said Scrooge's niece, clapping her hands. "He never finishes what he begins to say! He is such a ridiculous fellow!"

Scrooge's nephew revelled in another laugh, and as it was impossible to keep the infection off; though the plump sister tried hard to do it with aromatic vinegar; his example was unanimously followed.

"I was going to say," said Scrooge's nephew, "that the consequence of his taking a dislike to us, and not making merry with us, is, as I think, that he loses some pleasant moments, which could do him no harm. I am sure he loses pleasanter companions than he can find in his own thoughts, either in his mouldy old office, or his dusty chambers. I mean to give him the same chance every year, whether he likes it or not, for I pity him. He may rail at Christmas till he dies, but he can't help thinking better of it—I defy him—if he finds me going there, in good temper, year after year, and saying Uncle Scrooge, how are you? If it only puts him in the vein to leave his poor clerk fifty pounds, *that's* something; and I think I shook him, yesterday."

It was their turn to laugh now, at the notion of his shaking Scrooge. But being thoroughly good-natured, and not much caring what they laughed at, so that they laughed at any rate, he encouraged them in their merriment, and passed the bottle, joyously.

After tea, they had some music. For they were a musical family, and knew what they were about, when they sung a Glee or Catch, I can assure you: especially Topper, who could growl away in the bass like a good one, and never swell the large veins in his forehead, or get red in the face over it. Scrooge's niece played well upon the harp; and played among other tunes a simple little air (a mere nothing: you might learn to whistle it in two minutes), which had been familiar to the child who fetched Scrooge from the boarding-school, as he had been reminded by the Ghost of Christmas Past. When this strain of music sounded, all the things that Ghost had shown him, came upon his mind; he softened more and more; and thought that if he could have listened to it often, years ago, he might have cultivated the kindnesses of life for his own happiness with his own hands, without resorting to the sexton's spade that buried Jacob Marley.

But they didn't devote the whole evening to music. After a while they played at forfeits; for it is good to be children sometimes, and never better than at Christmas, when its mighty Founder was a child himself. Stop! There was first a game at blind-man's buff. Of course there was. And I no more believe Topper was really blind than I believe he had eyes in his boots. My opinion is, that it was a done thing between him and Scrooge's nephew; and that the Ghost of Christmas Present knew it. The way he went after that plump sister in the lace tucker, was an outrage on the credulity of human nature. Knocking down the fire-irons, tumbling over the chairs, bumping against the piano, smothering himself among the curtains, wherever she went, there went he. He always knew where the plump sister was. He wouldn't catch anybody else. If you had fallen up against him, as some of them did, and stood there; he would have made a feint of endeavouring to seize you, which would have been an affront to your understanding; and would instantly have sidled off in the direction of the plump sister. She often cried out that it wasn't fair; and it really was not. But when at last, he caught her; when, in spite of all her silken rustlings, and her rapid flutterings past him, he got her into a corner whence there was no escape; then his conduct was the most execrable. For his pretending not to know her; his pretending that it was necessary to touch her head-dress, and further to assure himself of her identity by pressing a certain ring upon her finger, and a certain chain about her neck; was vile, monstrous! No doubt she told him her opinion of it, when, another blind-man being in office, they were so very confidential together, behind the curtains.

Scrooge's niece was not one of the blind-man's buff party, but was made comfortable with a large chair and a footstool, in a snug corner, where the Ghost and Scrooge were close behind her. But she joined in the forfeits, and loved her love to admiration with all the letters of the alphabet. Likewise at the game of How, When, and Where, she was very great, and to the secret joy of Scrooge's nephew, beat her sisters hollow: though they were sharp girls too, as Topper could have told you. There might have been twenty people there, young and old, but they all played, and so did Scrooge; for wholly forgetting in the interest he had in what was going on, that his voice made no sound in their ears, he sometimes came out with his guess quite loud, and very often guessed quite right, too; for the sharpest needle, best Whitechapel, warranted not to cut in the eye, was not sharper than Scrooge: blunt as he took it in his head to be.

The Ghost was greatly pleased to find him in this mood, and looked upon him with such favour that he begged like a boy to be allowed to stay until the guests departed. But this the Spirit said could not be done.

"Here's a new game," said Scrooge. "One half hour, Spirit, only one!"

It was a Game called Yes and No, where Scrooge's nephew had to think of something, and the rest must find out what; he only answering to their questions yes or no as the case was. The brisk fire of questioning to which he was exposed, elicited from him that he was thinking of an animal, a live animal, rather a disagreeable animal, a savage animal, an animal that growled and grunted sometimes, and talked sometimes, and lived in London, and walked about the streets, and wasn't made a show of, and wasn't led by anybody, and didn't live in a menagerie, and was never killed in a market, and was not a horse, or an ass, or a cow, or a bull, or a tiger, or a dog, or a pig, or a cat, or a bear. At every fresh question that was put to him, this nephew burst into a fresh roar of laughter; and was so inexpressibly tickled, that he was obliged to get up off the sofa and stamp. At last the plump sister, falling into a similar state, cried out:

"I have found it out! I know what it is, Fred! I know what it is!"

"What is it?" cried Fred.

"It's your Uncle Scro-o-o-o-oge!"

Which it certainly was. Admiration was the universal sentiment, though some objected that the reply to "Is it a bear?" ought to have been "Yes"; inasmuch as an answer in the negative was sufficient to have diverted their thoughts from Mr. Scrooge, supposing they had ever had any tendency that way.

"He has given us plenty of merriment, I am sure," said Fred, "and it would be ungrateful not to drink his health. Here is a glass of mulled wine ready to our hand at the moment; and I say 'Uncle Scrooge!' "

"Well! Uncle Scrooge!" they cried.

"A Merry Christmas and a Happy New Year to the old man, whatever he is!" said Scrooge's nephew. "He wouldn't take it from me, but may he have it, nevertheless. Uncle Scrooge!"

Uncle Scrooge had imperceptibly become so gay and light of heart, that he would have pledged the unconscious company in return, and thanked them in an inaudible speech, if the Ghost had given him time. But the whole scene passed off in the breath of the last word spoken by his nephew; and he and the Spirit were again upon their travels.

Much they saw, and far they went, and many homes they visited, but always with a happy end. The Spirit stood beside sick beds, and they were cheerful; on foreign lands, and they were close at home; by struggling men, and they were patient in their greater hope; by poverty, and it was rich. In almshouse, hospital, and jail, in misery's every refuge, where vain man in his little brief authority had not made fast the door, and barred the Spirit out, he left his blessing, and taught Scrooge his precepts.

It was a long night, if it were only a night; but Scrooge had his doubts of this, because the Christmas Holidays appeared to be condensed into the space of time they passed together. It was strange, too, that while Scrooge remained unaltered in his outward form, the Ghost grew older, clearly older. Scrooge had observed this change, but never spoke of it, until they left a children's Twelfth Night party, when, looking at the Spirit as they stood together in an open place, he noticed that its hair was gray.

"Are spirits' lives so short?" asked Scrooge.

"My life upon this globe, is very brief," replied the Ghost. "It ends to-night."

"To-night!" cried Scrooge.

"To-night at midnight. Hark! The time is drawing near."

The chimes were ringing the three quarters past eleven at that moment.

"Forgive me if I am not justified in what I ask," said Scrooge, looking intently at the Spirit's robe, "but I see something strange, and not belonging to yourself, protruding from your skirts. Is it a foot or a claw!"

"It might be a claw, for the flesh there is upon it," was the Spirit's sorrowful reply. "Look here."

From the foldings of its robe, it brought two children; wretched, abject, frightful, hideous, miserable. They knelt down at its feet, and clung upon the outside of its garment.

"Oh, Man! look here. Look, look, down here!" exclaimed the Ghost.

They were a boy and girl. Yellow, meagre, ragged, scowling, wolfish; but prostrate, too, in their humility. Where graceful youth should have filled their features out, and touched them with its freshest tints, a stale and shrivelled hand, like that of age, had pinched, and twisted them, and pulled them into shreds. Where angels might have sat enthroned, devils lurked, and glared out menacing. No change, no degradation, no perversion of humanity, in any grade, through all the mysteries of wonderful creation, has monsters half so horrible and dread.

Scrooge started back, appalled. Having them shown to him in this way, he tried to say they were fine children, but the words choked themselves, rather than be parties to a lie of such enormous magnitude.

"Spirit! are they yours?" Scrooge could say no more.

"They are Man's," said the Spirit, looking down upon them. "And they cling to me, appealing from their fathers. This boy is Ignorance. This girl is Want. Beware them both, and all of their degree, but most of all beware this boy, for on his brow I see that written which is Doom, unless the writing be erased. Deny it!" cried the Spirit, stretching out its hand towards the city. "Slander those who tell it ye! Admit it for your factious purposes, and make it worse. And bide the end!"

"Have they no refuge or resource?" cried Scrooge.

"Are there no prisons?" said the Spirit, turning on him for the last time with his own words. "Are there no workhouses?"

The bell struck twelve.

Scrooge looked about him for the Ghost, and saw it not. As the last stroke ceased to vibrate, he remembered the prediction of old Jacob Marley, and lifting up his eyes, beheld a solemn Phantom, draped and hooded, coming, like a mist along the ground, towards him.

STAVE FOUR

THE LAST OF THE SPIRITS

The Phantom slowly, gravely, silently, approached. When it came near him, Scrooge bent down upon his knee; for in the very air through which this Spirit moved it seemed to scatter gloom and mystery.

It was shrouded in a deep black garment, which concealed its head, its face, its form, and left nothing of it visible save one outstretched hand. But for this it would have been difficult to detach its figure from the night, and separate it from the darkness by which it was surrounded.

He felt that it was tall and stately when it came beside him, and that its mysterious presence filled him with a solemn dread. He knew no more, for the Spirit neither spoke nor moved.

"I am in the presence of the Ghost of Christmas Yet To Come?" said Scrooge.

The Spirit answered not, but pointed onward with its hand.

"You are about to show me shadows of the things that have not happened, but will happen in the time before us," Scrooge pursued. "Is that so, Spirit?"

The upper portion of the garment was contracted for an instant in its folds, as if the Spirit had inclined its head. That was the only answer he received.

Although well used to ghostly company by this time, Scrooge feared the silent shape so much that his legs trembled beneath him, and he found that he could hardly stand when he prepared to follow it. The Spirit paused a moment, as observing his condition, and giving him time to recover.

But Scrooge was all the worse for this. It thrilled him with a vague uncertain horror, to know that behind the dusky shroud, there were ghostly eyes intently fixed upon him, while he, though he stretched his own to the utmost, could see nothing but a spectral hand and one great heap of black.

"Ghost of the Future!" he exclaimed, "I fear you more than any Spectre I have seen. But as I know your purpose is to do me good, and as I hope to live to be another man from what I was, I am prepared to bear you company, and do it with a thankful heart. Will you not speak to me?"

It gave him no reply. The hand was pointed straight before them.

"Lead on!" said Scrooge. "Lead on! The night is waning fast, and it is precious time to me, I know. Lead on, Spirit!"

The Phantom moved away as it had come towards him. Scrooge followed in the shadow of its dress, which bore him up, he thought, and carried him along.

They scarcely seemed to enter the city; for the city rather seemed to spring up about them, and encompass them of its own act. But there they were, in the heart of it; on 'Change, amongst the merchants; who hurried up and down, and chinked the money in their pockets, and conversed in groups, and looked at their watches, and trifled thoughtfully with their great gold seals; and so forth, as Scrooge had seen them often.

The Spirit stopped beside one little knot of business men. Observing that the hand was pointed to them, Scrooge advanced to listen to their talk.

"No," said a great fat man with a monstrous chin, "I don't know much about it, either way. I only know he's dead."

"When did he die?" inquired another.

"Last night, I believe."

"Why, what was the matter with him?" asked a third, taking a vast quantity of snuff out of a very large snuff-box. "I thought he'd never die."

"God knows," said the first, with a yawn.

"What has he done with his money?" asked a red-faced gentleman with a pendulous excrescence on the end of his nose, that shook like the gills of a turkey-cock.

"I haven't heard," said the man with the large chin, yawning again. "Left it to his Company, perhaps. He hasn't left it to *me*. That's all I know."

This pleasantry was received with a general laugh.

"It's likely to be a very cheap funeral," said the same speaker; "for upon my life I don't know of anybody to go to it. Suppose we make up a party and volunteer?"

"I don't mind going if a lunch is provided," observed the

gentleman with the excrescence on his nose. "But I must be fed, if I make one."

Another laugh.

"Well, I am the most disinterested among you, after all," said the first speaker, "for I never wear black gloves, and I never eat lunch. But I'll offer to go, if anybody else will. When I come to think of it, I'm not at all sure that I wasn't his most particular friend; for we used to stop and speak whenever we met. Bye, bye!"

Speakers and listeners strolled away, and mixed with other groups. Scrooge knew the men, and looked towards the Spirit for an explanation.

The Phantom glided on into a street. Its finger pointed to two persons meeting. Scrooge listened again, thinking that the explanation might lie here.

He knew these men, also, perfectly. They were men of business: very wealthy, and of great importance. He had made a point always of standing well in their esteem: in a business point of view, that is; strictly in a business point of view.

"How are you?" said one.

"How are you?" returned the other.

"Well!" said the first. "Old Scratch has got his own at last, hey?"

"So I am told," returned the second. "Cold, isn't it?"

"Seasonable for Christmas time. You're not a skaiter, I suppose?"

"No. No. Something else to think of. Good morning!"

Not another word. That was their meeting, their conversation, and their parting.

Scrooge was at first inclined to be surprised that the Spirit should attach importance to conversations apparently so trivial; but feeling assured that they must have some hidden purpose, he set himself to consider what it was likely to be. They could scarcely be supposed to have any bearing on the death of Jacob, his old partner, for that was Past, and this Ghost's province was the Future. Nor could he think of any one immediately connected with himself, to whom he could apply them. But nothing doubting that to whomsoever they applied they had some latent moral for his own improvement, he resolved to treasure up every word he heard, and everything he saw; and especially to observe the shadow of himself when it appeared. For he had an expectation that the conduct of his future self would give him the clue he missed, and would render the solution of these riddles easy.

He looked about in that very place for his own image; but another man stood in his accustomed corner, and though the clock pointed to his usual time of day for being there, he saw no likeness of himself among the multitudes that poured in through the Porch. It gave him little surprise, however; for he had been revolving in his mind a change of life, and thought and hoped he saw his new-born resolutions carried out in this.

Quiet and dark, beside him stood the Phantom, with its outstretched hand. When he roused himself from his thoughtful quest, he fancied from the turn of the hand, and its situation in reference to himself, that the Unseen Eyes were looking at him keenly. It made him shudder, and feel very cold.

They left the busy scene, and went into an obscure part of the town, where Scrooge had never penetrated before although he recognised its situation, and its bad repute. The ways were foul and narrow; the shops and houses wretched; the people half-naked, drunken, slipshod, ugly. Alleys and archways, like so many cesspools, disgorged their offences of smell, and dirt, and life, upon the straggling streets; and the whole quarter reeked with crime, with filth, and misery.

Far in this den of infamous resort, there was a low-browed, beetling shop, below a pent-house roof, where iron, old rags, bottles, bones, and greasy offal, were bought. Upon the floor within, were piled up heaps of rusty keys, nails, chains, hinges, files, scales, weights, and refuse iron of all kinds. Secrets that few would like to scrutinise were bred and hidden in mountains of unseemly rags, masses of corrupted fat, and sepulchres of bones. Sitting in among the wares he dealt in, by a charcoal-stove, made of old bricks, was a gray-haired rascal, nearly seventy years of age; who had screened himself from the cold air without, by a frousy curtaining of miscellaneous tatters, hung upon a line; and smoked his pipe in all the luxury of calm retirement.

Scrooge and the Phantom came into the presence of this man, just as a woman with a heavy bundle slunk into the shop. But she had scarcely entered, when another woman, similarly laden, came in too; and she was closely followed by a

man in faded black, who was no less startled by the sight of
them, than they had been upon the recognition of each other.
After a short period of blank astonishment, in which the old
man with the pipe had joined them, they all three burst into
a laugh.

"Let the charwoman alone to be the first!" cried she who
had entered first. "Let the laundress alone to be the second;
and let the undertaker's man alone to be the third. Look
here, old Joe, here's a chance! If we haven't all three met
here without meaning it."

"You couldn't have met in a better place," said old Joe,
removing his pipe from his mouth. "Come into the parlour.
You were made free of it long ago, you know; and the other
two an't strangers. Stop till I shut the door of the shop.
Ah! How it skreeks! There an't such a rusty bit of metal in the
place as its own hinges, I believe; and I'm sure there's no
such old bones here, as mine. Ha, ha! We're all suitable to
our calling, we're well matched. Come into the parlour.
Come into the parlour."

The parlour was the space behind the screen of rags. The
old man raked the fire together with an old stair-rod, and
having trimmed his smoky lamp (for it was night), with the
stem of his pipe, put it in his mouth again.

While he did this, the woman who had already spoken
threw her bundle on the floor and sat down in a flaunting
manner on a stool; crossing her elbows on her knees, and
looking with a bold defiance at the other two.

"What odds then! What odds, Mrs. Dilber?" said the woman.
"Every person has a right to take care of themselves. *He*
always did!"

"That's true, indeed!" said the laundress. "No man more
so."

"Why then, don't stand staring as if you was afraid, woman;
who's the wiser? We're not going to pick holes in each other's
coats, I suppose?"

"No, indeed!" said Mrs. Dilber and the man together. "We
should hope not."

"Very well, then!" cried the woman. "That's enough. Who's
the worse for the loss of a few things like these? Not a dead
man, I suppose."

"No, indeed," said Mrs. Dilber, laughing.

"If he wanted to keep 'em after he was dead, a wicked old

screw," pursued the woman, "why wasn't he natural in his lifetime? If he had been, he'd have had somebody to look after him when he was struck with Death, instead of lying gasping out his last there, alone by himself."

"It's the truest word that ever was spoke," said Mrs. Dilber. "It's a judgment on him."

"I wish it was a little heavier one," replied the woman; "and it should have been, you may depend upon it, if I could have laid my hands on anything else. Open that bundle, old Joe, and let me know the value of it. Speak out plain. I'm not afraid to be the first, nor afraid for them to see it. We knew pretty well that we were helping ourselves, before we met here, I believe. It's no sin. Open the bundle, Joe."

But the gallantry of her friends would not allow of this; and the man in faded black, mounting the breach first, produced *his* plunder. It was not extensive. A seal or two, a pencil-case, a pair of sleeve-buttons, and a brooch of no great value, were all. They were severally examined and appraised by old Joe, who chalked the sums he was disposed to give for each, upon the wall, and added them up into a total when he found there was nothing more to come.

"That's your account," said Joe, "and I wouldn't give another sixpence, if I was to be boiled for not doing it. Who's next?"

Mrs. Dilber was next. Sheets and towels, a little wearing apparel, two old-fashioned silver teaspoons, a pair of sugar-tongs, and a few boots. Her account was stated on the wall in the same manner.

"I always give too much to ladies. It's a weakness of mine, and that's the way I ruin myself," said old Joe. "That's your account. If you asked me for another penny, and made it an open question, I'd repent of being so liberal and knock off half-a-crown."

"And now undo *my* bundle, Joe," said the first woman.

Joe went down on his knees for the greater convenience of opening it, and having unfastened a great many knots, dragged out a large and heavy roll of some dark stuff.

"What do you call this?" said Joe. "Bed-curtains!"

"Ah!" returned the woman, laughing and leaning forward on her crossed arms. "Bed-curtains!"

"You don't mean to say you took 'em down, rings and all, with him lying there?" said Joe.

"Yes I do," replied the woman. "Why not?"

"You were born to make your fortune," said Joe, "and you'll certainly do it."

"I certainly shan't hold my hand, when I get anything in it by reaching it out, for the sake of such a man as He was, I promise you, Joe," returned the woman coolly. "Don't drop that oil upon the blankets, now."

"His blankets?" asked Joe.

"Whose else's do you think?" replied the woman. "He isn't likely to take cold without 'em, I dare say."

"I hope he didn't die of anything catching? Eh?" said old Joe, stopping in his work, and looking up.

"Don't you be afraid of that," returned the woman. "I an't so fond of his company that I'd loiter about him for such things, if he did. Ah! you may look through that shirt till your eyes ache; but you won't find a hole in it, nor a threadbare place. It's the best he had, and a fine one too. They'd have wasted it, if it hadn't been for me."

"What do you call wasting of it?" asked old Joe.

"Putting it on him to be buried in, to be sure," replied the woman with a laugh. "Somebody was fool enough to do it, but I took it off again. If calico an't good enough for such a purpose, it isn't good enough for anything. It's quite as becoming to the body. He can't look uglier than he did in that one."

Scrooge listened to this dialogue in horror. As they sat grouped about their spoil, in the scanty light afforded by the old man's lamp, he viewed them with a detestation and disgust, which could hardly have been greater, though they had been obscene demons, marketing the corpse itself.

"Ha, ha!" laughed the same woman, when old Joe, producing a flannel bag with money in it, told out their several gains upon the ground. "This is the end of it, you see! He frightened every one away from him when he was alive, to profit us when he was dead! Ha, ha, ha!"

"Spirit!" said Scrooge, shuddering from head to foot. "I see, I see. The case of this unhappy man might be my own. My life tends that way, now. Merciful Heaven, what is this!"

He recoiled in terror, for the scene had changed, and now he almost touched a bed: a bare, uncurtained bed: on which, beneath a ragged sheet, there lay a something covered up, which, though it was dumb, announced itself in awful language.

The room was very dark, too dark to be observed with any accuracy, though Scrooge glanced round it in obedience to a secret impulse, anxious to know what kind of room it was. A pale light, rising in the outer air, fell straight upon the bed; and on it, plundered and bereft, unwatched, unwept, uncared for, was the body of this man.

Scrooge glanced towards the Phantom. Its steady hand was pointed to the head. The cover was so carelessly adjusted that the slightest raising of it, the motion of a finger upon Scrooge's part, would have disclosed the face. He thought of it, felt how easy it would be to do, and longed to do it; but had no more power to withdraw the veil than to dismiss the spectre at his side.

Oh cold, cold, rigid, dreadful Death, set up thine altar here, and dress it with such terrors as thou hast at thy command: for this is thy dominion! But of the loved, revered, and honoured head, thou canst not turn one hair to thy dread purposes, or make one feature odious. It is not that the hand is heavy and will fall down when released; it is not that the heart and pulse are still; but that the hand WAS open, generous, and true; the heart brave, warm, and tender; and the pulse a man's. Strike, Shadow, strike! And see his good deeds springing from the wound, to sow the world with life immortal!

No voice pronounced these words in Scrooge's ears, and yet he heard them when he looked upon the bed. He thought, if this man could be raised up now, what would be his foremost thoughts? Avarice, hard dealing, griping cares? They have brought him to a rich end, truly!

He lay, in the dark empty house, with not a man, a woman, or a child, to say that he was kind to me in this or that, and for the memory of one kind word I will be kind to him. A cat was tearing at the door, and there was a sound of gnawing rats beneath the hearth-stone. What *they* wanted in the room of death, and why they were so restless and disturbed, Scrooge did not dare to think.

"Spirit!" he said, "this is a fearful place. In leaving it, I shall not leave its lesson, trust me. Let us go!"

Still the Ghost pointed with an unmoved finger to the head.

"I understand you," Scrooge returned, "and I would do it, if I could. But I have not the power, Spirit. I have not the power."

Again it seemed to look upon him.

"If there is any person in the town, who feels emotion caused by this man's death," said Scrooge quite agonised, "show that person to me, Spirit, I beseech you!"

The Phantom spread its dark robe before him for a moment, like a wing; and withdrawing it, revealed a room by daylight, where a mother and her children were.

She was expecting some one, and with anxious eagerness; for she walked up and down the room; started at every sound; looked out from the window; glanced at the clock; tried, but in vain, to work with her needle; and could hardly bear the voices of the children in their play.

At length the long-expected knock was heard. She hurried to the door, and met her husband; a man whose face was care-worn and depressed, though he was young. There was a remarkable expression in it now; a kind of serious delight of which he felt ashamed, and which he struggled to repress.

He sat down to the dinner that had been hoarding for him by the fire; and when she asked him faintly what news (which was not until after a long silence), he appeared embarrassed how to answer.

"Is it good," she said, "or bad?"—to help him.

"Bad," he answered.

"We are quite ruined?"

"No. There is hope yet, Caroline."

"If *he* relents," she said, amazed, "there is! Nothing is past hope, if such a miracle has happened."

"He is past relenting," said her husband. "He is dead."

She was a mild and patient creature if her face spoke truth; but she was thankful in her soul to hear it, and she said so, with clasped hands. She prayed forgiveness the next moment, and was sorry; but the first was the emotion of her heart.

"What the half-drunken woman whom I told you of last night, said to me, when I tried to see him and obtain a week's delay; and what I thought was a mere excuse to avoid me; turns out to have been quite true. He was not only very ill, but dying, then."

"To whom will our debt be transferred?"

"I don't know. But before that time we shall be ready with the money; and even though we were not, it would be bad fortune indeed to find so merciless a creditor in his successor. We may sleep to-night with light hearts, Caroline!"

Yes. Soften it as they would, their hearts were lighter. The children's faces, hushed and clustered round to hear what they so little understood, were brighter; and it was a happier house for this man's death! The only emotion that the Ghost could show him, caused by the event, was one of pleasure.

"Let me see some tenderness connected with a death," said Scrooge; "or that dark chamber, Spirit, which we left just now, will be for ever present to me."

The Ghost conducted him through several streets familiar to his feet; and as they went along, Scrooge looked here and there to find himself, but nowhere was he to be seen. They entered poor Bob Cratchit's house; the dwelling he had visited before; and found the mother and the children seated round the fire.

Quiet. Very quiet. The noisy little Cratchits were as still as statues in one corner, and sat looking up at Peter, who had a book before him. The mother and her daughters were engaged in sewing. But surely they were very quiet!

" 'And He took a child, and set him in the midst of them.' "

Where had Scrooge heard those words? He had not dreamed them. The boy must have read them out, as he and the Spirit crossed the threshold. Why did he not go on?

The mother laid her work upon the table, and put her hand up to her face.

"The colour hurts my eyes," she said.

The colour? Ah, poor Tiny Tim!

"They're better now again," said Cratchit's wife. "It makes them weak by candle-light; and I wouldn't show weak eyes to your father when he comes home, for the world. It must be near his time."

"Past it rather," Peter answered, shutting up his book. "But I think he's walked a little slower than he used, these few last evenings, mother."

They were very quiet again. At last she said, and in a steady, cheerful voice, that only faultered once:

"I have known him walk with—I have known him walk with Tiny Tim upon his shoulder, very fast indeed."

"And so have I," cried Peter. "Often."

"And so have I!" exclaimed another. So had all.

"But he was very light to carry," she resumed, intent upon her work, "and his father loved him so, that it was no trouble—no trouble. And there is your father at the door!"

She hurried out to meet him; and little Bob in his comforter—he had need of it, poor fellow—came in. His tea was ready for him on the hob, and they all tried who should help him to it most. Then the two young Cratchits got upon his knees and laid, each child a little cheek, against his face, as if they said, "Don't mind it, father. Don't be grieved!"

Bob was very cheerful with them, and spoke pleasantly to all the family. He looked at the work upon the table, and praised the industry and speed of Mrs. Cratchit and the girls. They would be done long before Sunday, he said.

"Sunday! You went to-day then, Robert?" said his wife.

"Yes, my dear," returned Bob. "I wish you could have gone. It would have done you good to see how green a place it is. But you'll see it often. I promised him that I would walk there on a Sunday. My little, little child!" cried Bob. "My little child!"

He broke down all at once. He couldn't help it. If he could have helped it, he and his child would have been farther apart perhaps than they were.

He left the room, and went up stairs into the room above, which was lighted cheerfully, and hung with Christmas. There was a chair set close beside the child, and there were signs of some one having been there, lately. Poor Bob sat down in it, and when he had thought a little and composed himself, he kissed the little face. He was reconciled to what had happened, and went down again quite happy.

They drew about the fire, and talked; the girls and mother working still. Bob told them of the extraordinary kindness of Mr. Scrooge's nephew, whom he had scarcely seen but once, and who, meeting him in the street that day, and seeing that he looked a little—"just a little down you know" said Bob, inquired what had happened to distress him. "On which," said Bob, "for he is the pleasantest-spoken gentleman you ever heard, I told him. 'I am heartily sorry for it, Mr. Cratchit,' he said, 'and heartily sorry for your good wife.' By the bye, how he ever knew *that*, I don't know."

"Knew what, my dear."

"Why, that you were a good wife," replied Bob.

"Everybody knows that!" said Peter.

"Very well observed, my boy!" cried Bob. "I hope they do. 'Heartily sorry,' he said, 'for your good wife. If I can be of any service to you in any way,' he said, giving me his card, 'that's where I live. Pray come to me.' Now, it wasn't," cried Bob, "for the sake of anything he might be able to do for us, so much as for his kind way, that this was quite delightful. It really seemed as if he had known our Tiny Tim, and felt with us."

"I'm sure he's a good soul!" said Mrs. Cratchit.

"You would be surer of it, my dear," returned Bob, "if you saw and spoke to him. I shouldn't be at all surprised, mark what I say, if he got Peter a better situation."

"Only hear that, Peter," said Mrs. Cratchit.

"And then," cried one of the girls, "Peter will be keeping company with some one, and setting up for himself."

"Get along with you!" retorted Peter, grinning.

"It's just as likely as not," said Bob, "one of these days; though there's plenty of time for that, my dear. But however and whenever we part from one another, I am sure we shall none of us forget poor Tiny Tim—shall we—or this first parting that there was among us?"

"Never, father!" cried they all.

"And I know," said Bob, "I know, my dears, that when we recollect how patient and how mild he was; although he was a little, little child; we shall not quarrel easily among ourselves, and forget poor Tiny Tim in doing it."

"No, never, father!" they all cried again.

"I am very happy," said little Bob, "I am very happy!"

Mrs. Cratchit kissed him, his daughters kissed him, the two young Cratchits kissed him, and Peter and himself shook hands. Spirit of Tiny Tim, thy childish essence was from God!

"Spectre," said Scrooge, "something informs me that our parting moment is at hand. I know it, but I know not how. Tell me what man that was whom we saw lying dead?"

The Ghost of Christmas Yet To Come conveyed him, as before—though at a different time, he thought: indeed, there seemed no order in these latter visions, save that they were in the Future—into the resorts of business men, but showed him not himself. Indeed, the Spirit did not stay for anything, but went straight on, as to the end just now desired, until besought by Scrooge to tarry for a moment.

"This court," said Scrooge, "through which we hurry now, is where my place of occupation is, and has been for a length of time. I see the house. Let me behold what I shall be, in days to come."

The Spirit stopped; the hand was pointed elsewhere.

"The house is yonder," Scrooge exclaimed. "Why do you point away?"

The inexorable finger underwent no change.

Scrooge hastened to the window of his office, and looked in. It was an office still, but not his. The furniture was not the same, and the figure in the chair was not himself. The Phantom pointed as before.

He joined it once again, and wondering why and whither he had gone, accompanied it until they reached an iron gate. He paused to look round before entering.

A churchyard. Here, then, the wretched man whose name he had now to learn, lay underneath the ground. It was a worthy place. Walled in by houses; overrun by grass and weeds, the growth of vegetation's death, not life; choked up with too much burying; fat with repleted appetite. A worthy place!

The Spirit stood among the graves, and pointed down to One. He advanced towards it trembling. The Phantom was exactly as it had been, but he dreaded that he saw new meaning in its solemn shape.

"Before I draw nearer to that stone to which you point," said Scrooge, "answer me one question. Are these the shadows of the things that Will be, or are they shadows of things that May be, only?"

Still the Ghost pointed downward to the grave by which it stood.

"Men's courses will foreshadow certain ends, to which, if persevered in, they must lead," said Scrooge. "But if the courses be departed from, the ends will change. Say it is thus with what you show me!"

The Spirit was immovable as ever.

Scrooge crept towards it, trembling as he went; and following the finger, read upon the stone of the neglected grave his own name, EBENEZER SCROOGE.

"Am I that man who lay upon the bed?" he cried, upon his knees.

The finger pointed from the grave to him, and back again.

"No, Spirit! Oh, no, no!"

The finger still was there.

"Spirit!" he cried, tight clutching at its robe, "hear me! I am not the man I was. I will not be the man I must have been but for this intercourse. Why show me this, if I am past all hope?"

For the first time the hand appeared to shake.

"Good Spirit," he pursued, as down upon the ground he fell before it: "Your nature intercedes for me, and pities me. Assure me that I yet may change these shadows you have shown me, by an altered life!"

The kind hand trembled.

"I will honour Christmas in my heart, and try to keep it all the year. I will live in the Past, Present, and the Future. The Spirits of all Three shall strive within me. I will not shut out the lessons that they teach. Oh, tell me I may sponge away the writing on this stone!"

In his agony, he caught the spectral hand. It sought to free itself, but he was strong in his entreaty, and detained it. The Spirit, stronger yet, repulsed him.

Holding up his hands in a last prayer to have his fate reversed, he saw an alteration in the Phantom's hood and dress. It shrunk, collapsed, and dwindled down into a bedpost.

STAVE FIVE

THE END OF IT

Yes! and the bedpost was his own. The bed was his own, the room was his own. Best and happiest of all, the Time before him was his own, to make amends in!

"I will live in the Past, the Present, and the Future!" Scrooge repeated, as he scrambled out of bed. "The Spirits of all Three shall strive within me. Oh Jacob Marley! Heaven, and the Christmas Time be praised for this! I say it on my knees, old Jacob; on my knees!"

He was so fluttered and so glowing with his good intentions, that his broken voice would scarcely answer to his call. He had been sobbing violently in his conflict with the Spirit, and his face was wet with tears.

"They are not torn down," cried Scrooge, folding one of his bed-curtains in his arms, "they are not torn down, rings and all. They are here: I am here: the shadows of the things that would have been, may be dispelled. They will be. I know they will!"

His hands were busy with his garments all this time: turning them inside out, putting them on upside down, tearing them, mislaying them, making them parties to every kind of extravagance.

"I don't know what to do!" cried Scrooge, laughing and crying in the same breath; and making a perfect Laocoön of himself with his stockings. "I am as light as a feather, I am as happy as an angel, I am as merry as a school-boy. I am as giddy as a drunken man. A merry Christmas to everybody! A happy New Year to all the world! Hallo here! Whoop! Hallo!"

He had frisked into the sitting-room, and was now standing there: perfectly winded.

"There's the saucepan that the gruel was in!" cried Scrooge, starting off again, and frisking round the fire-place. "There's the door, by which the Ghost of Jacob Marley entered! There's the corner where the Ghost of Christmas Present, sat! There's the window where I saw the wandering Spirits! It's all right, it's all true, it all happened. Ha ha ha!"

Really, for a man who had been out of practice for so many years, it was a splendid laugh, a most illustrious laugh. The father of a long, long line of brilliant laughs!

"I don't know what day of the month it is!" said Scrooge. "I don't know how long I've been among the Spirits. I don't know anything. I'm quite a baby. Never mind. I don't care. I'd rather be a baby. Hallo! Whoop! Hallo here!"

He was checked in his transports by the churches ringing out the lustiest peals he had ever heard. Clash, clang, hammer, ding, dong, bell. Bell, dong, ding, hammer, clang, clash! Oh, glorious, glorious!

Running to the window, he opened it, and put out his head. No fog, no mist; clear, bright, jovial, stirring, cold; cold, piping for the blood to dance to; Golden sunlight; Heavenly sky; sweet fresh air; merry bells. Oh, glorious. Glorious!

"What's to-day?" cried Scrooge, calling downward to a boy

in Sunday clothes, who perhaps had loitered in to look about him.

"Eh?" returned the boy, with all his might of wonder.

"What's to-day, my fine fellow?" said Scrooge.

"To-day!" replied the boy. "Why, CHRISTMAS DAY."

"It's Christmas Day!" said Scrooge to himself. "I haven't missed it. The Spirits have done it all in one night. They can do anything they like. Of course they can. Of course they can. Hallo, my fine fellow!"

"Hallo!" returned the boy.

"Do you know the Poulterer's, in the next street but one, at the corner?" Scrooge inquired.

"I should hope I did," replied the lad.

"An intelligent boy!" said Scrooge. "A remarkable boy! Do you know whether they've sold the prize Turkey that was hanging up there? Not the little prize Turkey: the big one?"

"What, the one as big as me?" returned the boy.

"What a delightful boy!" said Scrooge. "It's a pleasure to talk to him. Yes, my buck!"

"It's hanging there now," replied the boy.

"Is it?" said Scrooge. "Go and buy it."

"Walk-ER!" exclaimed the boy.

"No, no," said Scrooge, "I am in earnest. Go and buy it, and tell 'em to bring it here, that I may give them the direction where to take it. Come back with the man, and I'll give you a shilling. Come back with him in less than five minutes, and I'll give you half-a-crown!"

The boy was off like a shot. He must have had a steady hand at a trigger who could have got a shot off half so fast.

"I'll send it to Bob Cratchit's!" whispered Scrooge, rubbing his hands, and splitting with a laugh. "He shan't know who sends it. It's twice the size of Tiny Tim. Joe Miller never made such a joke as sending it to Bob's will be!"

The hand in which he wrote the address was not a steady one, but write it he did, somehow, and went down stairs to open the street door, ready for the coming of the poulterer's man. As he stood there, waiting his arrival, the knocker caught his eye.

"I shall love it, as long as I live!" cried Scrooge, patting it with his hand. "I scarcely ever looked at it before. What an honest expression it has in its face! It's a wonderful knocker!

—Here's the Turkey. Hallo! Whoop! How are you! Merry Christmas!"

It *was* a Turkey! He never could have stood upon his legs, that bird. He would have snapped 'em short off in a minute, like sticks of sealing-wax.

"Why, it's impossible to carry that to Camden Town," said Scrooge. "You must have a cab."

The chuckle with which he said this, and the chuckle with which he paid for the Turkey, and the chuckle with which he paid for the cab, and the chuckle with which he recompensed the boy, were only to be exceeded by the chuckle with which he sat down breathless in his chair again, and chuckled till he cried.

Shaving was not an easy task, for his hand continued to shake very much; and shaving requires attention, even when you don't dance while you are at it. But if he had cut the end of his nose off, he would have put a piece of sticking-plaister over it, and been quite satisfied.

He dressed himself "all in his best," and at last got out into the streets. The people were by this time pouring forth, as he had seen them with the Ghost of Christmas Present; and walking with his hands behind him, Scrooge regarded every one with a delighted smile. He looked so irresistibly pleasant, in a word, that three or four good-humoured fellows said, "Good morning, sir! A merry Christmas to you!" And Scrooge said often afterwards, that of all the blithe sounds he had ever heard, those were the blithest in his ears.

He had not gone far, when coming on towards him he beheld the portly gentleman, who had walked into his counting-house the day before and said, "Scrooge and Marley's, I believe?" It sent a pang across his heart to think how this old gentleman would look upon him when they met; but he knew what path lay straight before him, and he took it.

"My dear sir," said Scrooge, quickening his pace, and taking the old gentleman by both his hands. "How do you do? I hope you succeeded yesterday. It was very kind of you. A merry Christmas to you, sir!"

"Mr. Scrooge?"

"Yes," said Scrooge. "That is my name, and I fear it may not be pleasant to you. Allow me to ask your pardon. And will you have the goodness"—here Scrooge whispered in his ear.

"Lord bless me!" cried the gentleman, as if his breath were gone. "My dear Mr. Scrooge, are you serious?"

"If you please," said Scrooge. "Not a farthing less. A great many back-payments are included in it, I assure you. Will you do me that favour?"

"My dear sir," said the other, shaking hands with him. "I don't know what to say to such munifi—"

"Don't say anything, please," retorted Scrooge. "Come and see me. Will you come and see me?"

"I will!" cried the old gentleman. And it was clear he meant to do it.

"Thank'ee," said Scrooge. "I am much obliged to you. I thank you fifty times. Bless you!"

He went to church, and walked about the streets, and watched the people hurrying to and fro, and patted children on the head, and questioned beggars, and looked down into the kitchens of houses, and up to the windows; and found that everything could yield him pleasure. He had never dreamed that any walk—that anything—could give him so much happiness. In the afternoon, he turned his steps towards his nephew's house.

He passed the door a dozen times, before he had the courage to go up and knock. But he made a dash, and did it:

"Is your master at home, my dear?" said Scrooge to the girl. Nice girl! Very.

"Yes, sir."

"Where is he, my love?" said Scrooge.

"He's in the dining-room, sir, along with mistress. I'll show you up stairs, if you please."

"Thank'ee. He knows me," said Scrooge, with his hand already on the dining-room lock. "I'll go in here, my dear."

He turned it gently, and sidled his face in, round the door. They were looking at the table (which was spread out in great array); for these young housekeepers are always nervous on such points, and like to see that everything is right.

"Fred!" said Scrooge.

Dear heart alive, how his niece by marriage started! Scrooge had forgotten, for the moment, about her sitting in the corner with the footstool, or he wouldn't have done it, on any account.

"Why bless my soul!" cried Fred, "who's that?"

"It's I. Your uncle Scrooge. I have come to dinner. Will you let me in, Fred."

Let him in! It is a mercy he didn't shake his arm off. He was at home in five minutes. Nothing could be heartier. His niece looked just the same. So did Topper when *he* came. So did the plump sister, when *she* came. So did every one when *they* came. Wonderful party, wonderful games, wonderful unanimity, won-der-ful happiness!

But he was early at the office next morning. Oh, he was early there. If he could only be there first, and catch Bob Cratchit coming late! That was the thing he had set his heart upon.

And he did it; yes, he did! The clock struck nine. No Bob. A quarter past. No Bob. He was full eighteen minutes and a half, behind his time. Scrooge sat with his door wide open, that he might see him come into the Tank.

His hat was off, before he opened the door; his comforter too. He was on his stool in a jiffy; driving away with his pen, as if he were trying to overtake nine o'clock.

"Hallo!" growled Scrooge, in his accustomed voice as near as he could feign it. "What do you mean by coming here at this time of day?"

"I am very sorry, sir," said Bob. "I *am* behind my time."

"You are?" repeated Scrooge. "Yes. I think you are. Step this way, if you please."

"It's only once a year, sir," pleaded Bob, appearing from the Tank. "It shall not be repeated. I was making rather merry yesterday, sir."

"Now, I'll tell you what, my friend," said Scrooge, "I am not going to stand this sort of thing any longer. And therefore," he continued, leaping from his stool, and giving Bob such a dig in the waistcoat that he staggered back into the Tank again: "and therefore I am about to raise your salary!"

Bob trembled, and got a little nearer to the ruler. He had a momentary idea of knocking Scrooge down with it; holding him; and calling to the people in the court for help and a strait-waistcoat.

"A merry Christmas, Bob!" said Scrooge, with an earnestness that could not be mistaken, as he clapped him on the back. "A merrier Christmas, Bob, my good fellow, than I have given you, for many a year! I'll raise your salary, and endeavour to assist your struggling family, and we will discuss your affairs this very afternoon, over a Christmas bowl of smoking bishop, Bob! Make up the fires, and buy another coal-scuttle before you dot another i, Bob Cratchit!"

Scrooge was better than his word. He did it all, and infinitely more; and to Tiny Tim, who did NOT die, he was a second father. He became as good a friend, as good a master, and as good a man, as the good old city knew, or any other good old city, town, or borough, in the good old world. Some people laughed to see the alteration in him, but he let them laugh, and little heeded them; for he was wise enough to know that nothing ever happened on this globe, for good, at which some people did not have their fill of laughter in the outset; and knowing that such as these would be blind anyway, he thought it quite as well that they should wrinkle up their eyes in grins, as have the malady in less attractive forms. His own heart laughed: and that was quite enough for him.

He had no further intercourse with Spirits, but lived upon the Total Abstinence Principle, ever afterwards; and it was always said of him, that he knew how to keep Christmas well, if any man alive possessed the knowledge. May that be truly said of us, and all of us! And so, as Tiny Tim observed, God bless Us, Every One!

THE KING OF
THE GOLDEN RIVER

OR
THE BLACK BROTHERS
BY JOHN RUSKIN

I

HOW THE AGRICULTURAL SYSTEM OF THE BLACK BROTHERS WAS INTERFERED WITH BY SOUTH-WEST WIND, ESQUIRE

In a secluded and mountainous part of Stiria there was, in old time, a valley of the most surprising and luxuriant fertility. It was surrounded, on all sides, by steep and rocky mountains, rising into peaks, which were always covered with snow, and from which a number of torrents descended in constant cataracts. One of these fell westward, over the face of a crag so high, that, when the sun had set to everything else, and all below was darkness, his beams still shone full upon this waterfall, so that it looked like a shower of gold. It was, therefore, called by the people of the neighbourhood, the Golden River. It was strange that none of these streams fell into the valley itself. They all descended on the other side of the mountains, and wound away through broad plains and by populous cities. But the clouds were drawn so constantly to the snowy hills, and rested so softly in the circular hollow, that in time of drought and heat, when all the country round was burnt up, there was still rain in the little valley; and its crops were so heavy, and its hay so high, and its apples so red, and its grapes so blue, and its wine so rich, and its honey so sweet, that it was a marvel to every one who beheld it, and was commonly called the Treasure Valley.

The whole of this little valley belonged to three brothers, called Schwartz, Hans, and Gluck. Schwartz and Hans, the two elder brothers, were very ugly men, with over-hanging eyebrows and small dull eyes, which were always half shut, so that you couldn't see into *them*, and always fancied they saw very far into *you*. They lived by farming the Treasure Valley, and very good farmers they were. They killed everything that did not pay for its eating. They shot the blackbirds, because they pecked the fruit; and killed the hedgehogs, lest

81

they should suck the cows; they poisoned the crickets for eating the crumbs in the kitchen; and smothered the cicadas, which used to sing all summer in the lime trees. They worked their servants without any wages, till they would not work any more, and then quarrelled with them, and turned them out of doors without paying them. It would have been very odd, if with such a farm, and such a system of farming, they hadn't got very rich; and very rich they *did* get. They generally contrived to keep their corn by them till it was very dear, and then sell it for twice its value; they had heaps of gold lying about on their floors, yet it was never known that they had given so much as a penny or a crust in charity; they never went to mass; grumbled perpetually at paying tithes; and were, in a word, of so cruel and grinding a temper, as to receive from all those with whom they had any dealings, the nick-name of the "Black Brothers."

The youngest brother, Gluck, was as completely opposed, in both appearance and character, to his seniors as could possibly be imagined or desired. He was not above twelve years old, fair, blue-eyed, and kind in temper to every living thing. He did not, of course, agree particularly well with his brothers, or rather, they did not agree with *him*. He was usually appointed to the honourable office of turnspit, when there was anything to roast, which was not often; for, to do the brothers justice, they were hardly less sparing upon themselves than upon other people. At other times he used to clean the shoes, floors, and sometimes the plates, occasionally getting what was left on them, by way of encouragement, and a wholesome quantity of dry blows, by way of education.

Things went on in this manner for a long time. At last came a very wet summer, and everything went wrong in the country around. The hay had hardly been got in, when the hay-stacks were floated bodily down to the sea by an inundation; the vines were cut to pieces with the hail; the corn was all killed by a black blight; only in the Treasure Valley, as usual, all was safe. As it had rain when there was rain nowhere else, so it had sun when there was sun nowhere else. Everybody came to buy corn at the farm, and went away pouring maledictions on the Black Brothers. They asked what they liked, and got it, except from the poor people, who could only beg, and several of whom were starved at their very door, without the slightest regard or notice.

It was drawing towards winter, and very cold weather, when one day the two elder brothers had gone out, with their usual warning to little Gluck, who was left to mind the roast, that he was to let nobody in, and give nothing out. Gluck sat down quite close to the fire, for it was raining very hard, and the kitchen walls were by no means dry or comfortable looking. He turned and turned, and the roast got nice and brown. "What a pity," thought Gluck, "my brothers never ask anybody to dinner. I'm sure, when they've got such a nice piece of mutton as this, and nobody else has got so much as a piece of dry bread, it would do their hearts good to have somebody to eat it with them."

Just as he spoke, there came a double knock at the house door, yet heavy and dull, as though the knocker had been tied up—more like a puff than a knock.

"It must be the wind," said Gluck; "nobody else would venture to knock double knocks at our door."

No; it wasn't the wind: there it came again very hard, and what was particularly astounding, the knocker seemed to be in a hurry, and not to be in the least afraid of the consequences. Gluck went to the window, opened it, and put his head out to see who it was.

It was the most extraordinary looking little gentleman he had ever seen in his life. He had a very large nose, slightly brass-coloured; his cheeks were very round, and very red, and might have warranted a supposition that he had been blowing a refractory fire for the last eight-and-forty hours; his eyes twinkled merrily through long silky eyelashes, his moustaches curled twice round like a corkscrew on each side of his mouth, and his hair, of a curious mixed pepper-and-salt colour, descended far over his shoulders. He was about four-feet-six in height, and wore a conical pointed cap of nearly the same altitude, decorated with a black feather some three feet long. His doublet was prolonged behind into something resembling a violent exaggeration of what is now termed a "swallow tail," but was much obscured by the swelling folds of an enormous black, glossy-looking cloak, which must have been very much too long in calm weather, as the wind, whistling round the old house, carried it clear out from the wearer's shoulders to about four times his own length.

Gluck was so perfectly paralyzed by the singular appearance of his visitor, that he remained fixed without uttering a word, until the old gentleman, having performed another, and a more energetic concerto on the knocker, turned round to look after his fly-away cloak. In so doing he caught sight of Gluck's little yellow head jammed in the window, with its mouth and eyes very wide open indeed.

"Hollo!" said the little gentleman, "that's not the way to answer the door: I'm wet, let me in."

To do the little gentleman justice, he *was* wet. His feather hung down between his legs like a beaten puppy's tail, dripping like an umbrella; and from the ends of his moustaches the water was running into his waistcoat pockets, and out again like a mill stream.

"I beg pardon, sir," said Gluck, "I'm very sorry, but I really can't."

"Can't what?" said the old gentleman.

"I can't let you in, sir,—I can't indeed; my brothers would beat me to death, sir, if I thought of such a thing. What do you want, sir?"

"Want?" said the old gentleman, petulantly. "I want fire, and shelter; and there's your great fire there blazing, crackling, and dancing on the walls, with nobody to feel it. Let me in, I say; I only want to warm myself."

Gluck had had his head, by this time, so long out of the window, that he began to feel it was really unpleasantly cold, and when he turned, and saw the beautiful fire rustling and roaring, and throwing long bright tongues up the chimney, as if it were licking its chops at the savoury smell of the leg of mutton, his heart melted within him that it should be burning away for nothing. "He does look *very* wet," said little Gluck; "I'll just let him in for a quarter of an hour." Round he went to the door, and opened it; and as the little gentleman walked in, there came a gust of wind through the house, that made the old chimneys totter.

"That's a good boy," said the little gentleman. "Never mind your brothers. I'll talk to them."

"Pray, sir, don't do any such thing," said Gluck. "I can't let you stay till they come; they'd be the death of me."

"Dear me," said the old gentleman, "I'm very sorry to hear that. How long may I stay?"

"Only till the mutton's done, sir," replied Gluck, "and it's very brown."

Then the old gentleman walked into the kitchen, and sat himself down on the hob, with the top of his cap accommodated up the chimney, for it was a great deal too high for the roof.

"You'll soon dry there, sir," said Gluck, and sat down again to turn the mutton. But the old gentleman did *not* dry there, but went on drip, drip, dripping among the cinders, and the fire fizzed, and sputtered, and began to look very black, and uncomfortable: never was such a cloak; every fold in it ran like a gutter.

"I beg pardon, sir," said Gluck at length, after watching the water spreading in long, quicksilver-like streams over the floor for a quarter of an hour; "mayn't I take your cloak?"

"No, thank you," said the old gentleman.

"Your cap, sir?"

"I am all right, thank you," said the old gentleman, rather gruffly.

"But,—sir,—I'm very sorry," said Gluck, hesitatingly; "but— really, sir,—you're—putting the fire out."

"It'll take longer to do the mutton, then," replied his visitor, drily.

Gluck was very much puzzled by the behaviour of his guest; it was such a strange mixture of coolness and humility. He turned away at the string meditatively for another five minutes.

"That mutton looks very nice," said the old gentleman at length. "Can't you give me a little bit?"

"Impossible, sir," said Gluck.

"I'm very hungry," continued the old gentleman: "I've had nothing to eat yesterday, nor to-day. They surely couldn't miss a bit from the knuckle!"

He spoke in so very melancholy a tone, that it quite melted Gluck's heart. "They promised me one slice to-day, sir," said he; "I can give you that, but not a bit more."

"That's a good boy," said the old gentleman again.

Then Gluck warmed a plate, and sharpened a knife. "I don't care if I do get beaten for it," thought he. Just as he had cut a large slice out of the mutton, there came a tremendous rap at the door. The old gentleman jumped off the hob, as if it had suddenly become inconveniently warm. Gluck fitted the slice into the mutton again, with desperate efforts at exactitude, and ran to open the door.

"What did you keep us waiting in the rain for?" said Schwartz, as he walked in, throwing his umbrella in Gluck's face. "Ay! what for, indeed, you little vagabond?" said Hans, administering an educational box on the ear, as he followed his brother into the kitchen.

"Bless my soul!" said Schwartz when he opened the door.

"Amen," said the little gentleman, who had taken his cap off, and was standing in the middle of the kitchen, bowing with the utmost possible velocity.

"Who's that?" said Schwartz, catching up a rolling-pin, and turning to Gluck with a fierce frown.

"I don't know, indeed, brother," said Gluck in great terror.

"How did he get in?" roared Schwartz.

"My dear brother," said Gluck, deprecatingly, "he was so *very* wet!"

The rolling-pin was descending on Gluck's head; but, at the instant, the old gentleman interposed his conical cap, on which it crashed with a shock that shook the water out of it all over the room. What was very odd, the rolling-pin no sooner touched the cap, than it flew out of Schwartz's hand, spinning like a straw in a high wind, and fell into the corner at the further end of the room.

"Who are you, sir?" demanded Schwartz, turning upon him.

"What's your business?" snarled Hans.

"I'm a poor old man, sir," the little gentleman began very modestly, "and I saw your fire through the window, and begged shelter for a quarter of an hour."

"Have the goodness to walk out again, then," said Schwartz. "We've quite enough water in our kitchen, without making it a drying-house."

"It is a cold day to turn an old man out in, sir; look at my grey hairs." They hung down to his shoulders, as I told you before.

"Ay!" said Hans, "there are enough of them to keep you warm. Walk!"

"I'm very, very hungry, sir; couldn't you spare me a bit of bread before I go?"

"Bread, indeed!" said Schwartz; "do you suppose we've nothing to do with our bread but to give it to such red-nosed fellows as you?"

"Why don't you sell your feather?" said Hans, sneeringly. "Out with you!"

"A little bit," said the old gentleman.

"Be off!" said Schwartz.

"Pray, gentlemen——"

"Off, and be hanged!" cried Hans, seizing him by the collar. But he had no sooner touched the old gentleman's collar, than away he went after the rolling-pin, spinning round and round, till he fell into the corner on the top of it. Then Schwartz was very angry, and ran at the old gentleman to turn him out; but he also had hardly touched him, when away he went after Hans and the rolling-pin, and hit his head against the wall as he tumbled into the corner. And so there they lay, all three.

Then the old gentleman spun himself round with velocity in the opposite direction; continued to spin until his long cloak was all wound neatly about him; clapped his cap on his head, very much on one side (for it could not stand upright without going through the ceiling), gave an additional twist to his corkscrew moustaches, and replied with perfect coolness: "Gentlemen, I wish you a very good morning. At twelve o'clock to-night I'll call again; after such a refusal of hospitality as I have just experienced, you will not be surprised if that visit is the last I ever pay you."

"If ever I catch you here again," muttered Schwartz, coming, half frightened, out of the corner—but, before he could finish his sentence, the old gentleman had shut the house door behind him with a great bang: and there drove past the window, at the same instant, a wreath of ragged cloud, that whirled and rolled away down the valley in all manner of shapes; turning over and over in the air, and melting away at last in a gush of rain.

"A very pretty business, indeed, Mr. Gluck!" said Schwartz. "Dish the mutton, sir. If ever I catch you at such a trick again—bless me, why, the mutton's been cut!"

"You promised me one slice, brother, you know," said Gluck.

"Oh! and you were cutting it hot, I suppose, and going to

catch all the gravy. It'll be long before I promise you such a thing again. Leave the room, sir; and have the kindness to wait in the coal-cellar till I call you."

Gluck left the room melancholy enough. The brothers ate as much mutton as they could, locked the rest in the cupboard, and proceeded to get very drunk after dinner.

Such a night as it was! Howling wind, and rushing rain, without intermission. The brothers had just sense enough left to put up all the shutters, and double bar the door, before they went to bed. They usually slept in the same room. As the clock struck twelve, they were both awakened by a tremendous crash. Their door burst open with a violence that shook the house from top to bottom.

"What's that?" cried Schwartz, starting up in his bed.

"Only I," said the little gentleman.

The two brothers sat up on their bolster, and stared into the darkness. The room was full of water, and by a misty moonbeam, which found its way through a hole in the shutter, they could see in the midst of it an enormous foam globe, spinning round, and bobbing up and down like a cork, on which, as on a most luxurious cushion, reclined the little old gentleman, cap and all. There was plenty of room for it now, for the roof was off.

"Sorry to incommode you," said their visitor, ironically. "I'm afraid your beds are dampish; perhaps you had better go to your brother's room: I've left the ceiling on, there."

They required no second admonition, but rushed into Gluck's room, wet through, and in an agony of terror.

"You'll find my card on the kitchen table," the old gentleman called after them. "Remember, the *last* visit."

"Pray Heaven it may!" said Schwartz, shuddering. And the foam globe disappeared.

Dawn came at last, and the two brothers looked out of Gluck's little window in the morning. The Treasure Valley was one mass of ruin and desolation. The inundation had swept away trees, crops, and cattle, and left in their stead a waste of red sand and grey mud. The two brothers crept shivering and horror-struck into the kitchen. The water had gutted the whole first floor; corn, money, almost every movable thing had been swept away, and there was left only a small white card on the kitchen table. On it, in large, breezy, long-legged letters, were engraved the words:—

II

OF THE PROCEEDINGS OF THE THREE BROTHERS AFTER
THE VISIT OF SOUTH-WEST WIND, ESQUIRE; AND
HOW LITTLE GLUCK HAD AN INTERVIEW WITH
THE KING OF THE GOLDEN RIVER

South-West Wind, Esquire, was as good as his word. After the momentous visit above related, he entered the Treasure Valley no more; and, what was worse, he had so much influence with his relations, the Wet Winds in general, and used it so effectually, that they all adopted a similar line of conduct. So no rain fell in the valley from one year's end to another. Though everything remained green and flourishing in the plains below, the inheritance of the Three Brothers was a desert. What had once been the richest soil in the kingdom, became a shifting heap of red sand; and the brothers, unable longer to contend with the adverse skies, abandoned their valueless patrimony in despair, to seek some means of gaining a livelihood among the cities and people of the plains. All their money was gone, and they had nothing left but some curious old-fashioned pieces of gold plate, the last remnants of their ill-gotten wealth.

"Suppose we turn goldsmiths?" said Schwartz to Hans, as they entered the large city. "It is a good knave's trade; we can put a great deal of copper into the gold, without any one's finding it out."

The thought was agreed to be a very good one; they hired a furnace, and turned goldsmiths. But two slight circumstances affected their trade: the first, that people did not approve of the coppered gold; the second, that the two elder brothers, whenever they had sold anything, used to leave little Gluck to mind the furnace, and go and drink out the money in the ale-house next door. So they melted all their gold, without making money enough to buy more, and were at last reduced to one large drinking mug, which an uncle of his had given to little Gluck, and which he was very fond of, and would not have parted with for the world; though he never drank anything out of it but milk and water. The mug was a very odd mug to look at. The handle was formed of two wreaths of flowing golden hair, so finely spun that it looked more like silk than metal, and these wreaths descended into, and mixed with, a beard and whiskers of the same exquisite workmanship, which surrounded and decorated a very fierce little face, of the reddest gold imaginable, right in the front of the mug, with a pair of eyes in it which seemed to command its whole circumference. It was impossible to drink out of the mug without being subjected to an intense gaze out of the side of these eyes; and Schwartz positively averred, that once, after emptying it, full of Rhenish, seventeen times, he had seen them wink! When it came to the mug's turn to be made into spoons, it half broke poor little Gluck's heart; but the brothers only laughed at him, tossed the mug into the melting-pot, and staggered out to the ale-house: leaving him, as usual, to pour the gold into bars, when it was all ready.

When they were gone, Gluck took a farewell look at his old friend in the melting-pot. The flowing hair was all gone; nothing remained but the red nose, and the sparkling eyes, which looked more malicious than ever. "And no wonder," thought Gluck, "after being treated in that way." He sauntered disconsolately to the window, and sat himself down to catch the fresh evening air, and escape the hot breath of the furnace. Now this window commanded a direct view of the range of mountains, which, as I told you before, overhung the Treasure Valley, and more especially of the peak from which fell the Golden River. It was just at the close of the day, and when Gluck sat down at the window, he saw the rocks of the mountain tops, all crimson, and purple with the sunset; and there were bright tongues of fiery cloud burning and quivering about them; and the river, brighter than all, fell, in a waving column of pure gold, from precipice to precipice, with the double arch of a broad purple rainbow stretched across it, flushing and fading alternately in the wreaths of spray.

"Ah!" said Gluck aloud, after he had looked at it for a little while, "if that river were really all gold, what a nice thing it would be."

"No it wouldn't, Gluck," said a clear metallic voice, close at his ear.

"Bless me! what's that?" exclaimed Gluck, jumping up. There was nobody there. He looked round the room, and under the table, and a great many times behind him, but there was certainly nobody there, and he sat down again at the window. This time he didn't speak, but he couldn't help thinking again that it would be very convenient if the river were really all gold.

"Not at all, my boy," said the same voice, louder than before.

"Bless me!" said Gluck again, "what *is* that?" He looked again into all the corners and cupboards, and then began turning round, and round, as fast as he could in the middle of the room, thinking there was somebody behind him, when the same voice struck again on his ear. It was singing now very merrily, "Lala-lira-la"; no words, only a soft running effervescent melody, something like that of a kettle on the boil. Gluck looked out of the window. No, it was certainly in the house. Upstairs, and downstairs. No, it was certainly in that very room, coming in quicker time, and clearer notes, every moment. "Lala-lira-la." All at once it struck Gluck that it sounded louder near the furnace. He ran to the opening, and looked in: yes, he saw right, it seemed to be coming, not only out of the furnace, but out of the pot. He uncovered it, and ran back in a great fright, for the pot was certainly singing! He stood in the farthest corner of the room, with his hands up, and his mouth open, for a minute or two, when the singing stopped, and the voice became clear, and pronunciative.

"Hollo!" said the voice.

Gluck made no answer.

"Hollo! Gluck, my boy," said the pot again.

Gluck summoned all his energies, walked straight up to the crucible, drew it out of the furnace, and looked in. The gold was all melted, and its surface as smooth and polished as a river; but instead of reflecting little Gluck's head, as he looked in, he saw meeting his glance from beneath the gold the red nose and sharp eyes of his old friend of the mug, a thousand times redder and sharper than ever he had seen them in his life.

"Come, Gluck, my boy," said the voice out of the pot again, "I'm all right; pour me out."

But Gluck was too much astonished to do anything of the kind.

"Pour me out, I say," said the voice, rather gruffly.

Still Gluck couldn't move.

"*Will* you pour me out?" said the voice, passionately, "I'm too hot."

By a violent effort, Gluck recovered the use of his limbs, took hold of the crucible, and sloped it so as to pour out the gold. But instead of a liquid stream, there came out, first, a pair of pretty little yellow legs, then some coat tails, then a pair of arms stuck a-kimbo, and, finally, the well-known head of his friend the mug; all which articles, uniting as they rolled out, stood up energetically on the floor, in the shape of a little golden dwarf, about a foot and a half high.

"That's right!" said the dwarf, stretching out first his legs, and then his arms, and then shaking his head up and down, and as far round as it would go, for five minutes, without stopping; apparently with the view of ascertaining if he were quite correctly put together, while Gluck stood contemplating him in speechless amazement. He was dressed in a slashed doublet of spun gold, so fine in its texture, that the prismatic colours gleamed over it, as if on a surface of mother of pearl; and, over this brilliant doublet, his hair and beard fell full halfway to the ground, in waving curls, so exquisitely delicate, that Gluck could hardly tell where they ended; they seemed to melt into air. The features of the face, however, were by no means finished with the same delicacy; they were rather coarse, slightly inclining to coppery in complexion, and indicative, in expression, of a very pertinacious and intractable disposition in their small proprietor. When the dwarf had finished his self-examination, he turned his small sharp eyes full on Gluck, and stared at him deliberately for a minute or two. "No, it wouldn't, Gluck, my boy," said the little man.

This was certainly rather an abrupt and unconnected mode of commencing conversation. It might indeed be supposed to refer to the course of Gluck's thoughts, which had first produced the dwarf's observations out of the pot; but whatever it referred to, Gluck had no inclination to dispute the dictum.

"Wouldn't it, sir?" said Gluck, very mildly and submissively indeed.

"No," said the dwarf, conclusively. "No, it wouldn't." And with that, the dwarf pulled his cap hard over his brows, and took two turns, of three feet long, up and down the room, lifting his legs up very high, and setting them down very hard. This pause gave time for Gluck to collect his thoughts a little, and, seeing no great reason to view his diminutive visitor with dread, and feeling his curiosity overcome his amazement, he ventured on a question of peculiar delicacy.

"Pray, sir," said Gluck, rather hesitatingly, "were you my mug?"

On which the little man turned sharp round, walked straight up to Gluck, and drew himself up to his full height. "I," said the little man, "am the King of the Golden River." Whereupon he turned about again, and took two more turns, some six feet long, in order to allow time for the consternation which this announcement produced in his auditor to evaporate. After which, he again walked up to Gluck and stood still, as if expecting some comment on his communication.

Gluck determined to say something at all events. "I hope your Majesty is very well," said Gluck.

"Listen!" said the little man, deigning no reply to this polite inquiry. "I am the King of what you mortals call the Golden River. The shape you saw me in was owing to the malice of a stronger king, from whose enchantments you have this instant freed me. What I have seen of you, and your conduct to your wicked brothers, renders me willing to serve you; therefore, attend to what I tell you. Whoever shall climb to the top of that mountain from which you see the Golden River issue, and shall cast into the stream at its source three drops of holy water, for him, and for him only, the river shall turn to gold. But no one failing in his first, can succeed in a second attempt; and if any one shall cast unholy water into the river, it will overwhelm him, and he will become a black stone." So saying, the King of the Golden River turned away and deliberately walked into the centre of the hottest flame of the furnace. His figure became red, white, transparent, dazzling,—a blaze of intense light—rose, trembled, and disappeared. The King of the Golden River had evaporated.

"Oh!" cried poor Gluck, running to look up the chimney after him; "oh dear, dear, dear me! My mug! my mug! my mug!"

III

HOW MR. HANS SET OFF ON AN EXPEDITION TO THE GOLDEN RIVER, AND HOW HE PROSPERED THEREIN

The King of the Golden River had hardly made the extraordinary exit related in the last chapter, before Hans and Schwartz came roaring into the house, very savagely drunk. The discovery of the total loss of their last piece of plate had the effect of sobering them just enough to enable them to stand over Gluck, beating him very steadily for a quarter of an hour; at the expiration of which period they dropped into a couple of chairs, and requested to know what he had got to say for himself. Gluck told them his story, of which, of course, they did not believe a word. They beat him again, till their arms were tired, and staggered to bed. In the morning, however, the steadiness with which he adhered to his story obtained him some degree of credence; the immediate consequence of which was, that the two brothers, after wrangling a long time on the knotty question, which of them should try his fortune first, drew their swords and began fighting. The noise of the fray alarmed the neighbours, who, finding they could not pacify the combatants, sent for the constable.

Hans, on hearing this, contrived to escape, and hid himself; but Schwartz was taken before the magistrate, fined for breaking the peace, and, having drunk out his last penny the evening before, was thrown into prison till he should pay.

When Hans heard this, he was much delighted, and determined to set out immediately for the Golden River. How to get the holy water was the question. He went to the priest, but the priest could not give any holy water to so abandoned a character. So Hans went to vespers in the evening for the first time in his life, and, under pretence of crossing himself, stole a cupful, and returned home in triumph.

Next morning he got up before the sun rose, put the holy water into a strong flask, and two bottles of wine and some meat in a basket, slung them over his back, took his alpine staff in his hand, and set off for the mountains.

On his way out of the town he had to pass the prison, and as he looked in at the windows, whom should he see but Schwartz himself peeping out of the bars, and looking very disconsolate.

"Good morning, brother," said Hans; "have you any message for the King of the Golden River?"

Schwartz gnashed his teeth with rage, and shook the bars with all his strength; but Hans only laughed at him, and advising him to make himself comfortable till he came back again, shouldered his basket, shook the bottle of holy water in Schwartz's face till it frothed again, and marched off in the highest spirits in the world.

It was, indeed, a morning that might have made any one happy, even with no Golden River to seek for. Level lines of dewy mist lay stretched along the valley, out of which rose the massy mountains—their lower cliffs in pale grey shadow, hardly distinguishable from the floating vapour, but gradually ascending till they caught the sunlight, which ran in sharp touches of ruddy colour along the angular crags, and pierced, in long level rays, through their fringes of spear-like pine. Far above, shot up red splintered masses of castellated rock, jagged and shivered into myriads of fantastic forms, with here and there a streak of sunlit snow, traced down their chasms like a line of forked lightning; and, far beyond, and far above all these, fainter than the morning cloud, but purer and changeless, slept, in the blue sky, the utmost peaks of the eternal snow.

The Golden River, which sprang from one of the lower and snowless elevations, was now nearly in shadow; all but the uppermost jets of spray, which rose like slow smoke above the undulating line of the cataract, and floated away in feeble wreaths upon the morning wind.

On this object, and on this alone, Hans' eyes and thoughts were fixed; forgetting the distance he had to traverse, he set off at an imprudent rate of walking, which greatly exhausted him before he had scaled the first range of the green and low hills. He was, moreover, surprised, on surmounting them, to find that a large glacier, of whose existence, notwithstanding his previous knowledge of the mountains, he had been absolutely ignorant, lay between him and the source of the Golden River. He entered on it with the boldness of a practised mountaineer; yet he thought he had never traversed so strange or so dangerous a glacier in his life. The ice was excessively slippery, and out of all its chasms came wild sounds of gushing water; not monotonous or low, but changeful and loud, rising occasionally into drifting passages of wild melody, then breaking off into short melancholy tones, or sudden shrieks, resembling those of human voices in distress or pain. The ice was broken into thousands of confused shapes, but none, Hans thought, like the ordinary forms of splintered ice. There seemed a curious *expression* about all their outlines—a perpetual resemblance to living features distorted and scornful. Myriads of deceitful shadows, and lurid lights, played and floated about and through the pale blue pinnacles, dazzling and confusing the sight of the traveller; while his ears grew dull and his head giddy with the constant gush and roar of the concealed waters. These painful circumstances increased upon him as he advanced; the ice crashed and yawned into fresh chasms at his feet, tottering spires nodded around him, and fell thundering across his path; and though he had repeatedly faced these dangers on the most terrific glaciers, and in the wildest weather, it was with a new and oppressive feeling of panic terror that he leaped the last chasm, and flung himself, exhausted and shuddering, on the firm turf of the mountain.

He had been compelled to abandon his basket of food, which became a perilous incumbrance on the glacier, and had now no means of refreshing himself but by breaking off and eating some of the pieces of ice. This, however, relieved his thirst; an hour's repose recruited his hardy frame, and with the indomitable spirit of avarice, he resumed his laborious journey.

His way now lay straight up a ridge of bare red rocks,

without a blade of grass to ease the foot, or a projecting angle to afford an inch of shade from the south sun. It was past noon, and the rays beat intensely upon the steep path, while the whole atmosphere was motionless, and penetrated with heat. Intense thirst was soon added to the bodily fatigue with which Hans was now afflicted; glance after glance he cast on the flask of water which hung at his belt. "Three drops are enough," at last thought he; "I may, at least, cool my lips with it."

He opened the flask, and was raising it to his lips, when his eye fell on an object lying on the rock beside him; he thought it moved. It was a small dog, apparently in the last agony of death from thirst. Its tongue was out, its jaws dry, its limbs extended lifelessly, and a swarm of black ants were crawling about its lips and throat. Its eye moved to the bottle which Hans held in his hand. He raised it, drank, spurned the animal with his foot, and passed on. And he did not know how it was, but he thought that a strange shadow had suddenly come across the blue sky.

The path became steeper and more rugged every moment; and the high hill air, instead of refreshing him, seemed to throw his blood into a fever. The noise of the hill cataracts sounded like mockery in his ears; they were all distant, and his thirst increased every moment. Another hour passed, and he again looked down to the flask at his side; it was half empty; but there was much more than three drops in it. He stopped to open it, and again, as he did so, something moved in the path above him. It was a fair child, stretched nearly lifeless on the *rock*, its breast heaving with thirst, its eyes closed, and its lips parched and burning. Hans eyed it deliberately, drank, and passed on. And a dark grey cloud came over the sun, and long, snake-like shadows crept up along the mountain sides. Hans struggled on. The sun was sinking, but its descent seemed to bring no coolness; the leaden weight of the dead air pressed upon his brow and heart, but the goal was near. He saw the cataract of the Golden River springing from the hill-side, scarcely five hundred feet above him. He paused for a moment to breathe, and sprang on to complete his task.

At this instant a faint cry fell on his ear. He turned, and saw a grey-haired old man extended on the rocks. His eyes were sunk, his features deadly pale, and gathered into an expression of despair. "Water!" he stretched his arms to Hans, and cried feebly, "Water! I am dying."

"I have none," replied Hans; "thou hast had thy share of life." He strode over the prostrate body, and darted on. And a flash of blue lightning rose out of the East, shaped like a sword; it shook thrice over the whole heaven, and left it dark with one heavy, impenetrable shade. The sun was setting; it plunged towards the horizon like a red-hot ball.

The roar of the Golden River rose on Hans' ear. He stood at the brink of the chasm through which it ran. Its waves were filled with the red glory of the sunset: they shook their crests like tongues of fire, and flashes of bloody light gleamed along their foam. Their sound came mightier and mightier on his senses; his brain grew giddy with the prolonged thunder. Shuddering he drew the flask from his girdle, and hurled it into the centre of the torrent. As he did so, an icy chill shot through his limbs: he staggered, shrieked, and fell. The waters closed over his cry. And the moaning of the river rose wildly into the night, as it gushed over

THE BLACK STONE.

IV

HOW MR. SCHWARTZ SET OFF ON AN EXPEDITION TO THE GOLDEN RIVER, AND HOW HE PROSPERED THEREIN

Poor little Gluck waited very anxiously alone in the house for Hans' return. Finding he did not come back, he was terribly frightened, and went and told Schwartz in the prison all that had happened. Then Schwartz was very much pleased, and said that Hans must certainly have been turned into a black stone, and he should have all the gold to himself. But Gluck was very sorry, and cried all night. When he got up in the morning there was no bread in the house, nor any money; so Gluck went and hired himself to another goldsmith, and he worked so hard, and so neatly, and so long every day, that he soon got money enough together to pay his brother's fine, and he went and gave it all to Schwartz, and Schwartz got out of prison. Then Schwartz was quite pleased, and said he should have some of the gold of the river. But Gluck only begged he would go and see what had become of Hans.

Now when Schwartz had heard that Hans had stolen the holy water, he thought to himself that such a proceeding might not be considered altogether correct by the King of the Golden River, and determined to manage matters better. So he took some more of Gluck's money, and went to a bad priest, who gave him some holy water very readily for it. Then Schwartz was sure it was all quite right. So Schwartz got up early in the morning before the sun rose, and took some bread and wine in a basket, and put his holy water in a flask, and set off for the mountains. Like his brother, he was much surprised at the sight of the glacier, and had great difficulty in crossing it, even after leaving his basket behind him. The day was cloudless, but not bright: there was a heavy purple haze hanging over the sky, and the hills looked lowering and gloomy. And as Schwartz climbed the steep rock path, the thirst came upon him, as it had upon his brother, until he lifted his flask to his lips to drink. Then he saw the fair child lying near him on the rocks, and it cried to him, and moaned for water.

"Water, indeed," said Schwartz; "I haven't half enough for myself," and passed on. And as he went he thought the sunbeams grew more dim, and he saw a low bank of black cloud rising out of the West; and, when he had climbed for another hour the thirst overcame him again, and he would have drunk. Then he saw the old man lying before him on the path, and heard him cry out for water. "Water, indeed," said Schwartz; "I haven't half enough for myself," and on he went.

Then again the light seemed to fade from before his eyes, and he looked up, and, behold, a mist, of the colour of blood, had come over the sun; and the bank of black cloud had risen very high, and its edges were tossing and tumbling like the waves of the angry sea. And they cast long shadows, which flickered over Schwartz's path.

Then Schwartz climbed for another hour, and again his thirst returned; and as he lifted his flask to his lips, he thought he saw his brother Hans lying exhausted on the path before him, and, as he gazed, the figure stretched its arms to him and cried for water. "Ha, ha," laughed Schwartz, "are you there? remember the prison bars, my boy. Water, indeed! do you suppose I carried it all the way up here for *you*!" And he strode over the figure; yet, as he passed, he thought he saw a strange expression of mockery about its lips. And, when he had gone a few yards farther, he looked back; but the figure was not there.

And a sudden horror came over Schwartz, he knew not why; but the thirst for gold prevailed over his fear, and he rushed on. And the bank of black cloud rose to the zenith, and out of it came bursts of spiry lightning, and waves of darkness seemed to heave and float between their flashes over the whole heavens. And the sky where the sun was setting was all level, and like a lake of blood; and a strong wind came out of that sky, tearing its crimson clouds into fragments, and scattering them far into the darkness. And when Schwartz stood by the brink of the Golden River, its waves were black, like thunder clouds, but their foam was like fire; and the roar of the waters below, and the thunder above, met, as he cast the flask into the stream. And, as he did so, the lightning glared into his eyes, and the earth gave way beneath him, and the waters closed over his cry. And the moaning of the river rose wildly into the night, as it gushed over the

TWO BLACK STONES.

V

HOW LITTLE GLUCK SET OFF ON AN EXPEDITION TO THE GOLDEN RIVER, AND HOW HE PROSPERED THEREIN; WITH OTHER MATTERS OF INTEREST

When Gluck found that Schwartz did not come back he was very sorry, and did not know what to do. He had no money, and was obliged to go and hire himself again to the goldsmith, who worked him very hard, and gave him very little money. So, after a month or two, Gluck grew tired, and made up his mind to go and try his fortune with the Golden River. "The little king looked very kind," thought he. "I don't think he will turn me into a black stone." So he went to the priest, and the priest gave him some holy water as soon as he asked for it. Then Gluck took some bread in his basket, and the bottle of water, and set off very early for the mountains.

If the glacier had occasioned a great deal of fatigue to his brothers, it was twenty times worse for him, who was neither so strong nor so practised on the mountains. He had several very bad falls, lost his basket and bread, and was very much frightened at the strange noises under the ice. He lay a long time to rest on the grass, after he had got over, and began to climb the hill just in the hottest part of the day. When he had climbed for an hour, he got dreadfully thirsty, and was going to drink like his brothers, when he saw an old man coming down the path above him, looking very feeble, and leaning on a staff. "My son," said the old man, "I am faint with thirst, give me some of that water." Then Gluck looked at him, and when he saw that he was pale and weary, he gave him the water; "Only pray don't drink it all," said Gluck. But the old man drank a great deal, and gave him back the bottle two-thirds empty. Then he bade him good speed, and Gluck went on again merrily. And the path became easier to his feet, and two or three blades of grass appeared upon it, and some grasshoppers began singing on the bank beside it; and Gluck thought he had never heard such merry singing.

Then he went on for another hour, and the thirst increased on him so that he thought he should be forced to drink. But, as he raised the flask, he saw a little child lying panting by the roadside, and it cried out piteously for water. Then Gluck struggled with himself, and determined to bear the thirst a little longer; and he put the bottle to the child's lips, and it drank it all but a few drops. Then it smiled on him, and got up, and ran down the hill; and Gluck looked after it, till it became as small as a little star, and then turned and began climbing again. And then there were all kinds of sweet flowers growing on the rocks, bright green moss, with pale pink starry flowers, and soft belled gentians, more blue than the sky at its deepest, and pure white transparent lilies. And crimson and purple butterflies darted hither and thither, and

the sky sent down such pure light, that Gluck had never felt
so happy in his life.

Yet, when he had climbed for another hour, his thirst
became intolerable again; and, when he looked at his bottle,
he saw that there were only five or six drops left in it, and he
could not venture to drink. And, as he was hanging the flask
to his belt again, he saw a little dog lying on the rocks,
gasping for breath—just as Hans had seen it on the day of his
ascent. And Gluck stopped and looked at it, and then at the
Golden River, not five hundred yards above him; and he
thought of the dwarf's words, "that no one could succeed,
except in his first attempt"; and he tried to pass the dog, but
it whined piteously, and Gluck stopped again. "Poor beastie,"
said Gluck, "it'll be dead when I come down again, if I don't
help it." Then he looked closer and closer at it, and its eye
turned on him so mournfully, that he could not stand it.
"Confound the King and his gold too," said Gluck; and he
opened the flask, and poured all the water into the dog's
mouth.

The dog sprang up and stood on its hind legs. Its tail
disappeared, its ears became long, longer, silky, golden; its
nose became very red, its eyes became very twinkling; in
three seconds the dog was gone, and before Gluck stood his
old acquaintance, the King of the Golden River.

"Thank you," said the monarch; "but don't be frightened,
it's all right"; for Gluck showed manifest symptoms of consternation at this unlooked-for reply to his last observation. "Why
didn't you come before," continued the dwarf, "instead of
sending me those rascally brothers of yours, for me to have
the trouble of turning into stones? Very hard stones they
make too."

"Oh dear me!" said Gluck, "have you really been so cruel?"

"Cruel!" said the dwarf, "they poured unholy water into
my stream: do you suppose I'm going to allow that?"

"Why," said Gluck, "I am sure, sir—your majesty, I mean—
they got the water out of the church font."

"Very probably," replied the dwarf; "but," and his countenance grew stern as he spoke, "the water which has been
refused to the cry of the weary and dying, is unholy, though
it had been blessed by every saint in heaven; and the water
which is found in the vessel of mercy is holy, though it had
been defiled with corpses."

So saying, the dwarf stooped and plucked a lily that grew at his feet. On its white leaves there hung three drops of clear dew. And the dwarf shook them into the flask which Gluck held in his hand. "Cast these into the river," he said, "and descend on the other side of the mountains into the Treasure Valley. And so good speed."

As he spoke, the figure of the dwarf became indistinct. The playing colours of his robe formed themselves into a prismatic mist of dewy light; he stood for an instant veiled with them as with the belt of a broad rainbow. The colours grew faint, the mist rose into the air; the monarch had evaporated.

And Gluck climbed to the brink of the Golden River, and its waves were as clear as crystal, and as brilliant as the sun. And, when he cast the three drops of dew into the stream, there opened where they fell a small circular whirlpool, into which the waters descended with a musical noise.

Gluck stood watching it for some time, very much disappointed, because not only the river was not turned into gold, but its waters seemed much diminished in quantity. Yet he obeyed his friend the dwarf, and descended the other side of the mountains towards the Treasure Valley; and, as he went, he thought he heard the noise of water working its way under the ground. And, when he came in sight of the Treasure Valley, behold, a river, like the Golden River, was springing from a new cleft of the rocks above it, and was flowing in innumerable streams among the dry heaps of red sand.

And as Gluck gazed, fresh grass sprang beside the new streams, and creeping plants grew, and climbed among the moistening soil. Young flowers opened suddenly along the river sides, as stars leap out when twilight is deepening, and thickets of myrtle, and tendrils of vine, cast lengthening shadows over the valley as they grew. And thus the Treasure Valley became a garden again, and the inheritance, which had been lost by cruelty, was regained by love.

And Gluck went, and dwelt in the valley, and the poor were never driven from his door: so that his barns became full of corn, and his house of treasure. And, for him, the river had, according to the dwarf's promise, become a River of Gold.

And, to this day, the inhabitants of the valley point out the place where the three drops of holy dew were cast into the stream, and trace the course of the Golden River under the ground, until it emerges in the Treasure Valley. And at the top of the cataract of the Golden River, are still to be seen two BLACK STONES, round which the waters howl mournfully every day at sunset; and these stones are still called by the people of the valley

THE BLACK BROTHERS.

THE ROSE AND THE RING

OR

THE HISTORY OF PRINCE GIGLIO
AND PRINCE BULBO

BY WILLIAM MAKEPEACE THACKERAY

PRELUDE

It happened that the undersigned spent the last Christmas season in a foreign city where there were many English children.

In that city, if you wanted to give a child's party, you could not even get a magic-lantern or buy Twelfth-Night characters—those funny painted pictures of the King, the Queen, the Lover, the Lady, the Dandy, the Captain, and so on—with which our young ones are wont to recreate themselves at this festive time.

My friend Miss Bunch, who was governess of a large family that lived in the *Piano Nobile* of the house inhabited by myself and my young charges (it was the Palazzo Poniatowski at Rome, and Messrs. Spillmann, two of the best pastry-cooks in Christendom, have their shop on the ground-floor): Miss Bunch, I say, begged me to draw a set of Twelfth-Night characters for the amusement of our young people.

She is a lady of great fancy and droll imagination, and having looked at the characters, she and I composed a history about them, which was recited to the little folks at night, and served as our FIRE-SIDE PANTOMIME.

Our juvenile audience was amused by the adventures of Giglio and Bulbo, Rosalba and Angelica. I am bound to say the fate of the Hall Porter created a considerable sensation; and the wrath of Countess Gruffanuff was received with extreme pleasure.

If these children are pleased, thought I, why should not others be amused also? In a few days Dr. Birch's young friends will be expected to re-assemble at Rodwell Regis, where they will learn everything that is useful, and under the eyes of careful ushers continue the business of their little lives.

But, in the meanwhile, and for a brief holiday, let us laugh and be as pleasant as we can. And you elder folks—a little joking, and dancing, and fooling will do even you no harm. The author wishes you a Merry Christmas, and welcomes you to the Fireside Pantomime.

M. A. TITMARSH

December 1854

SHOWS HOW THE ROYAL FAMILY SAT
DOWN TO BREAKFAST

This is Valoroso XXIV, King of Paflagonia, seated with his Queen and only child at their royal breakfast-table, and receiving the letter which announces to his Majesty a proposed visit from Prince Bulbo, heir of Padella, reigning King of Crim Tartary. Remark the delight upon the monarch's royal features. He is so absorbed in the perusal of the King of Crim Tartary's letter, that he allows his eggs to get cold, and leaves his august muffins untasted.

"What! that wicked, brave, delightful Prince Bulbo!" cries Princess Angelica; "so handsome, so accomplished, so witty—the conqueror of Rimbombamento, where he slew ten thousand giants!"

"Who told you of him, my dear?" asks his Majesty.

"A little bird," says Angelica.

"Poor Giglio!" says mamma, pouring out the tea.

"Bother Giglio!" cries Angelica, tossing up her head, which rustled with a thousand curl-papers.

"I wish," growls the King—"I wish Giglio was—"

"Was better? Yes, dear, he is better," says the Queen. "Angelica's little maid, Betsinda, told me so when she came to my room this morning with my early tea."

"You are always drinking tea," said the monarch, with a scowl.

"It is better than drinking port or brandy-and-water," replies her Majesty.

"Well, well, my dear, I only said you were fond of drinking tea," said the King of Paflagonia, with an effort as if to command his temper. "Angelica! I hope you have plenty of new dresses; your milliners' bills are long enough. My dear Queen, you must see and have some parties. I prefer dinners, but of course you will be for balls. Your everlasting blue velvet quite tires me: and, my love, I should like you to have a new necklace. Order one. Not more than a hundred or a hundred and fifty thousand pounds."

"And Giglio, dear?" says the Queen.

"GIGLIO MAY GO TO THE—"

"Oh, sir!" screams her Majesty. "Your own nephew! our late King's only son."

"Giglio may go to the tailor's, and order the bills to be sent in to Glumboso to pay. Confound him. I mean bless his dear heart. He need not want for nothing; give him a couple of guineas for pocket-money, my dear: and you may as well order yourself bracelets while you are about the necklace, Mrs. V."

Her Majesty, or *Mrs. V.*, as the monarch facetiously called her (for even royalty will have its sport, and this august family were very much attached), embraced her husband, and, twining her arm round her daughter's waist, they quitted the breakfast-room in order to make all things ready for the princely stranger.

When they were gone, the smile that had lighted up the eyes of the *husband* and *father* fled—the pride of the *King* fled—the MAN was alone. Had I the pen of a G. P. R. James, I would describe Valoroso's torments in the choicest language; in which I would also depict his flashing eye, his distended nostril—his dressing-gown, pocket-handkerchief, and boots. But I need not say I have *not* the pen of that novelist; suffice it to say, Valoroso was alone.

He rushed to the cupboard, seizing from the table one of the many egg-cups with which his princely board was served for the matin meal, drew out a bottle of right Nantz or Cognac, filled and emptied the cup several times, and laid it down with a hoarse "Ha, ha, ha! now Valoroso is a man again.

"But oh!" he went on (still sipping, I am sorry to say), "ere I was a king, I needed not this intoxicating draught; once I detested the hot brandy wine, and quaffed no other fount but nature's rill. It dashes not more quickly o'er the rocks, than I did, as, with blunderbuss in hand, I brushed away the early morning dew, and shot the partridge, snipe, or antlered deer! Ah! well may England's dramatist remark, 'Uneasy lies the head that wears a crown!' Why did I steal my nephew's, my young Giglio's—? Steal! said I? no, no, no, not steal, not steal. Let me withdraw that odious expression. I took, and on my manly head I set, the royal crown of Paflagonia; I took, and with my royal arm I wield, the sceptral rod of Paflagonia; I took, and in my outstretched hand I hold, the royal orb of Paflagonia! Could a poor boy, a snivelling, drivelling boy— was in his nurse's arms but yesterday, and cried for sugar- plums and puled for pap—bear up the awful weight of crown, orb, sceptre? gird on the sword my royal fathers wore, and meet in fight the tough Crimean foe?"

And then the monarch went on to argue in his own mind (though we need not say that blank verse is not argument) that what he had got it was his duty to keep, and that, if at one time he had entertained ideas of a certain restitution, which shall be nameless, the prospect by a *certain marriage* of uniting two crowns and two nations which had been en- gaged in bloody and expensive wars, as the Paflagonians and the Crimeans had been, put the idea of Giglio's restoration to the throne out of the question: nay, were his own brother, King Savio, alive, he would certainly will away the crown from his own son in order to bring about such a desirable union.

Thus easily do we deceive ourselves! Thus do we fancy what we wish is right! The King took courage, read the papers, finished his muffins and eggs, and rang the bell for his Prime Minister. The Queen, after thinking whether she should go up and see Giglio, who had been sick, thought, "Not now. Business first; pleasure afterwards. I will go and see dear Giglio this afternoon; and now I will drive to the jeweller's, to look for the necklace and bracelets." The Princess went up into her own room, and made Betsinda, her maid, bring out all her dresses; and as for Giglio, they forgot him as much as I forget what I had for dinner last Tuesday twelve- month.

II

HOW KING VALOROSO GOT THE CROWN, AND PRINCE GIGLIO WENT WITHOUT

Paflagonia, ten or twenty thousand years ago, appears to have been one of those kingdoms where the laws of succession were not settled; for when King Savio died, leaving his brother regent of the kingdom, and guardian of Savio's orphan infant, this unfaithful regent took no sort of regard of the late monarch's will; had himself proclaimed sovereign of Paflagonia under the title of King Valoroso. XXIV, had a most splendid coronation, and ordered all the nobles of the kingdom to pay him homage. So long as Valoroso gave them plenty of balls at Court, plenty of money and lucrative places, the Paflagonian nobility did not care who was king; and, as for the people, in those early times they were equally indifferent. The Prince Giglio, by reason of his tender age at his royal father's death, did not feel the loss of his crown and empire. As long as he had plenty of toys and sweetmeats, a holiday five times a week, and a horse and gun to go out shooting when he grew a little older, and, above all, the company of his darling cousin, the King's only child, poor Giglio was perfectly contented; nor did he envy his uncle the royal robes and sceptre, the great hot uncomfortable throne of state, and the enormous cumbersome crown in which that monarch appeared from morning till night. King Valoroso's portrait has been left to us; and I think were you to see it you would agree with me that he must have been sometimes *rather tired* of his velvet, and his diamonds, and his ermine, and his grandeur. I shouldn't like to sit in a stifling robe, with such a thing as a heavy crown on my head.

No doubt, the Queen must have been lovely in her youth; for though she grew rather stout in after life, yet her features, as shown in her portrait, are certainly *pleasing*. If she was fond of flattery, scandal, cards, and fine clothes, let us deal gently with her infirmities; which, after all, may be no greater than our own. She was kind to her nephew; and if she had any scruples of conscience about her husband's taking the young Prince's crown, consoled herself by thinking that the King, though a usurper, was a most respectable man, and that at his death Prince Giglio would be restored to his throne, and share it with his cousin, whom he loved so fondly.

The Prime Minister was Glumboso, an old statesman, who most cheerfully swore fidelity to King Valoroso, and in whose hands the monarch left all the affairs of his kingdom. All Valoroso wanted was plenty of money, plenty of hunting, plenty of flattery, and as little trouble as possible. As long as he had his sport, this monarch cared little how his people paid for it: he engaged in some wars, and of course the Paflagonian newspapers announced that he gained prodigious victories: he had statues erected to himself in every city of the empire; and of course his pictures placed everywhere, and in all the print-shops: he was Valoroso the Magnanimous, Valoroso the Victorious, Valoroso the Great, and so forth; —for even in these early times courtiers and people knew how to flatter.

This royal pair had one only child, the Princess Angelica, who, you may be sure, was a paragon in the courtiers' eyes, in her parents', and in her own. It was said she had the longest hair, the largest eyes, the slimmest waist, the smallest foot, and the most lovely complexion of any young lady in the Paflagonian dominions. Her accomplishments were announced to be even superior to her beauty; and governesses used to shame their idle pupils by telling them what Princess Angelica could do. She could play the most difficult pieces of music at sight. She could answer any one of "Mangnall's Questions." She knew every date in the history of Paflagonia, and every other country. She knew French, English, Italian, German, Spanish, Hebrew, Greek, Latin, Cappadocian, Samothracian, Ægean, and Crim Tartar. In a word, she was a most accomplished young creature; and her governess and lady-in-waiting was the severe Countess Gruffanuff.

Being a countess, one might fancy that Gruffanuff must have been a person of the highest birth. She looked so haughty that one would have thought her a princess at the very least, with a pedigree reaching as far back as the Deluge.

But this lady was no better born than many other ladies who give themselves airs; and all sensible people laughed at her absurd pretensions. The fact is, she had been maid-servant to the Queen when her Majesty was only Princess, and her husband had been head footman; but after his death, or *disappearance*, of which you shall hear presently, this Mrs. Gruffanuff, by flattering, toadying, and wheedling her royal mistress, became a favorite with the Queen (who was rather a weak woman), and her Majesty gave her a title, and made her nursery governess to the Princess.

And now I must tell you about the Princess's learning and accomplishments, for which she had such a wonderful character. Clever Angelica certainly was, but as *idle as possible*. Play at sight, indeed! she could play one or two pieces, and pretend that she had never seen them before; she could answer half-a dozen "Mangnall's Questions"; but then you must take care to ask the *right* ones. As for her languages, she had masters in plenty, but I doubt whether she knew more than a few phrases in each, for all her pretence; and as for her embroidery and her drawing, she showed beautiful specimens, it is true, but *who did them*?

This obliges me to tell the truth, and to do so I must go back ever so far, and tell you about the FAIRY BLACKSTICK.

III

TELLS WHO THE FAIRY BLACKSTICK WAS, AND WHO
WERE EVER SO MANY GRAND PERSONAGES BESIDES

Between the kingdoms of Paflagonia and Crim Tartary, there lived a mysterious personage, who was known in those countries as the Fairy Blackstick, from the ebony wand or crutch which she carried: on which she rode to the moon sometimes, or upon other excursions of business or pleasure, and with which she performed her wonders.

When she was young, and had been first taught the art of conjuring, by the necromancer her father, she was always practising her skill, whizzing about from one kingdom to another upon her black stick, and conferring her fairy favors upon this prince or that. She had scores of royal godchildren; turned numberless wicked people into beasts, birds, millstones, clocks, pumps, bootjacks, umbrellas, or other absurd shapes; and, in a word, was one of the most active and officious of the whole college of fairies.

But after two or three thousand years of this sport, I suppose Blackstick grew tired of it. Or perhaps she thought, "What good am I doing by sending this princess to sleep for a hundred years? by fixing a black pudding on to that booby's nose? by causing diamonds and pearls to drop from one little girl's mouth, and vipers and toads from another's? I begin to think I do as much harm as good by my performances. I might as well shut my incantations up, and allow things to take their natural course.

"There were my two young goddaughters, King Savio's wife and Duke Padella's wife: I gave them each a present, which was to render them charming in the eyes of their husbands, and secure the affection of those gentlemen as long as they lived. What good did my Rose and my Ring do these two women? None on earth. From having all their whims indulged by their husbands, they became capricious, lazy, ill-humored, absurdly vain, and leered and languished, and fancied themselves irresistibly beautiful, when they were really quite old and hideous, the ridiculous creatures! They used actually to patronize me when I went to pay them a visit,—me, the Fairy Blackstick, who knows all the wisdom of the necromancers, and who could have turned them into baboons, and all their diamonds into strings of onions, by a single wave of my rod!" So she locked up her books in her cupboard, declined further magical performances, and scarcely used her wand at all except as a cane to walk about with.

So when Duke Padella's lady had a little son (the Duke was at that time only one of the principal noblemen in Crim Tartary), Blackstick, although invited to the christening, would not so much as attend; but merely sent her compliments and a silver papboat for the baby, which was really not worth a couple of guineas. About the same time the Queen of Paflagonia presented his Majesty with a son and heir; and guns were fired, the capital illuminated, and no end of feasts ordained to celebrate the young prince's birth. It was thought the Fairy, who was asked to be his godmother, would at least have presented him with an invisible jacket, a flying horse, a Fortunatus's purse, or some other valuable token of her favor; but instead, Blackstick went up to the cradle of the child Giglio, when everybody was admiring him and complimenting his royal papa and mamma, and said, "My poor child, the best thing I can send you is a little *misfortune*;" and this was all she would utter, to the disgust of Giglio's parents, who died very soon after; when Giglio's uncle took the throne, as we read in Chapter I.

In like manner, when CAVOLFIORE, King of Crim Tartary, had a christening of his only child, ROSALBA, the Fairy Blackstick, who had been invited, was not more gracious than in Prince Giglio's case. Whilst everybody was expatiating over the beauty of the darling child, and congratulating its parents, the Fairy Blackstick looked very sadly at the baby and its mother, and said, "My good woman"—(for the Fairy was very familiar, and no more minded a queen than a washer-woman)—"my good woman, these people who are following you will be the first to turn against you; and, as for this little lady, the best thing I can wish her is a *little misfortune*." So she touched Rosalba with her black wand, looked severely at the courtiers, motioned the queen an adieu with her hand, and sailed slowly up into the air out of window.

When she was gone, the Court people, who had been awed and silenced in her presence, began to speak. "What an odious Fairy she is," they said,—"a pretty fairy, indeed! Why, she went to the King of Paflagonia's christening, and pretended to do all sorts of things for that family; and what has happened—the Prince her godson has been turned off his throne by his uncle. Would we allow our sweet Princess to be deprived of her rights by any enemy? Never, never, never, never!"

And they all shouted in a chorus, "Never, never, never, never!"

Now, I should like to know how did these fine courtiers show their fidelity? One of King Cavolfiore's vassals, the Duke Padella just mentioned, rebelled against the King, who went out to chastise his rebellious subject. "Any one rebel against our beloved and august Monarch!" cried the courtiers; "any one resist *him*! Pooh! He is invincible, irresistible. He will bring home Padella a prisoner, and tie him to a donkey's tail, and drive him round the town, saying, 'This is the way the great Cavolfiore treats rebels.' "

The King went forth to vanquish Padella; and the poor Queen, who was a very timid, anxious creature, grew so frightened and ill, that I am sorry to say she died; leaving injunctions with her ladies to take care of the dear little Rosalba. Of course they said they would. Of course they vowed they would die rather than any harm should happen to the Princess. At first the "Crim Tartar Court Journal" stated that the King was obtaining great victories over the audacious rebel: then it was announced that the troops of the infamous Padella were in flight: then it was said that the royal army would soon come up with the enemy, and then—then the news came that King Cavolfiore was vanquished and slain by his Majesty, King Padella the First!

At this news, half the courtiers ran off to pay their duty to the conquering chief, and the other half ran away, laying hands on all the best articles in the palace; and poor little Rosalba was left there quite alone—quite alone: she toddled from one room to another, crying, "Countess! Duchess!" (only she said "Tountess, Duttess," not being able to speak plain) "bring me my mutton-sop; my Royal Highness hungry! Tountess! Duttess!" And she went from the private apartments into the throne-room, and nobody was there;—and thence into the ball-room, and nobody was there;—and thence into the pages' room, and nobody was there;—and she toddled down the great staircase into the hall, and nobody was there;—and the door was open, and she went into the court, and into the garden, and thence into the wilderness, and thence into the forest where the wild beasts live, and was never heard of any more!

A piece of her torn mantle and one of her shoes were found in the wood in the mouth of two lioness's cubs, whom KING PADELLA and a royal hunting-party shot—for he was King now, and reigned over Crim Tartary. "So the poor little Princess is done for," said he. "Well, what's done can't be helped. Gentlemen, let us go to luncheon!" And one of the courtiers took up the shoe and put it in his pocket. And there was an end of Rosalba!

IV

HOW BLACKSTICK WAS NOT ASKED TO THE
PRINCESS ANGELICA'S CHRISTENING

When the Princess Angelica was born, her parents not only did not ask the Fairy Blackstick to the christening party, but gave orders to their porter, absolutely to refuse her if she called. This porter's name was Gruffanuff, and he had been selected for the post by their Royal Highnesses because he was a very tall fierce man, who could say "Not at home" to a tradesman or an unwelcome visitor with a rudeness which frightened most such persons away. He was the husband of the Countess Gruffanuff, and as long as they were together they quarrelled from morning till night. Now this fellow tried his rudeness once too often, as you shall hear. For the Fairy Blackstick coming to call upon the Prince and Princess, who were actually sitting at the open drawing-room window, Gruffanuff not only denied them, but made the most *odious vulgar sign* as he was going to slam the door in the Fairy's face! "Git away, hold Blackstick!" said he. "I tell you, Master and Missis ain't at home to you": and he was, as we have said, *going* to slam the door.

But the Fairy, with her wand, prevented the door being shut; and Gruffanuff came out again in a fury, swearing in the most abominable way, and asking the Fairy "whether she thought he was a-going to stay at that there door hall day?"

"You *are* going to stay at that door all day and all night, and for many a long year," the Fairy said, very majestically; and Gruffanuff, coming out of the door, straddling before it with his great calves, burst out laughing, and cried "Ha, ha, ha! that *is* a good un! Ha—ah—what's this? Let me down—oh—o—h'm!" and then he was dumb!

For, as the Fairy waved her wand over him, he felt himself rising off the ground and fluttering up against the door, and then, as if a screw ran into his stomach, he felt a dreadful pain there, and was pinned to the door; and then his arms flew up over his head; and his legs, after writhing about wildly, twisted under his body; and he felt cold, cold growing over him, as if he was turning into metal; and he said, "Oh—o—h'm!" and could say no more, because he was dumb.

He *was* turned into metal! He was from being *brazen*, *brass*! He was neither more nor less than a knocker! And there he was, nailed to the door in the blazing summer day, till he burned almost red hot; and there he was, nailed to the door all the bitter winter nights, till his brass nose was dropping with icicles. And the postman came and rapped at him, and the vulgarest boy with a letter came and hit him up against the door. And the King and Queen (Princess and Prince they were then) coming home from a walk that evening, the King said, "Hullo, my dear! you have had a new knocker put on the door. Why, it's rather like our Porter in the face! What has become of that boozy vagabond?" And the housemaid came and scrubbed his nose with sandpaper; and once, when the Princess Angelica's little sister was born, he was tied up in an old kid-glove; and another night, some *larking* young men tried to wrench him off, and put him to the most excruciating agony with a turnscrew. And then the Queen had a fancy to have the color of the door altered, and the painters dabbed him over the mouth and eyes, and nearly choked him, as they painted him pea-green. I warrant he had leisure to repent of having been rude to the Fairy Blackstick!

As for his wife, she did not miss him; and as he was always guzzling beer at the public-house, and notoriously quarrelling with his wife, and in debt to the tradesmen, it was supposed he had run away from all these evils, and emigrated to Australia or America. And when the Prince and Princess chose to become King and Queen, they left their old house, and nobody thought of the Porter any more.

V

HOW PRINCESS ANGELICA TOOK A LITTLE MAID

One day, when the Princess Angelica was quite a little girl, she was walking in the garden of the palace, with Mrs. Gruffanuff, the governess, holding a parasol over her head, to keep her sweet complexion from the freckles, and Angelica was carrying a bun, to feed the swans and ducks in the royal pond.

They had not reached the duck-pond, when there came toddling up to them such a funny little girl. She had a great quantity of hair blowing about her chubby little cheeks, and looked as if she had not been washed or combed for ever so long. She wore a ragged bit of a cloak, and had only one shoe on.

"You little wretch, who let you in here?" asked Gruffanuff.

"Dive me dat bun," said the little girl, "me vely hungry."

"Hungry! what is that?" asked Princess Angelica, and gave the child the bun.

"Oh, Princess!" says Gruffanuff, "how good, how kind, how truly angelical you are! See, your Majesties," she said to the King and Queen, who now came up, along with their nephew, Prince Giglio, "how kind the Princess is! She met this little dirty wretch in the garden—I can't tell how she came in here, or why the guards did not shoot her dead at the gate!—and the dear darling of a Princess has given her the whole of her bun!"

"I didn't want it," said Angelica.

"But you are a darling little angel all the same," says the governess.

"Yes; I know I am," said Angelica. "Dirty little girl, don't you think I am very pretty?" Indeed, she had on the finest of little dresses and hats; and, as her hair was carefully curled, she really looked very well.

"Oh, pooty, pooty!" says the little girl, capering about,

laughing and dancing, and munching her bun; and as she ate it she began to sing, "O what fun to have a plum bun! how I wis it never was done!" At which, and her funny accent, Angelica, Giglio, and the King and Queen began to laugh very merrily.

"I can dance as well as sing," says the little girl. "I can dance, and I can sing, and I can do all sorts of ting." And she ran to a flower-bed, and, pulling a few polyanthuses, rhododendrons, and other flowers, made herself a little wreath, and danced before the King and Queen so drolly and prettily, that everybody was delighted.

"Who was your mother—who were your relations, little girl?" said the Queen.

The little girl said, "Little lion was my brudder; great big lioness my mudder; neber heard of any udder." And she capered away on her one shoe, and everybody was exceedingly diverted.

So Angelica said to the Queen, "Mamma, my parrot flew away yesterday out of its cage, and I don't care any more for any of my toys; and I think this funny little dirty child will amuse me. I will take her home, and give her some of my old frocks—"

"Oh, the generous darling!" says Gruffanuff.

"—which I have worn ever so many times, and am quite tired of," Angelica went on; "and she shall be my little maid. Will you come home with me, little dirty girl?"

The child clapped her hands and said, "Go home with you—yes! You pooty Princess! Have a nice dinner, and wear a new dress!"

And they all laughed again, and took home the child to the palace; where, when she was washed and combed, and had one of the Princess's frocks given to her, she looked as handsome as Angelica, almost. Not that Angelica ever thought so; for this little lady never imagined that anybody in the world could be as pretty, as good, or as clever as herself. In order that the little girl should not become too proud and conceited, Mrs. Gruffanuff took her old ragged mantle and one shoe, and put them into a glass box, with a card laid upon them, upon which was written, "These were the old clothes in which little BETSINDA was found when the great goodness and admirable kindness of her Royal Highness the Princess Angelica

received this little outcast." And the date was added, and the
box locked up.

For a while little Betsinda was a great favorite with the
Princess, and she danced, and sang, and made her little
rhymes, to amuse her mistress. But then the Princess got a
monkey, and afterwards a little dog, and afterwards a doll,
and did not care for Betsinda any more, who became very
melancholy and quiet, and sang no more funny songs, because nobody cared to hear her. And then, as she grew older,
she was made a little lady's-maid to the Princess; and though
she had no wages, she worked and mended, and put Angelica's
hair in papers, and was never cross when scolded, and was
always eager to please her mistress, and was always up early
and to bed late, and at hand when wanted, and in fact
became a perfect little maid. So the two girls grew up, and,
when the Princess came out, Betsinda was never tired of
waiting on her; and made her dresses better than the best
milliner, and was useful in a hundred ways. Whilst the Princess was having her masters, Betsinda would sit and watch
them; and in this way she picked up a great deal of learning;
for she was always awake, though her mistress was not, and
listened to the wise professors when Angelica was yawning or
thinking of the next ball. And when the dancing-master came,
Betsinda learned along with Angelica; and when the music-
master came, she watched him, and practised the Princess's
pieces when Angelica was away at balls and parties; and when
the drawing-master came, she took note of all he said and
did; and the same with French, Italian, and all other
languages—she learned them from the teacher who came to
Angelica. When the Princess was going out of an evening she
would say, "My good Betsinda, you may as well finish what I
have begun." "Yes, Miss," Betsinda would say, and sit down
very cheerful, not to *finish* what Angelica began, but to *do* it.

For instance, the Princess would begin a head of a warrior,
and Betsinda would complete it; then the Princess put her
name to the drawing; and the Court and King and Queen,
and above all poor Giglio, admired the picture of all things,
and said, "Was there ever a genius like Angelica?" So, I am
sorry to say, was it with the Princess's embroidery and other
accomplishments; and Angelica actually believed that she did
these things herself, and received all the flattery of the Court
as if every word of it was true. Thus she began to think that

there was no young woman in all the world equal to herself, and that no young man was good enough for her. As for Betsinda, as she heard none of these praises, she was not puffed up by them, and being a most graceful, good-natured girl, she was only too anxious to do everything which might give her mistress pleasure. Now you begin to perceive that Angelica had faults of her own, and was by no means such a wonder of wonders as people represented her Royal Highness to be.

VI

HOW PRINCE GIGLIO BEHAVED HIMSELF

And now let us speak about Prince Giglio, the nephew of the reigning monarch of Paflagonia. It has already been stated, in Chapter II, that as long as he had a smart coat to wear, a good horse to ride, and money in his pocket—or rather to take out of his pocket, for he was very good-natured—my young Prince did not care for the loss of his crown and sceptre, being a thoughtless youth, not much inclined to politics or any kind of learning. So his tutor had a sinecure. Giglio would not learn classics or mathematics, and the Lord Chancellor of Paflagonia, SQUARETOSO, pulled a very long face because the Prince could not be got to study the Paflagonian laws and constitution; but, on the other hand, the King's game-keepers and huntsmen found the Prince an apt pupil; the dancing-master pronounced that he was a most elegant and assiduous scholar; the First Lord of the Billiard Table gave the most flattering reports of the Prince's skill; so did the Groom of the Tennis Court; and as for the Captain of the Guard and Fencing-master, the *valiant* and *veteran* Count KUTASOFF HEDZOFF, he avowed that since he ran the General of Crim Tartary, the dreadful Grumbuskin, through the body, he never had encountered so expert a swordsman as Prince Giglio.

I hope you do not imagine that there was any impropriety

in the Prince and Princess walking together in the palace garden, and because Giglio kissed Angelica's hand in a polite manner. In the first place they are cousins; next, the Queen is walking in the garden too (you cannot see her, for she happens to be behind that tree), and her Majesty always wished that Angelica and Giglio should marry: so did Giglio: so did Angelica sometimes, for she thought her cousin very handsome, brave, and good-natured: but then you know she was so clever and knew so many things, and poor Giglio knew nothing, and had no conversation. When they looked at the stars, what did Giglio know of the heavenly bodies? Once, when on a sweet night in a balcony where they were standing Angelica said, "There is the Bear"—"Where?" says Giglio. "Don't be afraid, Angelica! if a dozen bears come, I will kill them rather than they shall hurt you." "Oh, you silly creature!" says she: "you are very good, but you are not very wise." When they looked at the flowers, Giglio was utterly unacquainted with botany, and had never heard of Linnæus. When the butterflies passed, Giglio knew nothing about them, being as ignorant of entomology as I am of algebra. So you see, Angelica, though she liked Giglio pretty well, despised him on account of his ignorance. I think she probably valued *her own learning* rather too much; but to think too well of one's self is the fault of people of all ages and both sexes. Finally, when nobody else was there, Angelica liked her cousin well enough.

King Valoroso was very delicate in health, and withal so fond of good dinners (which were prepared for him by his French cook, Marmitonio), that it was supposed he could not live long. Now the idea of anything happening to the King struck the artful Prime Minister and the designing old lady-in-waiting with terror. For, thought Glumboso and the Countess, "when Prince Giglio marries his cousin and comes to the throne, what a pretty position we shall be in, whom he dislikes, and who have always been unkind to him. We shall lose our places in a trice; Gruffanuff will have to give up all the jewels, laces, snuff-boxes, rings, and watches which belonged to the Queen, Giglio's mother; and Glumboso will be forced to refund two hundred and seventeen thousand millions, nine hundred and eighty-seven thousand, four hundred and thirty-nine pounds thirteen shillings and sixpence halfpenny, money left to Prince Giglio by his poor dear father." So the

Lady of Honor and the Prime Minister hated Giglio because they had done him a wrong; and these unprincipled people invented a hundred cruel stories about poor Giglio, in order to influence the King, Queen, and Princess against him: how he was so ignorant that he could not spell the commonest words, and actually wrote Valoroso Valloroso, and spelt Angelica with two *l*'s; how he drank a great deal too much wine at dinner, and was always idling in the stables with the grooms; how he owed ever so much money at the pastry-cook's and the haberdasher's; how he used to go to sleep at church; how he was fond of playing cards with the pages. So did the Queen like playing cards; so did the King go to sleep at church, and eat and drink too much; and, if Giglio owed a trifle for tarts, who owed him two hundred and seventeen thousand millions, nine hundred and eighty-seven thousand, four hundred and thirty-nine pounds thirteen shillings and sixpence halfpenny, I should like to know? Detractors and talebearers (in my humble opinion) had much better look at *home*. All this backbiting and slandering had effect upon Princess Angelica, who began to look coldly on her cousin, then to laugh at him and scorn him for being so stupid, then to sneer at him for having vulgar associates; and at Court balls, dinners, and so forth, to treat him so unkindly that poor Giglio became quite ill, took to his bed, and sent for the doctor.

His Majesty King Valoroso, as we have seen, had his own reasons for disliking his nephew; and as for those innocent readers who ask why?—I beg (with the permission of their dear parents) to refer them to Shakespeare's pages, where they will read why King John disliked Prince Arthur. With the Queen, his royal but weak-minded aunt, when Giglio was out of sight he was out of mind. While she had her whist and her evening-parties, she cared for little else.

I dare say *two villains*, who shall be nameless, wished Doctor Pildrafto, the Court Physician, had killed Giglio right out, but he only bled and physicked him so severely, that the Prince was kept to his room for several months, and grew as thin as a post.

Whilst he was lying sick in this way, there came to the Court of Paflagonia a famous painter, whose name was Tomaso Lorenzo, and who was Painter in Ordinary to the King of Crim Tartary, Paflagonia's neighbor. Tomaso Lorenzo painted all the Court, who were delighted with his works; for even Countess Gruffanuff looked young and Glumboso good-humored in his pictures. "He flatters very much," some people said. "Nay!" says Princess Angelica, "I am above flattery, and I think he did not make my picture handsome enough. I can't bear to hear a man of genius unjustly cried down, and I hope my dear papa will make Lorenzo a knight of his Order of the Cucumber."

The Princess Angelica, although the courtiers vowed her Royal Highness could draw so *beautifully* that the idea of her taking lessons was absurd, yet chose to have Lorenzo for a teacher, and it was wonderful, *as long as she painted in his studio*, what beautiful pictures she made! Some of the performances were engraved for the "Book of Beauty": others were sold for enormous sums at Charity Bazaars. She wrote the *signatures* under the drawings no doubt, but I think I know who did the pictures—this artful painter, who had come with other designs on Angelica than merely to teach her to draw.

One day Lorenzo showed the Princess a portrait of a young man in armor, with fair hair and the loveliest blue eyes, and an expression at once melancholy and interesting.

"Dear Signor Lorenzo, who is this?" asked the Princess. "I never saw any one so handsome," says Countess Gruffanuff (the old humbug).

"That," said the Painter, "that, Madam, is the portrait of my august young master, his Royal Highness Bulbo, Crown Prince of Crim Tartary, Duke of Acroceraunia, Marquis of Poluphloisboio, and Knight Grand Cross of the Order of the Pumpkin. That is the Order of the Pumpkin glittering on his manly breast, and received by his Royal Highness from his august father, his Majesty King PADELLA I, for his gallantry at the battle of Rimbombamento, when he slew with his own princely hand the King of Ograria and two hundred and eleven giants of the two hundred and eighteen who formed the King's body-guard. The remainder were destroyed by the brave Crim Tartar army after an obstinate combat, in which the Crim Tartars suffered severely."

"What a Prince!" thought Angelica: "so brave—so calm-looking—so young—what a hero!"

"He is as accomplished as he is brave," continued the Court Painter. "He knows all languages perfectly: sings deliciously: plays every instrument: composes operas which have been acted a thousand nights running at the Imperial Theatre of Crim Tartary, and danced in a ballet there before the King and Queen; in which he looked so beautiful, that his cousin, the lovely daughter of the King of Circassia, died for love of him."

"Why did he not marry the poor Princess?" asked Angelica, with a sigh.

"Because they were *first-cousins*, Madam, and the clergy forbid these unions," said the Painter. "And besides, the young Prince had given his royal heart *elsewhere*."

"And to whom?" asked her Royal Highness.

"I am not at liberty to mention the Princess's name," answered the Painter.

"But you may tell me the first letter of it," gasped out the Princess.

"That your Royal Highness is at liberty to guess," says Lorenzo.

"Does it begin with a Z?" asked Angelica.

The Painter said it wasn't a Z; then she tried a Y; then an X; then a W, and went so backwards through almost the whole alphabet.

When she came to D, and it wasn't D, she grew very much excited; when she came to C, and it wasn't C, she was still more nervous; when she came to B, *and it wasn't B*, "Oh, dearest Gruffanuff," she said, "lend me your smelling-bottle!" and, hiding her head in the Countess's shoulder, she faintly whispered, "Ah, Signor, can it be A?"

"It was A; and though I may not, by my Royal Master's orders, tell your Royal Highness the Princess's name, whom he fondly, madly, devotedly, rapturously loves, I may show you her portrait," says the slyboots: and leading the Princess up to a gilt frame, he drew a curtain which was before it.

Oh goodness! the frame contained A LOOKING-GLASS! and Angelica saw her own face!

VII

HOW GIGLIO AND ANGELICA HAD A QUARREL

The Court Painter of his Majesty the King of Crim Tartary
returned to that monarch's dominions, carrying away a number of sketches which he had made in the Paflagonian capital
(you know of course, my dears, that the name of that capital
is Blombodinga); but the most charming of all his pieces was a
portrait of the Princess Angelica, which all the Crim Tartar
nobles came to see. With this work the King was so delighted,
that he decorated the Painter with his Order of the Pumpkin
(sixth class), and the artist became Sir Tomaso Lorenzo, K.P.,
thenceforth.

King Valoroso also sent Sir Tomaso his Order of the
Cucumber, besides a handsome order for money; for he
painted the King, Queen, and principal nobility while at
Blombodinga, and became all the fashion, to the perfect rage
of all the artists in Paflagonia, where the King used to point to
the portrait of Prince Bulbo, which Sir Tomaso had left
behind him, and say, "Which among you can paint a picture
like that?"

It hung in the royal parlor over the royal sideboard, and
Princess Angelica could always look at it as she sat making the
tea. Each day it seemed to grow handsomer and handsomer,
and the Princess grew so fond of looking at it, that she would
often spill the tea over the cloth, at which her father and
mother would wink and wag their heads; and say to each
other, "Aha! we see how things are going."

In the meanwhile poor Giglio lay up stairs very sick in his
chamber, though he took all the doctor's horrible medicines
like a good young lad: as I hope *you* do, my dears, when you
are ill and mamma sends for the medical man. And the only
person who visited Giglio (besides his friend the Captain of
the Guard, who was almost always busy or on parade) was

little Betsinda the housemaid, who used to do his bedroom
and sitting-room out, bring him his gruel, and warm his bed.

When the little housemaid came to him in the morning and
evening, Prince Giglio used to say, "Betsinda, Betsinda, how
is the Princess Angelica?"

And Betsinda used to answer, "The princess is very well,
thank you, my lord." And Giglio would heave a sigh, and
think, "If Angelica were sick, I am sure *I* should not be very
well."

Then Giglio would say, "Betsinda, has the Princess Angelica asked for me to-day?" And Betsinda would answer, "No,
my lord, not to-day"; or, "She was very busy practising the
piano when I saw her"; or "She was writing invitations for an
evening-party and did not speak to me"; or make some excuse or other, not strictly consonant with truth: (for Betsinda
was such a good-natured creature, that she strove to do
everything to prevent annoyance to Prince Giglio, and even
brought him up roast-chicken and jellies from the kitchen
when the doctor allowed them, and Giglio was getting better),
saying "that the princess had made the jelly, or the bread-
sauce, with her own hands, on purpose for Giglio."

When Giglio heard this he took heart, and began to mend
immediately; and gobbled up all the jelly, and picked the last
bone of the chicken—drumsticks, merry-thought, sides'-bones,
back, pope's-nose, and all—thanking his dear Angelica: and
he felt so much better the next day, that he dressed and went
down stairs—where whom should he meet but Angelica going
into the drawing-room? All the covers were off the chairs, the
chandeliers taken out of the bags, the damask curtains
uncovered, the work and things carried away, and the
handsomest albums on the tables. Angelica had her hair in
papers. In a word, it was evident there was going to be a
party.

"Heavens, Giglio!" cries Angelica: "*you* here in such a
dress! What a figure you are!"

"Yes, dear Angelica, I am come down stairs, and feel so
well to-day, thanks to the *fowl* and the *jelly*."

"What do I know about fowls and jellies, that you allude to
them in that rude way?" says Angelica.

"Why, didn't—didn't you send them, Angelica dear?" says
Giglio.

"I send them indeed! Angelica dear! No, Giglio dear," says

she, mocking him. "*I* was engaged in getting the rooms ready for his Royal Highness the Prince of Crim Tartary, who is coming to pay my papa's court a visit."

"The—Prince—of—Crim—Tartary!" Giglio said, aghast.

"Yes, the Prince of Crim Tartary," says Angelica, mocking him. "I dare say you never heard of such a country. What *did* you ever hear of? You don't know whether Crim Tartary is on the Red Sea, or on the Black Sea, I dare say."

"Yes, I do: it's on the Red Sea," says Giglio; at which the Princess burst out laughing at him, and said, "Oh, you ninny! You are so ignorant, you are really not fit for society! You know nothing but about horses and dogs, and are only fit to dine in a mess-room with my Royal Father's heaviest dragoons. Don't look so surprised at me, sir: go and put your best clothes on to receive the Prince, and let me get the drawing-room ready."

Giglio said, "Oh, Angelica, Angelica, I didn't think this of you. *This* wasn't your language to me when you gave me this ring, and I gave you mine in the garden, and you gave me that k—"

But what k—was we never shall know, for Angelica, in a rage, cried, "Get out, you saucy, rude creature! How dare you to remind me of your rudeness! As for your little trumpery twopenny ring, there, sir—there!" And she flung it out of the window.

"It was my mother's marriage-ring," cried Giglio.

"*I* don't care whose marriage-ring it was," cries Angelica. "Marry the person who picks it up if she's a woman; you sha'n't marry *me*. And give me back *my* ring. I've no patience with people who boast about the things they give away. *I* know who'll give me much finer things than you ever gave me. A beggarly ring indeed, not worth five shillings!"

Now Angelica little knew that the ring which Giglio had given her was a fairy ring; if a man wore it, it made all the women in love with him; if a woman, all the gentlemen. The Queen, Giglio's mother, quite an ordinary-looking person, was admired immensely whilst she wore this ring, and her husband was frantic when she was ill. But when she called her little Giglio to her, and put the ring on his finger, King Savio did not seem to care for his wife so much any more, but transferred all his love to little Giglio. So did everybody love him as long as he had the ring; but when, as quite a child, he gave it to Angelica, people began to love and admire *her*; and Giglio, as the saying is, played only second fiddle.

"Yes," says Angelica, going on in her foolish ungrateful way, "*I* know who'll give me much finer things than your beggarly little pearl nonsense."

"Very good, Miss! You may take back your ring, too!" says Giglio, his eyes flashing fire at her; and then, as if his eyes had been suddenly opened, he cried out, "Ha! what does this mean? Is *this* the woman I have been in love with all my life? Have I been such a ninny as to throw away my regard upon *you*? Why—actually—yes—you are a little crooked!"

"Oh, you wretch!" cries Angelica.

"And, upon my conscience, you—you squint a little."

"Eh!" cries Angelica.

"And your hair is red—and you are marked with the small-pox—and what? you have three false teeth—and one leg shorter than the other!"

"You brute, you brute, you!" Angelica screamed out: and as she seized the ring with one hand, she dealt Giglio one, two, three smacks on the face, and would have pulled the hair off his head had he not started laughing, and crying,—

"Oh, dear me, Angelica! don't pull out *my* hair, it hurts! You might remove a great deal of *your own*, as I perceive, without scissors or pulling at all. Oh, ho, ho! ha, ha, ha! he, he, he!"

And he nearly choked himself with laughing, and she with rage; when, with a low bow, and dressed in his Court habit, Count Gambabella, the first lord-in-waiting, entered and said, "Royal Highnesses! Their Majesties expect you in the Pink Throne-room, where they await the arrival of the Prince of CRIM TARTARY."

VIII

HOW GRUFFANUFF PICKED THE FAIRY RING UP,
AND PRINCE BULBO CAME TO COURT

Prince Bulbo's arrival had set all the court in a flutter: everybody was ordered to put his or her best clothes on: the
footmen had their gala liveries; the Lord Chancellor his new
wig; the Guards their last new tunics; and Countess Gruffanuff,
you may be sure, was glad of an opportunity of decorating *her*
old person with her finest things. She was walking through
the court of the Palace on her way to wait upon their Majesties,
when she spied something glittering on the pavement, and
bade the boy in buttons, who was holding up her train, to go
and pick up the article shining yonder. He was an ugly little
wretch, in some of the late groom-porter's old clothes cut
down, and much too tight for him; and yet, when he had
taken up the ring (as it turned out to be), and was carrying it
to his mistress, she thought he looked like a little Cupid. He
gave the ring to her; it was a trumpery little thing enough,
but too small for any of her old knuckles, so she put it into
her pocket.

"Oh, Mum!" says the boy, looking at her, "how—how
beyoutiful you do look, Mum, to-day, Mum!"

"And you, too, Jacky," she was going to say; but, looking
down at him—no, he was no longer good-looking at all—but
only the carroty-haired little Jacky of the morning. However,
praise is welcome from the ugliest of men or boys, and
Gruffanuff, bidding the boy hold up her train, walked on in
high good-humor. The Guards saluted her with peculiar
respect. Captain Hedzoff, in the ante-room, said, "My dear
madam, you look like an angel to-day." And so, bowing and
smirking, Gruffanuff went in and took her place behind her
Royal Master and Mistress, who were in the throne-room,
awaiting the Prince of Crim Tartary. Princess Angelica sat at

their feet, and behind the King's chair stood Prince Giglio, looking very savage.

The Prince of Crim Tartary made his appearance, attended by Baron Sleibootz, his chamberlain, and followed by a black page, carrying the most beautiful crown you ever saw! He was dressed in his travelling costume, and his hair was a little in disorder. "I have ridden three hundred miles since breakfast," said he, "so eager was I to behold the Prin—the Court and august family of Paflagonia, and I could not wait one minute before appearing in your Majesties' presences."

Giglio, from behind the throne, burst out into a roar of contemptuous laughter; but all the Royal party, in fact, were so flurried, that they did not hear this little outbreak. "Your R.H. is welcome in any dress," says the King. "Glumboso, a chair for his Royal Highness."

"Any dress his Royal Highness wears *is* a Court-dress," says Princess Angelica, smiling graciously.

"Ah! but you should see my other clothes," said the Prince. "I should have had them on, but that stupid carrier has not brought them. Who's that laughing?"

It was Giglio laughing. "I was laughing," he said, "because you said just now that you were in such a hurry to see the Princess that you could not wait to change your dress; and now you say you come in those clothes because you have no others."

"And who are you?" says Prince Bulbo, very fiercely.

"My father was King of this country, and I am his only son, Prince!" replies Giglio, with equal haughtiness.

"Ha!" said the King and Glumboso, looking very flurried; but the former, collecting himself, said, "Dear Prince Bulbo, I forgot to introduce to your Royal Highness my dear nephew, his Royal Highness Prince Giglio! Know each other! Embrace each other! Giglio, give his Royal Highness your hand!" And Giglio, giving his hand, squeezed poor Bulbo's until the tears ran out of his eyes. Glumboso now brought a chair for the Royal visitor, and placed it on the platform on which the King, Queen, and Prince were seated; but the chair was on the edge of the platform, and as Bulbo sat down, it toppled over, and he with it, rolling over and over, and bellowing like a bull. Giglio roared still louder at this disaster, but it was with laughter; so did all the Court when Prince Bulbo got up; for though when he entered the room he appeared not very ridiculous, as he stood up from his fall, for a moment, he looked so exceedingly plain and foolish that nobody could help laughing at him. When he had entered the room, he was observed to carry a rose in his hand, which fell out of it as he tumbled.

"My rose! my rose!" cried Bulbo; and his chamberlain dashed forwards and picked it up, and gave it to the Prince, who put it in his waistcoat. Then people wondered why they had laughed; there was nothing particularly ridiculous in him. He was rather short, rather stout, rather red-haired, but, in fine, for a prince not so bad.

So they sat and talked, the royal personages together, the Crim Tartar officers with those of Paflagonia—Giglio very comfortable with Gruffanuff behind the throne. He looked at her with such tender eyes, that her heart was all in a flutter. "Oh, dear Prince," she said, "how could you speak so haughtily in presence of their Majesties? I protest I thought I should have fainted."

"I should have caught you in my arms," said Giglio, looking raptures.

"Why were you so cruel to Prince Bulbo, dear Prince?" says Gruff.

"Because I hate him," says Gil.

"You are jealous of him, and still love poor Angelica," cries Gruffanuff, putting her handkerchief to her eyes.

"I did, but I love her no more!" Giglio cried. "I despise her! Were she heiress to twenty thousand thrones, I would despise her and scorn her. But why speak of thrones? I have lost mine. I am too weak to recover it—I am alone, and have no friend."

"Oh, say not so, dear Prince!" says Gruffanuff.

"Besides," says he, "I am so happy here *behind the throne*, that I would not change my place, no, not for the throne of the world!"

"What are you two people chattering about there?" says the Queen, who was rather good-natured, though not over-burdened with wisdom. "It is time to dress for dinner. Giglio, show Prince Bulbo to his room. Prince, if your clothes have not come, we shall be very happy to see you as you are." But when Prince Bulbo got to his bedroom, his luggage was there and unpacked; and the hairdresser coming in, cut and curled him entirely to his own satisfaction; and when the dinner-bell rang, the royal company had not to wait above five-and-twenty minutes until Bulbo appeared, during which time the King, who could not bear to wait, grew as sulky as possible. As for Giglio, he never left Madam Gruffanuff all this time, but stood with her in the embrasure of a window, paying her compliments. At length the groom of the chambers announced his Royal Highness the Prince of Crim Tartary! and the noble company went into the royal dining-room. It was quite a small party; only the King and Queen, the Princess, whom Bulbo took out, the two Princes, Countess Gruffanuff, Glumboso the Prime Minister, and Prince Bulbo's chamberlain. You may be sure they had a very good dinner—let every boy or girl think of what he or she likes best, and fancy it on the table.[1]

The Princess talked incessantly all dinner-time to the Prince of Crimea, who ate an immense deal too much, and never took his eyes off his plate, except when Giglio, who was carving a goose, sent a quantity of stuffing and onion-sauce into one of them. Giglio only burst out a-laughing as the Crimean Prince wiped his shirt-front and face with his scented pocket-handkerchief. He did not make Prince Bulbo any apology. When the Prince looked at him, Giglio would not look that way. When Prince Bulbo said, "Prince Giglio, may I have the honor of taking a glass of wine with you?" Giglio *wouldn't* answer. All his talk and his eyes were for Countess Gruffanuff, who, you may be sure, was pleased with Giglio's attentions—the vain old creature! When he was not complimenting her, he was making fun of Prince Bulbo, so loud that Gruffanuff was always tapping him with her fan and saying, "Oh, you satirical Prince! Oh, fie, the Prince will hear!" "Well, I don't mind," says Giglio, louder still. The King and Queen luckily did not hear; for her Majesty was a little deaf, and the King thought so much about his own dinner, and, besides, made such a dreadful noise, hob-gobbling in eating it, that he heard nothing else. After dinner, his Majesty and the Queen went to sleep in their arm-chairs.

This was the time when Giglio began his tricks with Prince Bulbo, plying that young gentleman with port, sherry, madeira, champagne, marsala, cherry-brandy and pale ale, of all of

---

[1] Here a very pretty game may be played by all the children saying what they like best for dinner.

which Master Bulbo drank without stint. But in plying his guest, Giglio was obliged to drink himself, and I am sorry to say, took more than was good for him, so that the young men were very noisy, rude, and foolish when they joined the ladies after dinner; and dearly did they pay for that imprudence, as now, my darlings, you shall hear!

Bulbo went and sat by the piano, where Angelica was playing and singing, and he sang out of tune, and he upset the coffee when the footman brought it, and he laughed out of place, and talked absurdly, and fell asleep and snored horridly. Booh, the nasty pig! But as he lay there stretched on the pink satin sofa, Angelica still persisted in thinking him the most beautiful of human beings. No doubt the magic rose which Bulbo wore caused this infatuation on Angelica's part: but is she the first young woman who has thought a silly fellow charming?

Giglio must go and sit by Gruffanuff, whose old face he, too, every moment began to find more lovely. He paid the most outrageous compliments to her:—There never was such a darling. Older than he was?—Fiddle-de-dee! He would marry her—he would have nothing but her!

To marry the heir to the throne! Here was a chance! The artful hussy actually got a sheet of paper and wrote upon it,—

"This is to give notice that I, Giglio, only son of Savio, King of Paflagonia, hereby promise to marry the charming and virtuous Barbara Griselda Countess Gruffanuff, and widow of the late Jenkins Gruffanuff, Esq."

"What is it you are writing, you charming Gruffy?" says Giglio, who was lolling on the sofa by the writing-table.

"Only an order for you to sign, dear Prince, for giving coals and blankets to the poor, this cold weather. Look! the King and Queen are both asleep and your Royal Highness's order will do."

So Giglio, who was very good-natured, as Gruffy well knew, signed the order immediately; and, when she had it in her pocket, you may fancy what airs she gave herself. She was ready to flounce out of the room before the Queen herself, as now she was the wife of the *rightful* King of

Paflagonia! She would not speak to Glumboso, whom she thought a brute, for depriving her *dear husband* of the crown! And when candles came, and she had helped to undress the Queen and Princess, she went into her own room, and actually practised, on a sheet of paper, "Griselda Paflagonia," "Barbara Regina," "Griselda Barbara, Paf. Reg.," and I don't know what signatures besides, against the day when she should be Queen forsooth!

IX

HOW BETSINDA GOT THE WARMING-PAN

Little Betsinda came in to put Gruffanuff's hair in papers; and the Countess was so pleased, that, for a wonder, she complimented Betsinda. "Betsinda!" she said, "you dressed my hair very nicely to-day; I promised you a little present. Here are five sh—no, here is a pretty little ring that I picked—that I have had some time." And she gave Betsinda the ring she had picked up in the court. It fitted Betsinda exactly.

"It's like the ring the Princess used to wear," says the maid.

"No such thing," says Gruffanuff; "I have had it this ever so long. There—tuck me up quite comfortable: and now, as it's a very cold night" (the snow was beating in at the window), "you may go and warm dear Prince Giglio's bed, like a good girl, and then you may unrip my green silk, and then you can just do me up a little cap for the morning, and then you can mend that hole in my silk stocking, and then you can go to bed, Betsinda. Mind, I shall want my cup of tea at five o'clock in the morning."

"I suppose I had best warm both the young gentlemen's beds, Ma'am?" says Betsinda.

Gruffanuff, for reply, said, "Hau-an-ho!—Grau-haw-hoo! —Hong-hrho!" In fact, she was snoring sound asleep.

Her room, you know, is next to the King and Queen, and

the Princess is next to them. So pretty Betsinda went away
for the coals to the kitchen, and filled the royal warming-pan.

Now she was a very kind, merry, civil, pretty girl; but
there must have been something very captivating about her
this evening, for all the women in the servants'-hall began to
scold and abuse her. The housekeeper said she was a pert,
stuck-up thing: the upper-housemaid asked, how dare she
wear such ringlets and ribbons, it was quite improper! The
cook (for there was a woman-cook as well as a man-cook) said
to the kitchen-maid that *she* never could see anything in that
creetur: but as for the men, every one of them, Coachman,
John, Buttons the page, and Monsieur the Prince of Crim
Tartary's valet, started up and said,—

"My eyes!
"O mussey!
"O jemmany!   } what a pretty girl Betsinda is!"
"O ciel!

"Hands off; none of your impertinence, you vulgar, low
people!" says Betsinda, walking off with her pan of coals. She
heard the young gentlemen playing at billiards as she went
up stairs: first to Prince Giglio's bed, which she warmed, and
then to Prince Bulbo's room.

He came in just as she had done; and as soon as he saw
her, "O! O! O! O! O! O! what a beyou—oo—ootiful creature
you are! You angel—you Peri—you rosebud, let me be thy
bulbul—thy Bulbo, too! Fly to the desert, fly with me! I
never saw a young gazelle to glad me with its dark blue eye
that had eyes like thine. Thou nymph of beauty, take, take
this young heart. A truer never did itself sustain within a
soldier's waistcoat. Be mine! Be mine! Be Princess of Crim
Tartary! My Royal Father will approve our union: and as for
that little carroty-haired Angelica, I do not care a fig for her
any more."

"Go away, your Royal Highness, and go to bed, please,"
said Betsinda, with the warming-pan.

But Bulbo said, "No, never, till thou swearest to be mine,
thou lovely, blushing chambermaid divine! Here, at thy feet,
the royal Bulbo lies, the trembling captive of Betsinda's eyes."

And he went on, making himself so *absurd and ridiculous*,
that Betsinda, who was full of fun, gave him a touch with the
warming-pan, which, I promise you, made him cry "O-o-o-o!"
in a very different manner.

Prince Bulbo made such a noise that Prince Giglio, who heard him, from the next room, came in to see what was the matter. As soon as he saw what was taking place, Giglio, in a fury, rushed on Bulbo, kicked him in the rudest manner up to the ceiling, and went on kicking him till his hair was quite out of curl.

Poor Betsinda did not know whether to laugh or to cry; the kicking certainly must hurt the Prince, but then he looked so droll! When Giglio had done knocking him up and down to the ground, and whilst he went into a corner rubbing himself, what do you think Giglio does? He goes down on his own knees to Betsinda, takes her hand, begs her to accept his heart, and offers to marry her that moment. Fancy Betsinda's condition, who had been in love with the Prince ever since she first saw him in the palace garden, when she was quite a little child.

"Oh, divine Betsinda!" says the Prince, "how have I lived fifteen years in thy company without seeing thy perfections? What woman in all Europe, Asia, Africa, and America—nay, in Australia, only it is not yet discovered—can presume to be thy equal? Angelica? Pish! Gruffanuff? Phoo! The Queen? Ha, ha! Thou art my queen. Thou art the real Angelica, because thou art really angelic."

"Oh, Prince! I am but a poor chambermaid," says Betsinda, looking, however, very much pleased.

"Didst thou not tend me in my sickness, when all forsook me?" continues Giglio. "Did not thy gentle hand smooth my pillow, and bring me jelly and roast-chicken?"

"Yes, dear Prince, I did," says Betsinda, "and I sewed your Royal Highness's shirt-buttons on too, if you please, your Royal Highness," cries this artless maiden.

When poor Prince Bulbo, who was now madly in love with Betsinda, heard this declaration, when he saw the unmistakable glances which she flung upon Giglio, Bulbo began to cry bitterly, and tore quantities of hair out of his head, till it all covered the room like so much tow.

Betsinda had left the warming-pan on the floor while the Princes were going on with their conversation, and as they began now to quarrel and be very fierce with one another, she thought proper to run away.

"You great big blubbering booby, tearing your hair in the corner there! of course you will give me satisfaction for insulting Betsinda. *You* dare to kneel down at Princess Giglio's knees and kiss her hand!"

"She's not Princess Giglio!" roars out Bulbo. "She shall be Princess Bulbo, no other shall be Princess Bulbo."

"You are engaged to my cousin!" bellows out Giglio.

"I hate your cousin," says Bulbo.

"You shall give me satisfaction for insulting her!" cries Giglio in a fury.

"I'll have your life."

"I'll run you through."

"I'll cut your throat."

"I'll blow your brains out."

"I'll knock your head off."

"I'll send a friend to you in the morning."

"I'll send a bullet into you in the afternoon."

"We'll meet again," says Giglio, shaking his fist in Bulbo's face; and seizing up the warming-pan, he kissed it, because, forsooth, Betsinda had carried it, and rushed down stairs. What should he see on the landing but his Majesty talking to Betsinda, whom he called by all sorts of fond names. His Majesty had heard a row in the building, so he stated, and smelling something burning, had come out to see what the matter was.

"It's the young gentlemen smoking, perhaps, sir," says Betsinda.

"Charming chambermaid," says the King (like all the rest of them), "never mind the young men! Turn thy eyes on a middle-aged autocrat, who has been considered not ill-looking in his time."

"Oh, sir! what will her Majesty say?" cries Betsinda.

"Her Majesty!" laughs the Monarch. "Her Majesty be hanged! Am I not Autocrat of Paflagonia? Have I not blocks, ropes, axes, hangmen—ha? Runs not a river by my palace wall? Have I not sacks to sew up wives withal? Say but the word, that thou wilt be mine own,—your mistress straightway in a sack is sewn, and thou the sharer of my heart and throne."

When Giglio heard these atrocious sentiments, he forgot the respect usually paid to Royalty, lifted up the warming-pan, and knocked down the King as flat as a pancake; after which, Master Giglio took to his heels and ran away, and

Betsinda went off screaming, and the Queen, Gruffanuff, and the Princess, all came out of their rooms. Fancy their feelings on beholding their husband, father, sovereign, in such a posture.

X

HOW KING VALOROSO WAS IN A DREADFUL PASSION

As soon as the coals began to burn him, the King came to himself and stood up. "Ho! my Captain of the Guards!" his Majesty exclaimed, stamping his royal feet with rage. O piteous spectacle! the King's nose was bent quite crooked by the blow of Prince Giglio! His Majesty ground his teeth with rage. "Hedzoff," he said, taking a death-warrant out of his dressing-gown pocket,—"Hedzoff, good Hedzoff, seize upon the Prince. Thou'lt find him in his chamber two pair up. But now he dared, with sacrilegious hand, to strike the sacred nightcap of a king—Hedzoff, and floor me with a warming-pan! Away, no more demur, the villain dies! See it be done, or else—h'm!—ha!—h'm! mind thine own eyes!" And followed by the ladies, and lifting up the tails of his dressing-gown, the King entered his own apartment.

Captain Hedzoff was very much affected, having a sincere love for Giglio. "Poor, poor Giglio!" he said, the tears rolling over his manly face, and dripping down his mustaches. "My noble young Prince, is it my hand must lead thee to death?"

"Lead him to fiddlestick, Hedzoff," said a female voice. It was Gruffanuff, who had come out in her dressing-gown when she heard the noise. "The King said you were to hang the Prince. Well, hang the Prince."

"I don't understand you," says Hedzoff, who was not a very clever man.

"You Gaby! he didn't say which Prince," says Gruffanuff.

"No; he didn't say which, certainly," said Hedzoff.

"Well, then, take Bulbo, and hang him!"

When Captain Hedzoff heard this, he began to dance about for joy. "Obedience is a soldier's honor," says he. "Prince Bulbo's head will do capitally": and he went to arrest the Prince the very first thing next morning.

He knocked at the door. "Who's there?" says Bulbo. "Captain Hedzoff? Step in, pray, my good Captain; I'm delighted to see you; I have been expecting you."

"Have you?" says Hedzoff.

"Sleibootz, my Chamberlain, will act for me," says the Prince.

"I beg your Royal Highness's pardon, but you will have to act for yourself, and it's a pity to wake Baron Sleibootz."

The Prince Bulbo still seemed to take the matter very coolly. "Of course, Captain," says he, "you are come about that affair with Prince Giglio?"

"Precisely," says Hedzoff: "that affair of Prince Giglio."

"Is it to be pistols, or swords, Captain?" asks Bulbo. "I'm a pretty good hand with both, and I'll do for Prince Giglio as sure as my name is my Royal Highness Prince Bulbo."

"There's some mistake, my lord," says the Captain. "The business is done with *axes* among us."

"Axes? That's sharp work," says Bulbo. "Call my Chamberlain, he'll be my second, and in ten minutes I flatter myself you'll see Master Giglio's head off his impertinent shoulders. I'm hungry for his blood. Hoo-oo-aw!" and he looked as savage as an ogre.

"I beg your pardon, sir, but by this warrant I am to take you prisoner, and hand you over to—to the executioner."

"Pooh, pooh, my good man!—Stop, I say,—ho!—hulloa!" was all that this luckless Prince was enabled to say: for Hedzoff's guards seizing him, tied a handkerchief over his mouth and face, and carried him to the place of execution.

The King, who happened to be talking to Glumboso, saw him pass, and took a pinch of snuff, and said, "So much for Giglio. Now let's go to breakfast."

The Captain of the Guard handed over his prisoner to the Sheriff, with the fatal order.

"AT SIGHT CUT OFF THE BEARER'S HEAD.

VALOROSO XXIV"

"It's a mistake," says Bulbo, who did not seem to understand the business in the least.

"Poo-poo-pooh," says the Sheriff. "Fetch Jack Ketch instantly. Jack Ketch!"

And poor Bulbo was led to the scaffold, where an executioner with a block and a tremendous axe was always ready in case he should be wanted.

But we must now revert to Giglio and Betsinda.

XI

WHAT GRUFFANUFF DID TO GIGLIO AND BETSINDA

Gruffanuff, who had seen what had happened with the King, and knew that Giglio must come to grief, got up very early the next morning, and went to devise some plans for rescuing her darling husband, as the silly old thing insisted on calling him. She found him walking up and down the garden, thinking of a rhyme for Betsinda (*tinder* and *winda* were all he could find), and indeed having forgotten all about the past evening, except that Betsinda was the most lovely of beings.

"Well, dear Giglio?" says Gruff.

"Well, dear Gruffy?" says Giglio, only *he* was quite satirical.

"I have been thinking, darling, what you must do in this scrape. You must fly the country for a while."

"What scrape?—fly the country? Never without her I love, Countess," says Giglio.

"No, she will accompany you, dear Prince," she says in her most coaxing accents. "First, we must get the jewels belonging to our royal parents, and those of her and his present Majesty. Here is the key, duck; they are all yours, you know, by right, for you are the rightful King of Paflagonia, and your wife will be the rightful Queen."

"Will she?" says Giglio.

"Yes; and having got the jewels, go to Glumboso's apartment, where, under his bed, you will find sacks containing money to the amount of £217,000,000,987,439 13s 6½d., all belonging to you, for he took it out of your royal father's room on the day of his death. With this we will fly."

"*We* will fly?" says Giglio.

"Yes, you and your bride—your affianced love—your Gruffy!" says the Countess, with a languishing leer.

"*You* my bride!" says Giglio. "You, you hideous old woman!"

"Oh, you—you wretch! didn't you give me this paper promising marriage?" cries Gruff.

"Get away, you old goose! I love Betsinda, and Betsinda only!" And in a fit of terror he ran from her as quickly as he could.

"He! he! he!" shrieks out Gruff; "a promise is a promise, if there are laws in Paflagonia! And as for that monster, that wretch, that fiend, that ugly little vixen—as for that upstart, that ingrate, that beast Betsinda, Master Giglio will have no little difficulty in discovering her whereabouts. He may look very long before finding *her*, I warrant. He little knows that Miss Betsinda is—"

Is—what? Now, you shall hear. Poor Betsinda got up at five in winter's morning to bring her cruel mistress her tea; and instead of finding her in a good humor, found Gruffy as cross as two sticks. The Countess boxed Betsinda's ears half a dozen times whilst she was dressing; but as poor little Betsinda was used to this kind of treatment, she did not feel any special alarm. "And now," says she, "when her Majesty rings her bell twice, I'll trouble you, Miss, to attend."

So when the Queen's bell rang twice, Betsinda came to her Majesty and made a pretty little curtsy. The Queen, the Princess, and Gruffanuff were all three in the room. As soon as they saw her they began.

"You wretch!" says the Queen.

"You little vulgar thing!" says the Princess.

"You beast!" says Gruffanuff.

"Get out of my sight!" says the Queen.

"Go away with you, do!" says the Princess.

"Quit the premises!" says Gruffanuff.

Alas! and woe is me! very lamentable events had occurred to Betsinda that morning, and all in consequence of that fatal warming-pan business of the previous night. The King had offered to marry her; of course her Majesty the Queen was jealous: Bulbo had fallen in love with her; of course Angelica was furious: Giglio was in love with her, and oh, what a fury Gruffy was in!

"Take off that $\begin{Bmatrix} \text{cap} \\ \text{petticoat} \\ \text{gown} \end{Bmatrix}$ I gave you," they said, all at once,

and began tearing the clothes off poor Betsinda.

"How dare you flirt with $\begin{Bmatrix} \text{the King?"} \\ \text{Prince Bulbo?"} \\ \text{Prince Giglio?"} \end{Bmatrix}$ cried the Queen, the Princess, and Countess.

"Give her the rags she wore when she came into the house, and turn her out of it!" cries the Queen.

"Mind she does not go with *my* shoes on, which I lent her so kindly," says the Princess; and indeed the Princess's shoes were a great deal too big for Betsinda.

"Come with me, you filthy hussy!" and taking up the Queen's poker, the cruel Gruffanuff drove Betsinda into her room.

The Countess went to the glass box in which she had kept Betsinda's old cloak and shoe this ever so long, and said, "Take those rags, you little beggar creature, and strip off everything belonging to honest people, and go about your business." And she actually tore off the poor little delicate thing's back almost all her things, and told her to be off out of the house.

Poor Betsinda huddled the cloak round her back, on which were embroidered the letters PRIN . . . . ROSAL . . and then came a great rent.

As for the shoe, what was she to do with one poor little tootsey sandal? The string was still to it, so she hung it round her neck.

"Won't you give me a pair of shoes to go out in the snow, Mum, if you please, Mum?" cried the poor child.

"No, you wicked beast!" says Gruffanuff, driving her along with the poker—driving her down the cold stairs—driving her through the cold hall—flinging her out into the cold street, so that the knocker itself shed tears to see her!

But a kind Fairy made the soft snow warm for her little feet, and she wrapped herself up in the ermine of her mantle, and was gone!

*   *   *

"And now let us think about breakfast," says the greedy Queen.

"What dress shall I put on, Mamma? the pink or the pea-green?" says Angelica. "Which do you think the dear Prince will like best?"

"Mrs. V.!" sings out the King from his dressing-room, "let us have sausages for breakfast! Remember we have Prince Bulbo staying with us!"

And they all went to get ready.

Nine o'clock came, and they were all in the breakfast-room, and no Prince Bulbo as yet. The urn was hissing and humming: the muffins were smoking—such a heap of muffins! the eggs were done: there was a pot of raspberry jam, and coffee, and a beautiful chicken and tongue on the side-table. Marmitonio the cook brought in the sausages. Oh, how nice they smelt!

"Where is Bulbo?" said the King. "John, where is his Royal Highness?"

John said he had a took up his Roilighnessesses shaving-water, and his clothes and things, and he wasn't in his room, which he sposed his Royliness was just stepped hout.

"Stepped out before breakfast in the snow! Impossible!" says the King, sticking his fork into a sausage. "My dear, take one. Angelica, won't you have a saveloy?" The Princess took one, being very fond of them; and at this moment Glumboso entered with Captain Hedzoff, both looking very much disturbed. "I am afraid your Majesty—" cries Glumboso. "No business before breakfast Glum!" says the King. "Breakfast first, business next. Mrs. V., some more sugar!"

"Sire, I am afraid if we wait till after breakfast it will be too late," says Glumboso. "He—he—he'll be hanged at half-past nine."

"Don't talk about hanging and spoil my breakfast, you unkind vulgar man you," cries the Princess. "John, some mustard. Pray who is to be hanged?"

"Sire, it is the Prince," whispers Glumboso to the King.

"Talk about business after breakfast, I tell you!" says his Majesty, quite sulky.

"We shall have a war, Sire, depend on it," says the Minister. "His father, King Padella—"

"His father, King who?" says the King. "King Padella is not Giglio's father. My brother, King Savio, was Giglio's father."

"It's Prince Bulbo they are hanging, Sire, not Prince Giglio," says the Prime Minister.

"You told me to hang the Prince, and I took the ugly one," says Hedzoff. "I didn't, of course, think your Majesty intended to murder your own flesh and blood!"

The King for all reply flung the plate of sausages at Hedzoff's head. The Princess cried out, "Hee-karee-karee!" and fell down in a fainting-fit.

"Turn the cock of the urn upon her Royal Highness," said the King, and the boiling water gradually revived her. His Majesty looked at his watch, compared it by the clock in the parlor, and by that of the church in the square opposite; then he wound it up; then he looked at it again. "The great question is," says he, "am I fast or am I slow? If I'm slow, we may as well go on with breakfast. If I'm fast, why, there is just the possibility of saving Prince Bulbo. It's a doosid awkward mistake, and upon my word, Hedzoff, I have the greatest mind to have you hanged too."

"Sire, I did but my duty: a soldier has but his orders. I didn't expect, after forty-seven years of faithful service, that my sovereign would think of putting me to a felon's death!"

"A hundred thousand plagues upon you! Can't you see that while you are talking my Bulbo is being hung?" screamed the Princess.

"By Jove! she's always right, that girl, and I'm so absent," says the King, looking at his watch again. "Ha! Hark, there go the drums! What a doosid awkward thing though!"

"O Papa, you goose! Write the reprieve, and let me run with it," cries the Princess—and she got a sheet of paper, and pen and ink, and laid them before the King.

"Confound it! Where are my spectacles?" the Monarch exclaimed. "Angelica! Go up into my bedroom, look under my pillow, not your mamma's; there you'll see my keys. Bring them down to me, and—Well, well! what impetuous things these girls are!" Angelica was gone, and had run up panting to the bedroom and found the keys, and was back again before the King had finished a muffin. "Now, love," says he, "you must go all the way back for my desk, in which my spectacles are. If you *would* but have heard me out— Be hanged to her! There she is off again. Angelica! ANGELICA!" When his Majesty called in his *loud* voice, she knew she must obey, and came back.

"My dear, when you go out of a room, how often have I told you, *shut the door*? That's a darling. That's all." At last the keys and the desk and the spectacles were got, and the King mended his pen, and signed his name to a reprieve, and Angelica ran with it as swift as the wind. "You'd better stay, my love, and finish the muffins. There's no use going. Be sure it's too late. Hand me over that raspberry jam, please," said the Monarch. "Bong! Bawong! There goes the half-hour. I knew it was."

Angelica ran, and ran, and ran, and ran. She ran up Fore Street, and down High Street, and through the Market-place, and down to the left, and over the bridge, and up the blind ally, and back again, and round by the Castle, and so along by the haberdasher's on the right, opposite the lamp-post, and round the square, and she came—she came to the *Execution place*, where she saw Bulbo laying his head on the block!!! The executioner raised his axe, but at that moment the Princess came panting up and cried Reprieve. "Reprieve!" screamed the Princess. "Reprieve!" shouted all the people. Up the scaffold stairs she sprang, with the agility of a lighter of lamps; and flinging herself in Bulbo's arms, regardless of all ceremony, she cried out, "O my Prince! my lord! my love! my Bulbo! Thine Angelica has been in time to save thy precious existence, sweet rosebud; to prevent thy being nipped in thy young bloom! Had aught befallen thee, Angelica too had died, and welcomed death that joined her to her Bulbo."

"H'm! there's no accounting for tastes," said Bulbo, looking so very much puzzled and uncomfortable, that the Princess, in tones of tenderest strain, asked the cause of his disquiet.

"I tell you what it is, Angelica," said he: "since I came here, yesterday, there has been such a row, and disturbance, and quarrelling, and fighting, and chopping of heads off, and the deuce to pay, that I am inclined to go back to Crim Tartary."

"But with me as thy bride, my Bulbo! Though wherever thou art is Crim Tartary to me, my bold, my beautiful, my Bulbo!"

"Well, well, I suppose we must be married," says Bulbo. "Doctor, you came to read the Funeral Service—read the Marriage Service, will you? What must be, must. That will satisfy Angelica, and then, in the name of peace and quietness, do let us go back to breakfast."

Bulbo had carried a rose in his mouth all the time of the dismal ceremony. It was a fairy rose, and he was told by his mother that he ought never to part with it. So he had kept it between his teeth, even when he laid his poor head upon the block, hoping vaguely that some chance would turn up in his favor. As he began to speak to Angelica, he forgot about the rose, and of course it dropped out of his mouth. The romantic Princess instantly stooped and seized it. "Sweet rose!" she exclaimed, "that bloomed upon my Bulbo's lip, never, never will I part from thee!" and she placed it in her bosom. And you know Bulbo *couldn't* ask her to give the rose back again. And they went to breakfast; and as they walked, it appeared to Bulbo that Angelica became more exquisitely lovely every moment.

He was frantic until they were married; and now, strange to say, it was Angelica who didn't care about him! He knelt down, he kissed her hand, he prayed and begged; he cried with admiration; while she for her part said she really thought they might wait; it seemed to her he was not handsome any more—no, not at all, quite the reverse; and not clever, no, very stupid; and not well bred, like Giglio; no, on the contrary dreadfully vul—

What, I cannot say, for King Valoroso roared out "*Pooh*, stuff!" in a terrible voice. "We will have no more of this shilly-shallying! Call the Archbishop and let the Prince and Princess be married off-hand!"

So, married they were, and I am sure for my part I trust they will be happy.

XII

HOW BETSINDA FLED, AND WHAT BECAME
OF HER

Betsinda wandered on and on, till she passed through the town gates, and so on the great Crim Tartary road, the very way on which Giglio too was going. "Ah!" thought she, as the diligence passed her, of which the conductor was blowing a delightful tune on his horn, "how I should like to be on that coach!" But the coach and the jingling horses were very soon gone. She little knew who was in it, though very likely she was thinking of him all the time.

Then came an empty cart, returning from market; and the driver being a kind man, and seeing such a very pretty girl trudging along the road with bare feet, most good-naturedly gave her a seat. He said he lived on the confines of the forest, where his old father was a woodman, and, if she liked, he would take her so far on her road. All roads were the same to little Betsinda, so she very thankfully took this one.

And the carter put a cloth round her bare feet, and gave her some bread and cold bacon, and was very kind to her. For all that she was very cold and melancholy. When after travelling on and on, evening came, and all the black pines were bending with snow, and there, at last, was the comfortable light beaming in the woodman's windows; and so they arrived, and went into his cottage. He was an old man, and had a number of children, who were just at supper, with nice hot bread-and-milk, when their elder brother arrived with the cart. And they jumped and clapped their hands; for they were good children; and he had brought them toys from the town. And when they saw the pretty stranger, they ran to her, and brought her to the fire, and rubbed her poor little feet, and brought her bread-and-milk.

"Look, Father," they said to the old woodman, "look at this poor girl, and see what pretty cold feet she has. They are as white as our milk! And look and see what an odd cloak she has, just like the bit of velvet that hangs up in our cupboard, and which you found that day the little cubs were killed by King Padella, in the forest! And look, why, bless us all! she has got round her neck just such another little shoe as that you brought home, and have shown us so often—a little blue velvet shoe!"

"What," said the old woodman,—"What is all this about a shoe and a cloak?"

And Betsinda explained that she had been left, when quite a little child, at the town with this cloak and this shoe. And the persons who had taken care of her had—had been angry with her, for no fault, she hoped, of her own. And they had sent her away with her old clothes—and here, in fact, she was. She remembered having been in a forest—and perhaps it was a dream—it was so very odd and strange—having lived in a cave with lions there; and, before that, having lived in a very, very fine house, as fine as the King's, in the town.

When the woodman heard this he was so astonished, it was quite curious to see how astonished he was. He went to his cupboard, and took out of a stocking a five-shilling piece of King Cavolfiore, and vowed it was exactly like the young woman. And then he produced the shoe and the piece of velvet which he had kept so long, and compared them with the things which Betsinda wore. In Betsinda's little shoe was written, "Hopkins, maker to the Royal Family"; so in the other shoe was written, "Hopkins, maker to the Royal Family." In the inside of Betsinda's piece of cloak was embroidered, "PRIN ROSAL"; in the other piece of cloak was embroidered, "CESS BA. No. 246." So that when put together you read, "PRINCESS ROSALBA. No. 246."

On seeing this, the dear old woodman fell down on his knee, saying: "O my princess, O my gracious royal lady, O my rightful Queen of Crim Tartary,—I hail thee—I acknowledge thee—I do thee homage!" And in token of his fealty, he rubbed his venerable nose three times on the ground, and put the Princess's foot on his head.

"Why," said she, "my good woodman, you must be a nobleman of my royal father's Court!" for in her lowly retreat, and under the name of Betsinda, HER MAJESTY, ROSALBA, Queen of Crim Tartary, had read of the customs of all foreign courts and nations.

"Marry, indeed am I, my gracious liege—the poor Lord Spinachi once, the humble woodman these fifteen years syne—ever since the tyrant Padella (may ruin overtake the treacherous knave!) dismissed me from my post of First Lord."

"First Lord of the Toothpick and Joint Keeper of the Snuffbox? I mind me! Thou heldest these posts under our royal Sire. They are restored to thee, Lord Spinachi! I make thee knight of the second class of our Order of the Pumpkin (the first class being reserved for crowned heads alone). Rise, Marquis of Spinachi!" And with indescribable majesty, the Queen, who had no sword handy, waved the pewter spoon, with which she had been taking her bread-and-milk, over the bald head of the old nobleman, whose tears absolutely made a puddle on the ground, and whose dear children went to bed that night Lords and Ladies Bartolomeo, Ubaldo, Catarina, and Ottavia degli Spinachi!

The acquaintance HER MAJESTY showed with the history and *noble families* of her empire, was wonderful. "The House of Broccoli should remain faithful to us," she said; "they were ever welcome at our Court. Have the Articiocchi, as was their wont, turned to the Rising Sun? The family of Sauerkraut must sure be with us—they were ever welcome in the halls of King Cavolfiore." And so she went on enumerating quite a list of the nobility and gentry of Crim Tartary, so admirably had her Majesty profited by her studies while in exile.

The old Marquis of Spinachi said he could answer for them all; that the whole country groaned under Padella's tyranny, and longed to return to its rightful sovereign; and late as it was, he sent his children, who knew the forest well, to summon this nobleman and that; and when his eldest son, who had been rubbing the horse down and giving him his supper, came into the house for his own, the Marquis told him to put his boots on, and a saddle on the mare, and ride hither and thither to such and such people.

When the young man heard who his companion in the cart had been, he too knelt down and put her royal foot on his head; he too bedewed the ground with his tears; he was frantically in love with her, as everybody now was who saw her: so were the young Lords Bartolomeo and Ubaldo, who punched each other's little heads out of jealousy: and so, when they came from east and west at the summons of the Marquis degli Spinachi, were the Crim Tartar Lords who still remained faithful to the House of Cavolfiore. They were such very old gentlemen for the most part, that her Majesty never suspected their absurd passion, and went among them quite unaware of the havoc her beauty was causing, until an old blind Lord who had joined her party told her what the truth was; after which, for fear of making the people too much in love with her, she always wore a veil. She went about privately, from one nobleman's castle to another: and they visited amongst themselves again, and had meetings, and composed proclamations and counter-proclamations, and distributed all the best places of the kingdom amongst one another, and selected who of the opposition party should be executed when the Queen came to her own. And so in about a year they were ready to move.

The party of Fidelity was in truth composed of very feeble old fogies for the most part: they went about the country waving their old swords and flags, and calling "God save the Queen!" and King Padella happening to be absent upon an invasion, they had their own way for a little, and to be sure the people were very enthusiastic whenever they saw the Queen, otherwise the vulgar took matters very quietly—for they said, as far as they could recollect, they were pretty well as much taxed in Cavolfiore's time as now in Padella's.

XIII

HOW QUEEN ROSALBA CAME TO THE CASTLE OF
THE BOLD COUNT HOGGINARMO

Her Majesty, having indeed nothing else to give, made all her followers Knights of the Pumpkin, and Marquises, Earls, and Baronets; and they had a little court for her, and made her a little crown of gilt paper, and a robe of cotton velvet; and they quarrelled about the places to be given away in her court, and about rank and precedence and dignities;—you can't think how they quarrelled! The poor Queen was very tired of her honors before she had had them a month, and I dare say sighed sometimes even to be a lady's-maid again. But we must all do our duty in our respective stations, so the Queen resigned herself to perform hers.

We have said how it happened that none of the Usurper's troops came out to oppose this Army of Fidelity: it pottered along as nimbly as the gout of the principal commanders allowed: it consisted of twice as many officers as soldiers: and at length passed near the estates of one of the most powerful noblemen of the country, who had not declared for the Queen, but of whom her party had hopes, as he was always quarrelling with King Padella.

When they came close to his park gates, this nobleman sent to say he would wait upon her Majesty: he was a most powerful warrior, and his name was Count Hogginarmo, whose helmet it took two strong negroes to carry. He knelt down before her and said, "Madam and liege lady! it becomes the great nobles of the Crimean realm to show every outward sign of respect to the wearer of the Crown, whoever that may be. We testify to our own nobility in acknowledging yours. The bold Hogginarmo bends the knee to the first of the aristocracy of his country."

Rosalba said the bold Count of Hogginarmo was uncommonly kind; but she felt afraid of him, even while he was kneeling, and his eyes scowled at her from between his whiskers, which grew up to them.

"The first Count of the Empire, Madam," he went on, "salutes the Sovereign. The Prince addresses himself to the not more noble lady! Madam, my hand is free, and I offer it, and my heart and my sword, to your service! My three wives lie buried in my ancestral vaults. The third perished but a year since; and this heart pines for a consort! Deign to be mine, and I swear to bring to your bridal table the head of King Padella, the eyes and nose of his son Prince Bulbo, the right hand and ears of the usurping Sovereign of Paflagonia, which country shall henceforth be an appanage to your—to *our* Crown! Say yes; Hogginarmo is not accustomed to be denied. Indeed I cannot contemplate the possibility of a refusal; for frightful will be the result; dreadful the murders; furious the devastations; horrible the tyranny; tremendous the tortures, misery, taxation, which the people of this realm will endure, if Hogginarmo's wrath be aroused! I see consent in your Majesty's lovely eyes—their glances fill my soul with rapture!"

"Oh, sir!" Rosalba said, withdrawing her hand in great fright. "Your lordship is exceedingly kind; but I am sorry to tell you that I have a prior attachment to a young gentleman by the name of—Prince—Giglio—and never—never can marry any one but him."

Who can describe Hogginarmo's wrath at this remark? Rising up from the ground, he ground his teeth so that fire flashed out of his mouth, from which at the same time issued remarks and language, so *loud, violent, and improper*, that this pen shall never repeat them! "R-r-r-r-r-r—Rejected! Fiends and perdition! The bold Hogginarmo rejected! All the world shall hear of my rage; and you, Madam, you above all shall rue it!" And kicking the two negroes before him, he rushed away, his whiskers streaming in the wind.

Her Majesty's Privy Council was in a dreadful panic when they saw Hogginarmo issue from the royal presence in such a towering rage, making footballs of the poor negroes—a panic which the events justified. They marched off from Hogginarmo's park very crestfallen; and in another half-hour they were met by that rapacious chieftain with a few of his followers, who cut, slashed, charged, whacked, banged, and pommelled amongst them, took the Queen prisoner, and drove the Army of Fidelity to I don't know where.

Poor Queen! Hogginarmo, her conqueror, would not condescend to see her. "Get a horse-van!" he said to his grooms, "clap the hussy into it, and send her, with my compliments, to his Majesty King Padella."

Along with his lovely prisoner, Hogginarmo sent a letter full of servile compliments and loathsome flatteries to King Padella, for whose life, and that of his royal family, the *hypocritical humbug* pretended to offer the most fulsome prayers. And Hogginarmo promised speedily to pay his humble homage at his august master's throne, of which he begged leave to be counted the most loyal and constant defender. Such a *wary* old *bird* as King Padella was not to be caught by Master Hogginarmo's *chaff*, and we shall hear presently how the tyrant treated his upstart vassal. No, no; depend on't, two such rogues do not trust one another.

So this poor Queen was laid in the straw like Margery Daw, and driven along in the dark ever so many miles to the Court, where King Padella had now arrived, having vanquished all his enemies, murdered most of them, and brought some of the richest into captivity with him for the purpose of torturing them and finding out where they had hidden their money.

Rosalba heard their shrieks and groans in the dungeon in which she was thrust: a most awful black hole, full of bats, rats, mice, toads, frogs, mosquitoes, bugs, fleas, serpents, and every kind of horror. No light was let into it, otherwise the jailers might have seen her and fallen in love with her, as an owl that lived up in the roof of the tower did, and a cat, you know, who can see in the dark, and having set its green eyes on Rosalba, never would be got to go back to the turnkey's wife to whom it belonged. And the toads in the dungeon came and kissed her feet, and the vipers wound round her neck and arms, and never hurt her, so charming was this poor Princess in the midst of her misfortunes.

At last, after she had been kept in this place *ever so long,* the door of the dungeon opened, and the terrible KING PADELLA came in.

But what he said and did must be reserved for another chapter, as we must now back to Prince Giglio.

XIV

WHAT BECAME OF GIGLIO

The idea of marrying such an old creature as Gruffanuff, frightened Prince Giglio so, that he ran up to his room, packed his trunks, fetched in a couple of porters, and was off to the diligence office in a twinkling.

It was well that he was so quick in his operations, did not dawdle over his luggage, and took the early coach: for as soon as the mistake about Prince Bulbo was found out, that cruel Glumboso sent up a couple of policemen to Prince Giglio's room, with orders that he should be carried to Newgate, and his head taken off before twelve o'clock. But the coach was out of the Paflagonian dominions before two o'clock; and I dare say the express that was sent after Prince Giglio did not ride very quick, for many people in Paflagonia had a regard for Giglio, as the son of their old sovereign: a prince who, with all his weaknesses, was very much better than his brother, the usurping, lazy, careless, passionate, tyrannical reigning monarch. That Prince busied himself with the balls, fêtes, masquerades, hunting-parties and so forth, which he thought proper to give on occasion of his daughter's marriage to Prince Bulbo; and let us trust was not sorry in his own heart that his brother's son had escaped the scaffold.

It was very cold weather, and the snow was on the ground, and Giglio, who gave his name as simple Mr. Giles, was very glad to get a comfortable place in the coupé of the diligence, where he sat with the conductor and another gentleman. At the first stage from Blombodinga, as they stopped to change horses, there came up to the diligence a very ordinary, vulgar-looking woman, with a bag under her arm, who asked for a place. All the inside places were taken, and the young woman was informed that if she wished to travel, she must go upon the roof; and the passenger inside with Giglio (a rude person, I should think), put his head out of the window and said, "Nice weather for travelling outside! I wish you a pleasant journey, my dear." The poor woman coughed very much, and Giglio pitied her. "I will give up my place to her," says he, "rather than she should travel in the cold air with that horrid cough." On which the vulgar traveller said, "You'd keep her warm, I am sure, if it's a *muff* she wants." On which Giglio pulled his nose, boxed his ears, hit him in the eye, and gave this vulgar person a warning never to call him *muff* again.

Then he sprang up gayly on to the roof of the diligence, and made himself very comfortable in the straw. The vulgar traveller got down only at the next station, and Giglio took his place again, and talked to the person next to him. She appeared to be a most agreeable, well-informed, and entertaining female. They travelled together till night, and she gave Giglio all sorts of things out of the bag which she carried, and which indeed seemed to contain the most wonderful collection of articles. He was thirsty—out there came a pint-bottle of Bass's pale ale, and a silver mug! Hungry—she took out a cold fowl, some slices of ham, bread, salt, and a most delicious piece of cold plum-pudding, and a little glass of brandy afterwards.

As they travelled, this plain-looking, queer woman talked to Giglio on a variety of subjects, in which the poor Prince showed his ignorance as much as she did her capacity. He owned, with many blushes, how ignorant he was, on which the lady said, "My dear Gigl—my good Mr. Giles, you are a young man, and have plenty of time before you. You have nothing to do but to improve yourself. Who knows but that you may find use for your knowledge some day?—when—when you may be wanted at home, as some people may be."

"Good heavens, Madam!" says he, "do you know me?"

"I know a number of funny things," says the lady. "I have been at some people's christenings, and turned away from other folks' doors. I have seen some people spoiled by good fortune, and others, as I hope, improved by hardship. I advise you to stay at the town where the coach stops for the night. Stay there and study, and remember your old friend to whom you were kind."

"And who is my old friend?" asked Giglio.

"When you want anything," says the lady, "look in this bag, which I leave to you as a present, and be grateful to—"

"To whom, Madam?" says he.

"To the Fairy Blackstick," says the lady, flying out of the window. And when Giglio asked the conductor if he knew where the lady was?—

"What lady?" says the man. "There has been no lady in this coach, except the old woman who got out at the last stage." And Giglio thought he had been dreaming. But there was the bag which Blackstick had given him lying on his lap; and when he came to the town he took it in his hand and went into the inn.

They gave him a very bad bedroom, and Giglio, when he woke in the morning, fancying himself in the Royal Palace at home, called, "John, Charles, Thomas! My chocolate,—my dressing-gown—my slippers"; but nobody came. There was no bell, so he went and bawled out for waiter on the top of the stairs.

The landlady came up, looking very cross.

"What are you a-hollaring and a-bellaring for here, young man?" says she.

"There's no warm water—no servants; my boots are not even cleaned."

"He! he! Clean 'em yourself," says the landlady. "You young students give yourselves pretty airs. I never heard such impudence."

"I'll quit the house this instant," says Giglio.

"The sooner the better, young man. Pay your bill and be off. All my rooms is wanted for gentlefolks, and not for such as you."

"You may well keep the 'Bear Inn,'" says Giglio. "You should have yourself painted as the sign."

The landlady of the "Bear" went away growling. And Giglio returned to his room, where the first thing he saw was the fairy bag lying on the table, which seemed to give a little hop as he came in. "I hope it has some breakfast in it," says

Giglio, "for I have only a very little money left." But on opening the bag, what do you think was there? A blacking-brush and a pot of Warren's jet, and on the pot was written,—

> "Poor young men their boots must black:
> Use me and cork me and put me back."

So Giglio laughed and blacked his boots, and put back the brush and the bottle into the bag.

When he had done dressing himself, the bag gave another little hop, and he went to it and took out—

1. A tablecloth and a napkin.
2. A sugar-basin full of the best loaf-sugar.
4, 6, 8, 10. Two forks, two teaspoons, two knives, and a pair of sugar-tongs, and a butter-knife, all marked G.
11, 12, 13. A teacup, saucer, and slop-basin.
14. A jug full of delicious cream.
15. A canister with black tea and green.
16. A large tea-urn and boiling water.
17. A saucepan, containing three eggs nicely done.
18. A quarter of a pound of best Epping butter.
19. A brown loaf.

And if he hadn't enough now for a good breakfast, I should like to know who ever had one?

Giglio, having had his breakfast, popped all the things back into the bag, and went out looking for lodgings. I forgot to say that this celebrated university town was called Bosforo.

He took a modest lodging opposite the Schools, paid his bill at the inn, and went to his apartment with his trunk, carpet-bag, and not forgetting, we may be sure, his *other* bag.

When he opened his trunk, which the day before he had filled with his best clothes, he found it contained only books. And in the first of them which he opened there was written,—

> "Clothes for the back, books for the head:
> Read, and remember them when they are read."

And in his bag, when Giglio looked in it, he found a student's cap and gown, a writing-book full of paper, an inkstand, pens, and a Johnson's dictionary, which was very useful to him, as his spelling had been sadly neglected.

So he sat down and worked away, very, very hard, for a whole year, during which "Mr. Giles" was quite an example to all the students in the University of Bosforo. He never got into any riots or disturbances. The professors all spoke well of him, and the students liked him too; so that when at examination he took all the prizes, viz.:—

{ The Spelling Prize   { The French Prize
  The Writing Prize   The Arithmetic Prize
  The History Prize   The Latin Prize
  The Catechism Prize   The Good Conduct Prize,

all his fellow-students said, "Hurray! Hurray for Giles! Giles is the boy—the student's joy! Hurray for Giles!" And he brought quite a quantity of medals, crowns, books, and tokens of distinction home to his lodgings.

One day after the Examinations, as he was diverting himself at a coffee-house with two friends—(Did I tell you that in his bag, every Saturday night, he found just enough to pay his bills, with a guinea over for pocket-money! Didn't I tell you? Well, he did, as sure as twice twenty makes forty-five)—he chanced to look in the "Bosforo Chronicle," and read off quite easily (for he could spell, read, and write the longest words now) the following,—

"ROMANTIC CIRCUMSTANCE.—One of the most extraordinary adventures that we have ever heard has set the neighbouring country of Crim Tartary in a state of great excitement.

"It will be remembered that when the present revered sovereign of Crim Tartary, his Majesty King *Padella*, took possession of the throne, after having vanquished, in the terrific battle of Blunderbusco, the late King *Cavolfiore*, that Prince's only child, the Princess Rosalba, was not found in the royal palace, of which King Padella took possession, and, it was said, had strayed into the forest (being abandoned by all her attendants), where she had been eaten up by those ferocious lions, the last pair of which were captured some time since, and brought to the Tower, after killing several hundred persons.

"His Majesty King Padella, who has the kindest heart

in the world, was grieved at the accident which had occurred to the harmless little Princess, for whom his Majesty's known benevolence would certainly have provided a fitting establishment. But her death seemed to be certain. The mangled remains of a cloak, and a little shoe, were found in the forest, during a hunting-party, in which the intrepid sovereign of Crim Tartary slew two of the lions' cubs with his own spear. And these interesting relics of an innocent little creature were carried home and kept by their finder, the Baron Spinachi, formerly an officer in Cavolfiore's household. The Baron was disgraced in consequence of his known legitimist opinions, and has lived for some time, in the humble capacity of a wood-cutter, in a forest on the outskirts of the kingdom of Crim Tartary.

"Last Tuesday week Baron Spinachi and a number of gentlemen attached to the former dynasty appeared in arms, crying, 'God save Rosalba, the First Queen of Crim Tartary!' and surrounding a lady whom report describes as 'beautiful exceedingly.' Her history may be authentic, is certainly most romantic.

"The personage calling herself Rosalba states that she was brought out of the forest, fifteen years since, by a lady in a car drawn by dragons (this account is certainly improbable), that she was left in the Palace Garden of Blombodinga, where her Royal Highness the Princess Angelica, now married to his Royal Highness Bulbo, Crown Prince of Crim Tartary, found the child, and, with that elegant benevolence which has always distinguished the heiress of the throne of Paflagonia, gave the little outcast a shelter and a home! Her parentage not being known, and her garb very humble, the foundling was educated in the Palace in a menial capacity, under the name of Betsinda.

"She did not give satisfaction, and was dismissed, carrying with her, certainly, part of a mantle and a shoe which she had on when first found. According to her statement she quitted Blombodinga about a year ago, since which time she has been with the Spinachi family. On the very same morning the Prince Giglio, nephew to the King of Paflagonia, a young Prince whose character for *talent* and *order* were, to say truth, *none of the highest*, also quitted Blombodinga, and has not been since heard of!"

"What an extraordinary story!" said Smith and Jones, two young students, Giglio's especial friends.

"Ha! what is this?" Giglio went on, reading:—

"SECOND EDITION, EXPRESS.—We hear that the troop under Baron Spinachi has been surrounded, and utterly routed, by General Count Hogginarmo, and the *soidisant* Princess is sent a prisoner to the capital.

"UNIVERSITY NEWS.—Yesterday, at the Schools, the distinguished young student, Mr. Giles, read a Latin oration, and was complimented by the Chancellor of Bosforo, Dr. Prugnaro, with the highest University honor—the wooden spoon."

"Never mind that stuff," says *Giles*, greatly disturbed. "Come home with me, my friends. Gallant Smith! intrepid Jones! friends of my studies—partakers of my academic toils—I have that to tell shall astonish your honest minds."

"Go it, old boy!" cried the impetuous Smith.

"Talk away, my buck!" says Jones, a lively fellow.

With an air of indescribable dignity, Giglio checked their natural, but no more seemly, familiarity. "Jones, Smith, my good friends," said the PRINCE, "disguise is henceforth useless; I am no more the humble student Giles, I am the descendant of a royal line."

"*Atavis edite regibus*. I know, old co—," cried Jones. He was going to say "old cock," but a flash from the ROYAL EYE again awed him.

"Friends," continued the Prince, "I am that Giglio: I am, in fact, Paflagonia. Rise, Smith, and kneel not in the public street. Jones, thou true heart! My faithless uncle, when I was a baby, filched from me that brave crown my father left me, bred me, all young and careless of my rights, like unto hapless Hamlet, Prince of Denmark; and had I any thoughts about my wrongs, soothed me with promises of near redress. I should espouse his daughter, young Angelica; we two indeed should reign in Paflagonia. His words were false—false as Angelica's heart!—false as Angelica's hair, color, front teeth!

She looked with her skew eyes upon young Bulbo, Crim Tartary's stupid heir, and she preferred him. 'T was then I turned my eyes upon Betsinda—Rosalba, as she now is. And I saw in her the blushing sum of all perfection; the pink of maiden modesty; the nymph that my fond heart had ever woo'd in dreams," etc., etc.

(I don't give this speech, which was very fine, but very long; and though Smith and Jones knew nothing about the circumstances, my dear reader does: so I go on.)

The Prince and his young friends hastened home to his apartment, highly excited by the intelligence, as no doubt by the *royal narrator's* admirable manner of recounting it; and they ran up to his room, where he had worked so hard at his books.

On his writing-table was his bag, grown so long that the Prince could not help remarking it. He went to it, opened it, and what do you think he found in it?

A splendid long gold-handled, red-velvet-scabbarded cut-and-thrust sword, and on the sheath was embroidered "ROSALBA FOREVER!"

He drew out the sword, which flashed and illuminated the whole room, and called out "Rosalba forever!" Smith and Jones following him, but quite respectfully this time, and taking the time from his Royal Highness.

And now his trunk opened with a sudden pong, and out there came three ostrich feathers in a gold crown, surrounding a beautiful shining steel helmet, a cuirass, a pair of spurs, finally a complete suit of armor.

The books on Giglio's shelves were all gone. Where there had been some great dictionaries, Giglio's friends found two pairs of jack-boots labelled "Lieutenant Smith," "—— Jones, Esq.," which fitted them to a nicety. Besides, there were helmets, back and breast plates, swords, etc., just like in Mr. G.P.R. James's novels; and that evening three cavaliers might have been seen issuing from the gates of Bosforo, in whom the porters, proctors, etc., never thought of recognizing the young Prince and his friends.

They got horses at a livery-stable-keeper's, and never drew bridle until they reached the last town on the frontier before you come to Crim Tartary. Here, as their animals were tired, and the cavaliers hungry, they stopped and refreshed at an hostel. I could make a chapter of this if I were like some writers, but I like to cram my measure tight down, you see, and give you a great deal for your money. And, in a word, they had some bread-and-cheese and ale up stairs on the balcony of the inn. As they were drinking, drums and trumpets sounded nearer and nearer, the market-place was filled with soldiers, and his Royal Highness looking forth, recognized the Paflagonian banners, and the Paflagonian national air which the bands were playing.

The troops all made for the tavern at once, and as they came up, Giglio exclaimed, on beholding their leader, "Whom do I see? Yes!—no! It is, it is! —Phoo!—No, it can't be! Yes! it is my friend, my gallant, faithful veteran, Captain Hedzoff! Ho, Hedzoff! Knowest thou not thy Prince, thy Giglio? Good Corporal, methinks we once were friends. Ha, Sergeant, an my memory serves me right, we have had many a bout at singlestick."

"I' faith, we have a many, good my lord," says the Sergeant.

"Tell me what means this mighty armament," continued his Royal Highness from the balcony, "and whither march my Paflagonians?"

Hedzoff's head fell. "My lord," he said, "we march as the allies of great Padella, Crim Tartary's monarch."

"Crim Tartary's usurper, gallant Hedzoff! Crim Tartary's grim tyrant, honest Hedzoff!" said the Prince, on the balcony, quite sarcastically.

"A soldier, Prince, must needs obey his orders: mine are to help his Majesty Padella. And also (though alack that I should say it!) to seize wherever I should light upon him—"

"First catch your hare! ha, Hedzoff!" exclaimed his Royal Highness.

"—on the body of *Giglio*, whilom Prince of Paflagonia," Hedzoff went on, with indescribable emotion. "My Prince, give up your sword without ado. Look! we are thirty thousand men to one!"

"Give up my sword! Giglio give up his sword!" cried the Prince; and stepping well forward on to the balcony, the royal youth, *without preparation*, delivered a speech so magnificent, that no report can do justice to it. It was all in blank verse (in which, from this time, he invariably spoke, as more becoming his majestic station). It lasted for three days and three nights, during which not a single person who heard him was tired, or remarked the difference between daylight and dark. The

soldiers only cheering tremendously when occasionally—once
in nine hours—the Prince paused to suck an orange, which
Jones took out of the bag. He explained, in terms which we
say we shall not attempt to convey, the whole history of the
previous transaction, and his determination not only not to
give up his sword, but to assume his rightful crown; and at
the end of this extraordinary, this truly *gigantic* effort, Captain Hedzoff flung up his helmet and cried, "Hurray! Hurray!
Long live King Giglio!"

Such were the consequences of having employed his time
well at college!

When the excitement had ceased, beer was ordered out for
the army, and their Sovereign himself did not disdain a little!
And now it was with some alarm that Captain Hedzoff told
him his division was only the advanced guard of the Paflagonian
contingent hastening to King Padella's aid—the main force
being a day's march in the rear under his Royal Highness
Prince Bulbo.

"We will wait here, good friend, to beat the Prince," his
Majesty said, "and *then* will make his royal Father wince."

XV

WE RETURN TO ROSALBA

King Padella made very similar proposals to Rosalba to those
which she had received from the various Princes who, as we
have seen, had fallen in love with her. His Majesty was a
widower, and offered to marry his fair captive that instant,
but she declined his invitation in her usual polite gentle
manner, stating that Prince Giglio was her love, and that any
other union was out of the question. Having tried tears and
supplications in vain, this violent-tempered monarch men-
aced her with threats and tortures; but she declared she
would rather suffer all these than accept the hand of her
father's murderer, who left her finally, uttering the most

awful imprecations, and bidding her prepare for death on the following morning.

All night long the King spent in advising how he should get rid of this obdurate young creature. Cutting off her head was much too easy a death for her; hanging was so common in his Majesty's dominions that it no longer afforded him any sport: finally, he bethought himself of a pair of fierce lions which had lately been sent to him as presents, and he determined, with these ferocious brutes, to hunt poor Rosalba down. Adjoining his castle was an amphitheatre where the Prince indulged in bull-baiting, rat-hunting, and other ferocious sports. The two lions were kept in a cage under this place; their roaring might be heard over the whole city, the inhabitants of which, I am sorry to say, thronged in numbers to see a poor young lady gobbled up by two wild beasts.

The King took his place in the royal box, having the officers of the Court around and the Count Hogginarmo by his side, upon whom his Majesty was observed to look very fiercely: the fact is, royal spies had told the monarch of Hogginarmo's behavior, his proposals to Rosalba, and his offer to fight for the crown. Black as thunder looked King Padella at this proud noble, as they sat in the front seats of the theatre waiting to see the tragedy whereof poor Rosalba was to be the heroine.

At length that Princess was brought out in her night-gown, with all her beautiful hair falling down her back, and looking so pretty that even the beef-eaters and keepers of the wild animals wept plentifully at seeing her. And she walked with her poor little feet (only luckily the arena was covered with sawdust), and went and leaned up against a great stone in the centre of the amphitheatre, round which the Court and the people were seated in boxes, with bars before them, for fear of the great, fierce, red-maned, black-throated, long-tailed, roaring, bellowing, rushing lions.

And now the gates were opened, and with a "Wurrawar-rurawarar!" two great lean, hungry, roaring lions rushed out of their den, where they had been kept for three weeks on nothing but a little toast-and-water, and dashed straight up to the stone where poor Rosalba was waiting. Commend her to your patron saints, all you kind people, for she is in a dreadful state.

There was a hum and a buzz all through the circus, and the

fierce king Padella even felt a little compassion. But Count Hogginarmo, seated by his Majesty, roared out, "Hurray! Now for it! Soo-soo-soo!" that nobleman being uncommonly angry still at Rosalba's refusal of him.

But, O strange event! O remarkable circumstance! O extraordinary coincidence, which I am sure none of you could *by any possibility* have divined! When the lions came to Rosalba, instead of devouring her with their great teeth, it was with kisses they gobbled her up! They licked her pretty feet, they nuzzled their noses in her lap, they moo'd, they seemed to say, "Dear, dear sister, don't you recollect your brothers in the forest?" And she put her pretty white arms round their tawny necks, and kissed them.

King Padella was immensely astonished. The Count Hogginarmo was extremely disgusted. "Pooh!" the Count cried. "Gammon!" exclaimed his lordship. "These lions are tame beasts come from Wombwell's or Astley's. It is a shame to put people off in this way. I believe they are little boys dressed up in door-mats. They are no lions at all."

"Ha!" said the King, "you dare to say 'Gammon!' to your Sovereign, do you? These lions are no lions at all, aren't they? Ho, my beef-eaters! Ho, my body-guard! Take this Count Hogginarmo and fling him into the circus! Give him a sword and buckler, let him keep his armor on and his weather-eye out, and fight these lions."

The haughty Hogginarmo laid down his opera-glass and looked scowling round at the King and his attendants. "Touch me not, dogs!" he said, "or by St. Nicholas the Elder, I will gore you! Your Majesty thinks Hogginarmo is afraid? No, not of a hundred thousand lions! Follow me down into the circus, King Padella, and match thyself against one of yon brutes. Thou darest not? Let them both come on then!"

And opening a grating of the box, he jumped lightly down into the circus.

Wurra wurra wurra wur-aw-aw-aw!!!
In about two minutes
The Count Hogginarmo was
GOBBLED UP
by
those lions,

bones, boots, and all,
and
There was an
End of him.

At this the King said, "Serve him right, the rebellious ruffian! And now, as those lions won't eat that young woman—"

"Let her off! let her off!" cried the crowd.

"NO!" roared the King. "Let the beef-eaters go down and chop her into small pieces. If the lions defend her, let the archers shoot them to death. That hussy shall die in tortures!"

"A-a-ah!" cried the crowd. "Shame! shame!"

"Who dares cry out 'Shame'?" cried the furious potentate (so little can tyrants command their passions). "Fling any scoundrel who says a word down among the lions!" I warrant you there was a dead silence then, which was broken by a "Pang arang pang pangkarangpang!" and a Knight and a Herald rode in at the farther end of the circus; the Knight in full armor, with his visor up, and bearing a letter on the point of his lance.

"Ha!" exclaimed the King, "by my fay, 't is Elephant and Castle, pursuivant of my brother of Paflagonia; and the Knight, an' my memory serves me, is the gallant Captain Hedzoff? What news from Paflagonia, gallant Hedzoff? Elephant and Castle, beshrew me, thy trumpeting must have made thee thirsty. What will my trusty Herald like to drink?"

"Bespeaking first safe-conduct from your lordship," said Captain Hedzoff, "before we take a drink of anything, permit us to deliver our King's message."

"My lordship, ha!" said Crim Tartary, frowning terrifically. "That title soundeth strange in the anointed ears of a crowned King. Straightway speak out your message, Knight and Herald!"

Reining up his charger in a most elegant manner close under the King's balcony, Hedzoff turned to the Herald, and bade him begin.

Elephant and Castle, dropping his trumpet over his shoulder, took a large sheet of paper out of his hat, and began to read:—

"O Yes! O Yes! O Yes! Know all men by these presents, that we, Giglio, King of Paflagonia, Grand Duke of Cappadocia, Sovereign Prince of Turkey and

the Sausage Islands, having assumed our rightful throne
and title, long time falsely borne by our usurping uncle,
styling himself King of Paflagonia—"

"Ha!" growled Padella.

"Hereby summon the false traitor Padella, calling
himself King of Crim Tartary—"

The King's curses were dreadful. "Go on, Elephant and
Castle!" said the intrepid Hedzoff.

"—To release from cowardly imprisonment his liege
lady and rightful sovereign, ROSALBA, Queen of Crim
Tartary, and restore her to her royal throne: in default
of which, I, Giglio, proclaim the said Padella sneak,
traitor, humbug, usurper, and coward. I challenge him
to meet me, with fists or with pistols, with battle-axe
or sword, with blunderbuss or single-stick, alone or
at the head of his army, on foot or on horseback; and
will prove my words upon his wicked ugly body!"

"God save the King!" said Captain Hedzoff, executing a
demivolt, two semilunes, and three caracols.

"Is that all?" said Padella, with the terrific calm of concen-
trated fury.

"That, sir, is all my royal master's message. Here is his
Majesty's letter in autograph, and here is his glove; and if any
gentleman of Crim Tartary chooses to find fault with his
Majesty's expressions, I, Kutasoff Hedzoff, Captain of the
Guard, am very much at his service." And he waved his
lance, and looked at the assembly all round.

"And what says my good brother of Paflagonia, my dear
son's father-in-law, to this rubbish?" asked the King.

"The King's uncle hath been deprived of the crown he
unjustly wore," said Hedzoff gravely. "He and his ex-Minister,
Glumboso, are now in prison waiting the sentence of my
royal master. After the battle of Bombardaro—"

"Of what?" asked the surprised Padella.

"Of Bombardaro, where my liege, his present Majesty, would
have performed prodigies of valor, but that the whole of his

uncle's army came over to our side, with the exception of
Prince Bulbo—"

"Ah! my boy, my boy, my Bulbo was no traitor!" cried
Padella.

"Prince Bulbo, far from coming over to us, ran away, sir;
but I caught him. The Prince is a prisoner in our army, and
the most terrific tortures await him if a hair of the Princess
Rosalba's head is injured."

"Do they?" exclaimed the furious Padella, who was now
perfectly *livid* with rage. "Do they indeed? So much the
worse for Bulbo. I've twenty sons as lovely each as Bulbo.
Not one but is as fit to reign as Bulbo. Whip, whack, flog,
starve, rack, punish, torture Bulbo—break all his bones—
roast him or flay him alive—pull all his pretty teeth out one
by one! But justly dear as Bulbo is to me,—Joy of my eyes,
fond treasure of my soul!—Ha, ha, ha, ha! revenge is dearer
still. Ho! torturers, rackmen, executioners—light up the fires
and make the pincers hot! get lots of boiling lead!—Bring out
Rosalba!"

XVI

HOW HEDZOFF RODE BACK AGAIN TO KING GIGLIO

Captain Hedzoff rode away when King Padella uttered this
cruel command, having done his duty in delivering the message with which his royal master had intrusted him. Of course
he was very sorry for Rosalba, but what could he do?

So he returned to King Giglio's camp, and found the young
monarch in a disturbed state of mind, smoking cigars in the
royal tent. His Majesty's agitation was not appeased by the
news that was brought by his ambassador. "The brutal, ruthless ruffian royal wretch!" Giglio exclaimed. "As England's
poesy has well remarked, 'The man that lays his hand upon a
woman, save in the way of kindness, is a villain.' Ha, Hedzoff?"

"That he is, your Majesty," said the attendant.

"And didst thou see her flung into the oil? and didn't the

soothing oil—the emollient oil, refuse to boil, good Hedzoff—
and to spoil the fairest lady ever eyes did look on?"

" 'Faith, good my liege, I had no heart to look and see a
beauteous lady boiling down; I took your royal message to
Padella, and bore his back to you. I told him you would hold
Prince Bulbo answerable. He only said that he had twenty
sons as good as Bulbo, and forthwith he bade the ruthless
executioners proceed."

"O cruel father—O unhappy son," cried the King. "Go,
some of you, and bring Prince Bulbo hither."

Bulbo was brought in chains, looking very uncomfortable.
Though a prisoner, he had been tolerably happy, perhaps
because his mind was at rest, and all the fighting was over,
and he was playing at marbles with his guards, when the
King sent for him.

"Oh, my poor Bulbo," said his Majesty, with looks of
infinite compassion, "hast thou heard the news?" (for you see
Giglio wanted to break the thing gently to the Prince). "Thy
brutal father has condemned Rosalba—p-p-p-ut her to death,
P-p-p-prince Bulbo!"

"What, killed Betsinda! Boo-hoo-hoo!" cried out Bulbo.
"Betsinda! pretty Betsinda! dear Betsinda! She was the dearest
little girl in the world. I love her better twenty thousand
times even than Angelica." And he went on expressing his
grief in so hearty and unaffected a manner, that the King was
quite touched by it, and said, shaking Bulbo's hand, that he
wished he had known Bulbo sooner.

Bulbo, quite unconsciously, and meaning for the best, offered to come and sit with his Majesty, and smoke a cigar
with him, and console him. The *royal kindness* supplied
Bulbo with a cigar; he had not had one, he said, since he was
taken prisoner.

And now think what must have been the feelings of the
most *merciful of monarchs*, when he informed his prisoner
that, in consequence of King Padella's *cruel and dastardly
behavior* to Rosalba, Prince Bulbo must instantly be executed!
The noble Giglio could not restrain his tears, nor could the
Grenadiers, nor the officers, nor could Bulbo himself, when
the matter was explained to him; and he was brought to
understand that his Majesty's promise, of course, was *above
every*thing, and Bulbo must submit. So poor Bulbo was led
out,—Hedzoff trying to console him by pointing out that if he

had won the battle of Bombardaro, he might have hanged
Prince Giglio. "Yes! But that is no comfort to me now!" said
poor Bulbo; nor indeed was it, poor fellow.

He was told the business would be done the next morning
at eight, and was taken back to his dungeon, where every
attention was paid to him. The jailer's wife sent him tea, and
the turnkey's daughter begged him to write his name in
her album, where a many gentlemen had wrote it on like
occasions! "Bother your album!" says Bulbo. The undertaker
came and measured him for the handsomest coffin which money
could buy: even this didn't console Bulbo. The cook brought
him dishes which he once used to like; but he wouldn't touch
them: he sat down and began writing an adieu to Angelica, as
the clock kept always ticking and the hands drawing nearer to
the next morning. The barber came in at night, and offered to
shave him for the next day. Prince Bulbo kicked him away,
and went on writing a few words to Princess Angelica, as the
clock kept always ticking and the hands hopping nearer and
nearer to next morning. He got up on the top of a hat-box, on
the top of a chair, on the top of his bed, on the top of his
table, and looked out to see whether he might escape as the
clock kept always ticking and the hands drawing nearer, and
nearer, and nearer.

But looking out of the window was one thing, and jumping
another: and the town clock struck seven. So he got into bed
for a little sleep, but the jailer came and woke him, and
said, "Git up, your Royal Ighness, if you please, it's *ten
minutes to eight.*"

So poor Bulbo got up: he had gone to bed in his clothes
(the lazy boy), and he shook himself, and said he didn't mind
about dressing, or having any breakfast, thank you; and he
saw the soldiers who had come for him. "Lead on!" he said;
and they led the way, deeply affected; and they came into the
court-yard, and out into the square, and there was King
Giglio come to take leave of him, and his Majesty most kindly
shook hands with him, and the *gloomy procession* marched
on:—when hark!

"Haw—wurraw—wurraw—aworr!"

A roar of wild beasts was heard. And who should come
riding into the town, frightening away the boys, and even the
beadle and policeman, but ROSALBA!

The fact is, that when Captain Hedzoff entered into the

court of Snapdragon Castle, and was discoursing with King Padella, the lions made a dash at the open gate, gobbled up the six beef-eaters in a jiffy, and away they went with Rosalba on the back of one of them, and they carried her, turn and turn about, till they came to the city where Prince Giglio's army was encamped.

When the KING heard of the QUEEN'S arrival, you may think how he rushed out of his breakfast-room to hand her Majesty off her lion! The lions were grown as fat as pigs now, having had Hogginarmo and all those beef-eaters, and were so tame, anybody might pat them.

While Giglio knelt (most gracefully) and helped the Princess, Bulbo, for his part, rushed up and kissed the lion. He flung his arms round the forest monarch; he hugged him, and laughed and cried for joy. "Oh, you darling old beast—oh! how glad I am to see you, and the dear, dear Bets—that is, Rosalba."

"What, is it you, poor Bulbo?" said the Queen. "Oh, how glad I am to see you!" And she gave him her hand to kiss. King Giglio slapped him most kindly on the back, and said, "Bulbo my boy, I am delighted, for your sake, that her Majesty has arrived."

"So am I," said Bulbo; "and *you know why*." Captain Hedzoff here came up. "Sire, it is half-past eight: shall we proceed with the execution?"

"Execution? what for?" asked Bulbo.

"An officer only knows his orders," replied Captain Hedzoff, showing his warrant: on which his Majesty King Giglio smilingly said Prince Bulbo was reprieved this time, and most graciously invited him to breakfast.

XVII

HOW A TREMENDOUS BATTLE TOOK PLACE, AND WHO WON IT

As soon as King Padella heard—what we know already—that his victim, the lovely Rosalba, had escaped him, his Majesty's fury knew no bounds, and he pitched the Lord Chancellor, Lord Chamberlain, and every officer of the Crown whom he could set eyes on, into the caldron of boiling oil prepared for the Princess. Then he ordered out his whole army, horse, foot, and artillery; and set forth at the head of an innumerable host, and I should think twenty thousand drummers, trumpeters, and fifers.

King Giglio's advanced guard, you may be sure, kept that monarch acquainted with the enemy's dealings, and he was in nowise disconcerted. He was much too polite to alarm the Princess, his lovely guest, with any unnecessary rumors of battles impending; on the contrary, he did everything to amuse and divert her; gave her a most elegant breakfast, dinner, lunch, and got up a ball for her that evening, when he danced with her every single dance.

Poor Bulbo was taken into favor again, and allowed to go quite free now. He had new clothes given him, was called "My good cousin" by his Majesty, and was treated with the greatest distinction by everybody. But it was easy to see he was very melancholy. The fact is, the sight of Betsinda, who looked perfectly lovely in an elegant new dress, set poor Bulbo frantic in love with her again. And he never thought about Angelica, now Princess Bulbo, whom he had left at home, and who, as we know, did not care much about him.

The King, dancing the twenty-fifth polka with Rosalba, remarked with wonder the ring she wore; and then Rosalba told him how she had got it from Gruffanuff, who no doubt had picked it up when Angelica flung it away.

"Yes," says the Fairy Blackstick—who had come to see the

174

young people, and who had very likely certain plans regarding them—"that ring I gave the Queen, Giglio's mother, who was not, saving your presence, a very wise woman: it is enchanted, and whoever wears it looks beautiful in the eyes of the world. I made poor Prince Bulbo, when he was christened, the present of a rose which made him look handsome while he had it; but he gave it to Angelica, who instantly looked beautiful again, whilst Bulbo relapsed into his natural plainness."

"Rosalba needs no ring, I am sure," says Giglio, with a low bow. "She is beautiful enough, in my eyes, without any enchanted aid."

"Oh, sir!" said Rosalba.

"Take off the ring and try," said the King, and resolutely drew the ring off her finger. In *his* eyes she looked just as handsome as before!

The King was thinking of throwing the ring away, as it was so dangerous and made all the people so mad about Rosalba; but being a prince of great humor, and good-humor too, he cast eyes upon a poor youth who happened to be looking on very disconsolately, and said—

"Bulbo my poor lad! come and try on this ring. The Princess Rosalba makes it a present to you." The magic properties of this ring were uncommonly strong, for no sooner had Bulbo put it on, but lo and behold, he appeared a personable, agreeable young prince enough—with a fine complexion, fair hair, rather stout, and with bandy legs; but these were encased in such a beautiful pair of yellow morocco boots that nobody remarked them. And Bulbo's spirits rose up almost immediately after he had looked in the glass, and he talked to their Majesties in the most lively, agreeable manner, and danced opposite the Queen with one of the prettiest Maids of Honor, and after looking at her Majesty, could not help saying, "How very odd; she is very pretty, but not so *extraordinarily* handsome." "Oh, no, by no means!" says the Maid of Honor.

"But what care I, dear sir," says the Queen, who overheard them, "if *you* think I am good-looking enough?"

His Majesty's glance in reply to this affectionate speech was such that no painter could draw it. And the Fairy Blackstick said, "Bless you, my darling children! Now you are united and happy; and now you see what I said from the first, that a little misfortune has done you both good. *You*, Giglio, had you been bred in prosperity, would scarcely have learned to read or write; you would have been idle and extravagant, and could not have been a good King as you now will be. You, Rosalba, would have been so flattered, that your little head might have been turned like Angelica's, who thought herself too good for Giglio."

"As if anybody could be good enough for *him*," cried Rosalba.

"Oh, you, you darling!" says Giglio. And so she was; and he was just holding out his arms in order to give her a hug before the whole company, when a messenger came rushing in and said, "My lord, the enemy!"

"To arms!" cries Giglio.

"Oh, mercy!" says Rosalba, and fainted of course. He snatched one kiss from her lips, and rushed *forth to the field* of battle!

The Fairy had provided King Giglio with a suit of armor, which was not only embroidered all over with jewels, and blinding to your eyes to look at, but was water-proof, gun-proof, and sword-proof: so that, in the midst of the very hottest battles, his Majesty rode about as calmly as if he had been a British Grenadier at Alma. Were I engaged in fighting for my country, *I* should like such a suit of armor as Prince Giglio wore; but, you know, he was a prince of a fairy tale, and they always have these wonderful things.

Besides the fairy armor, the Prince had a fairy horse, which would gallop at any pace you please; and a fairy sword, which would lengthen, and run through a whole regiment of enemies at once. With such a weapon at command, I wonder, for my part, he thought of ordering his army out; but forth they all came, in magnificent new uniforms: Hedzoff and the Prince's two college friends each commanding a division, and his Majesty prancing in person at the head of them all.

Ah! if I had the pen of a Sir Archibald Alison, my dear friends, would I not now entertain you with the account of a most tremendous shindy? Should not fine blows be struck, dreadful wounds be delivered, arrows darken the air, cannon-balls crash through the battalions; cavalry charge infantry, infantry pitch into cavalry; bugles blow, drums beat, horses neigh, fifes sing, soldiers roar, swear, hurra; officers shout out, "Forward, my men!" "This way, lads!" "Give it 'em, boys!" "Fight for King Giglio and the cause of right!" "King Padella forever!" Would I not describe all this, I say, and in the very finest language too? But this humble pen does not possess the skill necessary for the description of combats. In a word, the overthrow of King Padella's army was so complete, that if they had been Russians you could not have wished them to be more utterly smashed and confounded.

As for that usurping monarch, having performed acts of valor much more considerable than could be expected of a royal ruffian and usurper, who had such a bad cause, and who was so cruel to women,—as for King Padella, I say, when his army ran away the King ran away too, kicking his first General, Prince Punchikoff, from his saddle, and galloping away on the Prince's horse, having, indeed, had twenty-five or twenty-six of his own shot under him. Hedzoff coming up, and finding Punchikoff down, as you may imagine, very speedily disposed of *him*. Meanwhile King Padella was scampering off as hard as his horse could lay legs to ground. Fast as he scampered, I promise you somebody else galloped faster; and that individual, as no doubt you are aware, was the royal Giglio, who kept bawling out, "Stay, traitor! Turn, miscreant, and defend thyself! Stand, tyrant, coward, ruffian, royal wretch, till I cut thy ugly head from thy usurping shoulders!" And, with his fairy sword, which elongated itself at will, his Majesty kept poking and prodding Padella in the back, until that wicked monarch roared with anguish.

When he was fairly brought to bay, Padella turned and dealt Prince Giglio a prodigious crack over the sconce with his battle-axe, a most enormous weapon, which had cut down I don't know how many regiments in the course of the afternoon. But law bless you! though the blow fell right down on his Majesty's helmet it made no more impression than if Padella had struck him with a pat of butter: his battle-axe crumpled up in Padella's hand, and the royal Giglio laughed for very scorn at the impotent efforts of that atrocious usurper.

At the ill success of his blow the Crim Tartar monarch was justly irritated. "If," says he to Giglio, "you ride a fairy horse, and wear fairy armor, what on earth is the use of my hitting you? I may as well give myself up a prisoner at once. Your Majesty won't, I suppose, be so mean as to strike a poor fellow who can't strike again?"

The justice of Padella's remark struck the magnanimous Giglio. "Do you yield yourself a prisoner, Padella?" says he.

"Of course I do," says Padella.

"Do you acknowledge Rosalba as your rightful Queen, and give up the crown and all your treasures to your rightful mistress?"

"If I must I must," says Padella, who was naturally very sulky.

By this time King Giglio's aides-de-camp had come up, whom his Majesty ordered to bind the prisoner. And they tied his hands behind him, and bound his legs tight under his horse, having set him with his face to the tail; and in this fashion he was led back to King Giglio's quarters, and thrust into the very dungeon where young Bulbo had been confined.

Padella (who was a very different person, in the depth of his distress, to Padella the proud wearer of the Crim Tartar crown), now most affectionately and earnestly asked to see his son—his dear eldest boy—his darling Bulbo; and that good-natured young man never once reproached his haughty parent for his unkind conduct the day before, when he would have left Bulbo to be shot without any pity, but came to see his father, and spoke to him through the grating of the door, beyond which he was not allowed to go; and brought him some sandwiches from the grand supper which his Majesty was giving above stairs, in honor of the brilliant victory which had just been achieved.

"I cannot stay with you long, sir," says Bulbo, who was in his best ball dress, as he handed his father in the prog. "I am engaged to dance the next quadrille with her Majesty Queen Rosalba, and I hear the fiddles playing at this very moment."

So Bulbo went back to the ball-room, and the wretched Padella ate his solitary supper in silence and tears.

All was now joy in King Giglio's circle. Dancing, feasting, fun, illuminations, and jollifications of all sorts ensued. The people through whose villages they passed were ordered to illuminate their cottages at night, and scatter flowers on the roads during the day. They were requested—and I promise you they did not like to refuse—to serve the troops liberally with eatables and wine; besides, the army was enriched by the immense quantity of plunder which was found in King Padella's camp, and taken from his soldiers; who (after they had given up everything) were allowed to fraternize with the conquerors; and the united forces marched back by easy stages towards King Giglio's capital, his royal banner and that of Queen Rosalba being carried in front of the troops. Hedzoff was made a Duke and a Field Marshal. Smith and Jones were promoted to be Earls; the Crim Tartar Order of the Pumpkin and the Paflagonian decoration of the Cucumber were freely distributed by their Majesties to the army. Queen Rosalba wore the Paflagonian Ribbon of the Cucumber across her riding-habit, whilst King Giglio never appeared without the grand Cordon of the Pumpkin. How the people cheered them as they rode along side by side! They were pronounced to be the handsomest couple ever seen: that was a matter of course; but they really *were* very handsome, and, had they been otherwise, would have looked so, they were so happy! Their Majesties were never separated during the whole day, but breakfasted, dined, and supped together always, and rode side by side, interchanging elegant compliments, and indulging in the most delightful conversation. At night, her Majesty's ladies of honor (who had all rallied round her the day after King Padella's defeat), came and conducted her to the apartments prepared for her; whilst King Giglio, surrounded by his gentlemen, withdrew to his own royal quarters. It was agreed they should be married as soon as they reached the capital, and orders were despatched to the Archbishop of Blombodinga, to hold himself in readiness to perform the interesting ceremony. Duke Hedzoff carried the message, and gave instructions to have the royal Castle splendidly refurnished and painted afresh. The Duke seized Glumboso, the ex-Prime Minister, and made him refund that considerable sum of money which the old scoundrel had secreted out of the late King's treasure. He also clapped Valoroso into prison (who, by the way, had been dethroned for some considerable period past), and when the ex-monarch weakly remonstrated, Hedzoff said, "A soldier, sir, knows but his duty; my orders are to lock you up along with the ex-King Padella, whom I have brought hither a prisoner under guard." So these two ex-royal personages were sent for a year to the House of Correction, and thereafter were obliged to become monks of the severest Order of Flagellants—in which state, by fasting, by vigils, by flogging (which they administered to one another, humbly but resolutely), no doubt they exhibited a repentance for their past misdeeds, usurpations, and private and public crimes.

As for Glumboso, that rogue was sent to the galleys, and never had an opportunity to steal any more.

XVIII

HOW THEY ALL JOURNEYED BACK TO THE CAPITAL

The Fairy Blackstick, by whose means this young King and Queen had certainly won their respective crowns back, would come not unfrequently to pay them a little visit—as they were riding in their triumphal progress towards Giglio's capital—change her wand into a pony, and travel by their Majesties' side, giving them the very best advice. I am not sure that King Giglio did not think the Fairy and her advice rather a bore, fancying it was his own valor and merits which had put him on his throne, and conquered Padella: and, in fine, I fear he rather gave himself airs towards his best friend and patroness. She exhorted him to deal justly by his subjects, to draw mildly on the taxes, never to break his promise when he had once given it,—and in all respects to be a good King.

"A good King, my dear Fairy!" cries Rosalba. "Of course he will. Break his promise! can you fancy my Giglio would ever do anything so improper, so unlike him? No! never!" And she looked fondly towards Giglio, whom she thought a pattern of perfection.

"Why is Fairy Blackstick always advising me, and telling me how to manage my government, and warning me to keep my word? Does she suppose that I am not a man of sense, and a man of honor?" asks Giglio, testily. "Methinks she rather presumes upon her position."

"Hush! dear Giglio," says Rosalba. "You know Blackstick has been very kind to us, and we must not offend her." But the Fairy was not listening to Giglio's testy observations: she had fallen back, and was trotting on her pony now, by Master

Bulbo's side—who rode a donkey, and made himself generally beloved in the army by his cheerfulness, kindness, and good-humor to everybody. He was eager to see his darling Angelica. He thought there never was such a charming being. Blackstick did not tell him it was the possession of the magic rose that made Angelica so lovely in his eyes. She brought him the very best accounts of his little wife, whose misfortunes and humiliations had indeed very greatly improved her; and you see, she could whisk off on her wand a hundred miles in a minute, and be back in no time, and so carry polite messages from Bulbo to Angelica, and from Angelica to Bulbo, and comfort that young man upon his journey.

When the Royal party arrived at the last stage before you reach Blombodinga, who should be in waiting, in her carriage there, with her lady of honor by her side, but the Princess Angelica? She rushed into her husband's arms, scarcely stopping to make a passing curtsy to the King and Queen. She had no eyes but for Bulbo, who appeared perfectly lovely to her on account of the fairy ring which he wore; whilst she herself, wearing the magic rose in her bonnet, seemed entirely beautiful to the enraptured Bulbo.

A splendid luncheon was served to the Royal party, of which the Archbishop, the Chancellor, the Duke Hedzoff, Countess Gruffanuff, and all our friends partook—the Fairy Blackstick being seated on the left of King Giglio, with Bulbo and Angelica beside. You could hear the joy-bells ringing in the capital, and the guns which the citizens were firing off in honor of their Majesties.

"What can have induced that hideous old Gruffanuff to dress herself up in such an absurd way? Did you ask her to be your bridesmaid, my dear?" says Giglio to Rosalba. "What a figure of fun Gruffy is!"

Gruffy was seated opposite their Majesties, between the Archbishop and the Lord Chancellor, and a figure of fun she certainly was, for she was dressed in a low white silk dress, with lace over, a wreath of white roses on her wig, a splendid lace veil, and her yellow old neck was covered with diamonds. She ogled the King in such a manner, that his Majesty burst out laughing.

"Eleven o'clock!" cries Giglio, as the great Cathedral bell of Blombodinga tolled that hour. "Gentlemen and ladies, we must be starting. Archbishop, you must be at church I think before twelve?"

"We must be at church before twelve," sighs out Gruffanuff in a languishing voice, hiding her old face behind her fan.

"And then I shall be the happiest man in my dominions," cries Giglio, with an elegant bow to the blushing Rosalba.

"Oh, my Giglio! Oh, my dear Majesty!" exclaims Gruffanuff; "and can it be that this happy moment at length has arrived—"

"Of course it has arrived," says the King.

"—And that I am about to become the enraptured bride of my adored Giglio!" continues Gruffanuff. "Lend me a smelling-bottle, somebody. I certainly shall faint with joy."

"*You* my bride?" roars out Giglio.

"*You* marry my Prince?" cries poor little Rosalba.

"Pooh! Nonsense! The woman's mad!" exclaims the King. And all the courtiers exhibited by their countenances and expressions, marks of surprise or ridicule, or incredulity or wonder.

"I should like to know who else is going to be married, if I am not?" shrieks out Gruffanuff. "I should like to know if King Giglio is a gentleman, and if there is such a thing as justice in Paflagonia? Lord Chancellor! my Lord Archbishop! will your lordships sit by and see a poor fond, confiding, tender creature put upon? Has not Prince Giglio promised to marry his Barbara? Is not this Giglio's signature? Does not this paper declare that he is mine, and only mine?" And she handed to his Grace the Archbishop the document which the Prince signed that evening when she wore the magic ring, and Giglio drank so much champagne. And the old Archbishop, taking out his eyeglasses, read,—

"This is to give notice that I, Giglio, only son of Savio, King of Paflagonia, hereby promise to marry the charming Barbara Griselda Countess Gruffanuff, and widow of the late Jenkins Gruffanuff, Esq."

"H'm," says the Archbishop, "the document is certainly a—a document."

"Phoo!" says the Lord Chancellor: "the signature is not in his Majesty's handwriting." Indeed, since his studies at Bosforo, Giglio had made an immense improvement in caligraphy.

"Is it your handwriting, Giglio?" cries the Fairy Blackstick, with an awful severity of countenance.

"Y—y—y—es," poor Giglio gasps out. "I had quite forgotten the confounded paper: she can't mean to hold me by it. You old wretch, what will you take to let me off? Help the Queen, some one—her Majesty has fainted."

"Chop her head off!"
"Smother the old witch!"
"Pitch her into the river!" } exclaim the impetuous Hedzoff, the ardent Smith, and the faithful Jones.

But Gruffanuff flung her arms round the Archbishop's neck and bellowed out, "Justice, justice, my Lord Chancellor!" so loudly, that her piercing shrieks caused everybody to pause. As for Rosalba, she was borne away lifeless by her ladies; and you may imagine the look of agony which Giglio cast towards that lovely being, as his hope, his joy, his darling, his all in all, was thus removed, and in her place the horrid old Gruffanuff rushed up to his side, and once more shrieked out, "Justice, justice!"

"Won't you take that sum of money which Glumboso hid?" says Giglio: "two hundred and eighteen thousand millions, or thereabouts. It's a handsome sum."

"I will have that and you too!" says Gruffanuff.

"Let us throw the crown jewels into the bargain," gasps out Giglio.

"I will wear them by my Giglio's side!" says Gruffanuff.

"Will half, three-quarters, five-sixths, nineteen-twentieths, of my kingdom do, Countess?" asks the trembling monarch.

"What were all Europe to me without *you*, my Giglio?" cries Gruff, kissing his hand.

"I won't, I can't, I sha'n't,—I'll resign the crown first," shouts Giglio, tearing away his hand; but Gruff clung to it.

"I have a competency, my love," she says, "and with thee and a cottage thy Barbara will be happy."

Giglio was half mad with rage by this time. "I will not marry her," says he. "Oh, Fairy, Fairy, give me counsel!" And as he spoke, he looked wildly round at the severe face of the Fairy Blackstick.

" 'Why is Fairy Blackstick always advising me, and warning me to keep my word? Does she suppose that I am not a man of honor?' " said the Fairy, quoting Giglio's own haughty words. He quailed under the brightness of her eyes: he felt that there was no escape for him from that awful Inquisition.

"Well, Archbishop," said he, in a dreadful voice that made his Grace start, "since this Fairy has led me to the height of happiness but to dash me down into the depths of despair, since I am to lose Rosalba, let me at least keep my honor. Get up, Countess, and let us be married; I can keep my word, but I can die afterwards."

"O dear Giglio," cries Gruffanuff, skipping up, "I knew, I knew I could trust thee—I knew that my Prince was the soul of honor. Jump into your carriages, ladies and gentlemen, and let us go to church at once; and as for dying, dear Giglio, no, no:—thou wilt forget that insignificant little chambermaid of a queen—thou wilt live to be consoled by thy Barbara! She wishes to be a Queen, and not a Queen Dowager, my gracious lord!" And hanging upon poor Giglio's arm, and leering and grinning in his face in the most disgusting manner, this old wretch tripped off in her white satin shoes, and jumped into the very carriage which had been got ready to convey Giglio and Rosalba to church. The cannons roared again, the bells pealed triple-bobmajors, the people came out flinging flowers upon the path of the royal bride and bridegroom, and Gruff looked out of the gilt coach window and bowed and grinned to them. Phoo! the horrid old wretch!

XIX

AND NOW WE COME TO THE LAST SCENE IN THE PANTOMIME

The many ups and down of her life had given the Princess Rosalba prodigious strength of mind, and that highly principled young woman presently recovered from her fainting-fit, out of which Fairy Blackstick, by a precious essence which the Fairy always carried in her pocket, awakened her. Instead of tearing her hair, crying, and bemoaning herself, and fainting again, as many young women would have done,

Rosalba remembered that she owed an example of firmness to her subjects; and though she loved Giglio more than her life, was determined, as she told the Fairy, not to interfere between him and justice, or to cause him to break his royal word.

"I cannot marry him, but I shall love him always," says she to Blackstick; "I will go and be present at his marriage with the Countess, and sign the book, and wish them happy with all my heart. I will see, when I get home, whether I cannot make the new Queen some handsome presents. The Crim Tartary crown diamonds are uncommonly fine, and I shall never have any use for them. I will live and die unmarried like Queen Elizabeth, and of course I shall leave my crown to Giglio when I quit this world. Let us go and see them married, my dear Fairy; let me say one last farewell to him; and then, if you please, I will return to my own dominions."

So the Fairy kissed Rosalba with peculiar tenderness and at once changed her wand into a very comfortable coach-and-four, with a steady coachman, and two respectable footmen behind, and the Fairy and Rosalba got into the coach, which Angelica and Bulbo entered after them. As for honest Bulbo, he was blubbering in the most pathetic manner, quite overcome by Rosalba's misfortune. She was touched by the honest fellow's sympathy, promised to restore to him the confiscated estates of Duke Padella his father, and created him, as he sat there in the coach, Prince, Highness, and First Grandee of the Crim Tartar Empire. The coach moved on, and, being a fairy coach, soon came up with the bridal procession.

Before the ceremony at church it was the custom in Paflagonia, as it is in other countries, for the bride and bridegroom to sign the Contract of Marriage, which was to be witnessed by the Chancellor, Minister, Lord Mayor, and principal officers of state. Now, as the royal palace was being painted and furnished anew, it was not ready for the reception of the King and his bride, who proposed at first to take up their residence at the Prince's palace, that one which Valoroso occupied when Angelica was born, and before he usurped the throne.

So the marriage-party drove up to the palace: the dignitaries got out of their carriages and stood aside: poor Rosalba stepped out of her coach, supported by Bulbo, and stood almost fainting up against the railings, so as to have a last look of her dear Giglio. As for Blackstick, she, according to her custom, had flown out of the coach window in some inscrutable manner, and was now standing at the palace-door.

Giglio came up the steps with his horrible bride on his arm, looking as pale as if he was going to execution. He only frowned at the Fairy Blackstick—he was angry with her, and thought she came to insult his misery.

"Get out of the way, pray," says Gruffanuff, haughtily. "I wonder why you are always poking your nose into other people's affairs?"

"Are you determined to make this poor young man unhappy?" says Blackstick.

"To marry him, yes! What business is it of yours? Pray, Madam, don't say 'you' to a queen," cries Gruffanuff.

"You won't take the money he offered you?"

"No."

"You won't let him off his bargain, though you know you cheated him when you made him sign the paper."

"Impudence! Policemen, remove this woman!" cries Gruffanuff. And the policemen were rushing forward, but with a wave of her wand the Fairy struck them all like so many statues in their places.

"You won't take anything in exchange for your bond, Mrs. Gruffanuff," cries the Fairy, with awful severity. "I speak for the last time."

"No!" shrieks Gruffanuff, stamping with her foot. "I'll have my husband, my husband, my husband!"

"YOU SHALL HAVE YOUR HUSBAND!" the Fairy Blackstick cried; and advancing a step, laid her hand upon the nose of the KNOCKER.

As she touched it, the brass nose seemed to elongate, the open mouth opened still wider, and uttered a roar which made everybody start. The eyes rolled wildly; the arms and legs uncurled themselves, writhed about, and seemed to lengthen with each twist; the knocker expanded into a figure in yellow livery, six feet high; the screws by which it was fixed to the door unloosed themselves, and JENKINS GRUFFANUFF once more trod the threshold off which he had been lifted more than twenty years ago!

"Master's not at home," says Jenkins, just in his old voice;

and Mrs. Jenkins, giving a dreadful *youp*, fell down in a fit, in which nobody minded her.

For everybody was shouting, "Huzza! huzza!" "Hip, hip, hurra!" "Long live the King and Queen!" "Were such things ever seen?" "No, never, never, never!" "The Fairy Blackstick forever!"

The bells were ringing double peals, the guns roaring and banging most prodigiously. Bulbo was embracing everybody; the Lord Chancellor was flinging up his wig and shouting like a madman; Hedzoff had got the Archbishop round the waist, and they were dancing a jig for joy; and as for Giglio, I leave you to imagine what he was doing, and if he kissed Rosalba once, twice—twenty thousand times, I'm sure I don't think he was wrong.

So Gruffanuff opened the hall-door with a low bow, just as he had been accustomed to do, and they all went in and signed the book, and then they went to church and were married, and the Fairy Blackstick sailed away on her cane, and was never more heard of in Paflagonia.

THE LIGHT PRINCESS
BY GEORGE MACDONALD

I

WHAT! NO CHILDREN?

Once upon a time, so long ago that I have quite forgotten the date, there lived a king and queen who had no children.

And the king said to himself, "All the queens of my acquaintance have children, some three, some seven, and some as many as twelve; and my queen has not one. I feel ill-used." So he made up his mind to be cross with his wife about it. But she bore it all like a good patient queen as she was. Then the king grew very cross indeed. But the queen pretended to take it all as a joke, and a very good one too.

"Why don't you have any daughters, at least?" said he. "I don't say *sons*; that might be too much to expect."

"I am sure, dear king, I am very sorry," said the queen.

"So you ought to be," retorted the king; "you are not going to make a virtue of *that*, surely."

But he was not an ill-tempered king, and in any matter of less moment would have let the queen have her own way with all his heart. This, however, was an affair of state.

The queen smiled.

"You must have patience with a lady, you know, dear king," said she.

She was, indeed, a very nice queen, and heartily sorry that she could not oblige the king immediately.

The king tried to have patience, but he succeeded very badly. It was more than he deserved, therefore, when, at last, the queen gave him a daughter—as lovely a little princess as ever cried.

II

WON'T I, JUST?

The day drew near when the infant must be christened. The king wrote all the invitations with his own hand. Of course somebody was forgotten.

Now it does not generally matter if somebody *is* forgotten, only you must mind who. Unfortunately, the king forgot without intending to forget; and so the chance fell upon the Princess Makemnoit, which was awkward. For the princess was the king's own sister; and he ought not to have forgotten her. But she had made herself so disagreeable to the old king, their father, that he had forgotten her in making his will; and so it was no wonder that her brother forgot her in writing his invitations. But poor relations don't do anything to keep you in mind of them. Why don't they? The king could not see into the garret she lived in, could he?

She was a sour, spiteful creature. The wrinkles of contempt crossed the wrinkles of peevishness, and made her face as full of wrinkles as a pat of butter. If ever a king could be justified in forgetting anybody, this king was justified in forgetting his sister, even at a christening. She looked very odd, too. Her forehead was as large as all the rest of her face, and projected over it like a precipice. When she was angry, her little eyes flashed blue. When she hated anybody, they shone yellow and green. What they looked like when she loved anybody, I do not know; for I never heard of her loving anybody but herself, and I do not think she could have managed that if she had not somehow got used to herself. But what made it highly imprudent in the king to forget her was—that she was awfully clever. In fact, she was a witch; when she bewitched anybody, he very soon had enough of it; for she beat all the wicked fairies in wickedness, and all the clever ones in cleverness. She despised all the modes we read of in history, in which offended fairies and witches have taken their revenges;

and therefore, after waiting and waiting in vain for an invitation, she made up her mind at last to go without one, and make the whole family miserable, like a princess as she was.

So she put on her best gown, went to the palace, was kindly received by the happy monarch, who forgot that he had forgotten her, and took her place in the procession to the royal chapel. When they were all gathered about the font, she contrived to get next to it, and threw something into the water; after which she maintained a very respectful demeanour till the water was applied to the child's face. But at that moment she turned round in her place three times, and muttered the following words, loud enough for those beside her to hear:—

> "Light of spirit, by my charms,
>   Light of body, every part,
> Never weary human arms—
>   Only crush thy parents' heart!"

They all thought she had lost her wits, and was repeating some foolish nursery rhyme; but a shudder went through the whole of them notwithstanding. The baby, on the contrary, began to laugh and crow; while the nurse gave a start and a smothered cry, for she thought she was struck with paralysis: she could not feel the baby in her arms. But she clasped it tight and said nothing.

The mischief was done.

III

SHE CAN'T BE OURS

Her atrocious aunt had deprived the child of all her gravity. If you ask me how this was effected, I answer, "In the easiest way in the world. She had only to destroy gravitation." For the princess was a philosopher, and knew all the *ins* and *outs* of the laws of gravitation as well as the *ins* and *outs* of her bootlace. And being a witch as well, she could abrogate those laws in a moment; or at least so clog their wheels and rust their bearings, that they would not work at all. But we have more to do with what followed than with how it was done.

The first awkwardness that resulted from this unhappy privation was, that the moment the nurse began to float the baby up and down, she flew from her arms towards the ceiling. Happily, the resistance of the air brought her ascending career to a close within a foot of it. There she remained, horizontal as when she left her nurse's arms, kicking and laughing amazingly. The nurse in terror flew to the bell, and begged the footman, who answered it, to bring up the house-steps directly. Trembling in every limb, she climbed upon the steps, and had to stand upon the very top, and reach up, before she could catch the floating tail of the baby's long clothes.

When the strange fact came to be known, there was a terrible commotion in the palace. The occasion of its discovery by the king was naturally a repetition of the nurse's experience. Astonished that he felt no weight when the child was laid in his arms, he began to wave her up and—not down; for she slowly ascended to the ceiling as before, and there remained floating in perfect comfort and satisfaction, as was testified by her peals of tiny laughter. The king stood staring up in speechless amazement, and trembled so that his beard shook like grass in the wind. At last, turning to the queen, who was just as horror-struck as himself, he said, gasping, staring, and stammering,—

"She *can't* be ours, queen!"

Now the queen was much cleverer than the king, and had begun already to suspect that "this effect defective came by cause."

"I am sure she is ours," answered she. "But we ought to have taken better care of her at the christening. People who were never invited ought not to have been present."

"Oh, oh!" said the king, tapping his forehead with his forefinger, "I have it all. I've found her out. Don't you see it, queen? Princess Makemnoit has bewitched her."

"That's just what I say," answered the queen.

"I beg your pardon, my love; I did not hear you.—John, bring the steps I get on my throne with."

For he was a little king with a great throne, like many other kings.

The throne-steps were brought, and set upon the dining-table, and John got upon the top of them. But he could not reach the little princess, who lay like a baby-laughter-cloud in the air, exploding continuously.

"Take the tongs, John," said his Majesty; and getting up on the table, he handed them to him.

John could reach the baby now, and the little princess was handed down by the tongs.

IV

WHERE IS SHE?

One fine summer day, a month after these her first adventures, during which time she had been very carefully watched, the princess was lying on the bed in the queen's own chamber, fast asleep. One of the windows was open, for it was noon, and the day so sultry that the little girl was wrapped in nothing less ethereal than slumber itself. The queen came into the room, and not observing that the baby was on the bed, opened another window. A frolicsome fairy wind, which had been watching for a chance of mischief, rushed in at the one window, and taking its way over the bed where the child was lying, caught her up, and rolling and floating her along like a piece of flue, or a dandelion-seed, carried her with it through the opposite window, and away. The queen went downstairs, quite ignorant of the loss she had herself occasioned.

When the nurse returned, she supposed that her Majesty had carried her off, and, dreading a scolding, delayed making inquiry about her. But hearing nothing, she grew uneasy, and went at length to the queen's boudoir, where she found her Majesty.

"Please, your Majesty, shall I take the baby?" said she.

"Where is she?" asked the queen.

"Please forgive me. I know it was wrong."

"What do you mean?" said the queen, looking grave.

"Oh! don't frighten me, your Majesty!" exclaimed the nurse, clasping her hands.

The queen saw that something was amiss, and fell down in a faint. The nurse rushed about the palace, screaming, "My baby! my baby!"

Every one ran to the queen's room. But the queen could give no orders. They soon found out, however, that the princess was missing, and in a moment the palace was like a beehive in a garden; and in one minute more the queen was brought to herself by a great shout and a clapping of hands. They had found the princess fast asleep under a rose-bush, to which the elvish little wind-puff had carried her, finishing its mischief by shaking a shower of red rose-leaves all over the little white sleeper. Startled by the noise the servants made, she woke, and, furious with glee, scattered the rose-leaves in all directions, like a shower of spray in the sunset.

She was watched more carefully after this, no doubt; yet it would be endless to relate all the odd incidents resulting from this peculiarity of the young princess. But there never was a baby in a house, not to say a palace, that kept the household in such constant good humour, at least below-stairs. If it was not easy for her nurses to hold her, at least she made neither their arms nor their hearts ache. And she was so nice to play at ball with! There was positively no danger of letting her fall. They might throw her down, or knock her down, or push her down, but couldn't *let* her down. It is true, they might let her fly into the fire or the coal-hole, or through the window; but none of these accidents had happened as yet. If you heard peals of laughter resounding from some unknown region, you might be sure enough of the cause. Going down into the kitchen, or *the room*, you would find Jane and Thomas, and Robert and Susan, all and sum, playing at ball with the little princess. She was the ball herself, and did not enjoy it the less for that. Away she went, flying from one to another, screeching with laughter. And the servants loved the ball itself better even than the game. But they had to take some care how they threw her, for if she received an upward direction, she would never come down again without being fetched.

V

WHAT IS TO BE DONE?

But above-stairs it was different. One day, for instance, after breakfast, the king went into his counting-house, and counted out his money.

The operation gave him no pleasure.

"To think," said he to himself, "that every one of these gold sovereigns weighs a quarter of an ounce, and my real, live, flesh-and-blood princess weighs nothing at all!"

And he hated his gold sovereigns, as they lay with a broad smile of self-satisfaction all over their yellow faces.

The queen was in the parlour, eating bread and honey. But at the second mouthful she burst out crying, and could not swallow it. The king heard her sobbing. Glad of anybody, but especially of his queen, to quarrel with, he clashed his gold sovereigns into his money-box, clapped his crown on his head, and rushed into the parlour.

"What is all this about?" exclaimed he. "What are you crying for, queen?"

"I can't eat it," said the queen, looking ruefully at the honey-pot.

"No wonder!" retorted the king. "You've just eaten your breakfast—two turkey eggs, and three anchovies."

"Oh, that's not it!" sobbed her Majesty. "It's my child, my child!"

"Well, what's the matter with your child? She's neither up the chimney nor down the draw-well. Just hear her laughing."

Yet the king could not help a sigh, which he tried to turn into a cough, saying,—

"It is a good thing to be light-hearted, I am sure, whether she be ours or not."

"It is a bad thing to be light-headed," answered the queen, looking with prophetic soul far into the future.

" 'Tis a good thing to be light-handed," said the king.

" 'Tis a bad thing to be light-fingered," answered the queen.

" 'Tis a good thing to be light-footed," said the king.

" 'Tis a bad thing——" began the queen; but the king interrupted her.

"In fact," said he, with the tone of one who concludes an argument in which he has had only imaginery opponents, and in which, therefore, he has come off triumphant—"in fact, it is a good thing altogether to be light-bodied."

"But it is a bad thing altogether to be light-minded," retorted the queen, who was beginning to lose her temper.

This last answer quite discomfited his Majesty, who turned on his heel, and betook himself to his counting-house again. But he was not half-way towards it, when the voice of his queen overtook him.

"And it's a bad thing to be light-haired," screamed she, determined to have more last words, now that her spirit was roused.

The queen's hair was black as night; and the king's had been, and his daughter's was, golden as morning. But it was not this reflection on his hair that arrested him; it was the double use of the word *light*. For the king hated all witticisms, and punning especially. And besides, he could not tell whether the queen meant light-*haired* or light-*heired*; for why might she not aspirate her vowels when she was ex-asperated herself?

He turned upon his other heel, and rejoined her. She looked angry still, because she knew that she was guilty, or, what was much the same, knew that he thought so.

"My dear queen," said he, "duplicity of any sort is exceedingly objectionable between married people of any rank, not to say kings and queens; and the most objectionable form duplicity can assume is that of punning."

"There!" said the queen, "I never made a jest, but I broke it in the making. I am the most unfortunate woman in the world!"

She looked so rueful, that the king took her in his arms; and they sat down to consult.

"Can you bear this?" said the king.

"No, I can't," said the queen.

"Well, what's to be done?" said the king.

"I'm sure I don't know," said the queen. "But might you not try an apology?"

"To my old sister, I suppose you mean?" said the king.

"Yes," said the queen.

"Well, I don't mind," said the king.

So he went the next morning to the house of the princess, and, making a very humble apology, begged her to undo the spell. But the princess declared, with a grave face, that she knew nothing at all about it. Her eyes, however, shone pink, which was a sign that she was happy. She advised the king and queen to have patience, and to mend their ways. The king returned disconsolate. The queen tried to comfort him.

"We will wait till she is older. She may then be able to suggest something herself. She will know at least how she feels, and explain things to us."

"But what if she should marry?" exclaimed the king, in sudden consternation at the idea.

"Well, what of that?" rejoined the queen.

"Just think! If she were to have children! In the course of a hundred years the air might be as full of floating children as of gossamers in autumn."

"That is no business of ours," replied the queen. "Besides, by that time they will have learned to take care of themselves."

A sigh was the king's only answer.

He would have consulted the court physicians; but he was afraid they would try experiments upon her.

VI

SHE LAUGHS TOO MUCH

Meantime, notwithstanding awkward occurrences, and griefs that she brought upon her parents, the little princess laughed and grew—not fat, but plump and tall. She reached the age of seventeen, without having fallen into any worse scrape than a chimney; by rescuing her from which, a little bird-nesting urchin got fame and a black face. Nor, thoughtless as she was, had she committed anything worse than laughter at everybody and everything that came in her way. When she was told, for the sake of experiment, that General Clanrunfort

was cut to pieces with all his troops, she laughed; when she
heard that the enemy was on his way to besiege her papa's
capital, she laughed hugely; but when she was told that the
city would certainly be abandoned to the mercy of the enemy's
soldiery—why, then she laughed immoderately. She never
could be brought to see the serious side of anything. When
her mother cried, she said,—

"What queer faces mamma makes! And she squeezes water
out of her cheeks! Funny mamma!"

And when her papa stormed at her, she laughed, and
danced round and round him, clapping her hands, and
crying,—

"Do it again, papa. Do it again! It's such fun! Dear, funny
papa!"

And if he tried to catch her, she glided from him in an
instant, not in the least afraid of him, but thinking it part of
the game not to be caught. With one push of her foot, she
would be floating in the air above his head; or she would go
dancing backwards and forwards and sideways, like a great
butterfly. It happened several times, when her father and
mother were holding a consultation about her in private, that
they were interrupted by vainly repressed outbursts of laughter over their heads; and looking up with indignation, saw her
floating at full length in the air above them, whence she
regarded them with the most comical appreciation of the
position.

One day an awkward accident happened. The princess had
come out upon the lawn with one of her attendants, who held
her by the hand. Spying her father at the other side of the
lawn she snatched her hand from the maid's and sped across
to him. Now when she wanted to run alone, her custom was
to catch up a stone in each hand, so that she might come
down again after a bound. Whatever she wore as part of her
attire had no effect in this way: even gold, when it thus
became as it were a part of herself, lost all its weight for the
time. But whatever she only held in her hands retained its
downward tendency. On this occasion she could see nothing
to catch up but a huge toad, that was walking across the lawn
as if he had a hundred years to do it in. Not knowing what
disgust meant, for this was one of her peculiarities, she
snatched up the toad and bounded away. She had almost
reached her father, and he was holding out his arms to

receive her, and take from her lips the kiss which hovered on them like a butterfly on a rosebud, when a puff of wind blew her aside into the arms of a young page, who had just been receiving a message from his Majesty. Now it was no great peculiarity in the princess that, once she was set agoing, it always cost her time and trouble to check herself. On this occasion there was no time. She *must* kiss—and she kissed the page. She did not mind it much; for she had no shyness in her composition; and she knew, besides, that she could not help it. So she only laughed, like a musical box. The poor page fared the worst. For the princess, trying to correct the unfortunate tendency of the kiss, put out her hands to keep her off the page; so that, along with the kiss, he received on the other cheek, a slap with the huge black toad, which she poked right into his eye. He tried to laugh, too, but the attempt resulted in such an odd contortion of countenance, as showed that there was no danger of his pluming himself on the kiss. As for the king, his dignity was greatly hurt, and he did not speak to the page for a whole month.

I may here remark that it was very amusing to see her run, if her mode of progression could properly be called running. For first she would make a bound; then, having alighted, she would run a few steps, and make another bound. Sometimes she would fancy she had reached the ground before she actually had, and her feet would go backwards and forwards, running upon nothing at all, like those of a chicken on its back. Then she would laugh like the very spirit of fun; only in her laugh there was something missing. What it was, I find myself unable to describe. I think it was a certain tone, depending upon the possibility of sorrow—*morbidezza,* perhaps. She never smiled.

VII

TRY METAPHYSICS

After a long avoidance of the painful subject, the king and queen resolved to hold a council of three upon it; and so they sent for the princess. In she came, sliding and flitting and gliding from one piece of furniture to another, and put herself at last in an arm-chair, in a sitting posture. Whether she could be said *to sit*, seeing she received no support from the seat of the chair, I do not pretend to determine.

"My dear child," said the king, "you must be aware by this time that you are not exactly like other people."

"Oh, you dear funny papa! I have got a nose, and two eyes, and all the rest. So have you. So has mamma."

"Now be serious, my dear, for once," said the queen.

"No, thank you, mamma; I had rather not."

"Would you not like to be able to walk like other people?" said the king.

"No indeed, I should think not. You only crawl. You are such slow coaches!"

"How do you feel, my child?" he resumed, after a pause of discomfiture.

"Quite well, thank you."

"I mean, what do you feel like?"

"Like nothing at all, that I know of."

"You must feel like something."

"I feel like a princess with such a funny papa, and such a dear pet of a queen-mamma!"

"Now really!" began the queen; but the princess interrupted her.

"Oh, yes," she added, "I remember. I have a curious feeling sometimes, as if I were the only person that had any sense in the whole world."

She had been trying to behave herself with dignity; but now she burst into a violent fit of laughter, threw herself backwards over the chair, and went rolling about the floor in an ecstasy of enjoyment. The king picked her up easier than one does a down quilt, and replaced her in her former relation to the chair. The exact preposition expressing this relation I do not happen to know.

"Is there nothing you wish for?" resumed the king, who had learned by this time that it was quite useless to be angry with her.

"Oh, you dear papa!—yes," answered she.

"What is it, my darling?"

"I have been longing for it—oh, such a time! Ever since last night."

"Tell me what it is."

"Will you promise to let me have it?"

The king was on the point of saying *Yes*, but the wiser queen checked him with a single motion of her head.

"Tell me what it is first," said he.

"No, no. Promise first."

"I dare not. What is it?"

"Mind, I hold you to your promise—It is—to be tied to the end of a string—a very long string indeed, and be flown like a kite. Oh, such fun! I would rain rose-water, and hail sugar-plums, and snow whipped-cream, and—and—and—"

A fit of laughing checked her; and she would have been off again over the floor, had not the king started up and caught her just in time. Seeing that nothing but talk could be got out of her, he rang the bell, and sent her away with two of her ladies-in-waiting.

"Now, queen," he said, turning to her Majesty, "what *is* to be done?"

"There is but one thing left," answered she. "Let us consult the college of Metaphysicians."

"Bravo!" cried the king; "we will."

Now at the head of this college were two very wise Chinese philosophers—by name, Hum-Drum, and Kopy-Keck. For them the king sent; and straightway they came. In a long speech he communicated to them what they knew very well already—as who did not?—namely, the peculiar condition of his daughter in relation to the globe on which she dwelt; and requested them to consult together as to what might be the cause and probable cure of her *infirmity*. The king laid stress upon the word, but failed to discover his own pun. The

queen laughed; but Hum-Drum and Kopy-Keck heard with
humility and retired in silence.

Their consultation consisted chiefly in propounding and
supporting, for the thousandth time, each his favourite theories.
For the condition of the princess afforded delightful scope for
the discussion of every question arising from the division of
thought—in fact, of all the Metaphysics of the Chinese Empire.
But it is only justice to say that they did not altogether
neglect the discussion of the practical question, *what was to
be done*.

Hum-Drum was a Materialist, and Kopy-Keck was a
Spiritualist. The former was slow and sententious; the latter
was quick and flighty: the latter had generally the first word;
the former the last.

"I reassert my former assertion," began Kopy-Keck, with a
plunge. "There is not a fault in the princess, body or soul;
only they are wrong put together. Listen to me now, Hum-
Drum, and I will tell you in brief that I think. Don't speak.
Don't answer me. I *won't* hear you till I have done.—At that
decisive moment, when souls seek their appointed habitations,
two eager souls met, struck, rebounded, lost their way, and
arrived each at the wrong place. The soul of the princess was
one of those, and she went far astray. She does not belong by
rights to this world at all, but to some other planet, probably
Mercury. Her proclivity to her true sphere destroys all the
natural influence which this orb would otherwise possess over
her corporeal frame. She cares for nothing here. There is no
relation between her and this world.

"She must therefore be taught, by the sternest compulsion,
to take an interest in the earth as the earth. She must study
every department of its history—its animal history; its vegeta-
ble history; its mineral history; its social history; its moral
history; its political history; its scientific history; its literary
history; its musical history; its artistical history; above all, its
metaphysical history. She must begin with the Chinese dynasty and end with Japan. But first of all she must study
geology, and especially the history of the extinct races of
animals—their natures, their habits, their loves, their hates,
their revenges. She must——"

"Hold, h-o-o-old!" roared Hum-Drum. "It is certainly my
turn now. My rooted and insubvertible conviction is, that the
causes of the anomalies evident in the princess's condition are

strictly and solely physical. But that is only tantamount to acknowledging that they exist. Hear my opinion.—From some cause or other, of no importance to our inquiry, the motion of her heart has been reversed. That remarkable combination of the suction and the force-pump works the wrong way—I mean in the case of the unfortunate princess: it draws in where it should force out, and forces out where it should draw in. The offices of the auricles and the ventricles are subverted. The blood is sent forth by the veins, and returns by the arteries. Consequently it is running the wrong way through all her corporeal organism—lungs and all. Is it then at all mysterious, seeing that such is the case, that on the other particular of gravitation as well, she should differ from normal humanity? My proposal for the cure is this:—

"Phlebotomize until she is reduced to the last point of safety. Let it be effected, if necessary, in a warm bath. When she is reduced to a state of perfect asphyxy, apply a ligature to the left ankle, drawing it as tight as the bone will bear. Apply, at the same moment, another of equal tension around the right wrist. By means of plates constructed for the purpose, place the other foot and hand under the receivers of two air-pumps. Exhaust the receivers. Exhibit a pint of French brandy, and await the result."

"Which would presently arrive in the form of grim Death," said Kopy-Keck.

"If it should, she would yet die in doing our duty," retorted Hum-Drum.

But their Majesties had too much tenderness for their volatile offspring to subject her to either of the schemes of the equally unscrupulous philosophers. Indeed, the most complete knowledge of the laws of nature would have been unserviceable in her case; for it was impossible to classify her. She was a fifth imponderable body, sharing all the other properties of the ponderable.

VIII

TRY A DROP OF WATER

Perhaps the best thing for the princess would have been to fall in love. But how a princess who had no gravity could fall into anything is a difficulty—perhaps *the* difficulty. As for her own feelings on the subject, she did not even know that there was such a beehive of honey and stings to be fallen into. But now I come to mention another curious fact about her.

The palace was built on the shore of the loveliest lake in the world; and the princess loved this lake more than father or mother. The root of this preference no doubt, although the princess did not recognize it as such, was, that the moment she got into it, she recovered the natural right of which she had been so wickedly deprived—namely, gravity. Whether this was owing to the fact that water had been employed as the means of conveying the injury, I do not know. But it is certain that she could swim and dive like the duck that her old nurse said she was. The manner in which this alleviation of her misfortune was discovered was as follows.

One summer evening, during the carnival of the country, she had been taken upon the lake by the king and queen, in the royal barge. They were accompanied by many of the courtiers in a fleet of little boats. In the middle of the lake she wanted to get into the lord chancellor's barge, for his daughter, who was a great favourite with her, was in it with her father. Now though the old king rarely condescended to make light of his misfortune, yet, happening on this occasion to be in a particularly good humour, as the barges approached each other, he caught up the princess to throw her into the chancellor's barge. He lost his balance, however, and, dropping into the bottom of the barge, lost his hold of his daughter; not, however, before imparting to her the downward tendency of his own person, though in a somewhat different direction; for, as the king fell into the boat, she fell into the water. With a burst of delighted laughter she disappeared in the lake. A cry of horror ascended from the boats. They had never seen the princess go down before. Half the men were under water in a moment; but they had all, one after another come up to the surface again for breath, when—tinkle, tinkle, babble, and gush! came the princess's laugh over the water from far away. There she was, swimming like a swan. Nor would she come out for king or queen, chancellor or daughter. She was perfectly obstinate.

But at the same time she seemed more sedate than usual. Perhaps that was because a great pleasure spoils laughing. At all events, after this, the passion of her life was to get into the water, and she was always the better behaved and the more beautiful the more she had of it. Summer and winter it was quite the same; only she could not stay so long in the water when they had to break the ice to let her in. Any day, from morning till evening in summer, she might be descried—a streak of white in the blue water—lying as still as the shadow of a cloud, or shooting along like a dolphin; disappearing, and coming up again far off, just where one did not expect her. She would have been in the lake of a night too, if she could have had her way; for the balcony of her window overhung a deep pool in it; and through a shallow reedy passage she could have swum out into the wide wet water, and no one would have been any the wiser. Indeed, when she happened to wake in the moonlight, she could hardly resist the temptation. But there was the sad difficulty of getting into it. She had as great a dread of the air as some children have of the water. For the slightest gust of wind would blow her away; and a gust might arise in the stillest moment. And if she gave herself a push towards the water and just failed of reaching it, her situation would be dreadfully awkward, irrespective of the wind; for at best there she would have to remain, suspended in her night-gown, till she was seen and angled for by somebody from the window.

"Oh! if I had my gravity," thought she, contemplating the water, "I would flash off this balcony like a long white seabird, headlong into the darling wetness. Heigh-ho!"

This was the only consideration that made her wish to be like other people.

Another reason for her being fond of the water was that in it alone she enjoyed any freedom. For she could not walk out without a *cortège*, consisting in part of a troop of light horse, for fear of the liberties which the wind might take with her. And the king grew more apprehensive with increasing years, till at last he would not allow her to walk abroad at all without some twenty silken cords fastened to as many parts of her dress, and held by twenty noblemen. Of course horseback was out of the question. But she bade good-bye to all this cere- mony when she got into the water.

And so remarkable were its effects upon her, especially in restoring her for the time to the ordinary human gravity, that Hum-Drum and Kopy-Keck agreed in recommending the king to bury her alive for three years; in the hope that, as the water did her so much good, the earth would do her yet more. But the king had some vulgar prejudices against the experiment, and would not give his consent. Foiled in this, they yet agreed in another recommendation; which, seeing that the one imported his opinions from China and the other from Thibet, was very remarkable indeed. They argued that, if water of external origin and application could be so efficacious, water from a deeper source might work a perfect cure; in short, that if the poor afflicted princess could by any means be made to cry, she might recover her lost gravity.

But how was this to be brought about? Therein lay all the difficulty—to meet which the philosophers were not wise enough. To make the princess cry was as impossible as to make her weigh. They sent for a professional beggar; com- manded him to prepare his most touching oracle of woe; helped him, out of the court charade-box, to whatever he wanted for dressing up, and promised great rewards in the event of his success. But it was all in vain. She listened to the mendicant artist's story, and gazed at his marvellous make-up, till she could contain herself no longer, and went into the most undignified contortions for relief, shrieking, positively screeching with laughter.

When she had a little recovered herself, she ordered her attendants to drive him away, and not give him a single copper; whereupon his look of mortified discomfiture wrought her punishment and his revenge, for it sent her into violent hysterics, from which she was with difficulty recovered.

But so anxious was the king that the suggestion should have a fair trial, that he put himself in a rage one day, and, rushing up to her room, gave her an awful whipping. Yet not a tear would flow. She looked grave, and her laughing sounded uncommonly like screaming—that was all. The good old tyrant, though he put on his best gold spectacles to look, could not discover the smallest cloud in the serene blue of her eyes.

IX

PUT ME IN AGAIN

It must have been about this time that the son of a king, who lived a thousand miles from Lagobel, set out to look for the daughter of a queen. He travelled far and wide, but as sure as he found a princess, he found some fault in her. Of course he could not marry a mere woman, however beautiful; and there was no princess to be found worthy of him. Whether the prince was so near perfection that he had a right to demand perfection itself, I cannot pretend to say. All I know is, that he was a fine, handsome, brave, generous, well-bred, and well-behaved youth, as all princes are.

In his wanderings he had come across some reports about our princess; but as everybody said she was bewitched, he never dreamed that she could bewitch him. For what indeed could a prince do with a princess that had lost her gravity? Who could tell what she might not lose next? She might lose her visibility, or her tangibility; or, in short, the power of making impressions upon the radical sensorium; so that he should never be able to tell whether she was dead or alive. Of course he made no further inquiries about her.

One day he lost sight of his retinue in a great forest. These forests are very useful in delivering princes from their courtiers, like a sieve that keeps back the bran. Then the princes get away to follow their fortunes. In this they have the advantage of the princesses, who are forced to marry before they have had a bit of fun. I wish our princesses got lost in a forest sometimes.

One lovely evening, after wandering about for many days, he found that he was approaching the outskirts of this forest;

for the trees had got so thin that he could see the sunset through them; and he soon came upon a kind of heath. Next he came upon signs of human neighbourhood; but by this time it was getting late, and there was nobody in the fields to direct him.

After travelling for another hour, his horse, quite worn out with long labour and lack of food, fell, and was unable to rise again. So he continued his journey on foot. At length he entered another wood—not a wild forest, but a civilized wood, through which a footpath led him to the side of a lake. Along this path the prince pursued his way through the gathering darkness. Suddenly he paused, and listened. Strange sounds came across the water. It was, in fact, the princess laughing. Now there was something odd in her laugh, as I have already hinted; for the hatching of a real hearty laugh requires the incubation of gravity; and perhaps this was how the prince mistook the laughter for screaming. Looking over the lake, he saw something white in the water; and, in an instant, he had torn off his tunic, kicked off his sandals, and plunged in. He soon reached the white object, and found that it was a woman. There was not light enough to show that she was a princess, but quite enough to show that she was a lady, for it does not want much light to see that.

Now I cannot tell how it came about,—whether she pretended to be drowning, or whether he frightened her, or caught her so as to embarrass her,—but certainly he brought her to shore in a fashion ignominious to a swimmer, and more nearly drowned than she had even expected to be; for the water had got into her throat as often as she had tried to speak.

At the place to which he bore her, the bank was only a foot or two above the water; so he gave her a strong lift out of the water, to lay her on the bank. But, her gravitation ceasing the moment she left the water, away she went up into the air, scolding and screaming.

"You naughty, *naughty*, NAUGHTY, NAUGHTY man!" she cried.

No one had ever succeeded in putting her into a passion before.—When the prince saw her ascend, he thought he must have been bewitched, and have mistaken a great swan for a lady. But the princess caught hold of the topmost cone upon a lofty fir. This came off; but she caught at another; and, in fact, stopped herself by gathering cones, dropping them as the stalks gave way. The prince, meantime, stood in the water, staring, and forgetting to get out. But the princess disappearing, he scrambled on shore, and went in the direction of the tree. There he found her climbing down one of the branches towards the stem. But in the darkness of the wood, the prince continued in some bewilderment as to what the phenomenon could be; until, reaching the ground, and seeing him standing there she caught hold of him, and said,—

"I'll tell papa."

"Oh no, you won't!" returned the prince.

"Yes, I will," she persisted. "What business had you to pull me down out of the water, and throw me to the bottom of the air? I never did you any harm."

"Pardon me. I did not mean to hurt you."

"I don't believe you have any brains; and that is a worse loss than your wretched gravity. I pity you."

The prince now saw that he had come upon the bewitched princess, and had already offended her. But before he could think what to say next, she burst out angrily, giving a stamp with her foot that would have sent her aloft again but for the hold she had of his arm,—

"Put me up directly."

"Put you up where, you beauty?" asked the prince.

He had fallen in love with her almost, already; for her anger made her more charming than any one else had ever beheld her; and, as far as he could see, which certainly was not far, she had not a single fault about her, except, of course, that she had not any gravity. No prince, however, would judge of a princess by weight. The loveliness of her foot he would hardly estimate by the depth of the impression it could make in mud.

"Put you up where, you beauty?" asked the prince.

"In the water, you stupid!" answered the princess.

"Come, then," said the prince.

The condition of her dress, increasing her usual difficulty in walking, compelled her to cling to him; and he could hardly persuade himself that he was not in a delightful dream, notwithstanding the torrent of musical abuse with which she overwhelmed him. The prince being therefore in no hurry, they came upon the lake at quite another part, where the bank was twenty-five feet high at least; and when they had reached the edge, he turned towards the princess, and said,—

"How am I to put you in?"

"That is your business," she answered, quite snappishly. "You took me out—put me in again."

"Very well," said the prince; and, catching her up in his arms, he sprang with her from the rock. The princess had just time to give one delighted shriek of laughter before the water closed over them. When they came to the surface, she found that, for a moment or two, she could not even laugh, for she had gone down with such a rush, that it was with difficulty she recovered her breath. The instant they reached the surface—

"How do you like falling in?" said the prince.

After some effort the princess panted out,—

"Is that what you call *falling in*?"

"Yes," answered the prince, "I should think it a very tolerable specimen."

"It seemed to me like going up," rejoined she.

"My feeling was certainly one of elevation too," the prince conceded.

The princess did not appear to understand him, for she retorted his question:—

"How do *you* like falling in?" said the princess.

"Beyond everything," answered he; "for I have fallen in with the only perfect creature I ever saw."

"No more of that: I am tired of it," said the princess.

Perhaps she shared her father's aversion to punning.

"Don't you like falling in, then?" said the prince.

"It is the most delightful fun I ever had in my life," answered she. "I never fell before. I wish I could learn. To think I am the only person in my father's kingdom that can't fall!"

Here the poor princess looked almost sad.

"I shall be most happy to fall in with you any time you like," said the prince, devotedly.

"Thank you. I don't know. Perhaps it would not be proper. But I don't care. At all events, as we have fallen in, let us have a swim together."

"With all my heart," responded the prince.

And away they went, swimming, and diving, and floating, until at last they heard cries along the shore, and saw lights glancing in all directions. It was now quite late, and there was no moon.

"I must go home," said the princess. "I am very sorry, for this is delightful."

"So am I," returned the prince. "But I am glad I haven't a home to go to—at least, I don't exactly know where it is."

"I wish I hadn't one either," rejoined the princess; "it is so stupid! I have a great mind," she continued, "to play them all a trick. Why couldn't they leave me alone? They won't trust me in the lake for a single night!—You see where that green light is burning? That is the window of my room. Now if you would just swim there with me very quietly, and when we are all but under the balcony, give me such a push—*up* you call it—as you did a little while ago, I should be able to catch hold of the balcony, and get in at the window; and then they may look for me till to-morrow morning!"

"With more obedience than pleasure," said the prince, gallantly; and away they swam, very gently.

"Will you be in the lake to-morrow-night?" the prince ventured to ask.

"To be sure I will. I don't think so. Perhaps," was the princess's somewhat strange answer.

But the prince was intelligent enough not to press her further; and merely whispered, as he gave her the parting lift, "Don't tell." The only answer the princess returned was a roguish look. She was already a yard above his head. The look seemed to say, "Never fear. It is too good fun to spoil that way."

So perfectly like other people had she been in the water, that even yet the prince could scarcely believe his eyes when he saw her ascend slowly, grasp the balcony, and disappear through the window. He turned, almost expecting to see her still by his side. But he was alone in the water. So he swam away quietly, and watched the lights roving about the shore for hours after the princess was safe in her chamber. As soon as they disappeared, he landed in search of his tunic and sword, and, after some trouble, found them again. Then he made the best of his way round the lake to the other side. There the wood was wilder, and the shore steeper—rising more immediately towards the mountains which surrounded the lake on all sides, and kept sending it messages of silvery streams from morning to night, and all night long. He soon found a spot whence he could see the green light in the princess's room, and where, even in the broad daylight, he would be in no danger of being discovered from the opposite shore. It was a sort of cave in the rock, where he provided himself a bed of withered leaves, and lay down too tired for hunger to keep him awake. All night long he dreamed that he was swimming with the princess.

X

LOOK AT THE MOON

Early the next morning the prince set out to look for something to eat, which he soon found at a forester's hut, where for many following days he was supplied with all that a brave prince could consider necessary. And having plenty to keep him alive for the present, he would not think of wants not yet in existence. Whenever Care intruded, this prince always bowed him out in the most princely manner.

When he returned from his breakfast to his watch-cave, he saw the princess already floating about in the lake, attended by the king and queen—whom he knew by their crowns— and a great company in lovely little boats, with canopies of all the colours of the rainbow, and flags and streamers of a great many more. It was a very bright day, and soon the prince, burned up with the heat, began to long for the cold water and the cool princess. But he had to endure till twilight; for the boats had provisions on board, and it was not till the sun went down that the gay party began to vanish. Boat after boat drew away to the shore, following that of the king and queen, till only one, apparently the princess's own boat, remained. But she did not want to go home even yet, and the prince thought he saw her order the boat to the shore without her. At all events, it rowed away; and now, of all the radiant company, only one white speck remained. Then the prince began to sing.

And this is what he sang;—

"Lady fair,
Swan-white,
Lift thine eyes,

"Banish night
By the might
Of thine eyes.

"Snowy arms,
Oars of snow,
Oar her hither,
Plashing low,
Soft and slow,
Oar her hither.

"Stream behind her
O'er the lake,
Radiant whiteness!
In her wake
Following, following for her sake,
Radiant whiteness!

"Cling about her,
Waters blue;
Part not from her,
But renew
Cold and true
Kisses round her.

"Lap me round,
Waters sad
That have left her;
Make me glad,
For ye had
Kissed her ere ye left her."

Before he had finished his song, the princess was just
under the place where he sat, and looking up to find him.
Her ears had led her truly.

"Would you like a fall, princess?" said the prince, looking
down.

"Ah! there you are! Yes, if you please, prince," said the princess, looking up.

"How do you know I am a prince, princess?" said the prince.

"Because you are a very nice young man, prince," said the princess.

"Come up then, princess."

"Fetch me, prince."

The prince took off his scarf, then his sword-belt, then his tunic, and tied them all together, and let them down. But the line was far too short. He unwound his turban, and added it to the rest, when it was all but long enough; and his purse completed it. The princess just managed to lay hold of the knot of money, and was beside him in a moment. This rock was much higher than the other, and the splash and the dive were tremendous. The princess was in ecstasies of delight, and their swim was delicious.

Night after night they met, and swam about in the dark clear lake; where such was the prince's gladness, that (whether the princess's way of looking at things infected him, or he was actually getting light-hearted) he often fancied that he was swimming in the sky instead of the lake. But when he talked about being in heaven, the princess laughed at him dreadfully.

When the moon came, she brought them fresh pleasure. Everything looked strange and new in her light, with an old, withered, yet unfading newness. When the moon was nearly full, one of their great delights was, to dive deep in the water, and then, turning round, look up through it at the great blot of light close above them, shimmering and trembling and wavering, spreading and contracting, seeming to melt away, and again grow solid. Then they would shoot up through the blot; and lo! there was the moon, far off, clear and steady and cold, and very lovely, at the bottom of a deeper and bluer lake than theirs, as the princess said.

The prince soon found out that while in the water the princess was very like other people. And besides this, she was not so forward in her questions or pert in her replies at sea as on shore. Neither did she laugh so much; and when she did laugh, it was more gently. She seemed altogether more modest and maidenly in the water than out of it. But when the prince, who had really fallen in love when he fell in the lake, began to talk to her about love, she always turned

her head towards him and laughed. After a while she began
to look puzzled, as if she were trying to understand what he
meant, but could not—revealing a notion that he meant
something. But as soon as ever she left the lake, she was so
altered, that the prince said to himself, "If I marry her, I see
no help for it: we must turn merman and mermaid, and go
out to sea at once."

XI

HISS!

The princess's pleasure in the lake had grown to a passion,
and she could scarcely bear to be out of it for an hour.
Imagine then her consternation, when, diving with the prince
one night, a sudden suspicion seized her that the lake was not
so deep as it used to be. The prince could not imagine what
had happened. She shot to the surface, and, without a word,
swam at full speed towards the higher side of the lake. He
followed, begging to know if she was ill, or what was the
matter. She never turned her head, or took the smallest
notice of his question. Arrived at the shore, she coasted the
rocks with minute inspection. But she was not able to come
to a conclusion, for the moon was very small, and so she
could not see well. She turned therefore and swam home,
without saying a word to explain her conduct to the prince, of
whose presence she seemed no longer conscious. He withdrew to his cave, in great perplexity and distress.

Next day she made many observations, which, alas! strength-
ened her fears. She saw that the banks were too dry; and that
the grass on the shore, and the trailing plants on the rocks,
were withering away. She caused marks to be made along the
borders, and examined them, day after day, in all directions
of the wind; till at last the horrible idea became a certain
fact—that the surface of the lake was slowly sinking.

The poor princess nearly went out of the little mind she
had. It was awful to her to see the lake, which she loved

more than any living thing, lie dying before her eyes. It sank away, slowly vanishing. The tops of rocks that had never been seen till now, began to appear far down in the clear water. Before long they were dry in the sun. It was fearful to think of the mud that would soon lie there baking and festering, full of lovely creatures dying, and ugly creatures coming to life, like the unmaking of a world. And how hot the sun would be without the lake! She could not bear to swim in it any more, and began to pine away. Her life seemed bound up with it; and ever as the lake sank, she pined. People said she would not live an hour after the lake was gone.

But she never cried.

Proclamation was made to all the kingdom, that whosoever should discover the cause of the lake's decrease, would be rewarded after a princely fashion. Hum-Drum and Kopy-Keck applied themselves to their physics and metaphysics; but in vain. Not even they could suggest a cause.

Now the fact was that the old princess was at the root of the mischief. When she heard that her niece found more pleasure in the water than any one else had out of it, she went into a rage, and cursed herself for her want of foresight.

"But," said she, "I will soon set all right. The king and the people shall die of thirst: their brains shall boil and frizzle in their skulls before I will lose my revenge."

And she laughed a ferocious laugh, that made the hairs on the back of her black cat stand erect with terror.

Then she went to an old chest in the room, and opening it, took out what looked like a piece of dried seaweed. This she threw into a tub of water. Then she threw some powder into the water, and stirred it with her bare arm, muttering over it words of hideous sound, and yet more hideous import. Then she set the tub aside, and took from the chest a huge bunch of a hundred rusty keys, that clattered in her shaking hands. Then she sat down and proceeded to oil them all. Before she had finished, out from the tub, the water of which had kept on a slow motion ever since she had ceased stirring it, came the head and half the body of a huge grey snake. But the witch did not look round. It grew out of the tub, waving itself backwards and forwards with a slow horizontal motion, till it reached the princess, when it laid its head upon her shoulders, and gave a low hiss in her ear. She started—but with joy; and seeing the head resting on her shoulder, drew it towards her and kissed it. Then she drew it all out of the tub, and wound it round her body. It was one of those dreadful creatures which few have ever beheld—the White Snakes of Darkness.

Then she took the keys and went down to her cellar; and as she unlocked the door she said to herself,—

"This *is* worth living for!"

Locking the door behind her, she descended a few steps into the cellar, and crossing it, unlocked another door into a dark, narrow passage. She locked this also behind her, and descended a few more steps. If any one had followed the witch-princess, he would have heard her unlock exactly one hundred doors, and descend a few steps after unlocking each. When she had unlocked the last, she entered a vast cave, the roof of which was supported by huge natural pillars of rock. Now this roof was the under side of the bottom of the lake.

She then untwined the snake from her body, and held it by the tail high above her. The hideous creature stretched up its head towards the roof of the cavern, which it was just able to reach. It then began to move its head backwards and forwards, with a slow oscillating motion, as if looking for something. At the same moment the witch began to walk round and round the cavern, coming nearer to the centre every circuit; while the head of the snake described the same path over the roof that she did over the floor, for she kept holding it up. And still it kept slowly oscillating. Round and round the cavern they went, ever lessening the circuit, till at last the snake made a sudden dart, and clung to the roof with its mouth.

"That's right, my beauty!" cried the princess; "drain it dry."

She let it go, left it hanging, and sat down on a great stone, with her black cat, which had followed her all round the cave, by her side. Then she began to knit and mutter awful words. The snake hung like a huge leech, sucking at the stone; the cat stood with his back arched, and his tail like a piece of cable, looking up at the snake; and the old woman sat and knitted and muttered. Seven days and seven nights they remained thus; when suddenly the serpent dropped from the roof as if exhausted, and shrivelled up till it was again like a piece of dried seaweed. The witch started to her feet, picked it up, put it in her pocket, and looked up at the roof. One drop of water was trembling on the spot where the snake had been sucking. As soon as she saw that, she turned and fled, followed by her cat. Shutting the door in a terrible hurry, she locked it, and having muttered some frightful words, sped to the next, which also she locked and muttered over; and so with all the hundred doors, till she arrived in her own cellar. There she sat down on the floor ready to faint, but listening with malicious delight to the rushing of the water, which she could hear distinctly through all the hundred doors.

But this was not enough. Now that she had tasted revenge, she lost her patience. Without further measures, the lake would be too long in disappearing. So the next night, with the last shred of the dying old moon rising, she took some of the water in which she had revived the snake, put it in a bottle, and set out, accompanied by her cat. Before morning she had made the entire circuit of the lake, muttering fearful words as she crossed every stream, and casting into it some of the water out of her bottle. When she had finished the circuit she muttered yet again, and flung a handful of water towards the moon. Thereupon every spring in the country ceased to throb and bubble, dying away like the pulse of a dying man. The next day there was no sound of falling water to be heard along the borders of the lake. The very courses were dry; and the mountains showed no silvery streaks down their dark sides. And not alone had the fountains of mother Earth ceased to flow; for all the babies throughout the country were crying dreadfully—only without tears.

XII

WHERE IS THE PRINCE?

Never since the night when the princess left him so abruptly had the prince had a single interview with her. He had seen her once or twice in the lake; but as far as he could discover, she had not been in it any more at night. He had sat and sung, and looked in vain for his Nereid; while she, like a true Nereid, was wasting away with her lake, sinking as it sank,

withering as it dried. When at length he discovered the
change that was taking place in the level of the water, he was
in great alarm and perplexity. He could not tell whether the
lake was dying because the lady had forsaken it; or whether
the lady would not come because the lake had begun to sink.
But he resolved to know so much at least.

He disguised himself, and, going to the palace, requested
to see the lord chamberlain. His appearance at once gained
his request; and the lord chamberlain, being a man of some
insight, perceived that there was more in the prince's solicita-
tion than met the ear. He felt likewise that no one could tell
whence a solution of the present difficulties might arise. So
he granted the prince's prayer to be made shoe-black to the
princess. It was rather cunning in the prince to request such
an easy post, for the princess could not possibly soil as many
shoes as other princesses.

He soon learned all that could be told about the princess.
He went nearly distracted; but after roaming about the lake
for days, and diving in every depth that remained, all that he
could do was to put an extra polish on the dainty pair of boots
that was never called for.

For the princess kept her room, with the curtains drawn to
shut out the dying lake. But she could not shut it out of
her mind for a moment. It haunted her imagination so that
she felt as if the lake were her soul, drying up within her,
first to mud, then to madness and death. She thus brooded
over the change, with all its dreadful accompaniments, till
she was nearly distracted. As for the prince, she had forgotten him. However much she had enjoyed his company in the
water, she did not care for him without it. But she seemed to
have forgotten her father and mother too.

The lake went on sinking. Small slimy spots began to
appear, which glittered steadily amidst the changeful shine of
the water. These grew to broad patches of mud, which wid-
ened and spread, with rocks here and there, and floundering
fishes and crawling eels swarming. The people went everywhere catching these, and looking for anything that might
have dropped from the royal boats.

At length the lake was all but gone, only a few of the
deepest pools remaining unexhausted.

It happened one day that a party of youngsters found
themselves on the brink of one of these pools in the very

centre of the lake. It was a rocky basin of considerable depth. Looking in, they saw at the bottom something that shone yellow in the sun. A little boy jumped in and dived for it. It was a plate of gold covered with writing. They carried it to the king. -

On one side of it stood these words:—

"Death alone from death can save.
Love is death, and so is brave.
Love can fill the deepest grave.
Love loves on beneath the wave."

Now this was enigmatical enough to the king and courtiers. But the reverse of the plate explained it a little. Its writing amounted to this:—

"If the lake should disappear, they must find the hole through which the water ran. But it would be useless to try to stop it by any ordinary means. There was but one effectual mode.—The body of a living man could alone stanch the flow. The man must give himself of his own will; and the lake must take his life as it filled. Otherwise the offering would be of no avail. If the nation could not provide one hero, it was time it should perish."

XIII

HERE I AM

This was a very disheartening revelation to the king—not that he was unwilling to sacrifice a subject, but that he was hopeless of finding a man willing to sacrifice himself. No time was to be lost, however, for the princess was lying motionless on her bed, and taking no nourishment but lake-water, which was now none of the best. Therefore the king caused the contents of the wonderful plate of gold to be published throughout the country.

No one, however, came forward.

The prince, having gone several days' journey into the forest, to consult a hermit whom he had met there on his way to Lagobel, knew nothing of the oracle till his return.

When he had acquainted himself with all the particulars, he sat down and thought,—

"She will die if I don't do it, and life would be nothing to me without her; so I shall lose nothing by doing it. And life will be pleasant to her as ever, for she will soon forget me. And there will be so much more beauty and happiness in the world!—To be sure, I shall not see it." (Here the poor prince gave a sigh.) "How lovely the lake will be in the moonlight, with that glorious creature sporting in it like a wild goddess!—It is rather hard to be drowned by inches, though. Let me see—that will be seventy inches of me to drown." (Here he tried to laugh, but could not.) "The longer the better, however," he resumed; "for can I not bargain that the princess shall be beside me all the time? So I shall see her once more, kiss her perhaps,—who knows? and die looking in her eyes. It will be no death. At least, I shall not feel it. And to see the lake filling for the beauty again!—All right! I am ready."

He kissed the princess's boot, laid it down, and hurried to the king's apartment. But feeling, as he went, that anything sentimental would be disagreeable, he resolved to carry off the whole affair with nonchalance. So he knocked at the door of the king's counting-house, where it was all but a capital crime to disturb him.

When the king heard the knock he started up, and opened the door in a rage. Seeing only the shoeblack, he drew his sword. This, I am sorry to say, was his usual mode of asserting his regality when he thought his dignity was in danger. But the prince was not in the least alarmed.

"Please your majesty, I'm your butler," said he.

"My Butler! you lying rascal? What do you mean?"

"I mean, I will cork your big bottle."

"Is the fellow mad?" bawled the king, raising the point of his sword.

"I will put a stopper—plug—what you call it, in your leaky lake, grand monarch," said the prince.

The king was in such a rage that before he could speak he had time to cool, and to reflect that it would be great waste to kill the only man who was willing to be useful in the present emergency, seeing that in the end the insolent fellow would be as dead as if he had died by his majesty's own hand.

"Oh!" said he at last, putting up his sword with difficulty, it was so long; "I am obliged to you, you young fool! Take a glass of wine?"

"No, thank you," replied the prince.

"Very well," said the king. "Would you like to run and see your parents before you make your experiment?"

"No, thank you," said the prince.

"Then we will go and look for the hole at once," said his majesty, and proceeded to call some attendants.

"Stop, please your majesty; I have a condition to make," interposed the prince.

"What!" exclaimed the king, "a condition! and with me! How dare you?"

"As you please," returned the prince, coolly. "I wish your majesty a good morning."

"You wretch! I will have you put in a sack, and stuck in the hole."

"Very well, your majesty," replied the prince, becoming a little more respectful, lest the wrath of the king should deprive him of the pleasure of dying for the princess. "But what good will that do your majesty? Please to remember that the oracle says the victim must offer himself."

"Well, you *have* offered yourself," retorted the king.

"Yes, upon one condition."

"Condition again!" roared the king, once more drawing his sword. "Begone! Somebody else will be glad enough to take the honour off your shoulders."

"Your majesty knows it will not be easy to get another to take my place."

"Well, what is your condition?" growled the king, feeling that the prince was right.

"Only this," replied the prince: "that, as I must on no account die before I am fairly drowned, and the waiting will be rather wearisome, the princess, your daughter, shall go with me, feed me with her own hands, and look at me now and then, to comfort me; for you must confess it *is* rather hard. As soon as the water is up to my eyes, she may go and be happy, and forget her poor shoeblack."

Here the prince's voice faltered, and he very nearly grew sentimental, in spite of his resolution.

"Why didn't you tell me before what your condition was? Such a fuss about nothing!" exclaimed the king.

"Do you grant it?" persisted the prince.

"Of course I do," replied the king.

"Very well. I am ready."

"Go and have some dinner, then, while I set my people to find the place."

The king ordered out his guards, and gave directions to the officers to find the hole in the lake at once. So the bed of the lake was marked out in divisions and thoroughly examined, and in an hour or so the hole was discovered. It was in the middle of a stone, near the centre of the lake, in the very pool where the golden plate had been found. It was a three-cornered hole of no great size. There was water all round the stone, but very little was flowing through the hole.

XIV

THIS IS VERY KIND OF YOU

The prince went to dress for the occasion, for he was resolved to die like a prince.

When the princess heard that a man had offered to die for her, she was so transported that she jumped off the bed, feeble as she was, and danced about the room for joy. She did not care who the man was; that was nothing to her. The hole wanted stopping; and if only a man would do, why, take one. In an hour or two more everything was ready. Her maid dressed her in haste, and they carried her to the side of the lake. When she saw it she shrieked, and covered her face with her hands. They bore her across to the stone, where they had already placed a little boat for her. The water was not deep enough to float it, but they hoped it would be, before long. They laid her on cushions, placed in the boat wines and fruits and other nice things, and stretched a canopy over all.

In a few minutes the prince appeared. The princess recognized him at once, but did not think it worth while to acknowledge him.

"Here I am," said the prince. "Put me in."

"They told me it was a shoeblack," said the princess.

"So I am," said the prince. "I blackened your little boots three times a day, because they were all I could get of you. Put me in."

The courtiers did not resent his bluntness, except by saying to each other that he was taking it out in impudence.

But how was he to be put in? The golden plate contained no instructions on this point. The prince looked at the hole, and saw but one way. He put both his legs into it, sitting on the stone and, stooping forward, covered the corner that remained open with his two hands. In this uncomfortable position he resolved to abide his fate, and turning to the people, said,—

"Now you can go."

The king had already gone home to dinner.

"Now you can go," repeated the princess after him, like a parrot.

The people obeyed her and went.

Presently a little wave flowed over the stone, and wetted one of the prince's knees. But he did not mind it much. He began to sing, and the song he sang was this:—

> "As a world that has no well,
>   Darkly bright in forest dell;
> As a world without the gleam
>   Of the downward-going stream;
> As a world without the glance
>   Of the ocean's fair expanse;
> As a world where never rain
>   Glittered on the sunny plain;—
> Such, my heart, thy world would be,
> If no love did flow in thee.
>
> "As a world without the sound
>   Of the rivulets underground;
> Or the bubbling of the spring
>   Out of darkness wandering;
> Or the mighty rush and flowing
>   Of the river's downward going;

Or the music-showers that drop
On the outspread beech's top;
Or the ocean's mighty voice,
When his lifted waves rejoice;—
Such, my soul, the world would be,
If no love did sing in thee.

"Lady, keep thy world's delight;
Keep the waters in thy sight.
Love had made me strong to go,
For thy sake, to realms below,
Where the water's shine and hum
Through the darkness never come:
Let, I pray, one thought of me
Spring, a little well, in thee;
Lest thy loveless soul be found
Like a dry and thirsty ground."

"Sing again, prince. It makes it less tedious," said the princess.

But the prince was too much overcome to sing any more, and a long pause followed.

"This is very kind of you, prince," said the princess at last, quite coolly, as she lay in the boat with her eyes shut.

"I am sorry I can't return the compliment," thought the prince; "but you are worth dying for, after all."

Again a wavelet, and another, and another flowed over the stone, and wetted both the prince's knees; but he did not speak or move. Two—three—four hours passed in this way, the princess apparently asleep, and the prince very patient. But he was much disappointed in his position, for he had none of the consolation he had hoped for.

At last he could bear it no longer.

"Princess!" said he.

But at the moment up started the princess, crying,—

"I'm afloat! I'm afloat!"

And the little boat bumped against the stone.

"Princess!" repeated the prince, encouraged by seeing her wide awake and looking eagerly at the water.

"Well?" said she, without looking round.

"Your papa promised that you should look at me, and you haven't looked at me once."

"Did he? Then I suppose I must. But I am so sleepy!"

"Sleep then, darling, and don't mind me," said the poor prince.

"Really, you are very good," replied the princess. "I think I will go to sleep again."

"Just give me a glass of wine and a biscuit first," said the prince, very humble.

"With all my heart," said the princess, and gaped as she said it.

She got the wine and the biscuit, however, and leaning over the side of the boat towards him, was compelled to look at him.

"Why, prince," she said, "you don't look well! Are you sure you don't mind it?"

"Not a bit," answered he, feeling very faint indeed. "Only I shall die before it is of any use to you, unless I have something to eat."

"There, then," said she, holding out the wine to him.

"Ah! you must feed me. I dare not move my hands. The water would run away directly."

"Good gracious!" said the princess; and she began at once to feed him with bits of biscuit and sips of wine.

As she fed him, he contrived to kiss the tips of her fingers now and then. She did not seem to mind it, one way or the other. But the prince felt better.

"Now, for your own sake, princess," said he, "I cannot let you go to sleep. You must sit and look at me, else I shall not be able to keep up."

"Well, I will do anything I can to oblige you," answered she, with condescension; and, sitting down, she did look at him, and kept looking at him with wonderful steadiness, considering all things.

The sun went down, and the moon rose, and, gush after gush, the waters were rising up the prince's body. They were up to his waist now.

"Why can't we go and have a swim?" said the princess. "There seems to be water enough just about here."

"I shall never swim more," said the prince.

"Oh, I forgot," said the princess, and was silent.

So the water grew and grew, and rose up and up on the prince. And the princess sat and looked at him. She fed him now and then. The night wore on. The waters rose and rose.

The moon rose likewise higher and higher, and shone full on the face of the dying prince. The water was up to his neck.

"Will you kiss me, princess?" said he feebly. The nonchalance was all gone now.

"Yes, I will," answered the princess, and kissed him with a long, sweet, cold kiss.

"Now," said he, with a sigh of content, "I die happy."

He did not speak again. The princess gave him some wine for the last time: he was past eating. Then she sat down again, and looked at him. The water rose and rose. It touched his chin. It touched his lower lip. It touched between his lips. He shut them hard to keep it out. The princess began to feel strange. It touched his upper lip. He breathed through his nostrils. The princess looked wild. It covered his nostrils. Her eyes looked scared, and shone strange in the moonlight. His head fell back; the water closed over it, and the bubbles of his last breath bubbled up through the water. The princess gave a shriek, and sprang into the lake.

She laid hold first of one leg, and then of the other, and pulled and tugged, but she could not move either. She stopped to take breath, and that made her think that he could not get any breath. She was frantic. She got hold of him, and held his head above the water, which was possible now his hands were no longer on the hole. But it was of no use, for he was past breathing.

Love and water brought back all her strength. She got under the water, and pulled and pulled with her whole might, till at last she got one leg out. The other easily followed. How she got him into the boat she never could tell; but when she did, she fainted away. Coming to herself, she seized the oars, kept herself steady as best she could, and rowed and rowed, though she had never rowed before. Round rocks, and over shallows, and through mud she rowed, till she got to the landing-stairs of the palace. By this time her people were on the shore, for they had heard her shriek. She made them carry the prince to her own room, and lay him in her bed, and light a fire, and send for the doctors.

"But the lake, your highness!" said the chamberlain, who, roused by the noise, came in, in his nightcap.

"Go and drown yourself in it!" she said.

This was the last rudeness of which the princess was ever

guilty; and one must allow that she had good cause to feel provoked with the lord chamberlain.

Had it been the king himself, he would have fared no better. But both he and the queen were fast asleep. And the chamberlain went back to his bed. Somehow, the doctors never came. So the princess and her old nurse were left with the prince. But the old nurse was a wise woman, and knew what to do.

They tried everything for a long time without success. The princess was nearly distracted between hope and fear, but she tried on and on, one thing after another, and everything over and over again.

At last, when they had all but given it up, just as the sun rose, the prince opened his eyes.

XV

LOOK AT THE RAIN!

The princess burst into a passion of tears, and *fell* on the floor. There she lay for an hour, and her tears never ceased. All the pent-up crying of her life was spent now. And a rain came on, such as had never been seen in that country. The sun shone all the time, and the great drops, which fell straight to the earth, shone likewise. The palace was in the heart of a rainbow. It was a rain of rubies, and sapphires, and emeralds, and topazes. The torrents poured from the mountains like molten gold; and if it had not been for its subterraneous outlet, the lake would have overflowed and inundated the country. It was full from shore to shore.

But the princess did not heed the lake. She lay on the floor and wept. And this rain within doors was far more wonderful than the rain out of doors. For when it abated a little, and she proceeded to rise, she found, to her astonishment, that she could not. At length, after many efforts, she succeeded in getting upon her feet. But she tumbled down again directly.

Hearing her fall, her old nurse uttered a yell of delight, and ran to her, screaming,—

"My darling child! she's found her gravity!"

"Oh, that's it! is it?" said the princess, rubbing her shoulder and her knee alternately. "I consider it very unpleasant. I feel as if I should be crushed to pieces."

"Hurrah!" cried the prince from the bed. "If you've come round, princess, so have I. How's the lake?"

"Brimful," answered the nurse.

"Then we're all happy."

"That we are indeed!" answered the princess, sobbing.

And there was rejoicing all over the country that rainy day. Even the babies forgot their past troubles, and danced and crowed amazingly. And the king told stories, and the queen listened to them. And he divided the money in his box, and she the honey in her pot, to all the children. And there was such jubilation as was never heard of before.

Of course the prince and princess were betrothed at once. But the princess had to learn to walk, before they could be married with any propriety. And this was not so easy at her time of life, for she could walk no more than a baby. She was always falling down and hurting herself.

"Is this the gravity you used to make so much of?" said she one day to the prince, as he raised her from the floor. "For my part, I was a great deal more comfortable without it."

"No, no, that's not it. This is it," replied the prince, as he took her up, and carried her about like a baby, kissing her all the time. "This is gravity."

"That's better," said she. "I don't mind that so much."

And she smiled the sweetest, loveliest smile in the prince's face. And she gave him one little kiss in return for all his; and he thought them overpaid, for he was beside himself with delight. I fear she complained of her gravity more than once after this, notwithstanding.

It was a long time before she got reconciled to walking. But the pain of learning it was quite counterbalanced by two things, either of which would have been sufficient consolation. The first was, that the prince himself was her teacher; and the second, that she could tumble into the lake as often as she pleased. Still, she preferred to have the prince jump in with her; and the splash they made before was nothing to the splash they made now.

The lake never sank again. In process of time, it wore the roof of the cavern quite through, and was twice as deep as before.

The only revenge the princess took upon her aunt was to tread pretty hard on her gouty toe the next time she saw her. But she was sorry for it the very next day, when she heard that the water had undermined her house, and that it had fallen in the night, burying her in its ruins; whence no one ever ventured to dig up her body. There she lies to this day.

So the prince and princess lived and were happy; and had crowns of gold, and clothes of cloth, and shoes of leather, and children of boys and girls, not one of whom was ever known, on the most critical occasion, to lose the smallest atom of his or her due proportion of gravity.

MOPSA THE FAIRY
BY JEAN INGELOW

I

ABOVE THE CLOUDS

"And can this be my own world?
　'Tis all gold and snow,
Save where scarlet waves are hurled
　Down yon gulf below."
" 'Tis thy world, 'tis my world,
　City, mead, and shore,
For he that hath his own world
　Hath many worlds more."

A boy, whom I knew very well, was once going through a
meadow which was full of buttercups. The nurse and his baby
sister were with him; and when they got to an old hawthorn,
which grew in the hedge and was covered with blossom, they
all sat down in its shade, and the nurse took out three slices
of plum cake, gave one to each of the children and kept one
for herself.

While the boy was eating he observed that this hedge was
very high and thick, and that there was a great hollow in the
trunk of the old thorn tree, and he heard a twittering, as if
there was a nest somewhere inside; so he thrust his head in,
twisted himself round and looked up.

It was a very great thorn tree, and the hollow was so large
that two or three boys could have stood upright in it; and
when he got used to the dim light in that brown, still place,
he saw that a good way above his head there was a nest—
rather a curious one too, for it was as large as a pair of
blackbirds would have built—and yet it was made of fine
white wool and delicate bits of moss; in short, it was like a
goldfinch's nest magnified three times.

Just then he thought he heard some little voices cry, "Jack!
Jack!" His baby sister was asleep, and the nurse was reading a
story book, so it could not have been either of them who

called. "I must get in here," said the boy. "I wish this hole was larger." So he began to wriggle and twist himself through, and just as he pulled in his last foot he looked up, and three heads which had been peeping over the edge of the nest suddenly popped down again.

"Those heads had no beaks, I am sure," said Jack, and he stood on tiptoe and poked in one of his fingers. "And the things have no feathers," he continued; so, the hollow being rather rugged, he managed to climb up and look in.

His eyes were not used yet to the dim light; but he was sure those things were not birds—no. He poked them, and they took no notice; but when he snatched one of them out of the nest it gave a loud squeak, and said: "Oh, don't, Jack!" as plainly as possible, upon which he was so frightened that he lost his footing, dropped the thing and slipped down himself. Luckily he was not hurt, nor the thing either; he could see it quite plainly now: it was creeping about like rather an old baby, and had on a little frock and pinafore.

"It's a fairy!" exclaimed Jack to himself. "How curious! and this must be a fairy's nest. Oh, how angry the old mother will be if this little thing creeps away and gets out of the hole!" So he looked down. "Oh, the hole is on the other side," he said; and he turned round, but the hole was not on the other side; it was not on any side; it must have closed up all on a sudden, while he was looking into the nest, for; look whichever way he would, there was no hole at all, excepting a very little one high up over the nest, which let in a very small sunbeam.

Jack was very much astonished, but he went on eating his cake, and was so delighted to see the young fairy climb up the side of the hollow and scramble again into her nest that he laughed heartily; upon which all the nestlings popped up their heads and, showing their pretty white teeth, pointed at the slice of cake.

"Well," said Jack, "I may have to stay inside here for a long time, and I have nothing to eat but this cake; however, your mouths are very small, so you shall have a piece"; and he broke off a small piece and put it into the nest, climbing up to see them eat it.

These young fairies were a long time dividing and munching the cake, and before they had finished it began to be rather dark, for a black cloud came over and covered the little sunbeam. At the same time the wind rose and rocked the boughs, and made the old tree creak and tremble. Then there was thunder and rain, and the little fairies were so frightened that they got out of the nest and crept into Jack's pockets. One got into each waistcoat pocket, and the other two were very comfortable, for he took out his handkerchief and made room for them in the pocket of his jacket.

It got darker and darker, till at last Jack could only just see the hole, and it seemed to be a very long way off. Every time he looked at it, it was farther off, and at last he saw a thin crescent moon shining through it.

"I am sure it cannot be night yet," he said; and he took out one of the fattest of the young fairies and held it up towards the hole.

"Look at that," said he; "what is to be done now? The hole is so far off that it's night up there, and down here I haven't done eating my lunch."

"Well," answered the young fairy, "then why don't you whistle?"

Jack was surprised to hear her speak in this sensible manner, and in the light of the moon he looked at her very attentively.

"When first I saw you in the nest," said he, "you had a pinafore on, and now you have a smart little apron, with lace round it."

"That is because I am much older now," said the fairy; "we never take such a long time to grow up as you do."

"But your pinafore?" said Jack.

"Turned into an apron, of course," replied the fairy, "just as your velvet jacket will turn into a tail-coat when you are old enough."

"It won't," said Jack.

"Yes, it will," answered the fairy, with an air of superior wisdom. "Don't argue with me; I am older now than you are—nearly grown up in fact. Put me into your pocket again, and whistle as loudly as you can."

Jack laughed, put her in, and pulled out another. "Worse and worse," he said; "why, this was a boy fairy, and now he has a moustache and a sword, and looks as fierce as possible!"

"I think I heard my sister tell you to whistle?" said this fairy very sternly.

"Yes, she did," said Jack. "Well, I suppose I had better do it." So he whistled very loudly indeed.

"Why did you leave off so soon?" said another of them, peeping out.

"Why, if you wish to know," answered Jack, "it was because I thought something took hold of my legs."

"Ridiculous child," cried the last of the four, "how do you think you are ever to get out, if she doesn't take hold of your legs?"

Jack thought he would rather have done a long-division sum than have been obliged to whistle; but he could not help doing it when they told him, and he felt something take hold of his legs again, and then give him a jerk, which hoisted him on to its back, where he sat astride, and wondered whether the thing was a pony; but it was not, for he presently observed that it had a very slender neck, and then that it was covered with feathers. It was a large bird, and he presently found that they were rising towards the hole, which had become so very far off, and in a few minutes she dashed through the hole, with Jack on her back and all the fairies in his pockets.

It was so dark that he could see nothing, and he twined his arms round the bird's neck, to hold on, upon which this agreeable fowl told him not to be afraid, and said she hoped he was comfortable.

"I should be more comfortable," replied Jack, "if I knew how I could get home again. I don't wish to go home just yet, for I want to see where we are flying to, but papa and mamma will be frightened if I never do."

"Oh no," replied the albatross (for she was an albatross), "you need not be at all afraid about that. When boys go to Fairyland, their parents never are uneasy about them."

"Really?" exclaimed Jack.

"Quite true," replied the albatross.

"And so we are going to Fairyland?" exclaimed Jack. "How delightful!"

"Yes," said the albatross; "the back way, mind; we are only going the back way. You could go in two minutes by the usual route; but these young fairies want to go before they are summoned, and therefore you and I are taking them." And she continued to fly on in the dark sky for a very long time.

"They seem to be all fast asleep," said Jack.

"Perhaps they will sleep till we come to the wonderful

river," replied the albatross; and just then she flew with a great bump against something that met her in the air.

"What craft is this that hangs out no light?" said a gruff voice.

"I might ask the same question of you," answered the albatross sullenly.

"I'm only a poor Will-o'-the-wisp," replied the voice, "and you know very well that I have but a lantern to show." Thereupon a lantern became visible, and Jack saw by the light of it a man who looked old and tired, and he was so transparent that you could see through him, lantern and all.

"I hope I have not hurt you, William," said the albatross; "I will light up immediately. Good night."

"Good night," answered the Will-o'-the-wisp. "I am going down as fast as I can; the storm blew me up, and I am never easy excepting in my native swamps."

Jack might have taken more notice of Will if the albatross had not begun to light up. She did it in this way. First one of her eyes began to gleam with a beautiful green light, which cast its rays far and near, and then, when it was as bright as a lamp, the other eye began to shine, and the light of that eye was red. In short, she was lighted up just like a vessel at sea.

Jack was so happy that he hardly knew which to look at first, there really were so many remarkable things.

"They snore," said the albatross; "they are very fast asleep, and before they wake I should like to talk to you a little."

She meant that the fairies snored, and so they did, in Jack's pockets.

"My name," continued the albatross, "is Jenny. Do you think you shall remember that? Because when you are in Fairyland and want someone to take you home again, and call 'Jenny,' I shall be able to come to you; and I shall come with pleasure, for I like boys better than fairies."

"Thank you," said Jack. "Oh yes, I shall remember your name, it is such a very easy one."

"If it is in the night that you want me, just look up," continued the albatross, "and you will see a green and a red spark moving in the air; you will then call Jenny, and I will come; but remember that I cannot come unless you do call me."

"Very well," said Jack; but he was not attending, because there was so much to be seen.

In the first place all the stars excepting a few large ones were gone, and they looked frightened; and as it got lighter one after the other seemed to give a little start in the blue sky and go out. And then Jack looked down and saw, as he thought, a great country covered with very jagged snow mountains with astonishingly sharp peaks. Here and there he saw a very deep lake—at least he thought it was a lake; but while he was admiring the mountains there came an enormous crack between two of the largest, and he saw the sun come rolling up among them, and it seemed to be almost smothered.

"Why, those are clouds!" exclaimed Jack. "And, oh, how rosy they have all turned! I thought they were mountains."

"Yes, they are clouds," said the albatross; and then they turned gold colour; and next they began to plunge and tumble, and every one of the peaks put on a glittering crown; and next they broke themselves to pieces and began to drift away. In fact Jack had been out all night, and now it was morning.

II

CAPTAIN JACK

It has been our lot to sail with many captains, not one of whom is fit to be a patch on your back.

Letter of the Ship's
Company of H.M.S.S. "Royalist"
to Captain W. T. Bate.

All this time the albatross kept dropping down and down like a stone till Jack was quite out of breath, and they fell or flew, whichever you like to call it, straight through one of the great chasms which he had thought were lakes, and he looked down as he sat on the bird's back to see what the world is like when you hang a good way above it at sunrise.

It was a very beautiful sight; the sheep and lambs were still fast asleep on the green hills, and the sea birds were asleep in long rows upon the ledges of the cliffs, with their heads under their wings.

"Are those young fairies awake yet?" asked the albatross.

"As sound asleep as ever," answered Jack; "but, Albatross, is not that the sea which lies under us? You are a sea bird, I know, but I am not a sea boy, and I cannot live in the water."

"Yes, that is the sea," answered the albatross. "Don't you observe that it is covered with ships?"

"I see boats and vessels," answered Jack, "and all their sails are set, but they cannot sail because there is no wind."

"The wind never does blow in this great bay," said the bird; "and those ships would all lie there becalmed till they dropped to pieces if one of them was not wanted now and then to go up the wonderful river."

"But how did they come there?" asked Jack.

"Some of them had captains who ill-used their cabin-boys, some were pirate ships and others were going out on evil errands. The consequence was that when they chanced to sail

241

within this great bay they got becalmed; the fairies came and picked all the sailors out and threw them into the water; they then took away the flags and pennons to make their best coats of, threw the ship-biscuits and other provisions to the fishes and set all the sails. Many ships which are supposed by men to have foundered lie becalmed in this quiet sea. Look at those five grand ones with high poops: they are moored close together, they were part of the Spanish Armada; and those open boats with blue sails belonged to the Romans, they sailed with Caesar when he invaded Britain."

By this time the albatross was hovering about among the vessels, making choice of one to take Jack and the fairies up the wonderful river.

"It must not be a large one," she said, "for the river in some places is very shallow."

Jack would have liked very much to have a fine three-master, all to himself; but then he considered that he did not know anything about sails and rigging, he thought it would be just as well to be contented with whatever the albatross might choose, so he let her set him down in a beautiful little open boat, with a great carved figurehead to it. There he seated himself in great state, and the albatross perched herself on the next bench and faced him.

"You remember my name?" asked the albatross.

"Oh yes," said Jack; but he was not attending—he was thinking what a fine thing it was to have such a curious boat all to himself.

"That's well," answered the bird; "then, in the next place, are those fairies awake yet?"

"No, they are not," said Jack; and he took them out of his pockets and laid them down in a row before the albatross.

"They are certainly asleep," said the bird. "Put them away again, and take care of them. Mind you don't lose any of them, for I really don't know what will happen if you do. Now I have one thing more to say to you, and that is, are you hungry?"

"Rather," said Jack.

"Then," replied the albatross, "as soon as you feel *very* hungry, lie down in the bottom of the boat and go to sleep. You will dream that you see before you a roasted fowl, some new potatoes and an apple pie. Mind you don't eat too much

in your dream, or you will be sorry for it when you wake.
That is all. Goodbye! I must go."

Jack put his arms round the neck of the bird and hugged
her; then she spread her magnificent wings and sailed slowly
away. At first he felt very lonely, but in a few minutes he
forgot that, because the little boat began to swim so fast.

She was not sailing, for she had no sail, and he was not
rowing, for he had no oars; so I am obliged to call her motion
swimming, because I don't know of a better word. In less
than a quarter of an hour they passed close under the bows of
a splendid three-decker, a seventy-gun ship. The gannets
who live in those parts had taken possession of her, and she
was so covered with nests that you could not have walked one
step on her deck without treading on them. The father birds
were aloft in the rigging, or swimming in the warm green
sea, and they made such a clamour when they saw Jack that
they nearly woke the fairies—nearly, but not quite, for the
little things turned round in Jack's pockets, and sneezed, and
began to snore again.

Then the boat swam past a fine brig. Some sea fairies had
just flung her cargo overboard, and were playing at leapfrog
on deck. These were not at all like Jack's own fairies; they
were about the same height and size as himself, and they had
brown faces, and red flannel shirts and red caps on. A large
fleet of the pearly nautilus was collected close under the
vessel's lee. The little creatures were feasting on what the sea
fairies had thrown overboard, and Jack's boat, in its eagerness
to get on, went plunging through them so roughly that several were capsized. Upon this the brown sea fairies looked
over, and called out angrily: "Boat ahoy!" and the boat stopped.

"Tell that boat of yours to mind what she is about," said the
fairy sea-captain to Jack.

Jack touched his cap, and said: "Yes, sir," and then called
out to his boat: "You ought to be ashamed of yourself, running down these little live fishing-vessels so carelessly. Go at
a more gentle pace."

So it swam more slowly; and Jack, being by this time
hungry, curled himself up in the bottom of the boat and fell
asleep.

He dreamt directly about a fowl and some potatoes, and he
ate a wing, and then he ate a merrythought, and then somebody said to him that he had better not eat any more, but he

did, he ate another wing; and presently an apple pie came, and he ate some of that, and then he ate some more, and then he immediately woke.

"Now that bird told me not to eat too much," said Jack, "and yet I have done it. I never felt so full in my life," and for more than half an hour he scarcely noticed anything.

At last he lifted up his head, and saw straight before him two great brown cliffs, and between them flowed in the wonderful river. Other rivers flow out, but this river flowed in, and took with it far into the land dolphins, swordfish, mullet, sunfish and many other strange creatures; and that is one reason why it was called the magic river, or the wonderful river.

At first it was rather wide, and Jack was alarmed to see what multitudes of soldiers stood on either side to guard the banks and prevent any person from landing.

He wondered how he should get the fairies on shore. However, in about an hour the river became much narrower, and then Jack saw that the guards were not real soldiers, but rose-coloured flamingoes. There they stood in long regiments among the reeds, and never stirred. They are the only foot-soldiers the fairies have in their pay; they are very fierce, and never allow anything but a fairy ship to come up the river.

They guarded the banks for miles and miles, many thousands of them, standing a little way into the water among the flags and rushes; but at last there were no more reeds and no soldier guards, for the stream became narrower, and flowed between such steep rocks that no one could possibly have climbed them.

III

WINDING-UP TIME

"Wake, baillie, wake! the crafts are out;
  Wake!" said the knight. "Be quick!
For high street, bystreet, over the town
  They fight with poker and stick."
Said the squire, "A fight so fell was ne'er
  In all thy bailliewick."
What said the old clock in the tower?
    "Tick, tick tick!"

"Wake, daughter, wake! the hour draws on;
  Wake!" quoth the dame. "Be quick!
The meats are set, the guests are coming,
  The fiddler's waxing his stick."
She said, "The bridegroom waiting and waiting
  To see thy face is sick."
What said the new clock in her bower?
    "Tick, tick, tick!"

Jack looked at these hot brown rocks, first on the left bank
and then on the right, till he was quite tired; but at last the
shore on the right bank became flat, and he saw a beautiful
little bay, where the water was still and where grass grew
down to the brink.

He was so much pleased at this change that he cried out
hastily: "Oh, how I wish my boat would swim into that bay
and let me land!" He had no sooner spoken than the boat
altered her course, as if somebody had been steering her, and
began to make for the bay as fast as she could go.

"How odd!" thought Jack. "I wonder whether I ought to
have spoken; for the boat certainly did not intend to come
into this bay. However, I think I will let her alone now, for I
certainly do wish very much to land here."

As they drew towards the strand the water got so shallow that you could see crabs and lobsters walking about at the bottom. At last the boat's keel grated on the pebbles; and just as Jack began to think of jumping on shore he saw two little old women approaching and gently driving a white horse before them.

The horse had panniers, one on each side; and when his feet were in the water he stood still; and Jack said to one of the old women: "Will you be so kind as to tell me whether this is Fairyland?"

"What does he say?" asked one old woman of the other.

"I asked if this was Fairyland," repeated Jack, for he thought the first old woman might have been deaf. She was very handsomely dressed in a red satin gown, and did not look in the least like a washerwoman, though it afterwards appeared that she was one.

"He says 'Is this Fairyland?' " she replied; and the other, who had a blue satin cloak, answered: "Oh, does he?" and then began to empty the panniers of many small blue and pink and scarlet shirts, and coats, and stockings; and when they had made them into two little heaps they knelt down and began to wash them in the river, taking no notice of him whatever.

Jack stared at them. They were not much taller than himself, and they were not taking the slightest care of their handsome clothes; then he looked at the old white horse, who was hanging his head over the lovely clear water with a very discontented air.

At last the blue washerwoman said: "I shall leave off now; I've got a pain in my works."

"Do," said the other. "We'll go home and have a cup of tea." Then she glanced at Jack, who was still sitting in the boat, and said: "Can you strike?"

"I can if I choose," replied Jack, a little astonished at this speech. And the red and blue washerwomen wrung out the clothes, put them again into the panniers and, taking the old horse by the bridle, began gently to lead him away.

"I have a great mind to land," thought Jack. "I should not wonder at all if this is Fairyland. So, as the boat came here to please me, I shall ask it to stay where it is, in case I should want it again."

So he sprang ashore, and said to the boat: "Stay just where

you are, will you?" and he ran after the old women, calling to them:

"Is there any law to prevent my coming into your country?"

"Wo!" cried the red-coated old woman, and the horse stopped, while the blue-coated woman repeated: "Any law? No, not that I know of; but if you are a stranger here you had better look out."

"Why?" asked Jack.

"You don't suppose, do you," she answered, "that our Queen will wind up strangers?"

While Jack was wondering what she meant, the other said:

"I shouldn't wonder if he goes eight days. Gee!" and the horse went on.

"No, wo!" said the other.

"No, no. Gee! I tell you," cried the first.

Upon this, to Jack's intense astonishment, the old horse stopped, and said, speaking through his nose:

"Now, then, which is it to be? I'm willing to gee, and I'm agreeable to wo; but what's a fellow to do when you say them both together?"

"Why, he talks!" exclaimed Jack.

"It's because he's got a cold in his head," observed one of the washerwomen; "he always talks when he's got a cold, and there's no pleasing him; whatever you say, he's not satisfied. Gee, Boney, do!"

"Gee it is, then," said the horse, and began to jog on.

"He spoke again!" said Jack, upon which the horse laughed, and Jack was quite alarmed.

"It appears that your horses don't talk?" observed the blue-coated woman.

"Never," answered Jack; "they can't."

"You mean they won't," observed the old horse; and though he spoke the words of mankind it was not in a voice like theirs. Still Jack felt that his was just the natural tone for a horse, and that it did not arise only from the length of his nose. "You'll find out some day, perhaps," he continued, "whether horses can talk or not."

"Shall I?" said Jack very earnestly.

"They'll TELL," proceeded the white horse. "I wouldn't be you when they tell how you've used them."

"Have you been ill used?" said Jack, in an anxious tone.

"Yes, yes, of course he has," one of the women broke in;

"but he has come here to get all right again. This is a very wholesome country for horses; isn't it, Boney?"

"Yes," said the horse.

"Well, then, jog on, there's a dear," continued the old woman. "Why, you will be young again soon, you know— young, and gamesome, and handsome; you'll be quite a colt by and by, and then we shall set you free to join your companions in the happy meadows."

The old horse was so comforted by this kind speech that he pricked up his ears and quickened his pace considerably.

"He was shamefully used," observed one washerwoman. "Look at him, how lean he is! You can see all his ribs."

"Yes," said the other, as if apologizing for the poor old horse. "He gets low-spirited when he thinks of all he has gone through; but he is a vast deal better already than he was. He used to live in London; his master always carried a long whip to beat him with, and never spoke civilly to him."

"London!" exclaimed Jack. "Why, that is in my country. How did the horse get here?"

"That's no business of yours," answered one of the women. "But I can tell you he came because he was wanted, which is more than you are."

"You let him alone," said the horse in a querulous tone. "I don't bear any malice."

"No; he has a good disposition, has Boney," observed the red old woman. "Pray, are you a boy?"

"Yes," said Jack.

"A real boy, that wants no winding up?" inquired the old woman.

"I don't know what you mean," answered Jack; "but I am a real boy, certainly."

"Ah!" she replied. "Well, I thought you were, by the way Boney spoke to you. How frightened you must be! I wonder what will be done to all your people for driving, and working, and beating so many beautiful creatures to death every year that comes? They'll have to pay for it some day, you may depend."

Jack was a little alarmed, and answered that he had never been unkind himself to horses, and he was glad that Boney bore no malice.

"They worked him, and often drove him about all night in the miserable streets, and never let him have so much as a canter in a green field," said one of the women; "but he'll be all right now, only he has to begin at the wrong end."

"What do you mean?" said Jack.

"Why, in this country," answered the old woman, "they begin by being terribly old and stiff, and they seem miserable and jaded at first, but by degrees they get young again, as you heard me reminding him."

"Indeed," said Jack; "and do you like that?"

"It has nothing to do with me," she answered. "We are only here to take care of all the creatures that men have ill used. While they are sick and old, which they are when first they come to us—after they are dead, you know—we take care of them, and gradually bring them up to be young and happy again."

"This must be a very nice country to live in then," said Jack.

"For horses it is," said the old lady significantly.

"Well," said Jack, "it does seem very full of haystacks certainly, and all the air smells of fresh grass."

At this moment they came to a beautiful meadow, and the old horse stopped and, turning to the blue-coated woman, said: "Faxa, I think I could fancy a handful of clover." Upon this Faxa snatched Jack's cap off his head, and in a very active manner jumped over a little ditch, and gathering some clover, presently brought it back full, handing it to the old horse with great civility.

"You shouldn't be in such a hurry," observed the old horse; "your weights will be running down some day, if you don't mind."

"It's all zeal," observed the red-coated woman.

Just then a little man, dressed like a groom, came running up, out of breath. "Oh, here you are, Dow!" he exclaimed to the red-coated woman. "Come along, will you? Lady Betty wants you; it's such a hot day, and nobody, she says, can fan her so well as you can."

The red-coated woman, without a word, went off with the groom, and Jack thought he would go with them, for this Lady Betty could surely tell him whether the country was called Fairyland, or whether he must get into his boat and go farther. He did not like either to hear the way in which Faxa and Dow talked about their works and their weights; so he asked Faxa to give him his cap, which she did, and he heard a curious sort of little ticking noise as he came close to her, which startled him.

"Oh, this must be Fairyland, I am sure," thought Jack, "for in my country our pulses beat quite differently from that."

"Well," said Faxa, rather sharply, "do you find any fault with the way I go?"

"No," said Jack, a little ashamed of having listened. "I think you walk beautifully; your steps are so regular."

"She's machine-made," observed the old horse, in a melancholy voice, and with a deep sigh. "In the largest magnifying glass you'll hardly find the least fault with her chain. She's not like the goods they turn out in Clerkenwell."

Jack was more and more startled, and so glad to get his cap and run after the groom and Dow to find Lady Betty, that he might be with ordinary human beings again; but when he got up to them he found that Lady Betty was a beautiful brown mare! She was lying in a languid and rather affected attitude, with a load of fresh hay before her, and two attendants, one of whom stood holding a parasol over her head, while the other was fanning her.

"I'm so glad you are come, my good Dow," said the brown mare. "Don't you think I am strong enough today to set off for the happy meadows?"

"Well," said Dow, "I'm afraid not yet; you must remember that it is no use your leaving us till you have quite got over the effects of the fall."

Just then Lady Betty observed Jack, and said: "Take that boy away; he reminds me of a jockey."

The attentive groom instantly started forward, but Jack was too nimble for him; he ran and ran with all his might, and only wished he had never left the boat. But still he heard the groom behind him; and in fact the groom caught him at last, and held him so fast that struggling was no use at all.

"You young rascal!" he exclaimed, as he recovered breath. "How you do run! It's enough to break your mainspring."

"What harm did I do?" asked Jack. "I was only looking at the mare."

"Harm!" exclaimed the groom. "Harm, indeed! Why, you reminded her of a jockey. It's enough to hold her back, poor thing!—and we trying so hard, too, to make her forget what a cruel end she came to in the old world."

"You need not hold me so tightly," said Jack. "I shall not

run away again; but," he added, "if this is Fairyland, it is not half such a nice country as I expected."

"Fairyland!" exclaimed the groom, stepping back with surprise. "Why, what made you think of such a thing? This is only one of the border countries, where things are set right again that people have caused to go wrong in the world. The world, you know, is what men and women call their own home."

"I know," said Jack; "and that's where I came from." Then, as the groom seemed no longer to be angry, he went on: "And I wish you would tell me about Lady Betty."

"She was a beautiful fleet creature, of the racehorse breed," said the groom; "and she won silver cups for her master, and then they made her run a steeplechase, which frightened her, but still she won it; and then they made her run another, and she cleared some terribly high hurdles, and many gates and ditches, till she came to an awful one, and at first she would not take it, but her rider spurred and beat her till she tried. It was beyond her powers, and she fell and broke her forelegs. Then they shot her. After she had died that miserable death we had her here, to make her all right again."

"Is this the only country where you set things right?" asked Jack.

"Certainly not," answered the groom; "they lie about in all directions. Why, you might wander for years and never come to the end of this one."

"I am afraid I shall not find the one I am looking for," said Jack, "if your countries are so large."

"I don't think our world is much larger than yours," answered the groom. "But come along; I hear the bell, and we are a good way from the palace."

Jack, in fact, heard the violent ringing of a bell at some distance; and when the groom began to run, he ran beside him, for he thought he should like to see the palace. As they ran, people gathered from all sides—fields, cottages, mills—till at last there was a little crowd, among whom Jack saw Dow and Faxa, and they were all making for a large house, the wide door of which was standing open. Jack stood with the crowd and peeped in. There was a woman sitting inside upon a rocking-chair, a tall, large woman, with a gold-coloured gown on, and beside her stood a table, covered with things that looked like keys.

"What is that woman doing?" said he to Faxa, who was standing close to him.

"Winding us up, to be sure," answered Faxa. "You don't suppose, surely, that we can go for ever?"

"Extraordinary!" said Jack. "Then are you wound up every evening, like watches?"

"Unless we have misbehaved ourselves," she answered; "and then she lets us run down."

"And what then?"

"What then?" repeated Faxa. "Why, then we have to stop and stand against a wall, till she is pleased to forgive us, and let our friends carry us in to be set going again."

Jack looked in, and saw the people pass in and stand close by the woman. One after the other she took by the chin with her left hand, and with her right hand found a key that pleased her. It seemed to Jack that there was a tiny keyhole in the back of their heads, and that she put the key in and wound them up.

"You must take your turn with the others," said the groom.

"There's no keyhole in my head," said Jack; "besides, I do not want any woman to wind me up."

"But you must do as others do," he persisted; "and if you have no keyhole, our Queen can easily have one made, I should think."

"Make one in my head!" exclaimed Jack. "She shall do no such thing."

"We shall see," said Faxa quietly. And Jack was so frightened that he set off, and ran back towards the river with all his might. Many of the people called to him to stop, but they could not run after him, because they wanted winding up. However, they would certainly have caught him if he had not been very quick, for before he got to the river he heard behind him the footsteps of those who had been first attended to by the Queen, and he had only just time to spring into the boat when they reached the edge of the water.

No sooner was he on board than the boat swung round, and got again into the middle of the stream; but he could not feel safe till not only was there a long reach of water between him and the shore, but till he had gone so far down river that the beautiful bay had passed out of sight and the sun was going down. By this time he began to feel very tired and sleepy; so, having looked at his fairies, and found that they were all safe and fast asleep, he laid down in the bottom of the boat, and fell into a doze, and then into a dream.

IV

BEES AND OTHER FELLOW CREATURES

The dove laid some little sticks,
    Then began to coo;
The gnat took his trumpet up
    To play the day through;
The pie chattered soft and long—
    But that she always does;
The bee did all he had to do,
    And only said "Buzz."

When Jack at length opened his eyes, he found that it was night, for the full moon was shining; but it was not at all a dark night, for he could see distinctly some black birds that looked like ravens. They were sitting in a row on the edge of the boat.

Now that he had fairies in his pockets he could understand bird-talk, and he heard one of these ravens saying: "There is no meat so tender; I wish I could pick their little eyes out."

"Yes," said another, "fairies are delicate eating indeed. We must speak Jack fair if we want to get at them." And she heaved up a deep sigh.

Jack lay still, and thought he had better pretend to be asleep; but they soon noticed that his eyes were open, and one of them presently walked up his leg and bowed, and asked if he was hungry.

Jack said: "No."

"No more am I," replied the raven; "not at all hungry." Then she hopped off his leg, and Jack sat up.

"And how are the sweet fairies that my young master is taking to their home?" asked another of the ravens. "I hope they are safe in my young master's pockets?"

Jack felt in his pockets. Yes, they were all safe; but he did not take any of them out, lest the ravens should snatch at them.

"Eh?" continued the raven, pretending to listen. "Did this dear young gentleman say that the fairies were asleep?"

"It doesn't amuse me to talk about fairies," said Jack; "but if you would explain some of the things in this country that I cannot make out, I should be very glad."

"What things?" asked the blackest of the ravens.

"Why," said Jack, "I see a full moon lying down there among the water-flags, and just going to set, and there is a half-moon overhead plunging among those great grey clouds, and just this moment I saw a thin crescent moon peeping out between the branches of that tree."

"Well," said all the ravens at once, "did the young master never see a crescent moon in the men and women's world?"

"Oh yes," said Jack.

"Did he never see a full moon?" asked the ravens.

"Yes, of course," said Jack; "but they are the same moon. I could never see all three of them at the same time."

The ravens were very much surprised at this, and one of them said:

"If my young master did not see the moons it must have been because he didn't look. Perhaps my young master slept in a room, and had only one window; if so, he couldn't see all the sky at once."

"I tell you, Raven," said Jack, laughing, "that I KNOW there is never more than one moon in my country, and sometimes there is no moon at all!"

Upon this all the ravens hung down their heads, and looked very much ashamed; for there is nothing that birds hate so much as to be laughed at, and they believed that Jack was saying this to mock them, and that he knew what they had come for. So first one and then another hopped to the other end of the boat and flew away, till at last there was only one left, and she appeared to be out of spirits, and did not speak again till he spoke to her.

"Raven," said Jack, "there's something very cold and slippery lying at the bottom of the boat. I touched it just now, and I don't like it at all."

"It's a water-snake," said the raven, and she stooped and picked up a long thing with her beak, which she threw out, and then looked over. "The water swarms with them, wicked, murderous creatures; they smell the young fairies, and they want to eat them."

Jack was so thrown off his guard that he snatched one fairy out, just to make sure that it was safe. It was the one with the moustache; and, alas! in one instant the raven flew at it, got it out of his hand and pecked off its head before it had time to wake or Jack to rescue it. Then, as she slowly rose, she croaked, and said to Jack: "You'll catch it for this, my young master!" and she flew to the bough of a tree, where she finished eating the fairy, and threw his little empty coat into the river.

On this Jack began to cry bitterly, and to think what a foolish boy he had been. He was the more sorry because he did not know that poor little fellow's name. But he had heard the others calling by name to their companions, and very grand names they were too. One was Jovinian—he was a very fierce-looking gentleman; the other two were Roxaletta and Mopsa.

Presently, however, Jack forgot to be unhappy, for two of the moons went down, and then the sun rose, and he was delighted to find that however many moons there might be, there was only one sun, even in the country of the wonderful river.

So on and on they went; but the river was very wide and the waves were boisterous. On the right brink was a thick forest of trees, with such heavy foliage that a little way off they looked like a bank, green and smooth and steep; but as the light became clearer Jack could see here and there the great stems, and see creatures like foxes, wild boars and deer come stealing down to drink in the river.

It was very hot here; not at all like the spring weather he had left behind. And as the low sunbeams shone into Jack's face he said hastily, without thinking of what would occur: "I wish I might land among those lovely glades on the left bank."

No sooner said than the boat began to make for the left bank, and the nearer they got towards it the more beautiful it became; but also the more stormy were the reaches of water they had to traverse.

A lovely country indeed! It sloped gently down to the water's edge, and beautiful trees were scattered over it, soft mossy grass grew everywhere, great old laburnum trees stretched their boughs down in patches over the water, and higher up camellias, almost as large as hawthorns, grew together and mingled their red and white flowers.

The country was not so open as a park—it was more like a half-cleared woodland; but there was a wide space just where the boat was steering for that had no trees, only a few flowering shrubs. Here groups of strange-looking people were bustling about, and there were shrill fifes sounding, and drums.

Farther back he saw rows of booths or tents under the shade of the trees.

In another place some people dressed like gipsies had made fires of sticks just at the skirts of the woodland, and were boiling their pots. Some of these had very gaudy tilted carts, hung all over with goods, such as baskets, brushes, mats, little glasses, pottery and beads.

It seemed to be a kind of fair, to which people had gathered from all parts; but there was not one house to be seen. All the goods were either hung upon the trees or collected in strange-looking tents.

The people were not all of the same race; indeed, he thought the only human beings were the gipsies, for the folks who had tents were no taller than himself.

How hot it was that morning! and as the boat pushed itself into a little creek, and made its way among the beds of yellow and purple iris which skirted the brink, what a crowd of dragon-flies and large butterflies rose from them!

"Stay where you are!" cried Jack to the boat; and at that instant such a splendid moth rose slowly that he sprang on shore after it, and quite forgot the fair and the people in his desire to follow it.

The moth settled on a great red honey-flower, and he stole up to look at it. As large as a swallow, it floated on before him. Its wings were nearly black, and they had spots of gold on them.

When it rose again Jack ran after it, till he found himself close to the rows of tents where the brown people stood; and they began to cry out to him: "What'll you buy? what'll you buy, sir?" and they crowded about him, so that he soon lost sight of the moth, and forgot everything else in his surprise at the booths.

They were full of splendid things—clocks and musical boxes, strange china ornaments, embroidered slippers, red caps and many kinds of splendid silks and small carpets. In other booths were swords and dirks, glittering with jewels; and the chatter of the people when they talked together was not in a language that Jack could understand.

Some of the booths were square, and evidently made of common canvas, for when you went into them and the sun shone you could distinctly see the threads.

But scattered a little farther on in groups were some round tents which were far more curious. They were open on all sides, and consisted only of a thick canopy overhead, which was supported by one beautiful round pillar in the middle.

Outside, the canopy was white or brownish; but when Jack stood under these tents he saw that they were lined with splendid flutings of brown or pink silk—what looked like silk, at least, for it was impossible to be sure whether these were real tents or gigantic mushrooms.

They varied in size, also, as mushrooms do, and in shape: some were large enough for twenty people to stand under them, and had flat tops with a brown lining; others had dome-shaped roofs; these were lined with pink, and would only shelter six or seven.

The people who sold in these tents were as strange as their neighbours; each had a little high cap on his head, in shape just like a beehive, and it was made of straw, and had a little hole in front. In fact Jack very soon saw bees flying in and out, and it was evident that these people had their honey made on the premises. They were chiefly selling country produce. They had cheeses so large as to reach to their waists, and the women trundled them along as boys do their hoops. They sold a great many kinds of seed too, in wooden bowls, and cakes and good things to eat, such as gilt gingerbread. Jack bought some of this, and found it very nice indeed. But when he took out his money to pay for it the little man looked rather strangely at it, and turned it over with an air of disgust. Then Jack saw him hand it to his wife, who also seemed to dislike it; and presently Jack observed that they followed him about, first on one side, then on the other. At last the little woman slipped her hand into his pocket, and Jack, putting his hand in directly, found his sixpence had been returned.

"Why, you've given me back my money!" he said.

The little woman put her hands behind her. "I do not like it," she said; "it's dirty; at least, it's not new."

"No, it's not new," said Jack, a good deal surprised, "but it is a good sixpence."

"The bees don't like it," continued the little woman. "They like things to be neat and new, and that sixpence is bent."

"What shall I give you then?" said Jack.

The good little woman laughed and blushed. "This young gentleman has a beautiful whistle round his neck," she observed politely, but did not ask for it.

Jack had a dog-whistle, so he took it off and gave it to her.

"Thank you, for the bees," she said. "They love to be called home when we've collected flowers for them."

So she made a pretty little curtsy, and went away to her customers.

There were some very strange creatures also, about the same height as Jack, who had no tents, and seemed there to buy, not to sell. Yet they looked poorer than the other folks and they were also very cross and discontented; nothing pleased them. Their clothes were made of moss, and their mantles of feathers; and they talked in a queer whistling tone of voice, and carried their skinny little children on their backs and on their shoulders.

They were treated with great respect by the people in the tents; and when Jack asked his friend to whom he had given the whistle what they were, and where they got so much money as they had, she replied that they lived over the hills, and were afraid to come in their best clothes. They were rich and powerful at home, and they came shabbily dressed, and behaved humbly, lest their enemies should envy them. It was very dangerous, she said, to fairies to be envied.

Jack wanted to listen to their strange whistling talk, but he could not for the noise and cheerful chattering of the brown folks, and more still for the screaming and talking of parrots.

Among the goods were hundreds of splendid gilt cages, which were hung by long gold chains from the trees. Each cage contained a parrot and his mate, and they all seemed to be very unhappy indeed.

The parrots could talk, and they kept screaming to the discontented women to buy things for them, and trying very hard to attract attention.

One old parrot made himself quite conspicuous by these

efforts. He flung himself against the wires of his cage, he squalled, he screamed, he knocked the floor with his bcak, till Jack and one of the customers came running up to see what was the matter.

"What do you make such a fuss for?" cried the discontented woman. "You've set your cage swinging with knocking yourself about; and what good does that do? I cannot break the spell and open it for you."

"I know that," answered the parrot, sobbing; "but it hurts my feelings so that you should take no notice of me now that I have come down in the world."

"Yes," said the parrot's mate, "it hurts our feelings."

"I haven't forgotten you," answered the woman, more crossly than ever; "I was buying a measure of maize for you when you began to make such a noise."

Jack thought this was the queerest conversation he had ever heard in his life, and he was still more surprised when the bird answered:

"I would much rather you would buy me a pocket-handkerchief. Here we are, shut up, without a chance of getting out, and with nobody to pity us; and we can't even have the comfort of crying, because we've got nothing to wipe our eyes with."

"But at least," replied the woman, "you CAN cry now if you please, and when you had your other face you could not."

"Buy me a handkerchief," sobbed the parrot.

"I can't afford both," whined the cross woman, "and I've paid now for the maize." So saying, she went back to the tent to fetch her present to the parrots, and as their cage was still swinging Jack put out his hand to steady it for them, and the instant he did so they became perfectly silent, and all the other parrots on that tree, who had been flinging themselves about in their cages, left off screaming and became silent too.

The old parrot looked very cunning. His cage hung by such a long gold chain that it was just on a level with Jack's face, and so many odd things had happened that day that it did not seem more odd than usual to hear him say, in a tone of great astonishment:

"It's a BOY, if ever there was one!"

"Yes," said Jack, "I'm a boy."

"You won't go yet, will you?" said the parrot.

"No, don't," said a great many other parrots. Jack agreed to stay a little while, upon which they all thanked him.

"I had no notion you were a boy till you touched my cage," said the old parrot.

Jack did not know how this could have told him, so he only answered: "Indeed!"

"I'm a fairy," observed the parrot, in a confidential tone. "We are imprisoned here by our enemies the gipsies."

"So we are," answered a chorus of other parrots.

"I'm sorry for that," replied Jack. "I'm friends with the fairies."

"Don't tell," said the parrot, drawing a film over his eyes, and pretending to be asleep. At that moment his friend in the moss petticoat and feather cloak came up with a little measure of maize, and poured it into the cage.

"Here, neighbour," she said; "I must say goodbye now, for the gipsy is coming this way, and I want to buy some of her goods."

"Well, thank you," answered the parrot, sobbing again; "but I could have wished it had been a pocket-handkerchief."

"I'll lend you my handkerchief," said Jack. "Here!" And he drew it out and pushed it between the wires.

The parrot and his wife were in a great hurry to get Jack's handkerchief. They pulled it in very hastily; but instead of using it they rolled it up into a ball, and the parrot-wife tucked it under her wing.

"It makes me tremble all over," said she, "to think of such good luck."

"I say!" observed the parrot to Jack. "I know all about it now. You've got some of my people in your pockets—not of my own tribe, but fairies."

By this Jack was sure that the parrot really was a fairy himself, and he listened to what he had to say the more attentively.

V

THE PARROT IN HIS SHAWL

That handkerchief
Did an Egyptian to my mother give:
She was a charmer, and could almost read
The thoughts of people.

Othello

"That gipsy woman who is coming with her cart," said the parrot, "is a fairy too, and very malicious. It was she and others of her tribe who caught us and put us into these cages, for they are more powerful than we. Mind you do not let her allure you into the woods, nor wheedle you or frighten you into giving her any of those fairies."

"No," said Jack; "I will not."

"She sold us to the brown people," continued the parrot. "Mind you do not buy anything of her, for your money in her palm would act as a charm against you."

"She has a baby," observed the parrot-wife scornfully.

"Yes, a baby," repeated the old parrot; "and I hope by means of that baby to get her driven away, and perhaps get free myself. I shall try to put her in a passion. Here she comes."

There she was indeed, almost close at hand. She had a little cart; her goods were hung all about it, and a small horse drew it slowly on, and stopped when she got a customer.

Several gipsy children were with her, and as the people came running together over the grass to see her goods, she sang a curious kind of song, which made them wish to buy them.

Jack turned from the parrot's cage as she came up. He had heard her singing a little way off, and now, before she began again, he felt that already her searching eyes had found him out, and taken notice that he was different from the other people.

When she began to sing her selling song he felt a most curious sensation. He felt as if there were some cobwebs before his face, and he put up his hand as if to clear them away. There were no real cobwebs, of course; and yet he again felt as if they floated from the gipsy-woman to him, like gossamer threads, and attracted him towards her. So he gazed at her, and she at him, till Jack began to forget how the parrot had warned him.

He saw her baby too, wondered whether it was heavy for her to carry and wished he could help her. I mean, he saw that she had a baby on her arm. It was wrapped in a shawl and had a handkerchief over its face. She seemed very fond of it, for she kept hushing it; and Jack softly moved nearer and nearer to the cart, till the gipsy-woman smiled, and suddenly began to sing:

> "My good man—he's an old, old man—
>   And my good man got a fall,
> To buy me a bargain so fast he ran
>   When he heard the gipsies call:
>   'Buy, buy brushes,
>   Baskets wrought o' rushes.
>   Buy them, buy them, take them, try them,
>   Buy, dames all.'
>
> "My old man, he has money and land,
>   And a young, young wife am I.
> Let him put the penny in my white hand
>   When he hears the gipsies cry:
>   'Buy, buy laces,
>   Veils to screen your faces.
>   Buy them, buy them, take and try them,
>   Buy, maids, buy.'"

When the gipsy had finished her song Jack felt as if he was covered all over with cobwebs; but he could not move away, and he did not mind them now. All his wish was to please her, and get close to her; so when she said, in a soft wheedling voice: "What will you please to buy, my pretty gentleman?" he was just going to answer that he would buy anything she recommended, when, to his astonishment and displeasure, for he thought it very rude, the parrot suddenly burst into a violent fit of coughing, which made all the customers stare. "That's to clear my throat," he said, in a most impertinent tone of voice; and then he began to beat time with his foot, and sing, or rather scream out, an extremely saucy imitation of the gipsy's song, and all his parrot friends in the other cages joined in the chorus.

> "My fair lady's a dear, dear lady—
>   I walked by her side to woo.
> In a garden alley, so sweet and shady,
>   She answered, 'I love not you,
>   John, John Brady,'
>   Quoth my dear lady,
> 'Pray now, pray now, go your way now,
>   Do, John, do!'"

At first the gipsy did not seem to know where that mocking song came from, but when she discovered that it was her prisoner, the old parrot, who was thus daring to imitate her, she stood silent and glared at him, and her face was almost white with rage.

When he came to the end of the verse he pretended to burst into a violent fit of sobbing and crying, and screeched out to his wife: "Mate! mate! hand up my handkerchief. Oh! oh! it's so affecting, this song is."

Upon this the other parrot pulled Jack's handkerchief from under her wing, hobbled up and began, with a great show of zeal, to wipe his horny beak with it. But this was too much for the gipsy; she took a large brush from her cart and flung it at the cage with all her might.

This set it violently swinging backwards and forwards, but did not stop the parrot, who screeched out: "How delightful it is to be swung!" And then he began to sing another verse in the most impudent tone possible, and with a voice that seemed to ring through Jack's head, and almost pierce it.

> "Yet my fair lady's my own, own lady,
>   For I passed another day;
> While making her moan, she sat all alone,
>   And thus and thus did she say:

'John, John Brady,'
Quoth my dear lady,
'Do now, do now, once more woo now,
Pray, John, pray!' "

"It's beautiful!" screeched the parrot-wife. "And so ap-pro-pri-ate." Jack was delighted when she managed slowly to say this long word with her black tongue, and he burst out laughing. In the meantime a good many of the brown people came running together, attracted by the noise of the parrots and the rage of the gipsy, who flung at his cage, one after the other, all the largest things she had in her cart. But nothing did the parrot any harm; the more violently his cage swung the louder he sang, till at last the wicked gipsy seized her poor little young baby, who was lying in her arms, rushed frantically at the cage as it flew swiftly through the air towards her and struck at it with the little creature's head. "Oh, you cruel, cruel woman!" cried Jack, and all the small mothers who were standing near with their skinny children on their shoulders screamed out with terror and indignation; but only for one instant, for the handkerchief flew off that had covered its face, and was caught in the wires of the cage, and all the people saw that it was not a real baby at all, but a bundle of clothes, and its head was a turnip.

Yes, a turnip! You could see that as plainly as possible, for though the green leaves had been cut off, their stalks were visible through the lace cap that had been tied on it.

Upon this all the crowd pressed closer, throwing her baskets, and brushes, and laces, and beads at the gipsy, and calling out: "We will have none of your goods, you false woman! Give us back our money, or we will drive you out of the fair. You've stuck a stick into a turnip, and dressed it up in baby clothes. You're a cheat! a cheat!"

"My sweet gentlemen, my kind ladies," began the gipsy; but baskets and brushes flew at her so fast that she was obliged to sit down on the grass and hold up the sham baby to screen her face.

While this was going on Jack felt that the cobwebs which had seemed to float about his face were all gone; he did not care at all any more about the gipsy, and began to watch the parrots with great attention.

He observed that when the handkerchief stuck between

the cage wires the parrots caught it, and drew it inside; and then Jack saw the cunning old bird himself lay it on the floor, fold it crosswise like a shawl, and put it on his wife.

Then she jumped upon the perch, and held it with one foot, looking precisely like an old lady with a parrot's head. Then he folded Jack's handkerchief in the same way, put it on and got upon the perch beside his wife, screaming out, in his most piercing tone:

"I like shawls; they're so becoming."

Now the gipsy did not care at all what those inferior people thought of her, and she was calmly counting out their money, to return it; but she was very desirous to make Jack forget her behaviour, and had begun to smile again, and tell him she had only been joking, when the parrot spoke and, looking up, she saw the two birds sitting side by side, and the parrot-wife was screaming in her mate's ear, though neither of them was at all deaf:

"If Jack lets her allure him into the woods, he'll never come out again. She'll hang him up in a cage, as she did us. I say, how does my shawl fit?"

So saying, the parrot-wife whisked herself round on the perch, and lo! in the corner of the handkerchief were seen some curious letters, marked in red. When the crowd saw these they drew a little farther off, and glanced at one another with alarm.

"You look charming, my dear; it fits well!" screamed the old parrot in answer. "A word in your ear: 'Share and share alike' is a fine motto."

"What do you mean by all this?" said the gipsy, rising, and going with slow steps to the cage, and speaking cautiously.

"Jack," said the parrot, "do they ever eat handkerchiefs in your part of the country?"

"No, never," answered Jack.

"Hold your tongue and be reasonable," said the gipsy, trembling. "What do you want? I'll do it, whatever it is."

"But do they never pick out the marks?" continued the parrot. "Oh, Jack! are you sure they never pick out the marks?"

"The marks?" said Jack, considering. "Yes, perhaps they do."

"Stop!" cried the gipsy, as the old parrot made a peck at the strange letters. "Oh! you're hurting me. What do you

want? I say again, tell me what you want, and you shall
have it."

"We want to get out," replied the parrot; "you must undo
the spell."

"Then give me my handkerchief," answered the gipsy, "to
bandage my eyes. I dare not say the words with my eyes
open. You had no business to steal it. It was woven by human
hands, so that nobody can see through it; and if you don't
give it to me, you'll never get out—no, never!"

"Then," said the old parrot, tossing his shawl off, "you may
have Jack's handkerchief; it will bandage your eyes just as
well. It was woven over the water, as yours was."

"It won't do!" cried the gipsy in terror; "give me my own."

"I tell you," answered the parrot, "that you shall have
Jack's handkerchief; you can do no harm with that."

By this time the parrots all around had become perfectly
silent, and none of the people ventured to say a word, for
they feared the malice of the gipsy. She was trembling
dreadfully, and her dark eyes, which had been so bright and
piercing, had become dull and almost dim; but when she
found there was no help for it, she said:

"Well, pass out Jack's handkerchief. I will set you free if
you will bring out mine with you."

"Share and share alike," answered the parrot; "you must
let all my friends out too."

"Then I won't let you out," answered the gipsy. "You shall
come out first, and give me my handkerchief, or not one of
their cages will I undo. So take your choice."

"My friends, then," answered the brave old parrot; and he
poked Jack's handkerchief out to her through the wires.

The wondering crowd stood by to look, and the gipsy
bandaged her eyes tightly with the handkerchief; and then,
stooping low, she began to murmur something and clap her
hands—softly at first, but by degrees more and more violently.
The noise was meant to drown the words she muttered; but
as she went on clapping, the bottom of cage after cage fell
clattering down. Out flew the parrots by hundreds, screaming and congratulating one another; and there was such a
deafening din that not only the sound of her spell but the
clapping of her hands was quite lost in it.

But all this time Jack was very busy; for the moment the
gipsy had tied up her eyes the old parrot snatched the real

handkerchief off his wife's shoulders and tied it round her neck. Then she pushed out her head through the wires, and the old parrot called to Jack, and said: "Pull!"

Jack took the ends of the handkerchief, pulled terribly hard, and stopped. "Go on! go on!" screamed the old parrot.

"I shall pull her head off," cried Jack.

"No matter," cried the parrot; "no matter—only pull."

Well, Jack did pull, and he actually did pull her head off! nearly tumbling backward himself as he did it; but he saw what the whole thing meant then, for there was another head inside—a fairy's head.

Jack flung down the old parrot's head and great beak, for he saw that what he had to do was to clear the fairy of its parrot covering. The poor little creature seemed nearly dead, it was so terribly squeezed in the wires. It had a green gown or robe on, with an ermine collar; and Jack got hold of this dress, stripped the fairy out of the parrot feathers, and dragged her through—velvet robe, and crimson girdle, and little yellow shoes. She was very much exhausted, but a kind brown woman took her instantly, and laid her in her bosom. She was a splendid little creature, about half a foot long.

"There's a brave boy!" cried the parrot. Jack glanced round, and saw that not all the parrots were free yet—the gipsy was still muttering her spell.

He returned the handkerchief to the parrot, who put it round his own neck, and again Jack pulled. But oh! what a tough old parrot that was, and how Jack tugged before his cunning head would come off! It did, however, at last; and just as a fine fairy was pulled through, leaving his parrot skin and the handkerchief behind him, the gipsy untied her eyes and saw what Jack had done.

"Give me my handkerchief!" she screamed in despair.

"It's in the cage, gipsy," answered Jack; "you can get it yourself. Say your words again."

But the gipsy's spell would only open places where she had confined fairies, and no fairies were in the cage now.

"No, no, no!" she screamed; "too late! Hide me! Oh, good people, hide me!"

But it was indeed too late. The parrots had been wheeling in the air, hundreds and hundreds of them, high above her head; and as she ceased speaking she fell shuddering on the ground, drew her cloak over her face, and down they came, swooping in one immense flock, and settled so thickly all over her that she was completely covered; from her shoes to her head not an atom of her was to be seen.

All the people stood gravely looking on. So did Jack, but he could not see much for the fluttering of the parrots, nor hear anything for their screaming voices; but at last he made one of the cross people hear when he shouted to her: "What are they going to do to the poor gipsy?"

"Make her take her other form," she replied; "and then she cannot hurt us while she stays in our country. She is a fairy, as we have just found out, and all fairies have two forms."

"Oh!" said Jack; but he had no time for more questions.

The screaming, and fighting, and tossing about of little bits of cloth and cotton ceased; a black lump heaved itself up from the ground among the parrots; and as they flew aside an ugly great condor, with a bare neck, spread out its wings and, skimming the ground, sailed slowly away.

"They have pecked her so that she can hardly rise," exclaimed the parrot fairy. "Set me on your shoulder, Jack, and let me see the end of it."

Jack set him there; and his little wife, who had recovered herself, sprang from her friend the brown woman and sat on the other shoulder. He then ran on—the tribe of brown people, and mushroom people, and the feather-coated folks running too—after the great black bird, who skimmed slowly on before them till she got to the gipsy carts, when out rushed the gipsies, armed with poles, milking-stools, spades and everything they could get hold of to beat back the people and the parrots from hunting their relation, who had folded her tired wings and was skulking under a cart with ruffled feathers and a scowling eye.

Jack was so frightened at the violent way in which the gipsies and the other tribes were knocking each other about that he ran off, thinking he had seen enough of such a dangerous country.

As he passed the place where that evil-minded gipsy had been changed he found the ground strewed with little bits of her clothes. Many parrots were picking them up and poking them into the cage where the handkerchief was; and presently another parrot came with a lighted brand, which she had pulled from one of the gipsies' fires.

"That's right," said the fairy on Jack's shoulder, when he

saw his friend push the brand between the wires of what had been his cage, and set the gipsy's handkerchief on fire, and all the bits of her clothes with it. "She won't find much of herself here," he observed, as Jack went on. "It will not be very easy to put herself together again."

So Jack moved away. He was tired of the noise and confusion; and the sun was just setting as he reached the little creek where his boat lay.

Then the parrot fairy and his wife sprang down, and kissed their hands to him as he stepped on board and pushed the boat off. He saw, when he looked back, that a great fight was still going on; so he was glad to get away, and he wished his two friends goodbye, and set off, the old parrot fairy calling after him: "My relations have put some of our favourite food on board for you." Then they again thanked him for his good help, and sprang into a tree, and the boat began to go down the wonderful river.

"This has been a most extraordinary day," thought Jack; "the strangest day I have had yet." And after he had eaten a good supper of what the parrots had brought he felt so tired and sleepy that he lay down in the boat, and presently fell fast asleep. His fairies were sound asleep too in his pockets, and nothing happened of the least consequence; so he slept comfortably till morning.

VI

THE TOWN WITH NOBODY IN IT

"Master," quoth the auld hound,
   "Where will ye go?"
"Over moss, over muir,
   To court my new jo."
"Master, though the night be merk,
   I'se follow through the snow.

"Court her, master, court her,
   So shall ye do weel;
But and ben she'll guide the house,
   I'se get milk and meal.
Ye'se get lilting while she sits
   With her rock and reel."

"For, oh! she has a sweet tongue,
   And een that look down,
A gold girdle for her waist,
   And a purple gown.
She has a good word forbye
   Fra a' folk in the town."

Soon after sunrise they came to a great city, and it was
perfectly still. There were grand towers and terraces, wharves,
too, and a large market, but there was nobody anywhere to
be seen. Jack thought that might be because it was so early in
the morning; and when the boat ran itself up against a wooden
wharf and stopped, he jumped ashore, for he thought this
must be the end of his journey. A delightful town it was, if
only there had been any people in it! The market-place was
full of stalls, on which were spread toys, baskets, fruit, butter,
vegetables and all the other things that are usually sold in a
market.

Jack walked about in it. Then he looked in at the open doors of the houses, and at last, finding that they were all empty, he walked into one, looked at the rooms, examined the picture-books, rang the bells and set the musical-boxes going. Then, after he had shouted a good deal, and tried in vain to make someone hear, he went back to the edge of the river where his boat was lying, and the water was so delightfully clear and calm that he thought he would bathe. So he took off his clothes, and folding them very carefully, so as not to hurt the fairies, laid them down beside a haycock and went in, and ran about and paddled for a long time—much longer than there was any occasion for; but then he had nothing to do.

When at last he had finished he ran to the haycock and began to dress himself; but he could not find his stockings, and after looking about for some time he was obliged to put on his clothes without them, and he was going to put his boots on his bare feet when, walking to the other side of the haycock, he saw a little old woman about as large as himself. She had a pair of spectacles on, and she was knitting.

She looked so sweet tempered that Jack asked her if she knew anything about his stockings.

"It will be time enough to ask for them when you have had your breakfast," said she. "Sit down. Welcome to our town. How do you like it?"

"I should like it very much indeed," said Jack, "if there was anybody in it."

"I'm glad of that," said the woman. "You've seen a good deal of it; but it pleases me to find that you are a very honest boy. You did not take anything at all. I am honest too."

"Yes," said Jack, "of course you are."

"And as I am pleased with you for being honest," continued the little woman, "I shall give you some breakfast out of my basket." So she took out a saucer full of honey, a roll of bread and a cup of milk.

"Thank you," said Jack, "but I am not a beggar-boy; I have got a half-crown, a shilling, a sixpence and two pence; so I can buy this breakfast of you, if you like. You look very poor."

"Do I?" said the little woman softly; and she went on knitting, and Jack began to eat the breakfast.

"I wonder what has become of my stockings," said Jack.

"You will never see them any more," said the old woman.
"I threw them into the river, and they floated away."

"Why did you?" asked Jack.

The little woman took no notice; but presently she had
finished a beautiful pair of stockings, and she handed them to
Jack and said:

"Is that like the pair you lost?"

"Oh no," said Jack, "these are much more beautiful stockings than mine."

"Do you like them as well?" asked the fairy woman.

"I like them much better," said Jack, putting them on.
"How clever you are!"

"Would you like to wear these," said the woman, "instead
of yours?"

She gave Jack such a strange look when she said this that
he was afraid to take them, and answered:

"I shouldn't like to wear them if you think I had better
not."

"Well," she answered, "I am very honest, as I told you;
and therefore I am obliged to say that if I were you I would
not wear those stockings on any account."

"Why not?" said Jack; for she looked so sweet tempered
that he could not help trusting her.

"Why not?" repeated the fairy. "Why, because when you
have those stockings on your feet belong to me."

"Oh!" said Jack. "Well, if you think that matters, I'll take
them off again. Do you think it matters?"

"Yes," said the fairy woman; "it matters, because I am a
slave, and my master can make me do whatever he pleases,
for I am completely in his power. So if he found out that I
had knitted those stockings for you he would make me order
you to walk into his mill—the mill which grinds the corn for
the town; and there you would have to grind and grind till I
got free again."

When Jack heard this he pulled off the beautiful stockings
and laid them on the old woman's lap. Upon this she burst
out crying as if her heart would break.

"If my fairies that I have in my pocket would only wake,"
said Jack, "I would fight your master; for if he is no bigger
than you are perhaps I could beat him, and get you away."

"No, Jack," said the little woman; "that would be of no use.
The only thing you could do would be to buy me; for my

cruel master has said that if ever I am late again he will sell
me in the slave-market to the brown people, who work
underground. And, though I am dreadfully afraid of my master,
I mean to be late today, in hopes (as you are kind, and as you
have some money) that you will come to the slave-market and
buy me. Can you buy me, Jack, to be your slave?"

"I don't want a slave," said Jack; "and, besides, I have
hardly any money to buy you with."

"But it is real money," said the fairy woman, "not like what
my master has. His money has to be made every week, for if
there comes a hot day it cracks, so it never has time to look
old, as your half-crown does; and that is how we know the
real money, for we cannot imitate anything that is old. Oh,
now, now it is twelve o'clock! now I am late again! and
though I said I would do it, I am so frightened!"

So saying, the little woman ran off towards the town,
wringing her hands, and Jack ran beside her.

"How am I to find your master?" he said.

"Oh, Jack, buy me! buy me!" cried the fairy woman. "You
will find me in the slave-market. Bid high for me. Go back
and put your boots on, and bid high."

Now Jack had nothing on his feet, so he left the poor little
woman to run into the town by herself, and went back to put
his boots on. They were very uncomfortable, as he had no
stockings; but he did not much mind that, and he counted his
money. There was the half-crown that his grandmamma had
given him on his birthday, there was a shilling, a sixpence,
and two pence, besides a silver fourpenny-piece which he
had forgotten. He then marched into the town; and now it
was quite full of people—all of them little men and women
about his own height. They thought he was somebody of
consequence, and they called out to him to buy their goods.
And he bought some stockings, and said: "What I want to buy
now is a slave."

So they showed him the way to the slave-market, and there
whole rows of odd-looking little people were sitting, while in
front of them stood the slaves.

Now Jack had observed as he came along how very disrespectful the dogs of that town were to the people. They had a
habit of going up to them and smelling at their legs, and even
gnawing their feet as they sat before the little tables selling
their wares; and what made this more surprising was that the

people did not always seem to find out when they were being gnawed. But the moment the dogs saw Jack they came and fawned on him, and two old hounds followed him all the way to the slave-market; and when he took a seat one of them lay down at his feet, and said: "Master, set your handsome feet on my back, that they may be out of the dust."

"Don't be afraid of him," said the other hound; "he won't gnaw your feet. He knows well enough that they are real ones."

"Are the other people's feet not real?" asked Jack.

"Of course not," said the hound. "They had a feud long ago with the fairies, and they all went one night into a great cornfield which belonged to these enemies of theirs, intending to steal the corn. So they made themselves invisible, as they are always obliged to do till twelve o'clock at noon; but before morning dawn, the wheat being quite ripe, down came the fairies with their sickles, surrounded the field and cut the corn. So all their legs of course got cut off with it, for when they are invisible they cannot stir. Ever since that they have been obliged to make their legs of wood."

While the hound was telling this story Jack looked about, but he did not see one slave who was in the least like his poor little friend, and he was beginning to be afraid that he should not find her, when he heard two people talking together.

"Good day!" said one. "So you have sold that good-for-nothing slave of yours?"

"Yes," answered a very cross-looking old man. "She was late again this morning, and came to me crying and praying to be forgiven, but I was determined to make an example of her, so I sold her at once to Clink-of-the-Hole, and he has just driven her away to work in his mine."

Jack, on hearing this, whispered to the hound at his feet: "If you will guide me to Clink's hole, you shall be my dog."

"Master, I will do my best," answered the hound; and he stole softly out of the market, Jack following him.

VII

HALF A CROWN

So useful it is to have money, heigh ho!
So useful it is to have money!
A. H. Clough

The old hound went straight through the town, smelling Clink's footsteps, till he came into a large field of barley; and there, sitting against a sheaf, for it was harvest time, they found Clink-of-the-Hole. He was a very ugly little brown man, and he was smoking a pipe in the shade; while crouched near him was the poor little woman, with her hands spread before her face.

"Good day, sir," said Clink to Jack. "You are a stranger here, no doubt?"

"Yes," said Jack; "I only arrived this morning."

"Have you seen the town?" asked Clink civilly. "There is a very fine market."

"Yes, I have seen the market," answered Jack. "I went into it to buy a slave, but I did not see one that I liked."

"Ah," said Clink; "and yet they had some very fine articles." Here he pointed to the poor little woman, and said: "Now that's a useful body enough, and I had her very cheap."

"What did you give for her?" said Jack, sitting down.

"Three pitchers," said Clink, "and fifteen cups and saucers, and two shillings in the money of the town."

"Is their money like this?" said Jack, taking out his shilling.

When Clink saw the shilling he changed colour, and said, very earnestly: "Where did you get that, dear sir?"

"Oh, it was given me," said Jack carelessly.

Clink looked hard at the shilling, and so did the fairy woman, and Jack let them look some time, for he amused himself with throwing it up several times and catching it. At last he put it back in his pocket, and then Clink heaved a deep sigh. Then Jack took out a penny, and began to toss that up, upon which, to his great surprise, the little brown man fell on his knees, and said: "Oh, a shilling and a penny—a shilling and a penny of mortal coin! What would I not give for a shilling and a penny!"

"I don't believe you have got anything to give," said Jack cunningly. "I see nothing but that ring on your finger, and the old woman."

"But I have a great many things at home, sir," said the brown man, wiping his eyes; "and besides, that ring would be cheap at a shilling—even a shilling of mortal coin."

"Would the slave be cheap at a penny?" said Jack.

"Would you give a penny for her, dear sir?" inquired Clink, trembling with eagerness.

"She is honest," answered Jack; "ask her whether I had better buy her with this penny."

"It does not matter what she says," replied the brown man; "I would sell twenty such as she is for a penny—a real one."

"Ask her," repeated Jack; and the poor little woman wept bitterly, but she said "No."

"Why not?" asked Jack; but she only hung down her head and cried.

"I'll make you suffer for this," said the brown man. But when Jack took out the shilling, and said: "Shall I buy you with this, slave?" his eyes actually shot out sparks, he was so eager.

"Speak!" he said to the fairy woman; "and if you don't say 'Yes,' I'll strike you."

"He cannot buy me with that," answered the fairy woman, "unless it is the most valuable coin he has got."

The brown man, on hearing this, rose up in a rage, and was just going to strike her a terrible blow, when Jack cried out: "Stop!" and took out his half-crown.

"Can I buy you with this?" said he; and the fairy woman answered: "Yes."

Upon this Clink drew a long breath, and his eyes grew bigger and bigger as he gazed at the half-crown.

"Shall she be my slave for ever, and not yours," said Jack, "if I give you this?"

"She shall," said the brown man. And he made such a low bow as he took the money that his head actually knocked the ground. Then he jumped up; and, as if he was afraid Jack should repent of his bargain, he ran off towards the hole in the hill with all his might, shouting for joy as he went.

"Slave," said Jack, "that is a very ragged old apron that you have got, and your gown is quite worn out. Don't you think we had better spend my shilling in buying you some new clothes? You look so very shabby."

"Do I?" said the fairy woman gently. "Well, master, you will do as you please."

"But you know better than I do," said Jack, "though you are my slave."

"You had better give me the shilling, then," answered the little old woman; "and then I advise you to go back to the boat, and wait there till I come."

"What!" said Jack. "Can you go all the way back into the town again? I think you must be tired, for you know you are so very old."

The fairy woman laughed when Jack said this, and she had such a sweet laugh that he loved to hear it; but she took the shilling, and trudged off to the town, and he went back to the boat, his hound running after him.

He was a long time going, for he ran a good many times after butterflies, and then he climbed up several trees; and altogether he amused himself for such a long while that when he reached the boat his fairy woman was there before him. So he stepped on board, the hound followed, and the boat immediately began to swim on.

"Why, you have not bought any new clothes!" said Jack to his slave.

"No, master," answered the fairy woman; "but I have bought what I wanted." And she took out of her pocket a little tiny piece of purple ribbon, with a gold-coloured satin edge, and a very small tortoiseshell comb.

When Jack saw these he was vexed, and said: "What do you mean by being so silly? I can't scold you properly, because I don't know what name to call you by, and I don't like to say 'Slave,' because that sounds so rude. Why, this bit of ribbon is such a little bit that it's of no use at all. It's not large enough even to make one mitten of."

"Isn't it?" said the slave. "Just take hold of it, master, and let us see if it will stretch."

So Jack did. And she pulled, and he pulled, and very soon the silk had stretched till it was nearly as large as a handkerchief; and then she shook it, and they pulled again. "This is very good fun," said Jack; "why, now it is as large as an apron."

So she shook it again, and gave it a twitch here and a pat there; and then they pulled again, and the silk suddenly stretched so wide that Jack was very nearly falling overboard. So Jack's slave pulled off her ragged gown and apron, and put it on. It was a most beautiful robe of purple silk, it had a gold border, and it just fitted her.

"That will do," she said. And then she took out the little tortoiseshell comb, pulled off her cap and threw it into the river. She had a little knot of soft grey hair, and she let it down and began to comb. And as she combed the hair got much longer and thicker, till it fell in waves all about her throat. Then she combed again, and it all turned gold colour, and came tumbling down to her waist; and then she stood up in the boat and combed once more, and shook out the hair, and there was such a quantity that it reached down to her feet, and she was so covered with it that you could not see one bit of her, excepting her eyes, which peeped out, and looked bright and full of tears.

Then she began to gather up her lovely locks; and when she had dried her eyes with them, she said: "Master, do you know what you have done? Look at me now!" So she threw back the hair from her face, and it was a beautiful young face; and she looked so happy that Jack was glad he had bought her with his half-crown—so glad that he could not help crying, and the fair slave cried too; and then instantly the little fairies woke, and sprang out of Jack's pockets. As they did so Jovinian cried out: "Madam, I am your most humble servant"; and Roxaletta said: "I hope your Grace is well"; but the third got on Jack's knee and took hold of the buttons of his waistcoat, and when the lovely slave looked at her she hid her face and blushed with pretty childish shyness.

"These are fairies," said Jack's slave; "but what are you?"

"Jack kissed me," said the little thing; "and I want to sit on his knee."

"Yes," said Jack, "I took them out, and laid them in a row, to see if they were safe, and this one I kissed, because she looked such a little dear."

"Was she not like the others, then?" asked the slave.

"Yes," said Jack; "but I liked her the best; she was my favourite."

Now the instant these three fairies sprang out of Jack's pockets they got very much larger; in fact, they became fully grown—that is to say, they measured exactly one foot one inch in height, which, as most people know, is exactly the proper height for fairies of that tribe. The two who had sprung out first were very beautifully dressed. One had a green velvet coat, and a sword, the hilt of which was encrusted with diamonds. The second had a white spangled robe, and the loveliest rubies and emeralds round her neck and in her hair; but the third, the one who sat on Jack's knee, had a white frock and a blue sash on. She had soft, fat arms, and a face just like that of a sweet little child.

When Jack's slave saw this she took the little creature on her knee, and said to her: "How comes it that you are not like your companions?"

And she answered, in a pretty, lisping voice: "It's because Jack kissed me."

"Even so it must be," answered the slave; "the love of a mortal works changes indeed. It is not often that we win anything so precious. Here, master, let her sit on your knee sometimes, and take care of her, for she cannot now take the same care of herself that others of her race are capable of."

So Jack let little Mopsa sit on his knee; and when he was tired of admiring his slave, and wondering at the respect with which the other two fairies treated her, and at their cleverness in getting water-lilies for her, and fanning her with feathers, he curled himself up in the bottom of the boat with his own little favourite, and taught her how to play at cat's-cradle.

When they had been playing some time, and Mopsa was getting quite clever at the game, the lovely slave said: "Master, it is a long time since you spoke to me."

"And yet," said Jack, "there is something that I particularly want to ask you about."

"Ask it, then," she replied.

"I don't like to have a slave," answered Jack; "and as you are so clever, don't you think you can find out how to be free again?"

"I am very glad you asked me about that," said the fairy woman. "Yes, master, I wish very much to be free; and as you were so kind as to give the most valuable piece of real money you possessed in order to buy me, I can be free if you can think of anything that you really like better than that half-crown, and if I can give it you."

"Oh, there are many things," said Jack. "I like going up this river to Fairyland much better."

"But you are going there, master," said the fairy woman; "you were on the way before I met with you."

"I like this little child better," said Jack; "I love this little Mopsa. I should like her to belong to me."

"She is yours," answered the fairy woman; "she belongs to you already. Think of something else."

Jack thought again, and was so long about it that at last the beautiful slave said to him: "Master, do you see those purple mountains?"

Jack turned round in the boat and saw a splendid range of purple mountains, going up and up. They were very great and steep, each had a crown of snow, and the sky was very red behind them, for the sun was going down.

"At the other side of those mountains is Fairyland," said the slave; "but if you cannot think of something that you should like better to have than your half-crown I can never enter in. The river flows straight up to yonder steep precipice, and there is a chasm in it which pierces it, and through which the river runs down beneath, among the very roots of the mountains, till it comes out at the other side. Thousands and thousands of the small people will come when they see the boat, each with a silken thread in his hand; but if there is a slave in it not all their strength and skill can tow it through. Look at those rafts on the river; on them are the small people coming up."

Jack looked, and saw that the river was spotted with rafts, on which were crowded brown fairy sailors, each one with three green stripes on his sleeve, which looked like good-conduct marks. All these sailors were chattering very fast, and the rafts were coming down to meet the boat.

"All these sailors to tow my slave!" said Jack. "I wonder, I do wonder, what you are?" But the fairy woman only smiled, and Jack went on: "I have thought of something that I should like much better than my half-crown. I should like to have a little tiny bit of that purple gown of yours with the gold border."

Then the fairy woman said: "I thank you, master. Now I can be free." So she told Jack to lend her his knife, and with it she cut off a very small piece of the skirt of her robe, and gave it to him. "Now mind," she said; "I advise you never to stretch this unless you want to make some particular thing of it, for then it will only stretch to the right size; but if you merely begin to pull it for your own amusement, it will go on stretching and stretching, and I don't know where it will stop."

VIII

A STORY

In the night she told a story,
    In the night and all night through,
While the moon was in her glory,
    And the branches dropped with dew.

'Twas my life she told, and round it
    Rose the years as from a deep;
In the world's great heart she found it,
    Cradled like a child asleep.

In the night I saw her weaving
    By the misty moonbeam cold,
All the weft her shuttle cleaving
    With a sacred thread of gold.

Ah! she wept me tears of sorrow,
    Lulling tears so mystic sweet;
Then she wove my last tomorrow,
    And her web lay at my feet.

Of my life she made the story:
    I must weep—so soon 'twas told!
But your name did lend it glory,
    And your love its thread of gold!

By this time, as the sun had gone down, and none of the moons
had risen, it would have been dark but that each of the rafts
was rigged with a small mast that had a lantern hung to it.

By the light of these lanterns Jack saw crowds of little
brown faces, and presently many rafts had come up to the
boat, which was now swimming very slowly. Every sailor in
every raft fastened to the boat's side a silken thread; then the

rafts were rowed to shore, and the sailors jumped out and began to tow the boat along.

These crimson threads looked no stronger than the silk that ladies sew with, yet by means of them the small people drew the boat along merrily. There were so many of them that they looked like an army as they marched in the light of the lanterns and torches. Jack thought they were very happy, though the work was hard, for they shouted and sang.

The fairy woman looked more beautiful than ever now, and far more stately. She had on a band of precious stones to bind back her hair, and they shone so brightly in the night that her features could be clearly seen.

Jack's little favourite was fast asleep, and the other two fairies had flown away. He was beginning to feel rather sleepy himself, when he was roused by the voice of his free lady, who said to him: "Jack, there is no one listening now, so I will tell you my story. I am the Fairy Queen!"

Jack opened his eyes very wide, but he was so much surprised that he did not say a word.

"One day, long, long ago," said the Queen, "I was discontented with my own happy country. I wished to see the world, so I set forth with a number of the one-foot-one fairies, and went down the wonderful river, thinking to see the world.

"So we sailed down the river till we came to that town which you know of; and there, in the very middle of the stream, stood a tower—a tall tower built upon a rock.

"Fairies are afraid of nothing but other fairies, and we did not think this tower was fairy work, so we left our ship and went up the rock and into the tower, to see what it was like; but just as we had descended into the dungeon keep we heard the gurgling of water overhead, and down came the tower. It was nothing but water enchanted into the likeness of stone, and we all fell down with it into the very bed of the river.

"Of course, we were not drowned, but there we were obliged to lie, for we have no power out of our own element; and the next day the townspeople came down with a net and dragged the river, picked us all out of the meshes, and made us slaves. The one-foot-one fairies got away shortly; but from that day to this, in sorrow and distress, I have had to serve my masters. Luckily my crown had fallen off in the water, so

I was not known to be the Queen; but till you came, Jack, I had almost forgotten that I had ever been happy and free, and I had hardly any hope of getting away."

"How sorry your people must have been," said Jack, "when they found you did not come home again."

"No," said the Queen; "they only went to sleep, and they will not wake till tomorrow morning, when I pass in again. They will think I have been absent for a day, and so will the apple-woman. You must not undeceive them; if you do, they will be very angry."

"And who is the apple-woman?" inquired Jack; but the Queen blushed, and pretended not to hear the question, so he repeated:

"Queen, who is the apple-woman?"

"I've only had her for a very little while," said the Queen evasively.

"And how long do you think you have been a slave, Queen?" asked Jack.

"I don't know," said the Queen. "I have never been able to make up my mind about that."

And now all the moons began to shine, and all the trees lighted themselves up, for almost every leaf had a glow-worm or a firefly on it, and the water was full of fishes that had shining eyes. And now they were close to the steep mountain-side; and Jack looked and saw an opening in it, into which the river ran. It was a kind of cave, something like a long, long church with a vaulted roof, only the pavement of it was that magic river, and a narrow towing-path ran on either side.

As they entered the cave there was a hollow murmuring sound, and the Queen's crown became so bright that it lighted up the whole boat; at the same time she began to tell Jack a wonderful story, which he liked very much to hear, but at every fresh thing she said he forgot what had gone before; and at last, though he tried very hard to listen, he was obliged to go to sleep; and he slept soundly and never dreamed of anything till it was morning.

He saw such a curious sight when he woke. They had been going through this underground cavern all night, and now they were approaching its opening on the other side. This opening, because they were a good way from it yet, looked like a lovely little round window of blue and yellow and green glass, but as they drew on he could see far-off mountains, blue sky and a country all covered with sunshine.

He heard singing too, such as fairies make; and he saw some beautiful people, such as those fairies whom he had brought with him. They were coming along the towing-path. They were all lady fairies; but they were not very polite, for as each one came up she took a silken rope out of a brown sailor's hand and gave him a shove which pushed him into the water. In fact the water became filled with such swarms of these sailors that the boat could hardly get on. But the poor little brown fellows did not seem to mind this conduct, for they plunged and shook themselves about, scattering a good deal of spray. Then they all suddenly dived, and when they came up again they were ducks—nothing but brown ducks, I assure you, with green stripes on their wings; and with a great deal of quacking and floundering they all began to swim back again as fast as they could.

Then Jack was a good deal vexed, and he said to himself: "If nobody thanks the ducks for towing us I will"; so he stood up in the boat and shouted: "Thank you, ducks; we are very much obliged to you!" But neither the Queen nor these new towers took the least notice, and gradually the boat came out of that dim cave and entered Fairyland, while the river became so narrow that you could hear the song of the towers quite easily; those on the right bank sang the first verse, and those on the left bank answered:

"Drop, drop from the leaves of lign aloes,
    O honey-dew! drop from the tree.
Float up through your clear river shallows,
    White lilies, beloved of the bee.

"Let the people, O Queen! say, and bless thee,
    Her bounty drops soft as the dew,
And spotless in honour confess thee,
    As lilies are spotless in hue.

"On the roof stands yon white stork awaking,
    His feathers flush rosy the while,
For, lo! from the blushing east breaking,
    The sun sheds the bloom of his smile.

"Let them boast of thy word, 'It is certain;
We doubt it no more,' let them say,
'Than tomorrow that night's dusky curtain
Shall roll back its folds for the day.' "

"Master," whispered the old hound, who was lying at Jack's feet.

"Well?" said Jack.

"They didn't invent that song themselves," said the hound; "the old apple-woman taught it to them—the woman whom they love because she can make them cry."

Jack was rather ashamed of the hound's rudeness in saying this; but the Queen took no notice. And now they had reached a little landing-place, which ran out a few feet into the river and was strewn thickly with cowslips and violets.

Here the boat stopped, and the Queen rose and got out.

Jack watched her. A whole crowd of one-foot-one fairies came down a garden to meet her, and he saw them conduct her to a beautiful tent with golden poles and a silken covering; but nobody took the slightest notice of him, or of little Mopsa, or of the hound, and after a long silence the hound said: "Well, master, don't you feel hungry? Why don't you go with the others and have some breakfast?"

"The Queen didn't invite me," said Jack.

"But do you feel as if you couldn't go?" asked the hound.

"Of course not," answered Jack; "but perhaps I may not."

"Oh yes, master," replied the hound; "whatever you *can* do in Fairyland you *may* do."

"Are you sure of that?" asked Jack.

"Quite sure, master," said the hound; "and I am hungry too."

"Well," said Jack, "I will go there and take Mopsa. She shall ride on my shoulder; you may follow."

So he walked up that beautiful garden till he came to the great tent. A banquet was going on inside. All the one-foot-one fairies sat down the sides of the table, and at the top sat the Queen on a larger chair; and there were two empty chairs, one on each side of her.

Jack blushed; but the hound whispering again: "Master, whatever you can do you may do," he came slowly up the table towards the Queen, who was saying as he drew near: "Where is our trusty and well-beloved the apple-woman?"

And she took no notice of Jack; so, though he could not help feeling rather red and ashamed, he went and sat in the chair beside her with Mopsa still on his shoulder. Mopsa laughed for joy when she saw the feast. The Queen said: "Oh, Jack, I am so glad to see you!" and some of the one-foot-one fairies cried out: "What a delightful little creature that is! She can laugh! Perhaps she can also cry!"

Jack looked about, but there was no seat for Mopsa; and he was afraid to let her run about on the floor, lest she should be hurt.

There was a very large dish standing before the Queen; for though the people were small the plates and dishes were exactly like those we use, and of the same size.

This dish was raised on a foot, and filled with grapes and peaches. Jack wondered at himself for doing it, but he saw no other place for Mopsa; so he took out the fruit, laid it round the dish, and set his own little one-foot-one in the dish.

Nobody looked in the least surprised; and there she sat very happily, biting an apple with her small white teeth.

Then, as they brought him nothing to eat, Jack helped himself from some of the dishes before him, and found that a fairy breakfast was very nice indeed.

In the meantime there was a noise outside, and in stumped an elderly woman. She had very thick boots on, a short gown of red print, an orange cotton handkerchief over her shoulders and a black silk bonnet. She was exactly the same height as the Queen—for of course nobody in Fairyland is allowed to be any bigger than the Queen; so, if they are not children when they arrive, they are obliged to shrink.

"How are you, dear?" said the Queen.

"I am as well as can be expected," answered the apple-woman, sitting down in the empty chair. "Now, then, where's my tea? They're never ready with my cup of tea."

Two attendants immediately brought a cup of tea and set it down before the apple-woman, with a plate of bread and butter; and she proceeded to pour it out into the saucer, and blow it, because it was hot. In so doing her wandering eyes caught sight of Jack and little Mopsa, and she set down the saucer and looked at them with attention.

Now Mopsa, I am sorry to say, was behaving so badly that Jack was quite ashamed of her. First she got out of her dish, took something nice out of the Queen's plate with her fingers and ate it; and then, as she was going back, she tumbled over a melon and upset a glass of red wine, which she wiped up with her white frock; after which she got into her dish again, and there she sat smiling, and daubing her pretty face with a piece of buttered muffin.

"Mopsa," said Jack, "you are very naughty; if you behave in this way, I shall never take you out to parties again."

"Pretty lamb!" said the apple-woman; "it's just like a child." And then she burst into tears, and exclaimed, sobbing: "It's many a long day since I've seen a child. Oh dear! Oh deary me!"

Upon this, to the astonishment of Jack, every one of the guests began to cry and sob too.

"Oh dear! Oh dear!" they said to one another, "we're crying; we can cry just as well as men and women. Isn't it delightful? What a luxury it is to cry, to be sure!"

They were evidently quite proud of it; and when Jack looked at the Queen for an explanation, she only gave him a still little smile.

But Mopsa crept along the table to the apple-woman, let her take her and hug her, and seemed to like her very much; for as she sat on her knee she patted her brown face with a little dimpled hand.

"I should like vastly well to be her nurse," said the apple-woman, drying her eyes, and looking at Jack.

"If you'll always wash her, and put clean frocks on her, you may," said Jack; "for just look at her—what a figure she is already!"

Upon this the apple-woman laughed for joy, and again everyone else did the same. The fairies can only laugh and cry when they see mortals do so.

IX

AFTER THE PARTY

Stephano. This will prove a brave kingdom to me,
Where I shall have my music for nothing.

The Tempest

When breakfast was over the guests got up, one after the
other, without taking the least notice of the Queen; and the
tent began to get so thin and transparent that you could see
the trees and the sky through it. At last it looked only like a
coloured mist, with blue and green and yellow stripes, and
then it was gone; and the table and all the things on it began
to go in the same way. Only Jack, and the apple-woman, and
Mopsa were left, sitting on their chairs, with the Queen
between them.

Presently the Queen's lips began to move, and her eyes
looked straight before her, as she sat upright in her chair.
Whereupon the apple-woman snatched up Mopsa and, seizing Jack's hand, hurried him off, exclaiming: "Come away!
Come away! She is going to tell one of her stories; and if you
listen you'll be obliged to go to sleep, and sleep nobody
knows how long."

Jack did not want to go to sleep; he wished to go down to
the river again and see what had become of his boat, for he
had left his cap and several other things in it.

So he parted from the apple-woman—who took Mopsa
with her, and said he would find her again when he wanted
her at her apple-stall—and went down to the boat, where he
saw that his faithful hound was there before him.

"It was lucky, master, that I came when I did," said the
hound, "for a dozen or so of those one-foot-one fellows were
just shoving it off, and you will want it at night to sleep in."

"Yes," said Jack; "and I can stretch the bit of purple silk to
make a canopy overhead—a sort of awning—for I should not

like to sleep in tents or palaces that are inclined to melt away."

So the hound with his teeth, and Jack with his hands, pulled and pulled at the silk till it was large enough to make a splendid canopy, like a tent; and it reached down to the water's edge, and roofed in all the after part of the boat.

So now he had a delightful little home of his own; and there was no fear of its being blown away, for no wind ever blows in Fairyland. All the trees are quite still, no leaf rustles and the flowers lie on the ground exactly where they fall.

After this Jack told the hound to watch his boat, and went himself in search of the apple-woman. Not one fairy was to be seen, any more than if he had been in his own country, and he wandered down the green margin of the river till he saw the apple-woman sitting at a small stall with apples on it, and cherries tied to sticks, and some dry-looking nuts. She had Mopsa on her knee, and had washed her face, and put a beautiful clean white frock on her.

"Where are all the fairies gone to?" asked Jack.

"I never take any notice of that common trash and their doings," she answered. "When the Queen takes to telling her stories they are generally frightened, and go and sit in the tops of the trees."

"But you seem very fond of Mopsa," said Jack, "and she is one of them. You will help me to take care of her, won't you, till she grows a little older?"

"Grows!" said the apple-woman, laughing. "Grows! Why you don't think, surely, that she will ever be any different from what she is now!"

"I thought she would grow up," said Jack.

"They never change so long as they last," answered the apple-woman, "when once they are one-foot-one high."

"Mopsa," said Jack, "come here, and I'll measure you."

Mopsa came dancing towards Jack, and he tried to measure her, first with a yard measure that the apple-woman took out of her pocket, and then with a stick, and then with a bit of string; but Mopsa would not stand steady, and at last it ended in their having a good game of romps together, and a race; but when he carried her back, sitting on his shoulder, he was sorry to see that the apple-woman was crying again, and he asked her kindly what she did it for.

"It is because," she answered, "I shall never see my own

country any more, nor any men and women and children, excepting such as by a rare chance stray in for a little while as you have done."

"I can go back whenever I please," said Jack. "Why don't you?"

"Because I came in of my own good will, after I had had fair warning that if I came at all it would end in my staying always. Besides, I don't know that I exactly wish to go home again—I should be afraid."

"Afraid of what?" asked Jack.

"Why, there's the rain and the cold, and not having anything to eat excepting what you earn. And yet," said the apple-woman, "I have three boys of my own at home; one of them must be nearly a man by this time, and the youngest is about as old as you are. If I went home I might find one or more of those boys in jail, and then how miserable I should be."

"But you are not happy as it is," said Jack. "I have seen you cry."

"Yes," said the apple-woman; "but now I live here I don't care about anything so much as I used to do. 'May I have a satin gown and a coach?' I asked when first I came. 'You may have a hundred and fifty satin gowns if you like,' said the Queen, 'and twenty coaches with six cream-coloured horses to each.' But when I had been here a little time, and found I could have everything I wished for, and change it as often as I pleased, I began not to care for anything; and at last I got so sick of all their grand things that I dressed myself in my own clothes that I came in, and made up my mind to have a stall and sit at it, as I used to do, selling apples. And I used to say to myself: 'I have but to wish with all my heart to go home, and I can go, I know that'; but oh dear! oh dear! I couldn't wish enough, for it would come into my head that I should be poor, or that my boys would have forgotten me, or that my neighbours would look down on me, and so I always put off wishing for another day. Now here is the Queen coming. Sit down on the grass and play with Mopsa. Don't let her see us talking together, lest she should think I have been telling you things which you ought not to know."

Jack looked, and saw the Queen coming slowly towards them, with her hands held out before her, as if it was dark.

She felt her way, yet her eyes were wide open, and she was telling her stories all the time.

"Don't you listen to a word she says," whispered the apple-woman, and then, in order that Jack might not hear what the Queen was talking about, she began to sing.

She had no sooner begun than up from the river came swarms of one-foot-one fairies to listen, and hundreds of them dropped down from the trees. The Queen, too, seemed to attend as they did, though she kept murmuring her story all the time; and nothing that any of them did appeared to surprise the apple-woman—she sang as if nobody was taking any notice at all:

"When I sit on market-days amid the comers and the goers,
    Oh! full oft I have a vision of the days without alloy,
And a ship comes up the river with a jolly gang of towers,
    And a 'pull'e haul'e, pull'e haul'e, yoy! heave, hoy!'

"There is busy talk around me, all about mine ears it
    hummeth,
    But the wooden wharves I look on, and a dancing
    heaving buoy,
For 'tis tidetime in the river, and she cometh—oh, she
    cometh!
    With a 'pull'e haul'e, pull'e haul'e, yoy! heave, hoy!'

"Then I hear the water washing, never golden waves
    were brighter,
    And I hear the capstan creaking—'tis a sound that
    cannot cloy.
Bring her to, to ship her lading, brig or schooner, sloop
    or lighter,
    With a 'pull'e haul'e, pull'e haul'e, yoy! heave, hoy!'

" 'Will ye step aboard, my dearest? for the high seas lie
    before us.'
    So I sailed adown the river in those days without alloy.
We are launched! But when, I wonder, shall a sweeter
    sound float o'er us
    Than yon 'pull'e haul'e, pull'e haul'e, yoy! heave, hoy!' "

As the apple-woman left off singing the Queen moved away, still murmuring the words of her story, and Jack said:

"Does the Queen tell stories of what has happened, or of what is going to happen?"

"Why, of what is going to happen, of course," replied the woman. "Anybody could tell the other sort."

"Because I heard a little of it," observed Jack. "I thought she was talking of me. She said: 'So he took the measure, and Mopsa stood still for once, and he found she was only one foot high, and she grew a great deal after that. Yes, she can grow.'"

"That's a fine hearing, and a strange hearing," said the apple-woman; "and what did she mutter next?"

"Of how she heard me sobbing," replied Jack; "and while you went on about stepping on board the ship, she said: 'He was very good to me, dear little fellow! But Fate is the name of my old mother, and she reigns here. Oh, she reigns! The fatal F is in her name, and I cannot take it out!'"

"Ah!" replied the apple-woman, "they all say that, and that they are fays, and that mortals call their history fable; they are always crying out for an alphabet without the fatal F."

"And then she told how she heard Mopsa sobbing too," said Jack; "sobbing among the reeds and rushes by the river side."

"There are no reeds and no rushes either here," said the apple-woman, "and I have walked the river from end to end. I don't think much of that part of the story. But you are sure she said that Mopsa was short of her proper height?"

"Yes, and that she would grow; but that's nothing. In my country we always grow."

"Hold your tongue about your country!" said the apple-woman sharply. "Do you want to make enemies of them all?"

Mopsa had been listening to this, and now she said: "I don't love the Queen. She slapped my arm as she went by, and it hurts."

Mopsa showed her little fat arm as she spoke, and there was a red place on it.

"That's odd too," said the apple-woman; "there's nothing red in a common fairy's veins. They have sap in them: that's why they can't blush."

Just then the sun went down, and Mopsa got up on the apple-woman's lap and went to sleep; and Jack, being tired, went to his boat and lay down under the purple canopy, his old hound lying at his feet to keep guard over him.

The next morning, when he woke, a pretty voice called to him: "Jack! Jack!" and he opened his eyes and saw Mopsa.

The apple-woman had dressed her in a clean frock and blue shoes, and her hair was so long! She was standing on the landing-place, close to him. "Oh, Jack! I'm so big," she said. "I grew in the night; look at me."

Jack looked. Yes, Mopsa had grown indeed; she had only just reached to his knee the day before, and now her little bright head, when he measured her, came as high as the second button of his waistcoat.

"But I hope you will not go on growing so fast as this," said Jack, "or you will be as tall as my mamma is in a week or two—much too big for me to play with."

X

MOPSA LEARNS HER LETTERS

A—apple-pie.
B—bit it.

"How ashamed I am," Jack said, "to think that you don't know even your letters!"

Mopsa replied that she thought that did not signify, and then she and Jack began to play at jumping from the boat on to the bank and back again; and afterwards, as not a single fairy could be seen, they had breakfast with the apple-woman.

"Where is the Queen?" asked Jack.

The apple-woman answered: "It's not the fashion to ask questions in Fairyland."

"That's a pity," said Jack, "for there are several things that I particularly want to know about this country. Mayn't I even ask how big it is?"

"How big?" said Mopsa—little Mopsa looking as wise as possible. "Why, the same size as your world, of course."

Jack laughed. "It's the same world that you call yours," continued Mopsa; "and when I'm a little older I'll explain it all to you."

"If it's our world," said Jack, "why are none of us in it, excepting me and the apple-woman?"

"That's because you've got something in your world that you call TIME," said Mopsa; "so you talk about NOW, and you talk about THEN."

"And don't you?" asked Jack.

"I do if I want to make you understand," said Mopsa.

The apple-woman laughed, and said: "To think of the pretty thing talking so queenlike already! Yes, that's right, and just what the grown-up fairies say. Go on, and explain it to him if you can."

"You know," said Mopsa, "that your people say there was a

time when there were none of them in the world—a time
before they were made. Well, THIS is that time. This IS long
ago."

"Nonsense!" said Jack. "Then how do I happen to be
here?"

"Because," said Mopsa, "when the albatross brought you
she did not fly with you a long way off, but a long way
back—hundreds and hundreds of years. This is your world, as
you can see; but none of your people are here, because they
are not made yet. I don't think any of them will be made for a
thousand years."

"But I saw the old ships," answered Jack, "in the enchanted bay."

"That was a border country," said Mopsa. "I was asleep
while you went through those countries; but these are the
real Fairylands."

Jack was very much surprised when he heard Mopsa say
these strange things; and as he looked at her he felt that a
sleep was coming over him, and he could not hold up his
head. He felt how delightful it was to go to sleep; and though
the apple-woman sprang to him when she observed that he
was shutting his eyes, and though he heard her begging and
entreating him to keep awake, he did not want to do so; but
he let his head sink down on the mossy grass, which was as
soft as a pillow, and there under the shade of a Guelder rose
tree, that kept dropping its white flowrets all over him, he
had this dream.

He thought that Mopsa came running up to him, as he
stood by the river, and that he said to her: "Oh, Mopsa, how
old we are! We have lived back to the times before Adam and
Eve!"

"Yes," said Mopsa; "but I don't feel old. Let us go down
the river, and see what we can find."

So they got into the boat, and it floated into the middle of
the river, and then made for the opposite bank, where the
water was warm and very muddy, and the river became so
very wide that it seemed to be afternoon when they got near
enough to see it clearly; and what they saw was a boggy
country, green, and full of little rills, but the water—which,
as I told you, was thick and muddy—the water was full of
small holes! YOU never saw water with eyelet-holes in it; but
Jack did. On all sides of the boat he saw holes moving about

in pairs, and some were so close that he looked and saw their lining; they were lined with pink, and they snorted! Jack was afraid, but he considered that this was such a long time ago that the holes, whatever they were, could not hurt him; but it made him start, notwithstanding, when a huge flat head reared itself up close to the boat, and he found that the holes were the nostrils of creatures who kept all the rest of themselves under water.

In a minute or two hundreds of ugly flat-heads popped up, and the boat danced among them as they floundered about in the water.

"I hope they won't upset us," said Jack. "I wish you would land."

Mopsa said she would rather not, because she did not like the hairy elephants.

"There are no such things as hairy elephants," said Jack, in his dream; but he had hardly spoken when out of a wood close at hand some huge creatures, far larger than our elephants, came jogging down to the water. There were forty or fifty of them, and they were covered with what looked like tow. In fact, so coarse was their shaggy hair that they looked as if they were dressed in doormats; and when they stood still and shook themselves such clouds of dust flew out, as it swept over the river, that it almost stifled Jack and Mopsa.

"Odious!" exclaimed Jack, sneezing. "What terrible creatures these are!"

"Well," answered Mopsa, at the other end of the boat (but he could hardly see her for the dust,) "then why do you dream of them?"

Jack had just decided to dream of something else when with a noise greater than fifty trumpets, the elephants, having shaken out all the dust, came thundering down to the water to bathe in the liquid mud. They shook the whole country as they plunged; but that was not all. The awful river-horses rose up and, with shrill screams, fell upon them, and gave them battle; while up from every rill peeped above the rushes frogs as large as oxen, and with blue and green eyes that gleamed like the eyes of cats.

The frogs' croaking and the shrill trumpeting of the elephants, together with the cries of the river-horses, as all these creatures fought with horn and tusk, and fell on one another, lashing the water into whirlpools, among which the boat danced up and down like a cork, the blinding spray, and the flapping about of great bats over the boat and in it—so confused Jack that Mopsa had spoken to him several times before he answered.

"Oh, Jack!" she said at last; "if you can't dream any better, I must call the Craken."

"Very well," said Jack. "I'm almost wrapped up and smothered in bats' wings, so call anything you please."

Thereupon Mopsa whistled softly, and in a minute or two he saw, almost spanning the river, a hundred yards off, a thing like a rainbow, or a slender bridge, or still more like one ring or coil of an enormous serpent; and presently the creature's head shot up like a fountain, close to the boat, almost as high as a ship's mast. It was the Craken; and when Mopsa saw it she began to cry, and said: "We are caught in this crowd of creatures, and we cannot get away from the land of dreams. Do help us, Craken."

Some of the bats that hung to the edges of the boat had wings as large as sails, and the first thing the Craken did was to stoop its lithe neck, pick two or three of them off, and eat them.

"You can swim your boat home under my coils where the water is calm," the Craken said, "for she is so extremely old now that if you do not take care she will drop to pieces before you get back to the present time."

Jack knew it was of no use saying anything to this formidable creature, before whom the river-horses and the elephants were rushing to the shore; but when he looked and saw down the river rainbow behind rainbow—I mean coil behind coil—glittering in the sun, like so many glorious arches that did not reach to the banks, he felt extremely glad that this was a dream, and besides that, he thought to himself: "It's only a fabled monster."

"No, it's only a fable to these times," said Mopsa, answering his thought; "but in spite of that we shall have to go through all the rings."

They went under one—silver, green, and blue, and gold. The water dripped from it upon them, and the boat trembled, either because of its great age or because it felt the rest of the coil underneath.

A good way off was another coil, and they went so safely under that that Jack felt himself getting used to Crakens, and not afraid. Then they went under thirteen more. These kept getting nearer and nearer together but, besides that, the four-teenth had not quite such a high span as the former ones; but there were a great many to come, and yet they got lower and lower.

Both Jack and Mopsa noticed this, but neither said a word. The thirtieth coil brushed Jack's cap off, then they had to stoop to pass under the two next, and then they had to lie down in the bottom of the boat, and they got through with the greatest difficulty; but still before them was another! The boat was driving straight towards it, and it lay so close to the water that the arch it made was only a foot high. When Jack saw it, he called out: "No! that I cannot bear. Somebody else may do the rest of this dream. I shall jump overboard!"

Mopsa seemed to answer in quite a pleasant voice, as if she was not afraid:

"No, you'd much better wake." And then she went on: "Jack! Jack! why don't you wake?"

Then all on a sudden Jack opened his eyes, and found that he was lying quietly on the grass, that little Mopsa really had asked him why he did not wake. He saw the Queen too, standing by, looking at him, and saying to herself: "I did not put him to sleep. _I_ did not put him to sleep."

"We don't want any more stories today, Queen," said the apple-woman, in a disrespectful tone, and she immediately began to sing, clattering some tea-things all the time, for a kettle was boiling on some sticks, and she was going to make tea out of doors:

> "The marten flew to the finch's nest,
> Feathers, and moss, and a wisp of hay:
> 'The arrow it sped to thy brown mate's breast;
> Low in the broom is thy mate today.'
>
> " 'Liest thou low, love? low in the broom?
> Feathers and moss, and a wisp of hay,
> Warm the white eggs till I learn his doom.'
> She beateth her wings, and away, away.
>
> " 'Ah, my sweet singer, thy days are told
> (Feathers and moss, and a wisp of hay)!
> Thine eyes are dim, and the eggs grow cold.
> O mournful morrow! O dark today!'

"The finch flew back to her cold, cold nest,
  Feathers and moss, and a wisp of hay.
Mine is the trouble that rent her breast,
  And home is silent, and love is clay."

Jack felt very tired indeed—as much tired as if he had
really been out all day on the river, and gliding under the
coils of the Craken. He, however, rose up when the apple-
woman called him, and drank his tea, and had some fairy
bread with it, which refreshed him very much.

After tea he measured Mopsa again, and found that she had
grown up to a higher button. She looked much wiser too, and
when he said she must be taught to read she made no
objection, so he arranged daisies and buttercups into the
forms of the letters, and she learnt nearly all of them that one
evening, while crowds of the one-foot-one fairies looked on,
hanging from the boughs and sitting in the grass, and shouting out the names of the letters as Mopsa said them. They
were very polite to Jack, for they gathered all these flowers
for him, and emptied them from their little caps at his feet as
fast as he wanted them.

XI

GOOD MORNING, SISTER

Sweet is childhood—childhood's over,
　　Kiss and part.
Sweet is youth; but youth's a rover—
　　So's my heart.
Sweet is rest; but by all showing
　　Toil is nigh.
We must go. Alas! the going,
　　Say "goodbye."

Jack crept under his canopy, went to sleep early that night and did not wake till the sun had risen, when the apple-woman called him, and said breakfast was nearly ready.

The same thing never happens twice in Fairyland, so this time the breakfast was not spread in a tent, but on the river. The Queen had cut off a tiny piece of her robe, the one-foot-one fairies had stretched it till it was very large, and then they had spread it on the water, where it floated and lay like a great carpet of purple and gold. One corner of it was moored to the side of Jack's boat; but he had not observed this, because of his canopy. However, that was now looped up by the apple-woman, and Jack and Mopsa saw what was going on.

Hundreds of swans had been towing the carpet along, and were still holding it with their beaks, while a crowd of doves walked about on it, smoothing out the creases and patting it with their pretty pink feet till it was quite firm and straight. The swans then swam away, and they flew away.

Presently troops of fairies came down to the landing-place, jumped into Jack's boat without asking leave, and so got on to the carpet, while at the same time a great tree which grew on the bank began to push out fresh leaves, as large as fans, and shoot out long branches, which again shot out others, till very

302

soon there was shade all over the carpet—a thick shadow as good as a tent, which was very pleasant, for the sun was already hot.

When the Queen came down the tree suddenly blossomed out with thousands of red and white flowers.

"You must not go on to that carpet," said the apple-woman; "let us sit still in the boat, and be served here." She whispered this as the Queen stepped into the boat.

"Good morning, Jack," said the Queen. "Good morning, dear." This was to the apple-woman; and then she stood still for a moment and looked earnestly at little Mopsa, and sighed.

"Well," she said to her, "don't you mean to speak to me?" Then Mopsa lifted up her pretty face and blushed very rosy red, and said, in a shy voice: "Good morning—sister."

"I said so!" exclaimed the Queen; "I said so!" and she lifted up her beautiful eyes, and murmured out: "What is to be done now?"

"Never mind, Queen dear," said Jack. "If it was rude of Mopsa to say that, she is such a little young thing that she does not know better."

"It was not rude," said Mopsa, and she laughed and blushed again. "It was not rude, and I am not sorry."

As she said this the Queen stepped on to the carpet, and all the flowers began to drop down. They were something like camellias, and there were thousands of them.

The fairies collected them in little heaps. They had no tables and chairs, nor any plates and dishes for this breakfast; but the Queen sat down on the carpet close to Jack's boat, and leaned her cheek on her hand, and seemed to be lost in thought. The fairies put some flowers into her lap, then each took some, and they all sat down and looked at the Queen, but she did not stir.

At last Jack said: "When is the breakfast coming?"

"This is the breakfast," said the apple-woman; "these flowers are most delicious eating. You never tasted anything so good in your life; but we don't begin till the Queen does."

Quantities of blossoms had dropped into the boat. Several fairies tumbled into it almost head over heels, they were in such a hurry, and they heaped them into Mopsa's lap, but took no notice of Jack, nor of the apple-woman either.

At last, when everyone had waited some time, the Queen pulled a petal off one flower, and began to eat, so everyone else began; and what the apple-woman had said was quite true. Jack knew that he never had tasted anything half so nice, and he was quite sorry when he could not eat any more. So, when everyone had finished, the Queen leaned her arm on the edge of the boat and, turning her lovely face towards Mopsa, said: "I want to whisper to you, sister."

"Oh!" said Mopsa. "I wish I was in Jack's waistcoat pocket again; but I'm so big now." And she took hold of the two sides of his velvet jacket, and hid her face between them.

"My old mother sent a message last night," continued the Queen, in a soft, sorrowful voice. "She is much more powerful than we are."

"What is the message?" asked Mopsa; but she still hid her face.

So the Queen moved over, and put her lips close to Mopsa's ear, and repeated it: "There cannot be two queens in one hive."

"If Mopsa leaves the hive, a fine swarm will go with her," said the apple-woman. "I shall, for one; that I shall!"

"No!" answered the Queen. "I hope not, dear; for you know well that this is my old mother's doing, not mine."

"Oh!" said Mopsa. "I feel as if I must tell a story too, just as the Queen does." But the apple-woman broke out in a very cross voice: "It's not at all like Fairyland, if you go on in this way, and I would as lief be out of it as in it." Then she began to sing, that she and Jack might not hear Mopsa's story:

"On the rocks by Aberdeen.
Where the whislin' wave had been,
As I wandered and at e'en
    Was eerie;
There I saw the sailing west,
And I ran with joy opprest—
Ay, and took out all my best,
    My dearie.

"Then I busked mysel' wi' speed,
And the neighbours cried, 'What need?
'Tis a lass in any weed
    Aye bonny!'
Now my heart, my heart is sair.
What's the good, though I be fair,
For thou'lt never see me mair,
    Man Johnnie!"

While the apple-woman sang Mopsa finished her story; and the Queen untied the fastening which held her carpet to the boat, and went floating upon it down the river.

"Goodbye," she said, kissing her hand to them. "I must go and prepare for the deputation."

So Jack and Mopsa played about all the morning, sometimes in the boat and sometimes on the shore, while the apple-woman sat on the grass, with her arms folded, and seemed to be lost in thought. At last she said to Jack: "What was the name of the great bird that carried you two here?"

"I have forgotten," answered Jack. "I've been trying to remember ever since we heard the Queen tell her first story, but I cannot."

"I remember," said Mopsa.

"Tell it, then," replied the apple-woman; but Mopsa shook her head.

"I don't want Jack to go," she answered.

"I don't want to go, nor that you should," said Jack.

"But the Queen said, 'There cannot be two Queens in one hive,' and that means that you are going to be turned out of this beautiful country."

"The other fairy lands are just as nice," answered Mopsa. "She can only turn me out of this one."

"I never heard of more than one Fairyland," observed Jack.

"It's my opinion," said the apple-woman, "that there are hundreds! And those one-foot-one fairies are such a saucy set that if I were you I should be very glad to get away from them. You've been here a very little while as yet, and you've no notion what goes on when the leaves begin to drop."

"Tell us," said Jack.

"Well, you must know," answered the apple-woman, "that fairies cannot abide cold weather; so, when the first rime frost comes, they bury themselves."

"Bury themselves?" repeated Jack.

"Yes, I tell you, they bury themselves. You've seen fairy rings, of course, even in your own country; and here the fields are full of them. Well, when it gets cold a company of fairies forms itself into a circle, and every one digs a little hole. The first that has finished jumps into his hole, and his next neighbour covers him up, and then jumps into his own little hole, and he gets covered up in his turn, till at last there is only one left, and he goes and joins another circle, hoping he shall have better luck than to be last again. I've often asked them why they do that, but no fairy can ever give a reason for anything. They always say that old Mother Fate makes them do it. When they come up again they are not fairies at all, but the good ones are mushrooms, and the bad ones are toadstools."

"Then you think there are no one-foot-one fairies in the other countries?" said Jack.

"Of course not," answered the apple-woman; "all the fairy lands are different. It's only the queens that are alike."

"I wish the fairies would not disappear for hours," said Jack. "They all seem to run off and hide themselves."

"That's their ways," answered the apple-woman. "All fairies are part of their time in the shape of human creatures, and the rest of it in the shape of some animal. These can turn themselves, when they please, to Guinea-fowl. In the heat of the day they generally prefer to be in that form, and they sit among the leaves of the trees.

"A great many are now with the Queen, because there is a deputation coming; but if I were to begin to sing, such a flock of Guinea-hens would gather round that the boughs of the trees would bend with their weight, and they would light on the grass all about so thickly that not a blade of grass would be seen as far as the song was heard."

So she began to sing, and the air was darkened by great flocks of these Guinea-fowl. They alighted just as she had said, and kept time with their heads and their feet, nodding like a crowd of mandarins; and yet it was nothing but a stupid old song that you would have thought could have no particular meaning for them.

LIKE A LAVEROCK IN THE LIFT

I

It's we two, it's we two, it's we two for aye,
All the world and we two, and Heaven be our stay.
Like a laverock in the lift, sing, O bonny bride!
All the world was Adam once, with Eve by his side.

II

What's the world, my lass, my love! what can it do?
I am thine, and thou art mine; life is sweet and new.
If the world have missed the mark, let it stand by,
For we two have gotten leave, and once more we'll try.

III

Like a laverock in the lift, sing, O bonny bride!
It's we two, it's we two, happy side by side.
Take a kiss from me thy man; now the song begins:
"All is made afresh for us, and the brave heart wins."

IV

When the darker days come, and no sun will shine,
Thou shalt dry my tears, lass, and I'll dry thine.
It's we two, it's we two, while the world's away,
Sitting by the golden sheaves on our wedding-day.

XII

THEY RUN AWAY FROM OLD MOTHER FATE

A land that living warmth disowns,
　　It meets my wondering ken;
A land where all the men are stones,
　　Or all the stones are men.

Before the apple-woman had finished Jack and Mopsa saw the
Queen coming in great state, followed by thousands of the
one-foot-one fairies, and leading by a ribbon round its neck a
beautiful brown doe. A great many pretty fawns were walking
among the fairies.

"Here's the deputation," said the apple-woman; but as the
Guinea-fowl rose like a cloud at the approach of the Queen,
and the fairies and fawns pressed forward, there was a good
deal of noise and confusion, during which Mopsa stepped up
close to Jack and whispered in his ear: "Remember, Jack,
whatever you can do you may do."

Then the brown doe lay down at Mopsa's feet, and the
Queen began:

"Jack and Mopsa, I love you both. I had a message last
night from my old mother, and I told you what it was."

"Yes, Queen," said Mopsa, "you did."

"And now," continued the Queen, "she has sent this beautiful brown doe from the country beyond the lake, where they
are in the greatest distress for a queen, to offer Mopsa the
crown; and, Jack, it is fated that Mopsa is to reign there, so
you had better say no more about it."

"I don't want to be a queen," said Mopsa, pouting; "I want
to play with Jack."

"You are a queen already," answered the real Queen; "at
least, you will be in a few days. You are so much grown, even
since the morning, that you come up nearly to Jack's shoulder.
In four days you will be as tall as I am; and it is quite

308

impossible that anyone of fairy birth should be as tall as a queen in her own country."

"But I don't see what stags and does can want with a queen," said Jack.

"They were obliged to turn into deer," said the Queen, "when they crossed their own border; but they are fairies when they are at home, and they want Mopsa, because they are always obliged to have a queen of alien birth."

"If I go," said Mopsa, "shall Jack go too?"

"Oh no," answered the Queen; "Jack and the apple-woman are my subjects."

"Apple-woman," said Jack, "tell us what you think; shall Mopsa go to this country?"

"Why, child," said the apple-woman, "go away from here she must; but she need not go off with the deer, I suppose, unless she likes. They look gentle and harmless; but it is very hard to get at the truth in this country, and I've heard queer stories about them."

"Have you?" said the Queen. "Well, you can repeat them if you like; but remember that the poor brown doe cannot contradict them."

So the apple-woman said: "I have heard, but I don't know how true it is, that in that country they shut up their queen in a great castle, and cover her with a veil, and never let the sun shine on her; for if by chance the least little sunbeam should light on her she would turn into a doe directly, and all the nation would turn with her, and stay so."

"I don't want to be shut up in a castle," said Mopsa.

"But is it true?" asked Jack.

"Well," said the apple-woman, "as I told you before, I cannot make out whether it's true or not, for all these stags and fawns look very mild, gentle creatures."

"I won't go," said Mopsa; "I would rather run away."

All this time the Queen with the brown doe had been gently pressing with the crowd nearer and nearer to the brink of the river, so that now Jack and Mopsa, who stood facing them, were quite close to the boat; and while they argued and tried to make Mopsa come away, Jack suddenly whispered to her to spring into the boat, which she did, and he after her, and at the same time he cried out:

"Now, boat, if you are my boat, set off as fast as you can, and let nothing of fairy birth get on board of you."

No sooner did he begin to speak than the boat swung itself away from the edge, and almost in a moment it was in the very middle of the river, and beginning to float gently down with the stream.

Now, as I have told you before, that river runs up the country instead of down to the sea, so Jack and Mopsa floated still farther up into Fairyland; and they saw the Queen, and the apple-woman, and all the crowd of fawns and fairies walking along the bank of the river, keeping exactly to the same pace that the boat went; and this went on for hours and hours, so that there seemed to be no chance that Jack and Mopsa could land; and they heard no voices at all, nor any sound but the baying of the old hound, who could not swim out to them, because Jack had forbidden the boat to take anything of fairy birth on board of her.

Luckily the bottom of the boat was full of those delicious flowers that had dropped into it at breakfast time, so there was plenty of nice food for Jack and Mopsa; and Jack noticed, when he looked at her towards evening, that she was now nearly as tall as himself, and that her lovely brown hair floated down to her ankles.

"Jack," she said, before it grew dusk, "will you give me your little purse that has the silver fourpence in it?"

Now Mopsa had often played with this purse. It was lined with a piece of pale green silk, and when Jack gave it to her she pulled the silk out, and shook it, and patted it, and stretched it, just as the queen had done, and it came into a most lovely cloak, which she tied round her neck. Then she twisted up her long hair into a coil, and fastened it round her head, and called to the fireflies which were beginning to glitter on the trees to come, and they came and alighted in a row upon the coil, and turned into diamonds directly. So now Mopsa had got a crown and a robe, and she was so beautiful that Jack thought he should never be tired of looking at her; but it was nearly dark now, and he was so sleepy and tired that he could not keep his eyes open, though he tried very hard, and he began to blink, and then he began to nod, and at last he fell fast asleep, and did not awake till morning.

Then he sat up in the boat, and looked about him. A wonderful country, indeed!—no trees, no grass, no houses, nothing but red stones and red sand—and Mopsa was gone. Jack jumped on shore, for the boat had stopped, and was

close to the brink of the river. He looked about for some
time, and at last, in the shadow of a pale brown rock, he
found her; and oh! delightful surprise, the apple-woman was
there too. She was saying: "Oh, my bones! Dearie, dearie
me, how they do ache!" That was not surprising, for she had
been out all night. She had walked beside the river with the
Queen and her tribe till they came to a little tinkling stream,
which divides their country from the sandy land, and there
they were obliged to stop; they could not cross it. But the
apple-woman sprang over, and, though the Queen told her
she must come back again in twenty-four hours, she did not
appear to be displeased. Now the Guinea-hens, when they
had come to listen, the day before, to the apple-woman's
song, had brought each of them a grain of maize in her beak,
and had thrown it into her apron; so when she got up she
carried it with her gathered up there, and now she had been
baking some delicious little cakes on a fire of dry sticks that
the river had drifted down, and Mopsa had taken a honey-
comb from the rock, so they all had a very nice breakfast.
And the apple-woman gave them a great deal of good advice,
and told them if they wished to remain in Fairyland, and not
be caught by the brown doe and her followers, they must cross
over the purple mountains.

"For on the other side of those peaks," she said, "I have
heard that fairies live who have the best of characters for
being kind and just. I am sure they would never shut up a
poor queen in a castle.

"But the best thing you could do, dear," she said to Mopsa,
"would be to let Jack call the bird, and make her carry you
back to his own country."

"The Queen is not at all kind," said Jack; "I have been very
kind to her, and she should have let Mopsa stay."

"No, Jack, she could not," said Mopsa; "but I wish I had
not grown so fast, and I don't like to go to your country. I
would rather run away."

"But who is to tell us where to run?" asked Jack.

"Oh," said Mopsa, "some of these people."

"I don't see anybody," said Jack, looking about him.

Mopsa pointed to a group of stones, and then to another
group, and as Jack looked he saw that in shape they were
something like people—stone people. One stone was a little
like an old man with a mantle over him, and he was sitting on

the ground with his knees up nearly to his chin. Another was like a woman with a hood on, and she seemed to be leaning her chin on her hand. Close to these stood something very much like a cradle in shape; and beyond were stones that resembled a flock of sheep lying down on the bare sand, with something that reminded Jack of the figure of a man lying asleep near them, with his face to the ground.

That was a very curious country; all the stones reminded you of people or of animals, and the shadows that they cast were much more like than the stones themselves. There were blocks with things that you might have mistaken for stone ropes twisted round them; but, looking at the shadows, you could see distinctly that they were trees, and that what coiled round were snakes. Then there was a rocky prominence, at one side of which was something like a sitting figure, but its shadow, lying on the ground, was that of a girl with a distaff. Jack was very much surprised at all this; Mopsa was not. She did not see, she said, that one thing was more wonderful than another. All the fairy lands were wonderful, but the men-and-women world was far more so. She and Jack went about among the stones all day, and as the sun got low both the shadows and the blocks themselves became more and more like people, and if you went close you could now see features, very sweet, quiet features, but the eyes were all shut.

By this time the apple-woman began to feel very sad. She knew she would soon have to leave Jack and Mopsa, and she said to Mopsa, as they finished their evening meal: "I wish you would ask the inhabitants a few questions, dear, before I go, for I want to know whether they can put you in the way of how to cross the purple mountains."

Jack said nothing, for he thought he would see what Mopsa was going to do; so when she got up, and went towards the shape that was like a cradle he followed, and the apple-woman too. Mopsa went to the figure that sat by the cradle. It was a stone yet, but when Mopsa laid her little warm hand on its bosom it smiled.

"Dear," said Mopsa, "I wish you would wake."

A curious little sound was now heard, but the figure did not move, and the apple-woman lifted Mopsa on to the lap of the statue; then she put her arms round its neck, and spoke to it again very distinctly: "Dear! why don't you wake? You had better wake now; the baby's crying."

Jack now observed that the sound he had heard was something like the crying of a baby. He also heard the figure answering Mopsa. It said: "I am only a stone!"

"Then," said Mopsa, "I am not a queen yet. I cannot wake her. Take me down."

"I am not warm," said the figure; and that was quite true, and yet she was not a stone now which reminded one of a woman, but a woman that reminded one of a stone.

All the west was very red with the sunset, and the river was red too, and Jack distinctly saw some of the coils of rope glide down from the trees and slip into the water; next he saw the stones that had looked like sheep raise up their heads in the twilight, and then lift themselves and shake their woolly sides. At that instant the large white moon heaved up her pale face between two dark blue hills, and upon this the statue put out its feet and gently rocked the cradle.

Then it spoke again to Mopsa: "What was it that you wished me to tell you?"

"How to find the way over those purple mountains," said Mopsa.

"You must set off in an hour, then," said the woman, and she had hardly anything of the stone about her now. "You can easily find it by night without any guide, but nothing can ever take you to it by day."

"But we would rather stay a few days in this curious country," said Jack; "let us wait at least till tomorrow night."

The statue at this moment rubbed her hands together as if they still felt cold and stiff. "You are quite welcome to stay," she observed; "but you had better not."

"Why not?" persisted Jack.

"Father," said the woman, rising and shaking the figure next to her by the sleeve. "Wake up!" What had looked like an old man was a real old man now, and he got up and began to gather sticks to make a fire, and to pick up the little brown stones which had been scattered about all day, but which now were berries of coffee; the larger ones, which you might find here and there, were rasped rolls. Then the woman answered Jack: "Why not? Why, because it's full moon tonight at midnight, and the moment the moon is past the full your Queen, whose country you have just left, will be able to cross over the little stream, and she will want to take you and that other mortal back. She can do it, of course, if she pleases; and we can afford you no protection, for by that time we shall be stones again. We are only people two hours out of the twenty-four."

"That is very hard," observed Jack.

"No,"-said the woman, in a tone of indifference; "it comes to the same thing, as we live twelve times as long as others do."

By this time the shepherd was gently driving his flock down to the water, and round fifty little fires groups of people were sitting roasting coffee, while cows were lowing to be milked, and girls with distaffs were coming to them slowly, for no one was in a hurry there. They say in that country that they wish to enjoy their day quietly, because it is so short.

"Can you tell us anything of the land beyond the mountains?" asked Jack.

"Yes," said the woman. "Of all fairy lands it is the best; the people are the gentlest and kindest."

"Then I had better take Mopsa there than down the river?" said Jack.

"You can't take her down the river," replied the woman; and Jack thought she laughed and was glad of that.

"Why not?" asked Jack. "I have a boat."

"Yes, sir," answered the woman, "but where is it now?"

XIII

MELON SEEDS

Rosalind. Well, this is the forest of Arden.

Touchstone. Ay, now am I in Arden: the more fool I;
when I was at home I was in a better place; but travellers
must be content.

As You Like It

"Where is it now?" said the stone woman; and when Jack
heard that he ran down to the river, and looked right and
looked left. At last he saw his boat—a mere speck in the
distance, it had floated so far.

He called it, but it was far beyond the reach of his voice;
and Mopsa, who had followed him, said:

"It does not signify, Jack, for I feel that no place is the right
place for me but that country beyond the purple mountains,
and I shall never be happy unless we go there."

So they walked back towards the stone people hand in
hand, and the apple-woman presently joined them. She was
crying gently, for she knew that she must soon pass over the
little stream and part with these whom she called her dear
children. Jack had often spoken to her that day about going
home to her own country, but she said it was too late to think
of that now, and she must end her days in the land of Faery.

The kind stone people asked them to come and sit by their
little fire; and in the dusk the woman whose baby had slept in
a stone cradle took it up and began to sing to it. She seemed
astonished when she heard that the apple-woman had power
to go home if she could make up her mind to do it; and as she
sang she looked at her with wonder and pity.

> "Little babe, while burns the west,
>   Warm thee, warm thee in my breast;
> While the moon doth shine her best,
>   And the dews distil not.

"All the land so sad, so fair—
Sweet its toils are, blest its care.
Child, we may not enter there!
Some there are that will not.

"Fain would I thy margins know,
Land of work, and land of snow;
Land of life, whose rivers flow
On, and on, and stay not.

"Fain would I thy small limbs fold,
While the weary hours are told,
Little babe in cradle cold.
Some there are that may not."

"You are not exactly fairies, I suppose?" said Jack. "If you were, you could go to our country when you pleased."

"No," said the woman; "we are not exactly fairies; but we shall be more like them when our punishment is over."

"I am sorry you are punished," answered Jack, "for you seem very nice, kind people."

"We were not always kind," answered the woman; "and perhaps we are only kind now because we have no time and no chance of being otherwise. I'm sure I don't know about that. We were powerful once, and we did a cruel deed. I must not tell you what it was. We were told that our hearts were all as cold as stones—and I suppose they were—and we were doomed to be stones all our lives, excepting for the two hours of twilight. There was no one to sow the crops, or water the grass, so it all failed, and the trees died, and our houses fell, and our possessions were stolen from us."

"It is a very sad thing," observed the apple-woman; and then she said that she must go, for she had a long way to walk before she would reach the little brook that led to the country of her own queen; so she kissed the two children, Jack and Mopsa, and they begged her again to think better of it, and return to her own land. But she said No; she had no heart for work now, and could not bear either cold or poverty.

Then the woman who was hugging her little baby, and keeping it cosy and warm, began to tell Jack and Mopsa that it was time they should begin to run away to the country over the purple mountains, or else the Queen would overtake

them and be very angry with them; so, with many promises
that they would mind her directions, they set off hand in
hand to run; but before they left her they could see plainly
that she was beginning to turn again into stone. However,
she had given them a slice of melon with the seeds in it. It
had been growing on the edge of the river, and was stone in
the day-time, like everything else. "When you are tired," she
said, "eat the seeds, and they will enable you to go running
on. You can put the slice into this little red pot, which has
string handles to it, and you can hang it on your arm. While
you have it with you it will not turn to stone, but if you lay it
down it will, and then it will be useless."

So, as I said before, Jack and Mopsa set off hand in hand to
run; and as they ran all the things and people gradually and
softly settled themselves to turn into stone again. Their cloaks
and gowns left off fluttering, and hung stiffly; and then they
left off their occupations, and sat down, or lay themselves
down; and the sheep and cattle turned stiff and stonelike too,
so that in a very little while all that country was nothing but
red stones and red sand, just as it had been in the morning.

Presently the full moon, which had been hiding behind a
cloud, came out, and they saw their shadows, which fell
straight before them; so they ran on hand in hand very
merrily till the half-moon came up, and the shadows she
made them cast fell sideways. This was rather awkward,
because as long as only the full moon gave them shadows
they had but to follow them in order to go straight towards
the purple mountains. Now they were not always sure which
were her shadows; and presently a crescent moon came, and
still further confused them; also the sand began to have tufts
of grass in it; and then, when they had gone a little farther,
there were beautiful patches of anemones, and hyacinths, and
jonquils, and crown imperials, and they stopped to gather
them; and they got among some trees, and then, as they had
nothing to guide them but the shadows, and these went all
sorts of ways, they lost a great deal of time, and the trees
became of taller growth; but they still ran on and on till they
got into a thick forest where it was quite dark, and here
Mopsa began to cry, for she was tired.

"If I could only begin to be a queen," she said to Jack,
"I could go wherever I pleased. I am not a fairy, and yet I am

not a proper queen. Oh, what shall I do? I cannot go any farther."

So Jack gave her some of the seeds of the melon, though it was so dark that he could scarcely find the way to her mouth, and then he took some himself, and they both felt that they were rested, and Jack comforted Mopsa.

"If you are not a queen yet," he said, "you will be by tomorrow morning; for when our shadows danced on before us yours was so very nearly the same height as mine that I could see hardly any difference."

When they reached the end of that great forest, and found themselves out in all sorts of moonlight, the first thing they did was to laugh—the shadows looked so odd, sticking out in every direction; and the next thing they did was to stand back to back, and put their heels together, and touch their heads together, to see by the shadow which was the taller; and Jack was still the least bit in the world taller than Mopsa; so they knew she was not a queen yet, and they ate some more melon seeds, and began to climb up the mountain.

They climbed till the trees of the forest looked no bigger than gooseberry bushes, and then they climbed till the whole forest looked only like a patch of moss; and then, when they got a little higher, they saw the wonderful river, a long way off, and the snow glittering on the peaks overhead; and while they were looking and wondering how they should find a pass, the moons all went down, one after the other, and, if Mopsa had not found some glow-worms, they would have been quite in the dark again. However, she took a dozen of them, and put them round Jack's ankles, so that when he walked he could see where he was going; and he found a little sheep-path, and she followed him.

Now they had noticed during the night how many shooting stars kept darting about from time to time, and at last one shot close by them, and fell in the soft moss on before. There it lay shining; and Jack, though he began to feel tired again, made haste to it, for he wanted to see what it was like.

It was not what you would have supposed. It was soft and round, and about the colour of a ripe apricot; it was covered with fur, and in fact it was evidently alive, and had curled itself up into a round ball.

"The dear little thing!" said Jack, as he held it in his hand, and showed it to Mopsa. "How its heart beats! Is it frightened?"

"Who are you?" said Mopsa to the thing. "What is your name?"

The little creature made a sound that seemed like "Wisp."

"Uncurl yourself, Wisp," said Mopsa. "Jack and I want to look at you."

So Wisp unfolded himself, and showed two little black eyes, and spread out two long filmy wings. He was like a most beautiful bat, and the light he shed out illuminated their faces.

"It is only one of the air fairies," said Mopsa. "Pretty creature! It never did any harm, and would like to do us good if it knew how, for it knows that I shall be a queen very soon. Wisp, if you like, you may go and tell your friends and relations that we want to cross over the mountains, and if they can they may help us."

Upon this Wisp spread out his wings, and shot off again; and Jack's feet were so tired that he sat down and pulled off one of his shoes, for he thought there was a stone in it. So he set the little red jar beside him, and quite forgot what the stone woman had said, but went on shaking his shoe, and buckling it, and admiring the glow-worms round his ankle, till Mopsa said: "Darling Jack, I am so dreadfully tired! Give me some more melon seeds." Then he lifted up the jar, and thought it felt very heavy; and when he put in his hand, jar, and melon, and seeds were all turned to stone together.

They were both very sorry, and they sat still for a minute or two, for they were much too tired to stir; and then shooting stars began to appear in all directions. The fairy bat had told his friends and relations, and they were coming. One fell at Mopsa's feet, another in her lap; more, more, all about, behind, before and over them. And they spread out long filmy wings, some of them a yard long, till Jack and Mopsa seemed to be enclosed in a perfect network of the rays of shooting stars, and they were both a good deal frightened. Fifty or sixty shooting stars, with black eyes that could stare enough, they thought, to frighten anybody.

"If we had anything to sit upon," said Mopsa, "they could carry us over the pass." She had no sooner spoken than the largest of the bats bit off one of his own long wings, and laid it at Mopsa's feet. It did not seem to matter much to him that he had parted with it, for he shot out another wing directly, just as a comet shoots out a ray of light sometimes when it approaches the sun.

Mopsa thanked the shooting fairy and, taking the wing, began to stretch it, till it was large enough for her and Jack to sit upon. Then all the shooting fairies came round it, took its edges in their mouths and began to fly away with it over the mountains. They went slowly, for Jack and Mopsa were heavy, and they flew very low, resting now and then; but in the course of time they carried the wing over the pass, and half way down the other side. Then the sun came up; and the moment he appeared all their lovely apricot-coloured light was gone, and they only looked like common bats, such as you can see every evening.

They set down Jack and Mopsa, folded up their long wings and hung down their heads.

Mopsa thanked them, and said they had been useful; but still they looked ashamed, and crept into little corners and crevices of the rock, to hide.

XIV

REEDS AND RUSHES

'Tis merry, 'tis merry in Fairyland,
    When Fairy birds are singing;
When the court doth ride by their monarch's side,
    With bit and bridle ringing.

Walter Scott

There were many fruit trees on that slope of the mountain, and Jack and Mopsa, as they came down, gathered some fruit for breakfast, and did not feel very tired, for the long ride on the wing had rested them.

They could not see the plain, for a slight blue mist hung over it; but the sun was hot already, and as they came down they saw a beautiful bed of high reeds, and thought they would sit awhile and rest in it. A rill of clear water ran beside the bed, so when they had reached it they sat down, and began to consider what they should do next.

"Jack," said Mopsa, "did you see anything particular as you came down with the shooting stars?"

"No, I saw nothing so interesting as they were," answered Jack. "I was looking at them and watching how they squeaked to one another, and how they had little hooks in their wings, with which they held the large wing that we sat on."

"But I saw something," said Mopsa. "Just as the sun rose I looked down, and in the loveliest garden I ever saw, and all among trees and woods, I saw a most beautiful castle. Oh, Jack! I am sure that castle is the place I am to live in, and now we have nothing to do but to find it. I shall soon be a queen, and there I shall reign."

"Then I shall be king there," said Jack; "shall I?"

"Yes, if you can," answered Mopsa. "Of course, whatever you can do you may do. And, Jack, this is a much better fairy country than either the stony land or the other that we first came to, for this castle is a real place! It will not melt away. There the people can work, they know how to love each other: common fairies cannot do that, I know. They can laugh and cry, and I shall teach them several things that they do not know yet. Oh, do let us make haste and find the castle!"

So they arose; but they turned the wrong way, and by mistake walked farther and farther in among the reeds, whose feathery heads puffed into Mopsa's face, and Jack's coat was all covered with the fluffy seed.

"This is very odd," said Jack. "I thought this was only a small bed of reeds when we stepped into it; but really we must have walked a mile already."

But they walked on and on, till Mopsa grew quite faint, and her sweet face became very pale, for she knew that the beds of reeds were spreading faster than they walked, and then they shot up so high that it was impossible to see over their heads; so at last Jack and Mopsa were so tired that they sat down, and Mopsa began to cry.

However, Jack was the braver of the two this time, and he comforted Mopsa, and told her that she was nearly a queen, and would never reach her castle by sitting still. So she got up and took his hand, and he went on before, parting the reeds and pulling her after him, till all on a sudden they heard the sweetest sound in the world: it was like a bell, and it sounded again and again.

It was the castle clock, and it was striking twelve at noon.

As it finished striking they came out at the farther edge of the great bed of reeds, and there was the castle straight before them—a beautiful castle, standing on the slope of a hill. The grass all about it was covered with beautiful flowers; two of the taller turrets were overgrown with ivy, and a flag was flying on a staff; but everything was so silent and lonely that it made one sad to look on. As Jack and Mopsa drew near they trod as gently as they could, and did not say a word.

All the windows were shut, but there was a great door in the centre of the building, and they went towards it, hand in hand.

What a beautiful hall! The great door stood wide open, and they could see what a delightful place this must be to live in: it was paved with squares of blue and white marble, and here and there carpets were spread, with chairs and tables upon them. They looked and saw a great dome overhead, filled with windows of coloured glass, and they cast down blue and golden and rosy reflections.

"There is my home that I shall live in," said Mopsa; and she came close to the door, and they both looked in, till at last she let go of Jack's hand, and stepped over the threshold.

The bell in the tower sounded again more sweetly than ever, and the instant Mopsa was inside there came from behind the fluted columns, which rose up on every side, the brown doe, followed by troops of deer and fawns!

"Mopsa! Mopsa!" cried Jack. "Come away! come back!" But Mopsa was too much astonished to stir, and something seemed to hold Jack from following; but he looked and looked, till, as the brown doe advanced, the door of the castle closed—Mopsa was shut in, and Jack was left outside.

So Mopsa had come straight to the place she thought she had run away from.

"But I am determined to get her away from those creatures," thought Jack; "she does not want to reign over deer." And he began to look about him, hoping to get in. It was of no use: all the windows in the front of the castle were high, and when he tried to go round, he came to a high wall with battlements. Against some parts of this wall the ivy grew, and looked as if it might have grown there for ages; its stems were thicker than his waist, and its branches were spread over the surface like network; so by means of them he hoped to climb to the top.

He immediately began to try. Oh, how high the wall was! First he came to several sparrows' nests, and very much frightened the sparrows were; then he reached starlings' nests, and very angry the starlings were; but at last, just under the coping, he came to jackdaws' nests, and these birds were very friendly, and pointed out to him the best little holes for him to put his feet into. At last he reached the top, and found to his delight that the wall was three feet thick, and he could walk upon it quite comfortably, and look down into a lovely garden, where all the trees were in blossom, and creepers tossed their long tendrils from tree to tree, covered with puffs of yellow, or bells of white, or bunches and knots of blue or rosy bloom.

He could look down into the beautiful empty rooms of the castle, and he walked cautiously on the wall till he came to the west front, and reached a little casement window that had latticed panes. Jack peeped in; nobody was there. He took his knife and cut away a little bit of lead to let out the pane, and it fell with such a crash on the pavement below that he wondered it did not bring the deer over to look at what he was about. Nobody came.

He put in his hand and opened the latchet, and with very little trouble got down into the room. Still nobody was to be seen. He thought that the room, years ago, might have been a fairies' schoolroom, for it was strewn with books, slates and all sorts of copybooks. A fine soft dust had settled down over everything—pens, papers and all. Jack opened a copybook: its pages were headed with maxims, just as ours are, which proved that these fairies must have been superior to such as he had hitherto come among. Jack read some of them:

Turn your back on the light, and you'll follow a shadow.
The deaf queen Fate has dumb courtiers.
If the hound is your foe, don't sleep in his kennel.
That that is, is.

And so on; but nobody came, and no sound was heard, so he opened the door, and found himself in a long and most splendid gallery, all hung with pictures, and spread with a most beautiful carpet, which was as soft and white as a piece of wool, and wrought with a beautiful device. This was the letter M, with a crown and sceptre, and underneath a beautiful little boat, exactly like the one in which he had come up the river. Jack felt sure that this carpet had been made for Mopsa, and he went along the gallery upon it till he reached a grand staircase of oak that was almost black with age, and he stole gently down it, for he began to feel rather shy, more especially as he could now see the great hall under the dome, and that it had a beautiful lady in it, and many other people, but no deer at all.

These fairy people were something like the one-foot-one fairies, but much larger and more like children, and they had very gentle, happy faces, and seemed to be extremely glad and gay. But seated on a couch, where lovely painted windows threw down all sorts of rainbow colours on her, was a beautiful fairy lady, as large as a woman. She had Mopsa in her arms, and was looking down upon her with eyes full of love, while at her side stood a boy, who was exactly and precisely like Jack himself. He had rather long light hair and grey eyes, and a velvet jacket. That was all Jack could see at first, but as he drew nearer the boy turned, and then Jack felt as if he was looking at himself in the glass.

Mopsa had been very tired, and now she was fast asleep, with her head on that lady's shoulder. The boy kept looking at her, and he seemed very happy indeed; so did the lady, and she presently told him to bring Jack something to eat.

It was rather a curious speech that she made to him: it was this:

"Jack, bring Jack some breakfast."

"What!" thought Jack to himself. "Has he got a face like mine, and a name like mine too?"

So that other Jack went away, and presently came back with a golden plate full of nice things to eat.

"I know you don't like me," he said, as he came up to Jack with the plate.

"Not like him?" repeated the lady; "and pray, what reason have you for not liking my royal nephew?"

"Oh, dame!" exclaimed the boy, and laughed.

The lady, on hearing this, turned pale, for she perceived that she herself had mistaken the one for the other.

"I see you know how to laugh," said the real Jack. "You are wiser people than those whom I went to first; but the reason I don't like you is that you are so exactly like me."

"I am not!" exclaimed the boy. "Only hear him, dame! You mean, I suppose, that you are so exactly like me. I am sure I don't know what you mean by it."

"Nor I either," replied Jack, almost in a passion.

"It couldn't be helped, of course," said the other Jack.

"Hush! hush!" said the fairy woman. "Don't wake our dear little Queen. Was it you, my royal nephew, who spoke last?"

"Yes, dame," answered the boy, and again he offered the plate; but Jack was swelling with indignation, and he gave the plate a push with his elbow, which scattered the fruit and bread on the ground.

"I won't eat it," he said; but when the other Jack went and picked it up again, and said: "Oh yes, do, old fellow; it's not my fault, you know," he began to consider that it was no use being cross in Fairyland; so he forgave his double, and had just finished his breakfast when Mopsa woke.

XV

THE QUEEN'S WAND

One, two, three, four; one, two, three, four;
  'Tis still one, two, three, four.
Mellow and silvery are the tones,
  But I wish the bells were more.

Southey

Mopsa woke: she was rather too big to be nursed, for she was the size of Jack, and looked like a sweet little girl of ten years, but she did not always behave like one; sometimes she spoke as wisely as a grown-up woman, and sometimes she changed again and seemed like a child.

Mopsa lifted up her head and pushed back her long hair: her coronet had fallen off while she was in the bed of reeds; and she said to the beautiful dame:

"I am a queen now."

"Yes, my sweet Queen," answered the lady, "I know you are."

"And you promise that you will be kind to me till I grow up," said Mopsa, "and love me, and teach me how to reign?"

"Yes," repeated the lady; "and I will love you too, just as if you were a mortal and I your mother."

"For I am only ten years old yet," said Mopsa, "and the throne is too big for me to sit upon; but I am a queen." And then she paused, and said: "Is it three o'clock?"

As she spoke the sweet clear bell of the castle sounded three times, and then chimes began to play; they played such a joyous tune that it made everybody sing. The dame sang, the crowd of fairies sang, the boy who was Jack's double sang and Mopsa sang—only Jack was silent—and this was the song:

"The prince shall to the chase again,
The dame has got her face again,
The king shall have his place again
    Aneath the fairy dome.

"And all the knights shall woo again,
And all the doves shall coo again,
And all the dreams come true again,
    And Jack shall go home."

"We shall see about that!" thought Jack to himself. And
Mopsa, while she sang those last words, burst into tears,
which Jack did not like to see; but all the fairies were so very
glad, so joyous and so delighted with her for having come to
be their queen, that after a while she dried her eyes, and said
to the wrong boy:

"Jack, when I pulled the lining out of your pocket-book
there was a silver fourpence in it."

"Yes," said the real Jack, "and here it is."

"Is it real money?" asked Mopsa. "Are you sure you brought
it with you all the way from your own country?"

"Yes," said Jack, "quite sure."

"Then, dear Jack," answered Mopsa, "will you give it to
me?"

"I will," said Jack, "if you will send this boy away."

"How can I?" answered Mopsa, surprised. "Don't you know
what happened when the door closed? Has nobody told you?"

"I did not see anyone after I got into the place," said Jack.
"There was no one to tell anything—not even a fawn, nor the
brown doe. I have only seen down here these fairy people,
and this boy, and this lady."

"The lady is the brown doe," answered Mopsa; "and this
boy and the fairies were the fawns." Jack was so astonished at
this that he stared at the lady and the boy and the fairies with
all his might.

"The sun came shining in as I stepped inside," said Mopsa,
"and a long beam fell down from the fairy dome across my
feet. Do you remember what the apple-woman told us—how
it was reported that the brown doe and her nation had a
queen whom they shut up, and never let the sun shine on
her? That was not a kind or true report, and yet it came from
something that really happened."

"Yes, I remember," said Jack; "and if the sun did shine they were all to be turned into deer."

"I dare not tell you all that story yet," said Mopsa; "but, Jack, as the brown doe and all the fawns came up to greet me, and passed by turns into the sunbeam, they took their own forms, every one of them, because the spell was broken. They were to remain in the disguise of deer till a queen of alien birth should come to them against her will. I am a queen of alien birth, and did not I come against my will?"

"Yes, to be sure," answered Jack. "We thought all the time that we were running away."

"If ever you come to Fairyland again," observed Mopsa, "you can save yourself the trouble of trying to run away from the old mother."

"I shall not 'come,'" answered Jack, "because I shall not go—not for a long while, at least. But the boy—I want to know why this boy turned into another ME?"

"Because he is the heir, of course," answered Mopsa.

"But I don't see that this is any reason at all," said Jack.

Mopsa laughed. "That's because you don't know how to argue," she replied. "Why, the thing is as plain as possible."

"It may be plain to you," persisted Jack, "but it's no reason."

"No reason!" repeated Mopsa. "No reason! when I like you the best of anything in the world, and when I am come here to be queen! Of course, when the spell was broken he took exactly your form on that account; and very right too."

"But why?" asked Jack.

Mopsa, however, was like other fairies in this respect—that she knew all about Old Mother Fate, but not about causes and reasons. She believed, as we do in this world, that

That that is, is,

but the fairies go further than this; they say:

That that is, is; and when it is, that is the reason that it is.

This sounds like nonsense to us, but it is all right to them.

So Mopsa, thinking she had explained everything, said again:

"And, dear Jack, will you give the silver fourpence to me?"

Jack took it out; and she got down from the dame's knee and took it in the palm of her hand, laying the other palm upon it.

"It will be very hot," observed the dame.

"But it will not burn me so as really to hurt, if I am a real queen," said Mopsa.

Presently she began to look as if something gave her pain.

"Oh, it's so hot!" she said to the other Jack; "so very hot!"

"Never mind, sweet Queen," he answered; "it will not hurt you long. Remember my poor uncle and all his knights."

Mopsa still held the little silver coin; but Jack saw that it hurt her, for two bright tears fell from her eyes; and in another moment he saw that it was actually melted, for it fell in glittering drops from Mopsa's hand to the marble floor, and there it lay as soft as quicksilver.

"Pick it up," said Mopsa to the other Jack; and he instantly did so, and laid it in her hand again; and she began gently to roll it backwards and forwards between her palms till she had rolled it into a very slender rod, two feet long, and not nearly so thick as a pin; but it did not bend, and it shone so brightly that you could hardly look at it.

Then she held it out towards the real Jack, and said: "Give this a name."

"I think it is a ——" began the other Jack; but the dame suddenly stopped him. "Silence, sirc! Don't you know that what it is first called that it will be?"

Jack hesitated; he thought if Mopsa was a queen the thing ought to be a sceptre; but it was certainly not at all like a sceptre.

"That thing is a wand," said he.

"You are a wand," said Mopsa, speaking to the silver stick, which was glittering now in a sunbeam almost as if it were a beam of light itself. Then she spoke again to Jack:

"Tell me, Jack, what can I do with a wand?"

Again the boy-king began to speak, and the dame stopped him, and again Jack considered. He had heard a great deal in his own country about fairy wands, but he could not remember that the fairies had done anything particular with them, so he gave what he thought was true, but what seemed to him a very stupid answer:

"You can make it point to anything that you please."

The moment he had said this, shouts of ecstasy filled the

hall, and all the fairies clapped their hands with such hurrahs
of delight that he blushed for joy.

The dame also looked truly glad, and as for the other Jack,
he actually turned head over heels, just as Jack had often
done himself on his father's lawn.

Jack had merely meant that Mopsa could point with the
wand to anything that she saw; but he was presently told that
what he had meant was nothing, and that his words were
everything.

"I can make it point now," said Mopsa, "and it will point
aright to anything I please, whether I know where the thing
is or not."

Again the hall was filled with those cries of joy, and the
sweet childlike fairies congratulated each other with "The
Queen has got a wand—a wand! and she can make it point
wherever she pleases!"

Then Mopsa rose and walked towards the beautiful staircase,
the dame and all the fairies following. Jack was going too, but
the other Jack held him.

"Where is Mopsa going? and why am I not to follow?"
inquired Jack.

"They are going to put on her robes, of course," answered
the other Jack.

"I am so tired of always hearing you say 'of course,'"
answered Jack; "and I wonder how it is that you always seem
to know what is going to be done without being told. However,
I suppose you can't help being odd people."

The boy-king did not make a direct answer; he only said: "I
like you very much, though you don't like me."

"Why do you like me?" asked Jack.

The other opened his eyes wide with surprise. "Most boys
say Sire to me," he observed; "at least they used to when
there were any boys here. However, that does not signify.
Why, of course I like you, because I am so tired of being
always a fawn, and you brought Mopsa to break the spell.
You cannot think how disagreeable it is to have no hands, and
to be all covered with hair. Now look at my hands; I can
move them and turn them everywhere, even over my head if
I like. Hoofs are good for nothing in comparison: and we
could not talk."

"Do tell me about it," said Jack. "How did you become
fawns?"

"I dare not tell you," said the boy; "and listen!—I hear Mopsa."

Jack looked, and certainly Mopsa was coming, but very strangely, he thought. Mopsa, like all other fairies, was afraid to whisper a spell with her eyes open; so a handkerchief was tied across them, and as she came on she felt her way, holding by the banisters with one hand, and with the other, between her finger and thumb, holding out the silver wand. She felt with her foot for the edge of the first stair; and Jack heard her say: "I am much older—ah! so much older, now I have got my wand. I can feel sorrow too, and *their* sorrow weighs down my heart."

Mopsa was dressed superbly in a white satin gown, with a long, long train of crimson velvet which was glittering with diamonds; it reached almost from one end of the great gallery to the other, and had hundreds of fairies to hold it and keep it in its place. But in her hair were no jewels, only a little crown made of daisies, and on her shoulders her robe was fastened with the little golden image of a boat. These things were to show the land she had come from and the vessel she had come in.

So she came slowly, slowly downstairs blindfold, and muttering to her wand all the time:

"Though the sun shine brightly,
    Wand, wand, guide rightly."

So she felt her way down to the great hall. There the wand turned half round in the hall towards the great door, and she and Jack and the other Jack came out on to the lawn in front with all the followers and train-bearers; only the dame remained behind.

Jack noticed now for the first time that, with the one exception of the boy king, all these fairies were lady fairies; he also observed that Mopsa, after the manner of fairy queens, though she moved slowly and blindfold, was beginning to tell a story. This time it did not make him feel sleepy. It did not begin at the beginning: their stories never do.

These are the first words he heard, for she spoke softly and very low, while he walked at her right hand, and the other Jack on her left:

"And so now I have no wings. But my thoughts can go up

(Jovinian and Roxaletta could not think). My thoughts are instead of wings; but they have dropped with me now, as a lark among the clods of the valley. Wand, do you bend? Yes, I am following, Wand.

"And after that the bird said: 'I will come when you call me.' I have never seen her moving overhead; perhaps she is out of sight. Flocks of birds hover over the world, and watch it high up where the air is thin. There are zones, but those in the lowest zone are far out of sight.

"I have not been up there. I have no wings.

"Over the highest of the birds is the place where angels float and gather the children's souls as they are set free.

"And so that woman told me—(Wand, you bend again, and I will turn at your bending)—that woman told me how it was: for when the new king was born, a black fairy with a smiling face came and sat within the doorway. She had a spindle, and would always spin. She wanted to teach them how to spin, but they did not like her, and they loved to do nothing at all. So they turned her out.

"But after her came a brown fairy, with a grave face, and she sat on the black fairy's stool and gave them much counsel. They liked that still less; so they got spindles and spun, for they said: 'She will go now, and we shall have the black fairy again.' When she did not go they turned her out also, and after her came a white fairy, and sat in the same seat. She did nothing at all, and she said nothing at all; but she had a sorrowful face, and she looked up. So they were displeased. They turned her out also; and she went and sat by the edge of the lake with her two sisters.

"And everything prospered over all the land; till, after shearing-time, the shepherds, because the king was a child, came to his uncle, and said: 'Sir, what shall we do with the old wool, for the new fleeces are in the bales, and there is no storehouse to put them in?' So he said: 'Throw them into the lake.'

"And while they threw them in, a great flock of finches flew to them, and said: 'Give us some of the wool that you do not want; we should be glad of it to build our nests with.'

"They answered: 'Go and gather for yourselves; there is wool on every thorn.'

"Then the black fairy said: 'They shall be forgiven this time, because the birds should pick wool for themselves.'

"So the finches flew away.

"Then the harvest was over, and the reapers came and said to the child king's uncle: 'Sir, what shall we do with the new wheat, for the old is not half eaten yet, and there is no room in the granaries?'

"He said: 'Throw that into the lake also.'

"While they were throwing it in, there came a great flight of the wood fairies, fairies of passage from over the sea. They were in the form of pigeons, and they alighted and prayed them: 'O cousins! we are faint with our long flight; give us some of that corn which you do not want, that we may peck it and be refreshed.'

"But they said: 'You may rest on our land, but our corn is our own. Rest awhile, and go and get food in your own fields.'

"Then the brown fairy said: 'They may be forgiven this once, but yet it is a great unkindness.'

"And as they were going to pour in the last sackful, there passed a poor mortal beggar, who had strayed in from the men and women's world, and she said: 'Pray give me some of that wheat, O fairy people! for I am hungry, I have lost my way, and there is no money to be earned here. Give me some of that wheat, that I may bake cakes, lest I and my baby should starve.'

"And they said: 'What is starve? We never heard that word before, and we cannot wait while you explain it to us.'

"So they poured it all into the lake; and then the white fairy said: 'This cannot be forgiven them'; and she covered her face with her hands and wept. Then the black fairy rose and drove them all before her—the prince, with his chief shepherd and his reapers, his courtiers and his knights; she drove them into the great bed of reeds, and no one had ever set eyes on them since. Then the brown fairy went into the palace where the king's aunt sat, with all her ladies and her maids about her, and with the child king on her knee.

"It was a very gloomy day.

"She stood in the middle of the hall, and said: 'Oh, you cold-hearted and most unkind! my spell is upon you, and the first ray of sunshine shall bring it down. Lose your present forms, and be of a more gentle and innocent race, till a queen of alien birth shall come to reign over you against her will.'

"As she spoke they crept into corners, and covered the

dame's head with a veil. And all that day it was dark and gloomy, and nothing happened, and all the next day it rained and rained; and they thrust the dame into a dark closet, and kept her there for a whole month, and still not a ray of sunshine came to do them any damage; but the dame faded and faded in the dark, and at last they said: 'She must come out, or she will die; and we do not believe the sun will ever shine in our country any more.' So they let the poor dame come out; and lo! as she crept slowly forth under the dome, a piercing ray of sunlight darted down upon her head, and in an instant they were all changed into deer, and the child king too.

"They are gentle now, and kind; but where is the prince? Where are the fairy knights and the fairy men?"

"Wand! why do you turn?"

Now while Mopsa told her story the wand continued to bend, and Mopsa, following, was slowly approaching the foot of a great precipice, which rose sheer up for more than a hundred feet. The crowd that followed looked dismayed at this: they thought the wand must be wrong; or even if it was right, they could not climb a precipice.

But still Mopsa walked on blindfold, and the wand pointed at the rock till it touched it, and she said: "Who is stopping me?"

They told her, and she called to some of her ladies to untie the handkerchief. Then Mopsa looked at the rock, and so did the two Jacks. There was nothing to be seen but a very tiny hole. The boy-king thought it led to a bees' nest, and Jack thought it was a keyhole, for he noticed in the rock a slight crack which took the shape of an arched door. Mopsa looked earnestly at the hole. "It may be a keyhole," she said, "but there is no key."

XVI

FAILURE

We are much bound to them that do succeed;
  But, in a more pathetic sense, are bound
  To such as fail. They all our loss expound;
They comfort us for work that will not speed,
And life—itself a failure. Ay, his deed,
  Sweetest in story, who the dusk profound
  Of Hades flooded with entrancing sound,
Music's own tears, was failure. Doth it read
Therefore the worse? Ah, no! So much to dare,
  He fronts the regnant Darkness on its throne.—
So much to do; impetuous even there,
  He pours out love's disconsolate sweet moan—
He wins; but few for that his deed recall:
Its power is in the look which costs him all.

At this moment Jack observed that a strange woman was standing among them, and that the train-bearing fairies fell back, as if they were afraid of her. As no one spoke, he did, and said: "Good morning!"

"Good afternoon!" she answered, correcting him. "I am the black fairy. Work is a fine thing. Most people in your country can work."

"Yes," said Jack.

"There are two spades," continued the fairy woman; "one for you, and one for your double."

Jack took one of the spades—it was small, and was made of silver; but the other Jack said with scorn:

"I shall be a king when I am old enough, and must I dig like a clown?"

"As you please," said the black fairy, and walked away.

Then they all observed that a brown woman was standing there; and she stepped up and whispered in the boy-king's ear. As he listened his sullen face became good tempered, and at last he said, in a gentle tone: "Jack, I'm quite ready to begin if you are."

"But where are we to dig?" asked Jack.

"There," said a white fairy, stepping up and setting her foot on the grass just under the little hole. "Dig down as deep as you can."

So Mopsa and the crowd stood back, and the two boys began to dig; and greatly they enjoyed it, for people can dig so fast in Fairyland.

Very soon the hole was so deep that they had to jump into it, because they could not reach the bottom with their spades. "This is very jolly indeed," said Jack, when they had dug so much deeper that they could only see out of the hole by standing on tiptoe.

"Go on," said the white fairy; so they dug till they came to a flat stone, and then she said: "Now you can stamp. Stamp on the stone, and don't be afraid." So the two Jacks began to stamp, and in such a little time that she had only half turned her head round, the flat stone gave way, for there was a hollow underneath it, and down went the boys, and utterly disappeared.

Then, while Mopsa and the crowd silently looked on, the white fairy lightly pushed the clods of earth towards the hole with the side of her foot, and in a very few minutes the hole was filled in, and that so completely and so neatly that when she had spread the turf on it, and given it a pat with her foot, you could not have told where it had been. Mopsa said not a word, for no fairy ever interferes with a stronger fairy; but she looked on earnestly, and when the white stranger smiled she was satisfied.

Then the white stranger walked away, and Mopsa and the fairies sat down on a bank under some splendid cedar trees. The beautiful castle looked fairer than ever in the afternoon sunshine; a lovely waterfall tumbled with a tinkling noise near at hand, and the bank was covered with beautiful wild flowers.

They sat for a long while, and no one spoke: what they were thinking of is not known, but sweet Mopsa often sighed.

At last a noise—a very, very slight noise, as of footsteps of people running—was heard inside the rock, and then a little quivering was seen in the wand. It quivered more and more

as the sound increased. At last that which had looked like a
door began to shake as if someone was pushing it from
within. Then a noise was distinctly heard as of a key turning
in the hole, and out burst the two Jacks, shouting for joy, and
a whole troop of knights and squires and serving-men came
rushing wildly forth behind them.

Oh, the joy of that meeting! Who shall describe it? Fairies
by dozens came up to kiss the boy-king's hand, and Jack
shook hands with everyone that could reach him. Then Mopsa
proceeded to the castle between the two Jacks, and the king's
aunt came out to meet them, and welcomed her husband
with tears of joy; for these fairies could laugh and cry when
they pleased, and they naturally considered this a great proof
of superiority.

After this a splendid feast was served under the great
dome. The other fairy feasts that Jack had seen were nothing
to it. The prince and his dame sat at one board, but Mopsa
sat at the head of the great table, with the two Jacks one on
each side of her.

Mopsa was not happy, Jack was sure of that, for she often
sighed; and he thought this strange. But he did not ask her
any questions, and he, with the boy-king, related their adventures to her: how, when the stone gave way, they tumbled
in and rolled down a sloping bank till they found themselves
at the entrance of a beautiful cave, which was all lighted up
with torches, and glittering with stars and crystals of all the
colours in the world. There was a table spread with what
looked like a splendid luncheon in this great cave, and chairs
were set round, but Jack and the boy-king felt no inclination
to eat anything, though they were hungry, for a whole nation
of ants were creeping up the honey-pots. There were snails
walking about over the tablecloth, and toads peeping out of
some of the dishes.

So they turned away and, looking for some other door to
lead them farther in, they at last found a very small one—so
small that only one of them could pass through at a time.

They did not tell Mopsa all that had occurred on this
occasion. It was thus:

The boy-king said: "I shall go in first, of course, because of
my rank."

"Very well," said Jack, "I don't mind. I shall say to myself
that you've gone in first to find the way for me, because

you're my double. Besides, now I think of it, our Queen always goes last in a procession; so it's grand to go last. Pass in, Jack."

"No," answered the other Jack; "now you have said that, I will not. You may go first."

So they began to quarrel and argue about this, and it is impossible to say how long they would have gone on if they had not begun to hear a terrible and mournful sort of moaning and groaning, which frightened them both and instantly made them friends. They took tight hold of one another's hand, and again there came a loud sighing, and a noise of all sorts of lamentation, and it seemed to reach them through the little door.

Each of the boys would now have been very glad to go back, but neither liked to speak. At last Jack thought anything would be less terrible than listening to those dismal moans, so he suddenly dashed through the door, and the other Jack followed.

There was nothing terrible to be seen. They found themselves in a place like an immensely long stable; but it was nearly dark, and when their eyes got used to the dimness they saw that it was strewn with quantities of fresh hay, from which curious things like sticks stuck up in all directions. What were they?

"They are dry branches of trees," said the boy-king.

"They are table legs turned upside down," said Jack; but then the other Jack suddenly perceived the real nature of the thing, and he shouted out: "No; they are antlers!"

The moment he said this the moaning ceased, hundreds of beautiful antlered heads were lifted up and the two boys stood before a splendid herd of stags; but they had had hardly time to be sure of this when the beautiful multitude rose and fled away into the darkness, leaving the two boys to follow as well as they could.

They were sure they ought to run after the herd, and they ran, but they soon lost sight of it, though they heard far on in front what seemed at first like a pattering of deers' feet, but the sound changed from time to time. It became heavier and louder, and then the clattering ceased, and it was evidently the tramping of a great crowd of men. At last they heard words, very glad and thankful words; people were crying to one another to make haste, lest the spell should come upon

hem again. Then the two Jacks, still running, came into a
grand hall, which was quite full of knights and all sorts of fairy
men, and there was the boy king's uncle, but he looked very
pale. "Unlock the door!" they cried. "We shall not be safe till
we see our new Queen. Unlock the door; we see light coming
through the keyhole."

The two Jacks came on to the front, and felt and shook the
door. At last the boy-king saw a little golden key glittering on
the floor, just where the one narrow sunbeam fell that came
through the keyhole; so he snatched it up. It fitted, and out
they all came, as you have been told.

When they had done relating their adventures, the new
Queen's health was drunk. And then they drank the health of
the boy king, who stood up to return thanks, and, as is the
fashion there, he sang a song. Jack thought it the most
ridiculous song he had ever heard; but as everybody else
looked extremely grave, he tried to be grave too. It was about
Cock Robin and Jenny Wren, how they made a wedding
feast, and how the wren said she should wear her brown
gown, and the old dog brought a bone to the feast.

> " 'He had brought them,' he said, 'some meat on a
>   bone:
>   They were welcome to pick it or leave it alone.' "

The fairies were very attentive to this song; they seemed, if
one may judge by their looks, to think it was rather a serious
one. Then they drank Jack's health, and afterwards looked at
him as if they expected him to sing too; but as he did not
begin, he presently heard them whispering, and one asking
another: "Do you think he knows manners?"

So he thought he had better try what he could do, and he
stood up and sang a song that he had often heard his nurse
sing in the nursery at home.

> "One morning, oh! so early, my beloved, my beloved,
>   All the birds were singing blithely, as if never they
>   would cease;
>   'Twas a thrush sang in my garden, 'Hear the story,
>   hear the story!'
>   And the lark sang, 'Give us glory!'
>   And the dove said, 'Give us peace!'

"Then I listened, Oh! so early, my beloved, my beloved,
To that murmur from the woodland of the dove, my
    dear, the dove;
When the nightingale came after, 'Give us fame to
    'sweeten duty!'
       When the wren sang, 'Give us beauty!'
       She made answer, 'Give us love!'

"Sweet is spring, and sweet the morning, my beloved,
    my beloved;
Now for us doth spring, doth morning, wait upon the
    year's increase,
And my prayer goes up, 'Oh, give us, crowned in youth
    with marriage glory,
       Give for all our life's dear story,
       Give us love, and give us peace!' "

"A very good song too," said the dame, at the other end of
the table; "only you made a mistake in the first verse. What
the dove really said was, no doubt, 'Give us peas.' All kinds of
doves and pigeons are very fond of peas."

"It isn't peas, though," said Jack. However, the court histo-
rian was sent for to write down the song, and he came with a
quill pen, and wrote it down as the dame said it ought to be.

Now all this time Mopsa sat between the two Jacks, and
she looked very mournful—she said hardly a word.

When the feast was over, and everything had vanished, the
musicians came in, for there was to be dancing; but while
they were striking up the white fairy stepped in, and, coming
up, whispered something in Jack's ear; but he could not hear
what she said, so she repeated it more slowly, and still he
could neither hear nor understand it.

Mopsa did not seem to like the white fairy: she leaned her
face on her hand and sighed; but when she found that Jack
could not hear the message, she said: "That is well. Cannot
you let things alone for this one day?" The fairy then spoke to
Mopsa, but she would not listen; she made a gesture of
dislike and moved away. So then this strange fairy turned and
went out again, but on the doorstep she looked round, and
beckoned to Jack to come to her. So he did; and then, as they
two stood together outside, she made him understand what
she had said. It was this:

"Her name was Jenny, her name was Jenny."

When Jack understood what she said he felt so sorrowful; he wondered why she had told him, and he longed to stay in that great place with Queen Mopsa—his own little Mopsa, whom he had carried in his pocket, and taken care of, and loved.

He walked up and down, up and down, outside, and his heart swelled and his eyes filled with tears. The bells had said he was to go home, and the fairy had told him how to go. Mopsa did not need him, she had so many people to take care of her now; and then there was that boy, so exactly like himself that she would not miss him. Oh, how sorrowful it all was! Had he really come up the fairy river, and seen those strange countries, and run away with Mopsa over those dangerous mountains, only to bring her to the very place she wished to fly from, and there to leave her, knowing that she wanted him no more, and that she was quite content?

No; Jack felt that he could not do that. "I will stay," he said; "they cannot make me leave her. That would be too unkind."

As he spoke he drew near to the great yawning door, and looked in. The fairy folk were singing inside; he could hear their pretty chirping voices, and see their beautiful faces, but he could not bear it, and he turned away.

The sun began to get low, and all the west was dyed with crimson. Jack dried his eyes, and, not liking to go in, took one turn more.

"I will go in," he said; "there is nothing to prevent me." He set his foot on the step of the door, and while he hesitated Mopsa came out to meet him.

"Jack," she said, in a sweet mournful tone of voice. But he could not make any answer; he only looked at her earnestly, because her lovely eyes were not looking at him, but far away towards the west.

"He lives there," she said, as if speaking to herself. "He will play there again, in his father's garden."

Then she brought her eyes down slowly from the rose-flush in the cloud, and looked at him and said: "Jack."

"Yes," said Jack; "I am here. What is it that you wish to say?"

She answered: "I am come to give you back your kiss."

So she stooped forward as she stood on the step, and kissed him, and her tears fell on his cheek.

"Farewell!" she said, and she turned and went up the steps and into the great hall; and while Jack gazed at her as she entered, and would fain have followed, but could not stir, the great doors closed together again, and he was left outside.

Then he knew, without having been told, that he should never enter them any more. He stood gazing at the castle; but it was still—no more fairy music sounded.

How beautiful it looked in the evening sunshine, and how Jack cried!

Suddenly he perceived that reeds were growing up between him and the great doors: the grass, which had all day grown about the steps, was getting taller; it had long spear-like leaves, it pushed up long pipes of green stem, and they whistled.

They were up to his ankles, they were presently up to his waist; soon they were as high as his head. He drew back that he might see over them; they sprang up faster as he retired, and again he went back. It seemed to him that the castle also receded; there was a long reach of these great reeds between it and him, and now they were growing behind also, and on all sides of him. He kept moving back and back: it was of no use, they sprang up and grew yet more tall, till very shortly the last glimpse of the fairy castle was hidden from his sorrowful eyes.

The sun was just touching the tops of the purple mountains when Jack lost sight of Mopsa's home; but he remembered how he had penetrated the bed of reeds in the morning, and he hoped to have the same good fortune again. So on and on he walked, pressing his way among them as well as he could, till the sun went down behind the mountains, and the rosy sky turned gold colour, and the gold began to burn itself away, and then all on a sudden he came to the edge of the reed-bed, and walked out upon a rising ground.

Jack ran up it, looking for the castle. He could not see it, so he climbed a far higher hill; still he could not see it. At last, after a toilsome ascent to the very top of the green mountain, he saw the castle lying so far, so very far off, that its peaks and battlements were on the edge of the horizon, and the evening mist rose while he was gazing, so that all its outlines were lost, and very soon they seemed to mingle with the shapes of the hill and the forest, till they had utterly vanished away.

Then he threw himself down on the short grass. The words of the white fairy sounded in his ears: "Her name was Jenny"; and he burst into tears again, and decided to go home.

He looked up into the rosy sky, and held out his arms, and called: "Jenny! O Jenny! come."

In a minute or two he saw a little black mark overhead, a small speck, and it grew larger, and larger, and larger still, as it fell headlong down like a stone. In another instant he saw a red light and a green light, then he heard the winnowing noise of the bird's great wings, and she alighted at his feet, and said: "Here I am."

"I wish to go home," said Jack, hanging down his head and speaking in a low voice, for his heart was heavy because of his failure.

"That is well," answered the bird. She took Jack on her back, and in three minutes they were floating among the clouds.

As Jack's feet were lifted up from Fairyland he felt a little consoled. He began to have a curious feeling, as if this had all happened a good while ago, and then half the sorrow he had felt faded into wonder, and the feeling still grew upon him that these things had passed some great while since, so that he repeated to himself: "It was a long time ago."

Then he fell asleep, and did not dream at all, nor know anything more till the bird woke him.

"Wake up now, Jack," she said; "we are at home."

"So soon!" said Jack, rubbing his eyes. "But it is evening; I thought it would be morning."

"Fairy time is always six hours in advance of your time," said the bird. "I see glow-worms down in the hedge, and the moon is just rising."

They were falling so fast that Jack dared not look; but he saw the church, and the wood, and his father's house, which seemed to be starting up to meet him. In two seconds more the bird alighted, and he stepped down from her back into the deep grass of his father's meadow.

"Goodbye!" she said. "Make haste and run in, for the dews are falling"; and before he could ask her one question, or even thank her, she made a wide sweep over the grass, beat her magnificent wings, and soared away.

It was all very extraordinary, and Jack felt shy and ashamed; but he knew he must go home, so he opened the little gate that led into the garden, and stole through the shrubbery, hoping that his footsteps would not be heard.

Then he came out on the lawn, where the flower-beds were, and he observed that the drawing-room window was open, so he came softly towards it and peeped in.

His father and mother were sitting there. Jack was delighted to see them, but he did not say a word, and he wondered whether they would be surprised at his having stayed away so long. The bird had said that they would not.

He drew a little nearer. His mother sat with her back to the open window, but a candle was burning, and she was reading aloud. Jack listened as she read, and knew that this was not in the least like anything that he had seen in Fairyland, nor the reading like anything that he had heard, and he began to forget the boy-king, and the apple-woman, and even his little Mopsa, more and more.

At last his father noticed him. He did not look at all surprised, but just beckoned to him with his finger to come in. So Jack did, and got upon his father's knee, where he curled himself up comfortably, laid his head on his father's waistcoat and wondered what he would think if he should be told about the fairies in somebody else's waistcoat pocket. He thought, besides, what a great thing a man was; he had never seen anything so large in Fairyland, nor so important; so, on the whole, he was glad he had come back, and felt very comfortable. Then his mother, turning over the leaf, lifted up her eyes and looked at Jack, but not as if she was in the least surprised, or more glad to see him than usual; but she smoothed the leaf with her hand, and began again to read, and this time it was about the Shepherd Lady:

I

"Who pipes upon the long green hill,
     Where meadow grass is deep?
The white lamb bleats but followeth on—
     Follow the clean white sheep.
The dear white lady in yon high tower,
     She hearkeneth in her sleep.

"All in long grass the piper stands,
  Goodly and grave is he;
Outside the tower, at dawn of day,
  The notes of his pipe ring free.
A thought from his heart doth reach to hers:
  'Come down, O lady! to me.'

"She lifts her head, she dons her gown:
  Ah! the lady is fair;
She ties the girdle on her waist,
  And binds her flaxen hair,
And down she stealeth, down and down,
  Down the turret stair.

"Behold him! With the flock he wons
  Along yon grassy lea.
'My shepherd lord, my shepherd love,
  What wilt thou, then, with me?
My heart is gone out of my breast,
  And followeth on to thee.'

II

" 'The white lambs feed in tender grass:
  With them and thee to bide,
How good it were,' she saith at noon;
  'Albeit the meads are wide.
Oh! well is me,' she saith when day
  Draws on to eventide.

"Hark! hark! the shepherd's voice. Oh, sweet!
  Her tears drop down like rain.
'Take now this crook, my chosen, my fere,
  And tend the flock full fain:
Feed them, O lady, and lose not one,
  Till I shall come again.'

"Right soft her speech: 'My will is thine,
  And my reward thy grace!'
Gone are his footsteps over the hill,
  Withdrawn his goodly face;
The mournful dusk begins to gather,
  The daylight wanes apace.

III

"On sunny slopes, ah! long the lady
   Feedeth her flock at noon;
She leads them down to drink at eve
   Where the small rivulets croon.
All night her locks are wet with dew,
   Her eyes outwatch the moon.

"Over the hills her voice is heard,
   She sings when light doth wane:
'My longing heart is full of love.
   When shall my loss be gain?
My shepherd lord, I see him not,
   But he will come again.' "

When she had finished Jack lifted his face and said,
"Mamma!" Then she came to him and kissed him, and his
father said: "I think it must be time this man of ours was in
bed."

So he looked earnestly at them both, and as they still asked
him no questions, he kissed and wished them goodnight; and
his mother said there were some strawberries on the sideboard in the dining-room, and he might have them for his
supper.

So he ran out into the hall, and was delighted to find all the
house just as usual, and after he had looked about him he
went into his own room, and said his prayers. Then he got
into his little white bed, and comfortably fell asleep.

That's all.

Bibliography

Other Christmas Stories and Tales for Children by Charles Dickens

The Chimes (1844)
The Cricket on the Hearth (1845)
The Battle of Life (1846)
The Haunted Man (1848)
"A Christmas Tree" (1850)
"What Christmas Is as We Grow Older" (1851)
The Holly Tree (1855)
"Prince Bull: A Fairy-Tale" (1855)
Holiday Romance (1868)
The Life of Our Lord Written for His Children (1934)

Critical Studies of *A Christmas Carol*

Butt, John E. "*A Christmas Carol*: Its Origin and Design." *Dickensian* 51 (1954): 15–18.

Dickens, Charles. *The Annotated Christmas Carol*, ed. Michael Patrick Hearn. New York: Clarkson N. Potter, 1976.

———, *A Christmas Carol: The Original Manuscript*. New York: Dover, 1971.

———, *A Christmas Carol: The Public Reading Version,* ed. Philip Collins. New York: New York Public Library, 1971.

Johnson, Edgar. "*A Christmas Carol* and the Economic Man." *American Scholar* 21 (1952): 91–98. Reprinted in *The Dickens Critics*, ed. G. H. Ford and L. Lane, Jr. Ithaca: Cornell University Press, 1961.

Patten, Robert L. "Dickens Time and Again." *Dickens Studies Annual* 2 (1972): 163–196.

Slater, Michael. "The Christmas Books." *Dickensian* 65 (1969): 17–24.

Stone, Harry. *Dickens and the Invisible World: Fairy Tales, Fantasy, and Novel-Making*. Bloomington and London: Indiana University Press, 1979.

Thackeray, W. M. "A Box of Novels." *Fraser's Magazine* 29 (1844): 166–69. Reprinted in *Dickens: The Critical Heritage*, ed. Philip Collins. London: Routledge and Kegan Paul, 1971.

Studies of Fairy Tales and Victorian Children's Books

Bettelheim, Bruno. *The Uses of Enchantment: The Meaning and Importance of Fairy Tales*. New York: Knopf, 1976.

Bratton, J. S. *The Impact of Victorian Children's Fiction*. Totowa, NJ: Barnes and Noble, 1981.

Coveney, Peter. *The Image of Childhood*. Hammondsworth: Penguin, 1967.

Filstrup, Jane Merrill. "Thirst for Enchanted Views in Ruskin's *The King of the Golden River*." *Children's Literature* 8 (1980): 68–79.

Green, Roger Lancelyn. *Tellers of Tales: Children's Books and Their Authors From 1800 to 1964*. London: Edmund Ward, 1965.

Grylls, David. *Guardians and Angels: Parents and Children in Nineteenth-Century Literature*. London and Boston: Faber & Faber, 1978.

Hein, Rolland. *The Harmony Within: The Spiritual Vision of George MacDonald*. Grand Rapids, MI: Christian University Press, 1982.

Jan, Isabelle. *On Children's Literature*. New York: Schocken, 1974.

Knoepflmacher, U. C. "The Balancing of Child and Adult: An Approach to Victorian Fantasies for Children." *Nineteenth-Century Fiction* 37 (1983): 497–530.

Lüthi, Max. *Once Upon A Time: On the Nature of Fairy Tales*. Bloomington: Indiana University Press, 1976.

McMaster, Juliet. "*The Rose and The Ring*: Quintessential Thackeray." *Mosaic* 9 (1976): 157–165.

Opie, Iona, and Peter Opie. *The Classic Fairy Tales*. London: Oxford University Press, 1974.

Pattison, Robert. *The Child Figure in English Literature*. Athens: University of Georgia Press, 1978.

Peters, Maureen. *Jean Ingelow: Victorian Poetess*. Ipswich: Boydell Press, 1972.

Postman, Neil. *The Disappearance of Childhood*. New York: Delacorte Press, 1982.

Prickett, Stephen. *Victorian Fantasy*. Bloomington: Indiana University Press, 1979.

Rabkin, Eric S. *The Fantastic in Literature*. Princeton: Princeton University Press, 1977.

Sale, Roger. *Fairy Tales and After: From Snow White to E. B. White*. Cambridge: Harvard University Press, 1978.

Salway, Lance, ed. *A Peculiar Gift: Nineteenth-Century Writings on Books for Children*. London: Kestrel, 1976.

Thackeray, W. M. *The Rose and The Ring Reproduced in Facsimile*, introd. Gordon N. Ray. New York: Pierpont Morgan Library, 1947.

Wolff, Robert Lee. *The Golden Key: A Study of the Fiction of George MacDonald*. New Haven: Yale University Press, 1961.

Zipes, Jack. *Breaking the Magic Spell: Radical Theories of Folk and Fairy Tale*. Austin: University of Texas Press, 1979.

Bantam Classics bring you the world's greatest literature—books that have stood the test of time—at specially low prices. These beautifully designed books will be proud additions to your bookshelf. You'll want all these time-tested classics for your own reading pleasure.